The Cambridge Introduction to
The American Short Story

This wide-ranging introduction to the short story tradition in the United States of America traces the genre from its beginnings in the early nineteenth century with Irving, Hawthorne and Poe via Fitzgerald, Hemingway and Faulkner to Flannery O'Connor and Raymond Carver. The major writers in the genre are covered in depth with a general view of their work and detailed discussion of a number of examples of individual stories. *The Cambridge Introduction to the American Short Story* offers a comprehensive and accessible guide to this rich literary tradition. It will be invaluable to students and readers looking for critical approaches to the short story and wishing to deepen their understanding of how authors have approached and developed this fascinating and challenging genre. Further reading suggestions are included to explore the subject in more depth. This is an invaluable overview for all students and readers of American fiction.

MARTIN SCOFIELD is Senior Lecturer in English and American Literature at the University of Kent.

Cambridge Introductions to Literature

This series is designed to introduce students to key topics and authors. Accessible and lively, these introductions will also appeal to readers who want to broaden their understanding of the books and authors they enjoy.

- Ideal for students, teachers, and lecturers
- Concise, yet packed with essential information
- Key suggestions for further reading

Titles in this series:

Bulson *The Cambridge Introduction to James Joyce*

Cooper *The Cambridge Introduction to T. S. Eliot*

Dillon *The Cambridge Introduction to Early English Theatre*

Goldman *The Cambridge Introduction to Virginia Woolf*

Holdeman *The Cambridge Introduction to W. B. Yeats*

McDonald *The Cambridge Introduction to Samuel Beckett*

Peters *The Cambridge Introduction to Joseph Conrad*

Scofield *The Cambridge Introduction to the American Short Story*

Thomson *The Cambridge Introduction to English Theatre, 1660–1900*

Todd *The Cambridge Introduction to Jane Austen*

The Cambridge Introduction to

The American Short Story

MARTIN SCOFIELD

CAMBRIDGE UNIVERSITY PRESS
Cambridge, New York, Melbourne, Madrid, Cape Town, Singapore,
São Paulo, Delhi, Dubai, Tokyo, Mexico City

Cambridge University Press
The Edinburgh Building, Cambridge CB2 8RU, UK

Published in the United States of America by Cambridge University Press, New York

www.cambridge.org
Information on this title: www.cambridge.org/9780521533812

First published 2006

A catalogue record for this publication is available from the British Library

ISBN 978-0-521-82643-3 Hardback
ISBN 978-0-521-53381-2 Paperback

Contents

Acknowledgements

I would like to thank warmly my wife Lyn Innes, and other present and former colleagues at the University of Kent and elsewhere, particularly the American literature specialists Keith Carabine, Henry Claridge, David Herd, Stuart Hutchinson, Lionel Kelly, Guy Reynolds and David Stirrup, for advice, loan of books, useful discussion and other support; the School of English at Kent for its generous provisions of study leave; and also all those past and present students taking my courses in the nineteenth- and twentieth-century American short story over the past several years, whose enthusiasm, co-operation and lively critical contribution to our seminars have helped me to formulate the ideas in this book. I would also like to pay grateful tribute to my editorial team at Cambridge University Press, in particular my commissioning editor Ray Ryan for his unfailing support and encouragement, my production editor Jayne Aldhouse, and my copy-editor Lucy Carolan for her meticulous work on my typescript.

Chapter 1
Introduction

The short story in America has for almost two centuries held a prominent, even pre-eminent place in the American literary tradition. It was the Irish writer Frank O'Connor, himself a noted writer of short stories, who said that for the Americans the short story had become 'a national art form'.[1] It could be argued, indeed, that around the 1820s and 1830s the Americans virtually invented what has come to be called 'the short story', in its modern literary sense (although one should of course note the parallel European tradition in, for instance, the development of the Russian short story from Gogol in the 1830s). Certainly the short story found its first theorist in one of its major early practitioners, Edgar Allan Poe; and the short story was for Poe his most successful and influential literary form. A number of other American writers in both the nineteenth and the twentieth centuries have, arguably, done their best work in that medium. Nathaniel Hawthorne's stories rank with his novel *The Scarlet Letter* as among his most outstanding achievements. Herman Melville's best short stories, such as 'Bartleby', may not outweigh the epic achievement of *Moby Dick*, but for many readers they are equally rewarding and more formed and finished as works of art. Stephen Crane's short fictions (like 'The Open Boat' and 'The Bride Comes to Yellow Sky') are as well known as his great novel *The Red Badge of Courage*. Henry James's short stories (as well as his novellas) are, in the view of almost all his critics, among his finest achievements. Sherwood Anderson's short story sequence, *Winesburg, Ohio*, is his finest work. Ernest Hemingway's short stories are as highly esteemed as his novels and, in the view of some of his critics, constitute the most successful part of his *oeuvre*. In the middle of the twentieth century writers like Flannery O'Connor and Eudora Welty did their most significant work in the short story form, and nearer to our own time writers as different as Donald Barthelme and Raymond Carver – writers who can be said to be among the most significant of their era – have made their considerable mark primarily through their short stories.

As well as European and Middle Eastern predecessors such as Boccaccio's *Decameron*, Chaucer's *Canterbury Tales*, and the *Thousand and One Nights* (which originated in tenth-century Persia and was known in an eighteenth-century translation to Poe and Hawthorne), there are more local predecessors for the first flowering of the literary short story from the 1820s. Washington Irving's *The Sketch-Book of Geoffrey Crayon, Gent.* (1819–20), which contains the seminal – virtually the founding – stories of the American tradition, 'Rip Van Winkle' and 'The Legend of Sleepy Hollow', is mainly a collection of essays and sketches about places and characters. As such it grows out of the genteel English tradition of Addison and Steele's *Spectator* magazine (1711–12 and 1714), which mingled essayistic observations on contemporary society with tales and anecdotes. Irving's stories themselves, however, derive from German folklore sources: 'Rip Van Winkle' from a story found most notably in Grimm's tale 'Peter Klaus the Goatherd' and 'The Legend of Sleepy Hollow' from Bürger's 'Der wilde Jäger' ('The Wild Huntsman'), which had been translated by Sir Walter Scott. The influence of German, and British, Romanticism is there too in Poe. Poe had read E. T. A. Hoffmann, and used Hoffmann's term 'fantasy-pieces' (*Fantasiestücke)* to describe his *Tales of the Grotesque and of the Arabesque* (1839).

American origins

Among the Koasati Native American people of what is today southwestern Louisiana and eastern Texas they tell a story which, it is likely, goes back centuries to the time before the arrival of Europeans.[2] Bear and Rabbit are friends, and Bear invites Rabbit to his house. Racking his brains to think of something to give Rabbit to eat Bear decides, because he is fat, to cut off some of his own stomach and give that to Rabbit ('Thereupon Rabbit really sat and watched'). Rabbit eats the food, and later invites Bear over to his house. To feed Bear, he too cuts a piece out of his own stomach. But he injures himself and cries out for help. Bear goes out to look for a doctor and finds Vulture, who says he will doctor Rabbit. Vulture makes Bear fence in the house with palmetto leaves, and then tells him to leave. Bear goes, but later hears Rabbit cry out. 'Why is he making a sound?' asks Bear. 'Because he does not want the medicine' says Vulture. But Bear goes in later and finds nothing but Rabbit's bones. He becomes very angry and taking a knife he goes out to look for

Vulture. When he finds him he throws the knife at him and it pierces him through the beak. And that is why vultures have pierced beaks.

The story is typical of a host of Native American oral stories about animals, particularly trickster figures like Rabbit (*Cokfi*). They are often 'origin stories' or stories explaining the features of the natural world, as here. They also often 'illustrate and reaffirm, through positive or negative examples, culturally appropriate behaviour'.[3] It is odd, perhaps, that the main trickster figure here is Rabbit, since he seems to be merely the victim in the story: presumably he illustrates here by a 'negative example'. So the story illustrates both how things have come about (the Vulture's pierced beak), and how not to behave. Bear has magical powers (as the audience would know) but Rabbit does not: so the moral of the story is presumably (like the warning at the end of a television magic show), 'Don't try this at home!' The story is a myth of origin and also a moral fable. It is part of a group of stories that anthropologists have called 'Bungling Host' stories, and related to another group, 'Sham Doctor' Stories. The former group has affinities with figures in the literary tradition, like the backwoods host in Twain's 'Story of a Speech'; and the 'sham doctors' in the literary short story range from Hawthorne's Dr Heidegger in 'Dr Heidegger's Experiment' (1837) and Poe's 'Doctor Tarr and Professor Fether' (1845) to O. Henry's Jeff Peters in 'Jeff Peters as a Personal Magnet' (1908).

In its mythical and moral aspects this story has many of the features that we will find in the literary American short story. The moral fable and the figure of the trickster are two of its staple elements, as we shall see in the coming pages, and the trickster reappears in late twentieth-century Native American literary stories like those of Gerald Vizenor.[4] Early settlers often had close contact with Native American peoples, and certain stories certainly found their way into mainstream American Culture (Longfellow's long verse narrative *Hiawatha* is the most famous example). So it is likely that these stories played at least some part in the formation of the mental attitudes that gave rise to the literary short story. The African American slave story is also part of the cultural ambience of the literary short story, and received its first major literary treatment in Joel Chandler Harris's stories of Brer Rabbit and Brer Fox and others in *Uncle Remus: His Songs and His Sayings* (1881).

Genre

Any discussion of the short story has, sooner rather than later, to deal at least briefly with the vexed question of genre or 'kind'. How do we define the short story so that we know broadly what kind of work we are dealing with, and how far do we need to? Short story criticism has perhaps, as more than one critic has suggested, been overly concerned with genre definition.[5] Attempts have been made to identify the short story form with particular modes of cognition or attitudes to life, but these usually stumble over counter-instances. For example, the 'modern' short story (broadly, that developed in the later nineteenth century and brought to fruition in the early part of the twentieth) has been identified with 'epiphanic' perceptions of reality, which focus on lyric evocation and revelatory moments rather than plot or linear narrative and development,[6] or it has been associated with a view of life that transcends the material facts of the world and tries to establish some mythical or even sacred perspective.[7] But it is usually easy to come up with instances that contradict or at least trouble the principles laid down. The plot-driven stories of O. Henry upset any theory which sees the modern short story as simply presenting a fragment of life. Many broadly 'realist' stories (for instance many of Hemingway's, like 'Cross–Country Snow' or 'The Three Day Blow' or 'Fathers and Sons') narrate their chosen incidents and accumulate their varying significances without reaching any great single moment of revelation. Nor would such stories, or those of other writers who often (though by no means always) work in a broadly realist mode, like John Cheever in the 1950s or Raymond Carver in the 1970s and 1980s, easily be corralled under the heading of 'metaphoric' or 'symbolic': modes where the emphasis is on some figuration of reality which works by substitution rather than literal presentation. To be sure, a critic may want to value or stress the importance of one mode or another, and his or her critical preferences may lie in one direction or the other; but it seems ultimately counter-productive and restrictive to try to establish the validity of these preferences by way of generic definition.

Genres, it has been said, are not essences,[8] and we may give ourselves unnecessary labour if we try to identify *one* element or principle which defines the short story. Firstly, what is 'short'? Here one can only be pragmatic and relativistic: shortness has come to be defined in relation to the longer form, the novel, and when it comes to fictional prose means in practice anything between five hundred and fifteen thousand words, or between one and forty average printed pages.

But there is also the case of what has come to be known most often as the 'novella' or the long story – that form of between about fifty and hundred and fifty pages (or 20,000 and 40,000 words), too long for a 'short story' and too short for a novel. The novella often covers more narrative ground, often deals with a large number of characters rather than focusing on one or two, and is often divided into parts or chapters. As a brief pointer to usage, Melville's 'Bartleby' (around 20,000 words) is usually described as a short story, *Benito Cereno* and *Billy Budd* (about 35,000 words each) as novellas, and Stephen Crane's *The Red Badge of Courage* (around 60,000 words) as a short novel. *Novella* is an Italian term, used in that language simply for story or tale; its specific application in English to the long story comes via the German *Novelle*, in use since the early nineteenth century (when it was introduced by Goethe) to classify an important genre of longer stories from Kleist to Thomas Mann. Henry James preferred the French *nouvelle* for the more expansive form in which he himself excelled, speaking of 'the blest *nouvelle*' and praising its 'shapely' dimensions.[9] Recently 'long story' itself, workmanlike and vernacular, has been used and argued for in an outstanding anthology of twentieth-century pieces edited by Richard Ford.[10] There are many fine novellas in the American tradition (Herman Melville's *Billy Budd*, Stephen Crane's *Maggie: A Girl of the Streets*, and Henry James's *The Turn of the Screw*, to name only three), but for the sake of focus and economy this study will confine itself to the short story.

One notion (among others) of the short story which I would like to keep in mind during the exploration of the many different kinds of story which follow is that of 'the idea as hero'. The term was coined by the novelist Kingsley Amis in his critical book on Science Fiction, *New Maps of Hell* (1960), where he applied it to novels as much as short stories, and used it to point to works of fiction where a leading idea about a future state of society governed the development of the whole. But the phrase can suggest more broadly a mode of story in which the overall idea, rather than character, plot or 'themes' in the usual sense, dominates the conception of the work and gives it its unity or deliberate disunity. And it seems particularly applicable to the short story, which is often motivated by a single idea or image (whereas the novel can incorporate several and chart the relation between them). Poe wrote of how 'the idea of the tale' can be 'presented unblemished, because undisturbed, and this is an end unattainable by the novel'.[11] The 'idea as hero' should not suggest a 'thesis-driven' or polemical work, or one that works discursively rather than poetically, but rather a work that is dominated by a single guiding idea or mood and achieves a perceptible overall aesthetic coherence. It may well stay in the mind as an 'image' as much as an idea. Henry James insisted on this fusion of idea and image when he wrote of his story 'The Real Thing': 'It must be an idea – it can't be a story in the vulgar sense of the word. It must be a picture; it must illustrate something.'[12] The short story cannot, of course, entirely dispense with 'story' without becoming a sketch or prose poem or some other form, but its relation to story is that of the artist rather than the anecdotalist. Structure, diction, imagery and tone will all be conceived with a purpose which is more important than merely 'communicating the story'. To put it a simpler way, and to use a common phrase which is perhaps more suggestive analytically than its casual use would suggest, what the short story writer's art tries to convey is the 'point' of a story: that moment of understanding or cognition in which we grasp not so much 'what the writer was getting at', in the old phrase, as what the *story* may get at in its collaboration with the mind of the reader reading.

The literary and social context of the early American short story

Ralph Waldo Emerson, in his celebrated and seminal essay 'The American Scholar' (1837), wrote: 'Each age, it is found, must write its own books; or rather, each generation for the next succeeding. The books of an older period will not fit this.'[13] And this desire to 'make it new' (in Ezra Pound's phrase) is no small part of the emphasis on the short story in American literature from the 1820s.

Washington Irving, after the success of *The Sketch-Book of Geoffrey Crayon, Gent.*, wrote in a letter in 1824:

> I have preferred adopting a mode of sketches & short tales rather than long work, because I chose to take a line of writing peculiar to myself; rather than fall into the manner or school of any other writer; and there is a constant activity of thought and a nicety of execution required in writings of the kind, more than the world appears to imagine . . .[14]

Conditions of writing and publication in the first half of the century also encouraged the publication of short pieces. International copyright laws allowed publishers to pirate British work and print it cheaply, putting original American novels at a disadvantage. This inequity was not finally removed until 1891.[15] As a result a writer like Edgar Allan Poe with the ambitions to create an independent American tradition turned to magazine publication as the best means of creating both a literature and a reading public. It was particularly during the economic Depression of 1837 that he began to see 'the magazine, rather than the book, as the appropriate expression of American culture',[16] and he wrote to a prospective sponsor:

> I perceived that the whole energetic, busy spirit of the age tended wholly to the Magazine literature – to the curt, the terse, the well-timed, and the readily diffused, in preference to the old forms of the verbose, the ponderous and the inaccessible.[17]

For Poe, the medium of the magazine, with its concomitant stress on short pieces of writing, lyric poetry, essays and short stories, was central to his vision of his own career and of the whole future of American literature. Poe's important contribution to the aesthetic argument for the short story will be considered in a later chapter, but its connection with this broad cultural aim should not be underestimated. As Andrew Levy comments: 'For Poe the magazine project was an ideological end, not a means; the magazine's success per se would constitute a revolution, or the culmination of one.'[18]

Another insight into the suitability of the short story for American cultural conditions, though a notably more measured and less exalted one than Poe's, can be found in the remarkably astute and prescient comments of the contemporary French historian and cultural critic Alexis de Tocqueville in his *Democracy in America* (1843). De Tocqueville considers the question of what kind of literature can be expected of a new democracy in conditions where 'Classes are intermingled and confused' and 'knowledge as well as power is infinitely divided up and, if I may so put it, scattered all around'. Most of those who read will go into business or politics or 'adopt some profession which leaves but short, stolen hours for the pleasures of the mind'. He goes on:

> With but short time to spend on books they want it all to be profitable. They like books which are easily got and quickly read, requiring no learned research to understand them . . .; above all they like things unexpected and new . . . [W]hat they want is vivid, lively emotions, sudden revelations, brilliant truths, or errors able to rouse them up and plunge them, almost by violence, into the middle of the subject . . . Short works will be commoner than long books, wit than erudition, imagination than depth.[19]

Despite the European condescension in the tone, it is remarkable how penetrating De Tocqueville is here, and how well he predicts the strengths (as well as some of the potential weaknesses) of literature in a new democracy. He predicts with uncanny accuracy the qualities of a popular commercial literature (and seems to look forward to film and television). His accompanying analysis that 'formal qualities will be neglected' in literature does not, of course, do justice to Poe's zealous theorizing about form in his review of Hawthorne (1842) (about which De Tocqueville could scarcely have known by 1843) or 'The Philosophy of Composition' (1846), but nevertheless the passage I have quoted seem precisely to predict the short stories of Poe himself.

Looking forward to the development of the American short story across the nineteenth century and beyond, one might consider further this idea of the 'democracy' of the form. Apart from its association with magazine publication (which persists in the present, although often in élite or coterie publications as well as popular ones) and its appeal to busy readers, the form has been held to have characteristics which associate particularly with 'the man in the street'. Partly because of its length and the time taken to read it, it has been seen as the precursor of the one-hour television play or the two-hour film, those staples of culture from the mid-twentieth century onwards. Frank O'Connor, in his fine study of the short story *The Lonely Voice*, has seen the short story as the ideal form for treating the life of the isolated individual, the 'Little Man' and the 'submerged population group';[20]and while this definition may be restrictive, there is a sense in which the form does lend itself to the examination of scenes from the life of the common man or woman, episodes and crises which are typical of those of ordinary life but hardly demand the developed treatment of the novel. The emphasis of democracy was on what Emerson called 'the new importance given to the single person'.[21] And this emphasis, in nineteenth-century America, favoured the cultivation of the short story.

But it is perhaps the 'lightness' and mobility of the short story, above all, that suits it to the preoccupations of a fast developing rural and urban culture, characterized by the diversity of its traditions and the mixed nature of its population. As we shall see, the short story was to be associated in the period immediately following the Civil War with what became known as 'local colour' literature (of which Bret Harte's story 'The Luck of Roaring Camp', 1868, is perhaps the first example), which emphasized the varied customs and local flavour of different regions of the United States, like the newly settled Far West, the South-West or the Deep South. The short story was frequently the form chosen by writers introducing such new areas to a still predominantly East Coast reading public: it could give brief and vivid glimpses of new and 'exotic' places and ways of life in short narratives which wakened the imagination to new scenes and new experiences without subjecting readers to the extended treatment of a novel. Even today, when we are more aware of the variety of population groups within single societies, the short story is notable for the leading part it has played in the fictional treatment of Native American, African, Jewish, Hispanic, Asian and other ethnic groups within American society: disseminating ideas of cultural diversity and bringing these groups into various relations to each other and to the often challenged concept of a literary 'mainstream'.

Henry James once wrote that the novel required a society with long-established traditions: 'It takes an old civilization to set a novelist in motion.'[22] It might be said in contrast that a new civilization is likely to turn to the short story, which gives the writer an ability swiftly to change his focus on a variety of topics, places, figures. Elsewhere James implicitly likened his attitude as a short story writer to that of the photographer who can move through society with swiftness and agility capturing representative scenes. To Robert Louis Stevenson (another practitioner and critic of the form), James wrote: 'I want to leave a multitude of pictures of my time, projecting my small circular frame upon as many different spots as possible.'[23]

It is perhaps this sense of both mobility and democratic openness to experience that most characterizes the short story in America. The genre speaks in a host of different voices – as we shall see, the sense of 'voice', the closeness to the scene of an oral narrator is a strong strand in the web of the American short story – and has the freedom to tackle an immense variety of subjects in almost as many different modes. An approach to it cannot be centred on any one mode (romantic 'tale', realist story, 'tall tale', anecdote, sketch, or parable) but must take account of them all. In a fast developing society the genre as a whole, and the individual writer, may gain immeasurably from the short story's ability to move fast, to register the fleeting as well as to work experience more slowly into the careful constructions of a clearly defined art. Raymond Carver's advice to himself during a difficult time in his progress as a writer was advice that stayed with him, and it could be taken as one motto for the American short story writer: 'Get in, get out. Don't linger. Go on.'[24]

Chapter 2

The short story as ironic myth: Washington Irving and William Austin

Two writers at the very beginning of the American short story tradition, Washington Irving (1783–1859) and William Austin (1778–1843), produced stories which not only constitute the foundations of a genre but also deal with the foundations of modern American society itself. Other stories by Irving and Austin approach the genre by way of Romance, parable and sketch, and prepared the ground for the greater achievement of Nathaniel Hawthorne. Irving's 'Rip Van Winkle' (1819) and Austin's 'Peter Rugg, the Missing Man' (1824) also provide paradigmatic examples of the way the short story frequently – one might almost say typically – takes a moment of crisis as its subject matter: the moment which marks a radical change in the life of an individual, a group or, as here, a whole nation. Their small handful of other stories also tend to deal with crisis, usually psychological or moral, by way of 'Romance' (defined by Hawthorne as 'a neutral territory, somewhere between the real world and fairy-land, where the Actual and the imaginary may meet, and each imbue itself with the nature of the other')[1] or the semi-supernatural or 'fantastic'.[2] The term 'tale' was commonly used in the nineteenth century for this kind of story.

Washington Irving

Irving's 'Rip Van Winkle' is one of only three short stories or tales, as he more often called them, in *The Sketch-Book of Geoffrey Crayon, Gent.* (1819–20), a collection mostly made up of essays, sketches and anecdotes, many of which are not on American topics but grew out of Irving's travels in Britain between 1815 and 1817. In 'Rip Van Winkle' on the other hand Irving writes, one might say, the myth of the ordinary unheroic American. Rip lives at home with his nagging wife, avoiding his domestic duties, helping neighbours with odd tasks, telling stories to village children and whiling his time away with the village 'club of the sages', other idle males who sit around mulling over the public events of the day. Rip goes out one morning into the 'Kaatskill' Mountains in with his gun and his dog. He sees a man in antiquated garb toiling up the mountain with a great flagon. The man beckons for help, and then leads Rip to a remote amphitheatre among the cliffs where a group of men, dressed like old Dutch settlers of the seventeenth century, are playing nine-pins. Rip drinks too much of the 'excellent Hollands' (Dutch gin) and falls asleep. When he awakes his dog has disappeared and his gun is worm-eaten and rusty. Back in the village all is changed: the sign on his favourite inn has changed from the picture of King George III to the picture of a man in a cocked hat with the words General Washington underneath. He comes upon a political orator talking of elections and 'Bunker's Hill', who inquires on which side he voted. Utterly perplexed by all this he seeks his own house and finds his wife has died and his daughter is married with a small child, young Rip. He has been asleep for twenty years, years which encompassed the War of Independence, and has returned to a new society.

The crisis of the American Revolution is one that has passed him by: he has missed the Boston Tea Party and wakes up to find the world changed. He represents the common man who cares little for national politics, who avoids work as much as possible, and who likes nothing better than to spend his life talking with his fellows in the inn; or he is like the figure in the cinema Western who sits on the back porch with his hat over his eyes, chewing a stalk of grass. As critics have pointed out, he is one stereotype or mythic representation of the American male, the opposite of the Paul Bunyan type of pioneering hero who is famed for his mighty prowess as a lumberjack and backwoods explorer.[3]

Another aspect of his life before his long sleep also makes him representative. For Rip is 'a hen-pecked husband' with 'a termagant wife'. Indeed, this is given an emphasis in the story which is hardly necessary for the basic tale (as sketched above) but which is an essential part of its humour and its point. It is to escape his wife that he goes out on his ramble into the mountains. When he returns and is told his wife has died, the narrator comments: 'There was a drop of comfort, at least, in this intelligence.' As a kind of archetype of the hen-pecked husband, Rip might be taken to represent a strain of male exclusivity and sometimes misogyny (however genial and humorous it is in this story) that runs through nineteenth-century mainstream American literature. There is an element of it in Hawthorne; in Poe's poems women are idealized into paragons and in his stories are mainly the victims of his mad protagonists; the protagonists in Melville's novels and stories are almost exclusively male; Twain's Huckleberry Finn finds his primary ideological opponent in Miss Watson. It is only when we look at the flourishing but until recently largely occluded writing by women in nineteenth-century America (much of it in the short story – a topic to be explored in later chapters), or when we come to the treatment of women in many of Henry James's finest novels and stories, that we see the counterbalance to this tendency. Here in 'Rip Van Winkle', it should be stressed again, the 'misogyny' is hardly registered as such because of the genial and comic tone – though humorous geniality can itself, of course, be a powerful agent of conservatism in the matter of sexual inequality.

As well as the kernel of the story – the 'mythic' tale of the man out of his time, the man who goes to sleep and wakes up in a new world – there is a play of picturesque and humorous detail, which serves to orient the attitude of the story towards a humorous but nostalgic conservatism. Irving's technique, as he said in the letter quoted on p. 18 below, was one in which the story was in some ways less important than 'the way in which it is told':

> It is the play of thought, and sentiment and language; the weaving in of characters, lightly yet expressively delineated; the familiar and faithful exhibition of scenes in common life; and the half concealed vein of humour that is often playing through the whole – these are among what I aim at, and upon which I felicitate myself in proportion as I think I succeed.[4]

So in 'Rip Van Winkle' the play of thought and the weaving in of characters serves in a sense to cocoon the story of revolution in a pleasant web of observation and description. The political realities of scarcely two generations before are distanced into myth and legend; 'crisis' is softened by the mists of time. By giving the eponymous hero, too, a Dutch name, and emphasizing the Dutch ancestry of the State of New York, Irving looks back to an older period and older European origins than the more recent dominance of British rule, and so ignores the harsher realities of the anti-colonial struggle. An air of play (the 'play of thought' and the 'humour playing through the whole' of the letter) breathes through the whole story. Rip Van Winkle himself is the American male at play (teaching the children of the village 'to fly kites and shoot marbles'), and it is no accident of detail that when Rip encounters them in the mountains, the founding fathers themselves, Hendrick Hudson and his men, are drinking gin and playing ninepins. During much later historical crises, American Rip Van Winkles would be drinking beer down at the bowling alley.

One other story in *The Sketch Book*, at first seemingly supernatural, is 'The Spectre Bridegroom', this time set in Germany and heavily influenced by the German poet Bürger's 'Lenore' and 'The Wild Huntsman' (both translated by Sir Walter Scott, the versions which Irving probably knew). It has the trappings of a Gothic landscape and the promise of a ghostly conclusion, but the spectre bridegroom turns out to be not a spectre but the bridegroom's friend and the tale resolves itself into a romantic love story. 'The Pride of the Village' is a little anecdote of blighted love in an English village setting, would-be Wordsworthian in its simplicity and quiet tragedy, but falling into sentimentality and inadvertent melodrama in its abrupt and implausible ending. Neither of these stories has the rich and archetypal American quality of 'Rip Van Winkle'. But one other story, again significantly with an American setting, has that quality.

'The Legend of Sleepy Hollow' is another humorous and supernatural – or this time, rather, mock-supernatural – story which can be seen as being about the opposition of two American types, and which in its crisis is a kind of symbol of the fate of New England Puritanism. Ichabod Crane, the protagonist, is a comic version of one kind of Yankee, descended from the original New England Puritans, 'a native of Connecticut; a state which supplies the Union with pioneers for the mind as well as for the forest, and sends forth yearly its legions of frontier woodsmen and country schoolmasters'. Ichabod is one of the latter, a grotesque and ungainly figure with a small head, 'huge ears, large green glassy eyes, and a long snipe nose' like 'the genius of famine descending upon the earth, or some scarecrow eloped from a cornfield'. He is esteemed for his learning ('for he had read several books quite through') and 'was a perfect master of Cotton Mather's History of New England Witchcraft, in which, by the way, he most potently and firmly believed'. Ichabod is the victim of a hoax ghost – supposedly the headless horseman or Galloping Hessian of local lore – when he competes with a rival for the hand of the village beauty, Katrina van Tassel. If Ichabod is the lean and scholarly New England type, the rival Brom Van Brunt, nicknamed 'BROM BONES', is 'broad shouldered and double-jointed, with short, curly black hair, and a bluff, but not unpleasant countenance,' possessing 'a Herculean frame and great powers of limb' and 'famed for great knowledge and skill in horsemanship'. He is, perhaps, the precursor in epitomized Romance form of that species – however varied in different cases – of bluff, 'average sensual men' of later fiction, from James's Caspar Goodwood through the typical Hemingway hero to Updike's 'Rabbit' Angstrom and Ford's Frank Bascombe. By contrast, Ichabod, who supposedly ends up as a politician, journalist and justice in a small claims court, represents in his caricatural way the clerkly, intellectual or reflective type, the type treated (with considerably more fullness and seriousness, to be sure) in Hawthorne's Goodman Brown or Arthur Dimmesdale; and, however more sophisticatedly, the minor men of letters in Henry James's novels and stories.

The routing of Ichabod by the fake apparition of the headless horseman symbolizes the comic crisis of the Puritan tradition of belief in witchcraft and the supernatural, the final routing of Romance and superstition by the hard-headed practicality of Brom Bones. Irving's imagination here is much less sophisticated than Hawthorne's on similar kinds of topic, as we shall see in the next chapter (Hawthorne had a far more inward sense of the Puritan tradition, its strengths as well as it subtle weaknesses and extravagances). Like 'Rip Van Winkle' but with less subtlety of suggestion, 'The Legend of Sleepy Hollow' paints the crisis of a certain type of American figure and a certain situation in a way that affably reduces it to a pleasant fireside tale. The rigours and horrors of the Puritan legacy are made matter for a humorous 'ghost' story by Irving's essentially comfortable imagination, and at the end of the story a world of fantastic learning and religious enthusiasm is removed to a pleasant and picturesque distance by Irving's elegiac nostalgia (with shades of Gray's 'Elegy'):

> The school-house being deserted, soon fell to decay, and was reported to be haunted by the ghost of the unfortunate pedagogue; and the plough-boy, loitering homeward of a still summer evening, has often fancied his voice at a distance, chanting a melancholy psalm tune among the tranquil solitudes of Sleepy Hollow.

William Austin

Until very recently, little was current either of William Austin's life or of his work. F. L. Pattee's *The Development of the American Short Story* (1923) relates that he was a Boston lawyer and a graduate of Harvard University and mentions just two other stories that he was known to have written, as well as according high praise to 'Peter Rugg'. Until the welcome publication of an edition of *The Man with the Cloaks* in 1988,[5] 'Peter Rugg, the Missing Man' was his only story recently in print, and that only in one anthology, Joyce Carol Oates's *Oxford Book of American Short Stories.* The absence elsewhere is regrettable, and yet there is something melancholically apt about the homelessness of this great story of the loss of home. It is absolutely of its time and place – a significant piece of myth-making about the effect of the

American Revolution – and yet it has a considered artistry of tone and structure, and a haunting universality of theme (loss of place in the world), that looks forward (as Oates has suggested) to Kafka's metaphysically displaced protagonists. Like Irving's 'Rip Van Winkle' and much of Hawthorne's work, it combines history and Romance in a way that makes it at once an acute comment on its age, a founding story in the American short story tradition, and a work that stands independently of its context.

The story is told in 1820 by one Jonathan Dunwell of New York, in a letter to a friend. This remnant of eighteenth-century epistolary tradition creates the effect of historical verisimilitude which roots the story in its place and time. The narrative device of having several informants, from whom Dunwell gradually finds out more about the mysterious figure of Peter Rugg, also gives the story the air of popular tradition and local lore; while the device of the sceptical primary narrator – often used by writers of the supernatural, including Hawthorne and Poe – creates the effect of ambiguity (akin to Todorov's category of 'the Fantastic'),[6] as the reader's belief hovers suspended between the realm of the actual and that of the supernatural.

The story that Dunwell gradually gleans is of a figure travelling with his ten-year-old daughter in a small horse-drawn post-chaise, and followed by a storm, along the roads around Boston and then further and further afield. From one informant, Dunwell learns that Rugg's daughter Jenny was ten in 1770, at the time of the Boston Massacre (the reprisal by British troops after merchants boycotted trade in protest at Britain's taxing of the colonies). So Rugg has been travelling for fifty years. 'If the present generation know little of him, the next will know less, and Peter and his child will have no hold on the world.' Like Rip Van Winkle (with whom Rugg also shares a descent from Dutch settlers), Peter Rugg, having 'missed' the Revolution, finds himself in an America he no longer knows.

Dunwell eventually learns the origin of Rugg's disorientation: one night on the way back to Boston during a storm he stopped in the town of Menotomy and was urged to stay the night; whereupon: '"*Let the storm increase*", said Rugg, with a fearful oath. "*I will see home to-night, in spite of the last tempest, or may I never see home!*"' And like the traditional motif of the playful jest or casual oath in a fairy-tale or a Kafka story, Rugg's impatient exclamation doomed him to a life of wandering.

The details of Rugg's journeys link the story, implicitly but precisely, to events in the American Revolution. The original storm overtook Peter Rugg at Menotomy, *en route* between Charlestown and Lexington, the scenes of the first major engagements of the War of Independence in 1775. It is perhaps not clear how precise an allegory is at issue in the story, but it is certainly full of potent symbolic suggestions. At the end the narrator finds himself outside the land opposite Middle Street, on which Peter Rugg's house once stood, at the moment it is about to be sold at auction. The auctioneer is drawing the crowd's attention to the illustrious history that surrounds it: '[T]here, around that corner, lived James Otis; here Samuel Adams; there, Joseph Warren; and around that other corner, Josiah Quincy. Here was the birthplace of Freedom; here Liberty was born, and nursed, and grew to manhood.' A moment later the auctioneer announces that a piece of the estate will soon be compulsorily bought in order to widen Ann Street and praises the government fulsomely for its generosity. The irony is plain: liberty means the right to have your land forcibly purchased.

Beyond these local allusions there are the more timeless elements of folk superstition: at a horse race in Virginia it is discovered that the great black horse driven by Rugg leaves the imprint of hooves that are cloven (like the devil's). Dunwell tells one of his informants that 'It appears to me that Rugg's horse has some control of the chair, and that Rugg is, in some sort, under the control of his horse'; which recalls the idea traditional to moralists and emblem books that man's passions are like an impetuous horse and that Reason is the rider that should control it. The story also suggests the mythical figure of the Wandering Jew. In Hawthorne's later sketch, 'A Virtuoso's Collection', the Virtuoso is the Wandering Jew and his door-keeper is one Peter Rugg. To be the door-keeper to the Wandering Jew is to be doubly displaced: not only to be constantly on the move, but also at the service of a lord whose domicile is constantly changing. And as the narrator of the sketch enters Peter Rugg speaks: '"I beseech you kind sir," he said in a cracked, melancholy tone, "have pity on the most unfortunate man in the world. For Heaven's sake, answer me a single question: is this the town of Boston?"'[7]

Pattee feels that 'Peter Rugg', for all its force, is uneconomical and badly told, since the number of narrators and the order of events is confusing.[8] I suggest, however, that these qualities add to the effectiveness of a story which is half attested fact and half superstition, half history and half allegory. And as well as his narrative mode, Austin has a command of a language that can combine Dickensian grotesque with Biblical sonority. Dunwell describes Rugg's ruined house in Boston:

> The house seemed conscious of its fate; and as though tired of standing there, the front was fast retreating from the rear, and waiting the next south wind to project itself into the street. If the most wary animals had sought a place of refuge, here they would have rendezvoused. Here,

> under the ridge-pole, the crow would have perched in security; and in the recesses below, you might have caught the fox and the weasel asleep. 'The hand of destiny,' said I, has pressed heavy on this spot; still heavier on the former owners. Strange that so large a lot of land as this should want an heir! Yet Peter Rugg, at this day, might pass by his own door-stone, and ask, "Who once lived here?"'

The short story form is clearly ideal for this allegorical piece of invented folklore. A novel, on the other hand, would need to expand on Peter's life, his relations with his wife and daughter, his job and so on (would, in short, tend towards realism); and would thus lose the focus on the image of the outcast wanderer. The short story (in a way we shall often find in this study) lends itself to the symbolic or the emblematic. The crisis it records is approached obliquely, but gradually comes to light like a hidden trauma. It is the crisis of the American Revolution which has left Peter (and doubtless many other reactionaries) a stranger in his own country. But more than that it is also a universal tale of sudden impatience, leading, like Kafka's 'Knock at the Manor Gate', to a train of consequences far beyond its seeming triviality.

None of Austin's other stories has the haunting power of 'Peter Rugg', but they nevertheless deserve to be better known. They also reinforce the fact, apparent in Irving and Hawthorne, that the American short story has its roots very much in romance-parable. 'The Man With the Cloaks: a Vermont Legend' (1836) is a weirdly comic story (reminiscent of Wordsworth's Lyrical Ballad 'Goody Blake and Harry Gill' of 1798) about a miser who refuses to give his cast-off cloak to a poor man on a bitter winter day and suffers a torment of increasing cold as a result, needing more and more overcoats, another one for every day of the year. He eventually needs a telescope to peer down 'the long avenue of his many cloaks'. At one point, venturing outside, he topples from his doorstep and rolls down the snowy hill, accumulating snow until he becomes a giant snowball which slides right across the frozen lake at the bottom of the hill; and his neighbours take two days to hack him out. Only when he finds the poor men to take his cloaks does his heart begin to grow warmer and warm his body. The moral is clear and satisfying, but what gives the story its comedy and charm is its imaginative fantasy and grotesquerie. In 'Martha Gardner: or, Moral Reaction' a story about a woman in Charlestown who loses her house twice – once to a fire during the battle of Bunker Hill and later to the greed of the Corporation of Charles River Bridge – Austin, as in 'Peter Rugg', plays teasingly with the supernatural (a river post cut down by the Corporation wanders the seven seas but floats back to Martha's quayside, and a curse on the bridge makes it forever economically blighted) but under cover of the folk-tale writes a sharp and still timely satire on corporate greed ('conscience is a non-corporate word'). And in 'Some Account of the Sufferings of a Country Schoolmaster' (1825) Austin satirizes town authorities' mean treatment of schoolteachers in a story that comically exaggerates the 'sufferings' to the point of grotesquerie, and (it has been argued) provides an ironic commentary on Irving's more idyllic rural setting in 'The Legend of Sleepy Hollow'.[9]

Chapter 3

Nathaniel Hawthorne

Hawthorne's predilection for the mode of 'Romance' was undoubtedly one of the main factors in leading him towards the short story form. Romance, as understood by Hawthorne and later by Henry James, encourages an imaginative freedom with ordinary everyday circumstance and also a higher degree of metaphoric meaning, symbolism and allegory, and it can be argued that these elements are more easily embodied in the short story or tale than in the novel. It could even be argued that the greatest of Hawthorne's novels, *The Scarlet Letter*, is essentially an expanded short story, or at least a novella. The central image of the woman with the A embroidered on her dress was, in fact, first sketched by Hawthorne in the short story 'Endicott and the Red Cross' (1837), where the woman is the last and most suggestive figure in a sketch of various guilty individuals in the town of Salem 'whose punishment would be lifelong'. The central symbol of the letter, with its moral paradox, is the heart of the novel, 'the idea as hero'.[1]

Hawthorne began his career as a writer of short pieces. His first published short story 'The Hollow of the Three Hills', appeared in *The Salem Gazette* in 1830, and throughout the thirties and forties a host of stories followed in that and other magazines like *The Token*, *The New England Magazine* and *The Democratic Review*.[2] His first book collections of the stories were *Twice-Told Tales* (1837) and *Twice-Told Tales* (Second Series) (1842). These volumes, with the subsequent *Mosses from an Old Manse* (1846), really established his contemporary reputation as a short story writer, and contain the bulk of the stories on which that reputation rests today. The stories cover a great range of subjects, illustrating from the outset of the American tradition the mobility and variety of the form. But in order to focus on what is most distinctive about Hawthorne's art of the short story I shall divide my discussion into three areas (sometimes overlapping): stories examining Puritan history, those preoccupied with the psychological complexities of sin and guilt, and those which explore the nature of art and science.

Tales of Puritan history

Hawthorne's mind was deeply imbued, one might say formed, by Puritan tradition, but it was a tradition to which he stood in an ambivalent and ironic relationship. He was descended from a prominent New England family, and his great-great-grandfather, John Hathorne (sic), had been one of the presiding judges at the Salem witch trials of 1692. A famous passage from the first chapter of *The Scarlet Letter* expresses the inescapable sense of duty and admiration which mingles with Hawthorne's ironic sense of Puritan gloom and fanaticism, and asks how his own vocation as a writer stands in relation to his ancestors' moral seriousness:

> 'What is he?' murmurs one gray shadow of my forefathers to the other. 'A writer of storybooks! . . . Why, the degenerate fellow might as well have been a fiddler!'[3]

The mixture of irony and respect expressed in this passage extended beyond Hawthorne's attitude to his ancestors and imbues the very fabric of his literary imagination. And one might say that the appeal and interest of his writing today (beyond any mere historical interest) lies in its subtle mingling of the aesthetic and the moral attitudes to experience. Henry James, in his book on Hawthorne, identified the way in which Hawthorne had a Puritan sensibility 'minus the conviction', in which 'The old Puritan moral sense' is judged 'from the poetic and aesthetic point of view, the point of view of entertainment and irony'.[4]

That seems exactly right: yet one should not play down the moral seriousness of Hawthorne's stories in contrast to their 'poetic' and 'aesthetic' effects, their vividly pictorial style (James called it 'picturesque') and their playful humour. One might even say that Hawthorne's task, particularly in his short stories, is to critique the old Puritan ethic, questioning its superstitions and its rigid moral categories, yet preserving its fundamental seriousness. Hawthorne's stories still make us think seriously about moral issues, about sin and guilt and society's need for regularity and code, but in a way that subjects them to humour and irony – the irony that is aware of the perils of moral judgement, and the need of a kind of lightness of touch in the processes of moral reflection.

The treatment, in its broader aspects of 'sin and guilt', in Hawthorne's stories will be the subject of the next section. Firstly I want to look at some stories which treat more specifically the matter of Puritan history and Hawthorne's sense of its legacy. The pictorial element of Hawthorne's historical imagination, and the way his short stories are often about, or analogous to, pictures, is finely exemplified in 'Endicott and the Red Cross' (1837), which describes how in 1634 Governor Endicott of Massachusetts publicly defied new powers imposed from England and a loss of colonial liberties. One subtle and vivid scene in which Endicott is standing in the town square in Salem before his soldiers, mustered for martial exercise, is described as reflected in the breastplate of the Governor, 'so highly polished, that the whole surrounding scene had its image in the glittering steel'. The reflection includes the meeting house, with the head of a recently slain wolf nailed to its porch, 'the blood . . . still plashing on the doorstep'; the whipping post, 'that important engine of Puritanic authority'; the pillory with 'the head of an Episcopalian and suspected Catholic' encased in it, and the stocks holding a man who had drunk the health of the King; and several other figures, including the woman with the scarlet A on her gown.

This vivid picture is a complex image of Puritan authority, full of ironic reminders of the tyranny and violence of a society which the story is ultimately celebrating as a precursor of American liberties. And the breastplate itself is an Old Testament emblem of the theocratic state,[5] as well as, in the later scene of Endicott's anger, virtually a part of Endicott's own body ('nor was it unnatural to suppose that his breastplate would likewise become red-hot, with the angry fire of the bosom which it covered'). So this specular image of violent authority is both the heart of Endicott and the heart of the Puritan state. The irony qualifies the story's admiration of the Puritans, but it is also directed at the world of the reader. The subsequent paragraph points out that the scene illustrates that Puritan desire 'to search out the most secret sins and expose them to shame . . . Were such the custom now, perchance we might find materials for no less piquant a sketch than the above.' Hawthorne's imagination, in this concentrated short story image, reflects critically on the present as well as on the past.

In 'The Maypole of Merrymount' the imaging of a representative cultural moment is done in a more legend-like form.[6] The subtitle of the story when it first appeared in the magazine *The Token* in 1836 was 'A Parable', which suggests also a wider moral application than that of a merely historical tale. For the story is not just about Endicott and the Puritan repression of pagan customs, but about the clash of two attitudes to life, sensuous happiness against stern moral seriousness. The Maypole is the emblem of all the ancient

English pagan customs which survived into the Christian era, and it becomes in the story also the emblem of art and sexual love.

The inhabitants of Merrymount with their Maypole and seasonal rituals come into conflict with the sterner Puritans led by Endicott. Merrymount is associated with Nature and a kind of eternal spring where festivity rules all the year round. It is a garden of the 'Golden age', or Eden, and it has its Adam and Eve in the figures of two lovers, the Lord and Lady of the May, who are about to be married: a wedlock 'more serious than most affairs of Merrymount, where jest and delusion, trick and fantasy, kept up a continual carnival'. The darker side to the atmosphere is reflected in the carnival figures, the man with a stag's antlers, the man in the likeness of a bear, the real bear from the dark forest, the 'Salvage' or savage man, 'hairy as a baboon, and girdled with green leaves', and the mock Indian hunter. And the leader of the revellers is 'the very Comus of the Crew', a reference to the tempter in Homer's *Odyssey* and Milton's poem.

The conclusion of the story, although it sees the end of the Merrymount community, allows at least for the lovers a kind of middle way between the playful irresponsibility of the revellers and the harshness of the Puritans. Endicott's repression means that many of the revellers are taken away to be whipped. 'Yet the deepening twilight could not altogether conceal that the iron man was softened; he smiled at the fair spectacle of early love; he almost sighed for the inevitable blight of early hopes.' He commands that the lovers be dealt with gently, perceiving that they both have qualities that his community needs, and in a final emblematic gesture, he 'lifted the wreath of roses from the ruin of the Maypole, and threw it . . . over the heads of the Lord and Lady of the May'.

Hawthorne's art here creates a legend which both represents a historical and cultural moment and has a universal application. The play of light and shadow, the contrasts of innocent paganism with darker sensuality, of moral clarity with gloomy harshness, are delicately and pictorially done, so that the meaning is conveyed with lightness and charm. History for Hawthorne is here a matter of the emblematic event which embodies more than its own moment. The parable does not have the darker ambiguity of Hawthorne's more complex psychological tales of sin and guilt, and is perhaps limited by its focus on the charm of the picturesque, but it is typical of his delicate art and playful humour.

One of his most striking and representative stories of pre-revolutionary history, 'My Kinsman, Major Molineux' (1832), is a treatment of revolution and crisis and a paradigmatic example of the short story form in its Romance mode. It is also, like 'Peter Rugg', a Boston story, in which history and universality combine and which is at once personal and national, psychological and cultural. The story tells of a country youth, Robin, who comes to the metropolis in search of his father's cousin, Major Molineux. He encounters various townspeople: all are in various ways hostile or mocking, and Robin can get no information about his kinsman. Eventually he hears the sounds of merriment and festivity: he encounters figures dressed like Indians; behind them, borne along in a cart 'in tar-and-feathery dignity', his face pale and his forehead 'contracted in his agony', comes his kinsman, the government official deposed and humiliated by the revolutionary crowd. Robin is at first appalled, and then is caught up in the atmosphere of mirth and festivity so that he sends forth 'a shout of laughter' that joins with the universal merriment.

The summer night is central to a wonderfully evoked atmosphere, somewhere between dream and reality, the ominous and the comic. There is an almost theatrical play of light throughout the story: the light of the ferryman's lantern; the light which falls 'from the open door and windows of a barber's shop'; the moonlight on a man with a face painted in red and black; the moon in the street where Robin waits. This play of natural and artificial light culminates in the great theatrical blaze of the revolutionary procession, paradoxically illuminating and concealing (like the details of Robin's encounters in the story so far). And finally, at the climax of Robin's and the crowd's hilarity, 'the cloud-spirits peeped from their silvery islands', and the Man in the Moon looks down on the scene.

Throughout the story Hawthorne maintains a finely balanced irony which weighs comedy against tragedy, a sense of the pain of individual and social maturation against its laughable errors and an ultimately hilarious sense of release. That Robin is a 'shrewd youth' is one of the ironic motifs of the story, and at its close, the kindly gentleman Robin has met just before his encounter with the major pays Robin the compliment which, though still tinged with irony, is predominantly genial and encouraging: '"Some few days hence, if you wish it, I will speed you on your journey. Or, if you prefer to remain with us, perhaps, as you are a shrewd youth, you may rise in the world without the help of your kinsman, Major Molineux."'

What needs to be stressed is the complex 'image' or aesthetic idea which Hawthorne's unique vision and artistry creates. In 'My Kinsman, Major Molineux', Hawthorne produces a poetic and dramatic image of a moment of crisis, an image which encompasses both tragedy and comedy. Hawthorne's view of Robin (and of the good-natured gentleman) is fundamentally sympathetic, but his view of the political events in the story is richly ambivalent, balanced between a sense of the inevitability and 'comedy' of political change (taking 'comedy' in one of its fundamental senses of a story with a happy ending), and the sense of tragedy which that change involves. Indeed, the picture of the humiliation of the major himself, 'the foul disgrace of a head grown gray in honour', is the most powerful moment in the story, and explicitly tragic, evoking in Robin a feeling of 'pity and terror'.

Hawthorne's brilliant story epitomizes the crisis of the coming of age of Robin and of America and illustrates in its mastery of tone and precision of imagery the powerful potentialities of the short story. If in the short story the idea is hero, an idea of revolutionary change and its relation to 'the common man' dominates here. But it is realized as an aesthetic artefact which embodies rather than expounds this idea. What matters is its precise realization of narrative, scene and human figure (rather than 'character' in sense of the developed portrait belonging to the novel), its poetic precision of language.

Tales of sin and guilt

Hawthorne's contemporary, Herman Melville, in his essay 'Hawthorne and his Mosses' (1850), famously characterized one of Hawthorne's most powerful qualities as 'the power of blackness':

> For spite of all the Indian-summer sunlight on the hither side of Hawthorne's soul, the other side – like the dark half of the physical sphere – is shrouded in a blackness, ten times black.[7]

It is notable how Melville writes, appropriately for Hawthorne's work, in pictorial terms of light and darkness, 'lights and shades'; and in his wondering whether Hawthorne simply uses this 'mystical blackness' for aesthetic effect he is close to Henry James's later view of Hawthorne's aestheticizing of Puritan moral values. But he also senses the possibility of a 'Puritanic gloom' in Hawthorne, and closes with the sense that there is in his work a serious preoccupation with Original Sin.

This preoccupation is nowhere more marked that in what is perhaps Hawthorne's most famous story, 'Young Goodman Brown', first published in 1835. The story's mode lies somewhere between ghostly tale and parable, and it might be described as recording a vision of universal guilt. Goodman Brown sets out into the forest one night from Salem village on an initially unspecified errand, despite the pleas of his wife, the 'aptly-named' Faith, that he should stay with her 'this night . . . of all nights in the year': in retrospect it becomes clear that this must be the night of 31 October, All Saints' Eve or Hallowe'en.[8] On the road he meets a second traveller, a worldly gentleman of middle age with a staff 'which bore the likeness of a great black snake'. He comes upon a space in the forest where felled trunks and branches have been set on fire, with a rock altar or pulpit set between four blazing pines. He looks around and sees a great company of men and woman, among whom he sees all the most pious and respectable people of the village, mingled with the criminal and dissolute and with Indian priests or pow-wows. A voice cries: 'Bring forth the converts', Brown steps forward and a 'sable form' makes a speech of welcome, telling him 'It shall be yours to penetrate, in every bosom, the deep mystery of sin.' He finds himself before the altar, and beside him is his wife. '"Faith, Faith," cried the husband, "look up to heaven and resist the wicked one!"'; and at the next moment he is alone in the calm night. The following morning he is back in the village but he shrinks from the minister, his neighbours and even Faith with her pink ribbons who rushes to greet him. Thereafter he is 'a stern, a sad, a darkly meditative, a distrustful, if not a desperate, man'. And the story ends: 'And when he had lived long, and was borne to the grave, a hoary corpse, followed by Faith, an aged woman, and children and grandchildren, a goodly procession, besides neighbours not a few, they carved no hopeful verse upon his tombstone; for his dying hour was gloom.'

What is the meaning of this story? As I have already suggested, it could be described as a vision of universal guilt and hypocrisy, of universal human evil. But if so, it is the vision of Goodman Brown rather than of Hawthorne himself. Hawthorne's irony (one returns inescapably to that quality) keeps the story in the mode of Romance, and hence the question of belief at a distance, though still in play. The question towards the end of the story, 'Had Goodman Brown fallen asleep in the forest, and only dreamed a wild dream of a witch-meeting?' is perhaps an unnecessary one (a recourse to the ploy of the naive teller of a fantastic story). Whether dream or not, the fictional effect and the meaning of Brown's adventure remain the same. But the mode of witty dubiety in the details of the tale serves as a more sophisticated teasing of the reader with the trope of 'aporia' or doubt between fantasy and reality, as in the description of the worldly gentleman's staff – 'so curiously wrought that it might almost be seen to twist and wriggle itself like a living serpent. This, of course, must have been an ocular deception, assisted by the uncertain light.' Here the rationalistic disclaimer seems to appeal to our everyday mode of perception, but also teases us with the idea that this is *merely* a rationalization, and there is a deeper supernatural reality underneath. And even though the vision of evil is Brown's rather than Hawthorne's, and the mode of the story is archaic or folkloric superstition, its effect is to make us think about the nature of evil and the relation between mythic fantasy and moral reality. Perhaps such old fantastic stories, so 'quaint' in their supernatural accoutrements, have a truth in them that rationalistic accounts of human life cannot easily encompass.

'The Minister's Black Veil' (subtitled 'A Parable') is less solemn in its tone of quizzical scepticism about the motives of its protagonist, the Reverend Mr Hooper, who one day dons a black veil which he refuses to remove, and strikes fear and consternation into the hearts of his parishioners. As explanation, in so far as he gives one, he preaches a sermon which 'had reference to secret sin, and those sad mysteries which we hide from our nearest and dearest, and would fain conceal from our own consciousness', and just before he dies at the end of the story he reiterates the idea in more chilling terms:

> What, but the mystery which it obscurely typifies, has made this piece of crape so awful? When his friend shows his inmost heart to his friend; the lover to his best beloved; when man does not vainly shrink from the eye of his Creator, loathsomely treasuring up the secret of his sin; then deem me a monster, for the symbol beneath which I have lived, and die! I look around me, and, lo! on every visage a Black Veil!

But the story is not to be restricted to Hooper's own moral. There is an uncanny sense that the minister's gesture is itself a kind of madness, or represents a kind of diabolical pride, either one of superior knowingness, or one of concealing a sin more terrible than any known to his congregation, a pride indicated by the 'glimmering of a melancholy smile' on the 'placid mouth' which the veil still leaves exposed.[9] Poe triumphantly suggested that he alone had penetrated to the reality of Hooper's sin, as having reference to some crime committed against the young woman at whose funeral Hooper presides, uncannily holding his veil close to his face as he bends over her ('Could Mr Hooper be fearful of her glance . . .?', the narrator comments). But surely Poe (unless he is simply being mischievous) is crudely reductive here, exercising the detective-story side to his mentality rather than responding adequately to the suggestions of the tale, which gains its power precisely by not specifying or revealing. J. Hillis Miller, indeed, sees it as exemplifying the postmodern aporia of interpretation: a sense of the impossibility of getting 'inside' the outward signs of meaning, whether these are in the mode of allegory or realism.[10] In aesthetic rather than cognitive terms the story employs a kind of macabre wit to stir a frisson of horror at the uncanniness of Hooper's wilful self-veiling. There is a tactile horror in the way the veil stirs with his breath, and the final detail adds a touch of Poe-like melodrama in the last sentence (particularly if it preserves the capitals of Hawthorne's original text): 'and good Mr Hooper's face is dust; but awful is the thought, that it mouldered beneath THE BLACK VEIL'. There is black humour as well as horror in this, and it confirms the way in which the tale makes us consider both seriously and sceptically the tortuous psychological labyrinths of a hyper-scrupulous morality.

Art and science

The theme of the dangers of experimenting with human nature, whether in religion, art or science, are explored further in several of Hawthorne's stories. 'The Birthmark' (1843) records the fatal experiment of Aylmer to remove a birthmark from the face of his beautiful young wife. If Aylmer here is the type of the overweening scientist, he is also the tormented Puritan: the birthmark, in the shape of a tiny hand, becomes also the mark of an Original Sin. Aylmer has a terrible dream in which he imagines himself carrying out the operation: '[B]ut the deeper went the knife, the deeper sank the hand, until at length its tiny grasp appeared to have caught hold of Georgiana's heart; whence, however, her husband was inexorably resolved to cut or wrench it away.' The disturbing violence of this is a measure of how far Aylmer's scientific, aesthetic and even religious quest for perfection has dehumanized him. And the figure of Aminadab, Aylmer's servant, despite – or perhaps because of – his name (an anagram of 'I a bad man') represents ordinary unregenerate human nature and shows an earthy, humorous scepticism at Aylmer's experiment, muttering '"If she were my wife, I'd never part with that birthmark."'

The conflict between artistic (and scientific) aspiration and common human values is again the theme of 'An Artist of the Beautiful'. Owen Warland is a watchmaker who turns his back on the mundane world of watchmaking and aspires to create a work of ideal beauty from his mechanisms. He is mocked by the scepticism of an older colleague, Roger Hovenden, who sees something perhaps dangerous as well as impractical in his aspirations (at one point he associates them, if jokingly, with witchcraft). The rest of the town thinks he may be mad. Even the girl he loves, Hovenden's daughter Annie, though she is initially sympathetic to his efforts, is in the end won to marriage with the strong, practical blacksmith Roger Danforth. Spurred by his reaction to even more intense and solitary creative effort, Owen finally creates a beautiful mechanical butterfly, so delicate that its beauty apes that of nature and so light that it can fly. Roger exclaims wonderingly that it 'does beat all nature!', but Hovenden sees it as just a pretty toy. Even Annie has a secret scorn for Owen's achievement. And Annie's and Roger's little child, 'with his grandsire's sharp and shrewd expression in his face', makes a snatch at the toy and destroys it utterly.

From one point of view the story is a simple parable of the Romantic artist's doomed struggle to create in the face of a hostile and uncomprehending society. And the very end of the story seems to authorize an idealist or transcendent view of art in which for the artist the idea is all, and 'the symbol by which he made it perceptible to mortal senses became of little value in his eyes', so that Owen is indifferent to the destruction of the butterfly. But the story as a whole suggests a more ambiguous significance. The narrator seems sympathetic to Owen's efforts, but also conveys the feeling that his aspiration is too rarefied. Annie's incomprehension is seen as regrettable but is not scorned; and the child is 'a little personage who had come mysteriously out of the infinite, but with something so sturdy and real in his composition that he seemed moulded out of the densest substance that earth could supply' – 'mysterious' yet strongly physical too, unlike the butterfly. Annie is described as 'admiring her own infant, and with good reason, far more than the artistic butterfly'. So it is possible to see an irony in this story which partly undermines the apparent moral of the transcendent and essentially unworldly beauty of art.

There is a darker obscurity of subject in a final example from this group, 'Rappaccini's Daughter', the story of a beautiful young woman in a poisonous garden. Beatrice's father, the scientist Professor Rappaccini of Padua, has brought her up from childhood among the deadly plants and flowers which he himself has 'created' in order to endow her with 'marvellous gifts against which no power or strength could avail an enemy'. A young man, Giovanni, not knowing the secrets of the garden, is deeply attracted by her luxuriant beauty and her intimate closeness to the beautiful flowers. He gradually becomes aware of the deadly nature of the garden, but not heeding the warnings of Rappaccini's rival Baglioni he still pursues her, so that he too takes on her deadly power. When he realizes the full extent of her and his contamination he urges her to drink with him the antidote prepared by Baglioni. But she drinks first, and 'as poison had been life, so the powerful antidote was death', and Baglioni ends the story with the horrified and triumphant cry: '"Rappaccini! Rappaccini! and is *this* the upshot of your experiment?"'

This rich and darkly morbid story shows Hawthorne's art at its most sensuous and florid. The fatal luxuriance of the garden, its gorgeous and lethal beauty, is wonderfully done; and the growing signs of the deadliness of its flowers and the destructiveness of Beatrice and finally Giovanni himself accumulate with a sinister insistence, a quality enhanced rather than mitigated by Giovanni's doubts of his own perception. At the same time the story is rich in symbolic suggestion. The initial situation – the lover seeing from a window the beautiful woman in a garden – is a resonant *topos* of medieval Romance (*The Romance of the Rose*, or Chaucer's *Knight's Tale*, of which there are verbal echoes in the story), but here it is sinisterly subverted. The garden is also 'that Eden of poisonous flowers'. And if the garden is Eden, the narrator asks, is Rappaccini the Adam?

The question is not just rhetorical. If Rappaccini is the Adam, there is a buried suggestion of an incestuous closeness with the Eve of the garden, Beatrice. Or is he the God of the garden, since he 'created' the flowers; or, indeed, the serpent, since it was he who introduced the evil into the garden? The story is not a precise allegory, but has, rather, the suggestiveness of symbolism, and its rich ambiguity is the essence of its power. It is also, of course, about the fatal power of science (linking it with the other stories in this group), where Rappaccini is the mad scientist, and Baglioni, in his bitter rivalry with Rappaccini, is partly responsible for the death of Beatrice, since it is he who provides the too-powerful antidote. Rappaccini is also seen as an artist, who creates a dangerous beauty and who manipulates human lives so that at the end he gazes on them 'as might an artist who should spend his life in achieving a picture or a group of statuary, and finally be satisfied with his success'.

But the central ambiguity of the story lies in Beatrice and in the story's imagining of sexuality. In an ironic prologue (and in the subtitle of the story) the narrator claims that he has translated the story from one by a French author, M. de l'Aubépine (French for 'hawthorn'), where the title was 'La Belle Empoisonneuse' ('The Beautiful Poisoner'). In this version of the title the emphasis is put on Beatrice's agency, her responsibility for the poisoning of Giovanni; whereas the English title makes Rappaccini the dominant figure. Is the story, it has been asked, not so much about perverted science or art, as about the corruption of sexuality itself? Giovanni's attraction to Beatrice is described as 'not love . . . but a wild offspring of both love and horror'. And since Beatrice is most immediately responsible for this corruption (at the least she does not try to resist her father's influence), is the story taking a dark view of specifically female sexuality?

It is possible to read it this way. But Hawthorne writes that Giovanni '*fancied* her spirit to be imbued with the same baneful essence' as her physical frame (my italics), and there are other signs in the story that Hawthorne is resisting the suggestion that Beatrice is essentially corrupted, or that Giovanni is himself guiltless. There are several suggestions that Giovanni's perception may help to constitute the corruption rather than simply recording it. And at the end Beatrice in turn accuses him: 'Oh, was there not, from the first, more poison in thy nature than in mine?' There is the strong suggestion in the story that Hawthorne is trying to mitigate, at least, the misogynistic elements that it undoubtedly contains. Feminist critics have also tended to emphasize the agency of the dark figure of Rappaccini, who also suggests to some contemporary readers the 'law of the father' that both forms the structure of society and yet blights it with its repressive authority.

But whatever our final interpretative emphasis, the fertile subtlety of Hawthorne's short story art is not in doubt. 'Rappaccini's Daughter' is a fine example of that concentrated mode of parable, symbolism or allegory (it has elements of all three) which the form of the Romance short story allowed him. The lightness and 'popular' ambition of the form (Hawthorne's desire to 'open up an intercourse with the world') lends itself to these pieces which are pictorial and atmospheric as well as intellectually complex. Their treatment of symbolism, particularly the symbolism of nature, illustrates but also challenges Emerson's claim that 'Every natural fact is also a spiritual fact . . . A lamb is innocence, a snake is subtle spite, flowers express to us the delicate affections.'[11] Emerson's symbolism is morally clear-cut, but 'Rappaccini's Daughter', with its re-reading of flowers, is about moral ambiguity. Overall Hawthorne's stories constitute a challenge (more variously and more tellingly than any of his longer work with the exception of *The Scarlet Letter*) to the yea-saying and sometimes ponderous Emersonian optimism of the age. Hawthorne 'says No! in thunder', said Melville in a letter (16 April 1851). And the form of the Romance short story allowed that element of allegory, that fusing of idea and symbol which, far from being a debilitating distraction from realism as the realist Henry James suggested,[12] is essential to that challenge.

Chapter 4

Edgar Allan Poe

Poe and the aesthetics of the short story

As well as being one of its first and greatest American practitioners, Poe is the first theorist of the short story as a literary form. In his review of Hawthorne's *Twice-Told Tales* (1842) he elaborates his idea of the aesthetics of the short story, declaring that 'the tale proper, in our opinion, affords unquestionably the fairest field for the exercise of the loftiest talent, which can be afforded by the wide domain of mere prose.'[1] He focuses above all on the tale's ability to achieve 'unity of effect and impression' which relies on the fact that it can be read 'at one sitting'. The novel, by contrast, 'deprives itself . . . of the immense force derivable from *totality*' (italics in the original here and elsewhere in quotations from Poe). He continues with his ideal of the short story writer's practice:

> A skilful literary artist has constructed a tale. If wise, he has not fashioned his thoughts to accommodate his incidents; but having conceived, with deliberate care, a certain unique or single *effect* to be wrought out, he then invests such incidents – he then combines such events as may best aid him in establishing this preconceived effect. If his very initial sentence tend not to the outbringing of this effect, then he has failed in his first step. In the whole composition there should be no word written, of which the tendency, direct and indirect, is not to the one pre-established design. And by such means, with such care and skill, a picture is at length painted which leaves in the mind of him who contemplates it with a kindred art, a sense of the fullest satisfaction. The

> idea of the tale has been presented unblemished because undisturbed; and this is an end unattainable by the novel.[2]

This ideal of unity of effect and impression has been remarkably influential on the idea of the short story, and was repeated and recast by a number of critics (most notably Brander Matthews in his 'Philosophy of the Short-Story', 1885).[3] It was not seriously challenged until the twentieth century, and then rather more by the practice of writers who apparently ignored unity in Poe's sense than by any explicit theorizing; although the value of unity has been variously challenged by modernist and postmodernist aesthetics in general.

The review of Hawthorne, and still more his essay 'The Philosophy of Composition' (in which he relates somewhat implausibly the highly calculated way he composed his poem 'The Raven', starting from the aim for an 'effect' of Beauty and Melancholy and working backwards by supposedly inevitable steps towards a talking raven), is highly revealing of an essential quality in Poe: his profound need to give a semblance of rationality and calculation to the strange and irrational creations of his artistic imagination.[4] Poe's great topic in his short stories (however variedly presented in detective stories, science fiction and even comic parody) is horror, a dark vision of the irrational side of the human mind and its tendency to self-destruction. And his way of controlling this is to construct a theory of the artist's absolute rational command over his materials. Not only this, but the theme of rational control and explanation – with a protagonist often desperate to control his listeners or readers and to persuade them of his sanity – is central to many of the stories themselves.

The deaths of beautiful women

In his essay 'The Philosophy of Composition' Poe wrote that 'The death . . . of a beautiful woman is, unquestionably, the most poetical topic in the world';[5] and it is the recurring topic of a set of stories – 'Morella', 'Berenicë', 'Ligeia' and 'Eleonora' – which show an unusual element of psychological repetition.[6] In 'Morella' (1835) the narrator marries the woman of the title, though his love for her is not sexual: he becomes, rather, 'her pupil'. (In all these stories the relation to the woman is very much that of child to mother or older woman.) Eventually she dies, but just before her death she gives birth to a daughter, who grows to resemble her mother exactly; and the narrator's love for her is mingled with fear at the 'too perfect *identity*' of her smile and eyes with her mother's. Nevertheless at her baptism he is prompted ('What fiend spoke from the recesses of my soul?') to whisper to the priest the name

'Morella': at which the face of the child is convulsed and she falls back with the words 'I am here!' and dies.

The best and most complex of this group of tales is 'Ligeia' (1838). Again, the narrator marries a beautiful woman whom he met perhaps 'in some decaying city near the Rhine' (though he cannot remember 'how, when, or even precisely where' – the narrator's strange vagueness is again significant, raising a doubt about the degree of fantasy in his memories). His description of her is typical of Poe's deliberately mannered, hyperbolic style, full of esoteric references – it was 'Lord Verulam' (i.e Francis Bacon) who described the idea of 'strangeness' in beauty which her features are said to illustrate – and pseudo-references. As with Morella, Ligeia's learning is 'immense' and her mental acquisitions 'gigantic': 'Without Ligeia I was but as a child, groping benighted.' When she dies (as one has come to expect), the narrator 'in a moment of mental alienation' marries her spiritual and physical opposite, 'the fair-haired and blue-eyed lady Rowena Trevanion, of Tremaine.' But a perverse hatred of his second wife leads him to confine her to a castle room with strange, wild decorations and furnishings which evoke the Gothic and Druidic, and also the Oriental (a Saracenic censer, a gigantic black sarcophagus from Luxor): Poe utilizes all the trappings of the fear of 'the other'. Rowena soon sickens, and while giving her wine to revive her the narrator is aware of a presence in the room (though he has, however, had 'an immoderate dose of opium'), and he sees 'drops of a brilliant and ruby-colored fluid' falling into the glass. Rowena's condition quickly worsens, then revives, then sinks into what seems death. Then at last she revives again: but masses of *black* hair stream from the unwrapped cerements, and her slowly opened eyes are 'the full, and the black, and the wild eyes – of my lost love – of the lady – of the LADY LIGEIA!'

D. H. Lawrence saw Poe as a writer of 'the will': the will to experience 'extreme spiritual love . . . against the whole of the limitations of nature';[7] the will to force this experience even to the point of self-destruction. And he found 'the clue to him' in the epigraph to 'Ligeia' (attributed by Poe to the seventeenth-century philosopher Joseph Glanville, but not to be found in the latter's works and probably invented by Poe – another of his pieces of pseudo-scholarship), which concludes: 'Man doth not yield himself to the angels, nor unto death utterly, save only through the weakness of his feeble will.' So Poe can be seen as a writer who, in his narrators, pushes the 'will' to experience the most extreme states – deep crime, madness, the experience of death itself – and wills his own imagination to the limits of these experiences. And in 'Ligeia' he records the wilful assertion of Ligeia herself against death, so that the struggle at the end is her struggle to resume life through Rowena's body. There is, of course, an ambiguity: the narrator speaks of his 'immoderate dose of opium', and it is possible to see the ghostly presence and the return of Ligeia as products of his fantasy. One interpretation has it that he poisons Rowena's wine himself.[8] But there is no need to reduce the story to a merely rationalistic explanation (though Poe himself interpreted Hawthorne's 'The Minister's Black Veil' in that same 'detective' manner).[9] The story is in the mode of Todorov's 'fantastic', hovering between a supernatural and natural meaning.[10] And however we take it – as supernatural symbol or study of the narrator's madness – its relation to a lust of the will still remains. Psychoanalytic interpretations, too – the trauma of the loss of the mother, the desire to find a replacement for her and the repressed hatred of her substitutes – are persuasive. Once again the short story is a genre of crisis, here of psychological crisis.

The imp of the perverse

Poe is fascinated by the will, but particularly by its perverse impulse to self-destruction, and also its morbid fear of fear itself. In 'The Imp of the Perverse' (1845) the narrator analyses what he sees as man's perverse propensity to spite himself. Baudelaire, a passionate admirer and translator of Poe, saw this as Poe's version of the belief in man's innate evil, or Original Sin. This may be so, but the imp seems more trivially playful and undignified than this grand concept suggests. It is the imp, for example, which prompts men to go on talking and elaborating their circumlocution though they know their words are infuriating their listeners (Poe's narrator is here the striking precursor of Dostoyevsky's self-tormenting 'Underground Man');[11] or which compels men to venture nearer and nearer to the edge of an abyss, possessed by a fascination with what would be the sensations of falling, a thought which compels with 'the delight of its horror'. 'To indulge for a moment, in any attempt at *thought*, is to be inevitably lost.' It is difficult to believe that anyone has ever thrown themselves from a cliff from just these motives (though of course the question is unverifiable!). But it is possible to enter into, to *imagine*, the idea taking hold in this way. Poe explores our capacity to imagine madness and perversity. In this story, significantly, the narrator concludes by revealing that he is under sentence of death for a murder which he had committed with no chance of discovery, but which a perverse self-satisfaction, a kind of violent access of over-confidence, caused him to reveal. There is here what might be called a curious will to revelation, even a will to confession, working against the narrator. As often in Poe, the imp of the perverse works in ways that can have surprisingly moral effects.

D. H. Lawrence wrote that Poe's 'morbid' tales were written because 'old things need to die and disintegrate, because the old white psyche has to be gradually broken down before anything else can come to pass'. The idea may in the end be more relevant to Lawrence himself than to Poe: there is not much sense in Poe of anything else coming to pass. But the idea of man being 'stripped even of himself', 'a painful, sometimes a ghastly process', is certainly applicable to Poe. And perhaps one could see the violence and destruction of Poe's stories as, oddly enough, the paroxysm of a revolt against the American Puritan imagination, a return of obsessions repressed first by a fanatical theology and later by the bland moralism of its successors: Poe was brought up in the pious and genteel Episcopalian household of his stepfather John Allan.

Man 'stripped even of himself', and the destruction of a whole dynastic tradition (the tradition of Europe, perhaps, since the cultural associations within the house are from a wide range of European sources) are symbolized nowhere more vividly than in Poe's best-known and probably his greatest story, 'The Fall of House of Usher' (1839). It is a story of the fear of fear itself: Roderick Usher is terrified his life will end in 'some struggle with the grim phantasm, FEAR'. The House of Usher is both the building and the dynastic line, and Roderick Usher and his sister Madeline are the last surviving scions of the family. The house itself is rendered strangely sentient, so that Usher and the house become like one organic entity: it has 'vacant eye-like windows' and the 'tangled web-work' of the fungi on the eaves is echoed in Roderick's 'hair of a more than web-like softness and tenuity'. The house and it domain seems to the narrator to be 'enveloped in an atmosphere peculiar to themselves . . . and atmosphere which had no affinity with the air of heaven'; and later the house is enveloped in a storm which seems confined to the environs of the house itself. Roderick, in the grip of a nameless fear, involves the narrator, who visits him at his urgent request, in burying in a deep vault in the house his sister Madeline whom the narrator has glimpsed once or twice before her death. But, while the narrator is reading a medieval story of the 'Mad Trist' of Sir Launcelot Canning (an invention of Poe's), in which Sir Launcelot confronts and kills the dragon, the sounds in the story are mingled and confused with sounds from the vault: Madeline appears and collapses 'with a low, moaning cry' upon her brother, and '[bears] him to the floor a corpse'. The narrator flees from the house, and looking back sees the House split by a zigzag fissure and collapse with 'a long tumultuous shouting sound like the voice of a thousand waters' into the 'tarn'.

This is a story where the narrator is distinct from the victim, unlike the first-person narrators of 'Ligeia' or 'The Imp of the Perverse' and other stories. Here the mind of Poe (for his protagonists always bear some relation to his own mind) divides itself into two parts, that of the afflicted victim and that of the rational commentator and witness.[12] Roderick Usher represents a decadent refinement and debilitation of the European tradition of romantic excess or 'Romantic Agony'.[13] (There is even something of a Shelleyan refinement about Roderick, and shades of Byron in his quasi-incestuous relationship with Madeline – though nothing of the Byronic energy.) He is surrounded by esoteric works of art and literature, and plays long dirges on his 'speaking guitar', including 'a perversion and amplification of the wild air of the last waltz of Von Weber'.

In the reading of the 'Mad Trist', the story also comments subtly on itself. The coincidence of the details of this wild and almost comic parody of a medieval romance with the events of the primary story suggests a dangerous mingling of art and life, the events of fiction almost bringing about the events in the 'real' world. The narrator calls it one of Roderick's 'favourite romances', and though he says this 'more in jest than in earnest' the description is revealing and the disclaimer (as often with the disclaimers of Poe's narrators) not entirely convincing. At any rate, the story of the 'trist' is echoed in reality: Madeline escapes from her coffin and kills Roderick, just as Ethelred kills the dragon. The shadowy figure that Roderick has buried alive (metaphorically, the guilt that he has buried) returns to destroy him. There may even be a 'perverse' way in which Poe is commenting on the dangers of his own preoccupation with the morbid; and his death in a mysterious, never fully explained, state of dementia in Baltimore in 1849, has uncanny echoes of the fate of many of his protagonists.

The story symbolizes the collapse of a mind, a lineage, and even a whole culture, as well as, unconsciously, Poe's own psychological history (his dangerous states of inebriation, his marriage to his thirteen-year-old cousin). Among other stories of real and symbolic self-destruction, this time with the revealing element of compulsive self-exposure or confession, are 'William Wilson' (1839) and 'The Tell-Tale Heart' (1843). The first is a study of the psychological double, a theme with a precursor in Hogg's *Confessions of a Justified Sinner* and several descendants: most notably Stevenson's *Dr Jekyll and Mr Hyde* and Wilde's *The Picture of Dorian Grey*. In 'The Tell-Tale Heart' the narrator's mind is divided between his initial irrational and murderous hatred and his subsequent compulsive desire to confess. But there is no contrition: the telling of the tale is a kind of desperate attempt to persuade us of his sanity. The first sentence is one of Poe's most arresting openings; the reader is gripped immediately by the direct address of a disturbing voice: 'True! – nervous – very, very dreadfully nervous I had been and am; but why *will* you say that I am mad?' As one critic has said, Poe's murderers 'are not so much obsessive killers, as obsessive talkers'; mere 'communication for these speakers is a kind of salvation'.[14] But it is not the salvation that might come with remorse: the narrator simply wants us to share his experience. The narrator's murder of the old man (a father figure, as the Freudian reading would have it?) is driven by a mad hatred: 'I think it was his eye! yes, it was this! One of his eyes resembled that of a vulture – a pale blue eye, with a film over it!' ('I think. . .': like Iago, Poe's narrator's are rarely certain of their own motives). The murder is carried out with an obsessive, almost comical, slowness and calculation (after momentarily disturbing the old man, 'For a whole hour I did not move a muscle'), and he urges us to feel with him ('you cannot imagine how stealthily, stealthily. . .'). But as in 'The Imp of the Perverse' he is driven to reveal his crime to the police, as he hears the beating of his dead victim's heart (or is it his own? This story, like others, equivocates between natural and supernatural); and the telling builds to the climax of his shrieked revelation. It is a tour-de-force of compulsive rhetoric: the narrator re-enacts his drama in front of us and compels our appalled and unwilling empathy.

Detection and ratiocination

Poe was an inventor, responsible for the science fiction story, the modern horror story (it is Poe who adds the interiorized, psychological ingredient missing – with the exception of James Hogg – from most of the Gothic tradition) and not least the modern detective story. Arthur Conan Doyle, creator of the world's most famous detective Sherlock Holmes, was generous in his acknowledgement to Poe,[15] and Holmes borrows many characteristics from Poe's master-detective, C. Auguste Dupin: the preternatural powers of observation, and even the essential prop of his inspired reveries, the violin. And like Poe, Conan Doyle worked primarily in the form of the short story: its capacity for intense, sustained drama is matched by its suitability for the working out of a single concentrated problem arising from the enigma of the crime. In both writers, too, but particularly in Poe, the ratiocinative power of the detective – the power of reason itself – is pitted against the dark forces of unreason: and the latter are as much a part of the appeal as the former. There is a subversive force in Poe's detective stories: reason pits itself against violence and the irrational, but its victory is not always, in the final effect, complete.

'The Murders in the Rue Morgue' (1841), Poe's first detective story, takes as its fantastic pretext – though it is one that we do not learn of until the end of the story – the murder of two women by a demented orang-utan. Dupin proceeds to solve the crime by a series of minute steps, involving locked or unlocked doors and windows, the size of hand-marks on one of the women's throats, the tuft of red hair found in the room, and so on. One or two of the more notable clues contribute not simply to the 'ratiocinative' aspect of the story but to its disturbing psychological charge. For instance, the several witnesses speak of hearing the sounds of a 'foreign' voice, but they cannot agree on the language. Dupin concludes it is a non-human voice, but for a moment the fear of the 'other', whether the incomprehensible foreigner or the animal in man, has been set up. Then the corpse of one of the women is found forced feet first 'up the narrow aperture' of the chimney with such force that it takes five men to drag it down, which Dupin finds '*excessively outré*' – something altogether irreconcilable with our common notions of human action. This strange detail, mentioned several times, stays in the mind as a peculiar horror – setting up the sense of some psychological significance which we cannot quite interpret. From such details Dupin arrives at his conclusion and solution of the crime.

Poe himself made an obvious point about the 'ingenuity' of the story when he professed himself irritated by those who confused that of the detective with that of the author ('Where is the ingenuity of unravelling a web which you yourself. . .have woven for the express purpose of unravelling?').[16] We are nevertheless impressed by Dupin's ingenuity, but the emotional charge of the story comes from its bizarre premise and its violent details. The fear of the non-human or sub-human within the human (or vice-versa) is activated by the more than natural orang-utan (who imitates his master shaving and who, Dupin infers, is '[c]onscious of having deserved punishment': the beast is actually more like a madman than an animal). The violence done to the women has an inevitable sexual element (Poe's murder victims, it might be noted, are nearly always women). And even the body in the chimney has a weirdly sexual connotation. The overall effect of the story, then, is seemingly to persuade the reader that the strange and irrational has been controlled and solved by the sheer mental acuity of Dupin. The realistic detail of the story (the Parisian setting, the description of the witnesses, the minute description of the rooms) also serves to disguise its fundamentally fantastic quality. But the fantastic premise, and the violence which is inexplicable in realistic terms, leave the reader with a sense of unsolved problems and uncomprehended forces which insist on some kind of symbolic interpretation. G. K. Chesterton once suggested that the Detective was the modern knight of romance, questing in the labyrinths of the murky city and bringing to light and slaying its dragons not by force but by sheer ingenuity.[17] But in Poe the dragons seem to remain lurking in the depths.

'The Gold-Bug' (1843), while not strictly a detective story (there is no Dupin), is a story of detection, the finding of treasure by elaborate clues provided by a pirate's coded message, but it too plays with a fantastic premise: the discovery of the eponymous bug, which leads to the accidental discovery of the message on the parchment. The bug itself remains ambiguous – was it a real bug or just a scarab artefact? Or is it just a metaphor (the 'gold-bug' or gold-fever was just what was soon to intoxicate large numbers of California-bound gold prospectors in 1848)? Whatever else, it seems to be an object which Legrand, the owner and leader of the gold-hunting expedition, uses simply to mystify his companions with an air of magic because he is annoyed at their thinking he might be mad (and thus, of course, making them think so even more). But at the beginning of the story it is presented by Legrand as a real insect; and even at the end, when Legrand is explaining the mystery of how he found the parchment message, he says the creature gave him 'a sharp bite'. The element of the mysterious and the irrational or supernatural is not removed. Louise J. Kaplan speaks of Poe's 'fundamental antagonism to representational reality': the gold-bug seems to hover between the categories of natural and supernatural, literal and metaphoric, and between signifier and signified.[18] Poe is fond of puns and the misleadingness of words, and the phonetic status of words is momentarily highlighted by his black servant Jupiter, when he interrupts Legrand's talk of the bug's antennae with 'Dey aint *no* tin in him, Massa Will.' Language for Poe is often a deceptive screen between its user and reality.

One interest of 'The Mystery of Marie Roget' (1842–3) is that Poe had to change the details of the story before book publication because the outcome of the real-life case on which it was based proved Dupin's original theory wrong (Poe's ratiocination had to be proved right). But Dupin triumphs, of course, in the entirely fictional final detective story, 'The Purloined Letter', and his triumph is made up partly of the element of revenge (another favourite theme of Poe's, as in 'The Cask of Amontillado' and 'Hop-Frog'). The Prefect of Police comes to Dupin for help The minister D— has stolen a letter, containing the most sensitive information, from under the eyes of a female 'personage of most exalted station' in the royal boudoir (we infer it is the Queen), who could not prevent it because they were joined by another 'exalted personage' from whom she wished to conceal it (we infer this is the King). The Police have searched D—'s apartment in the most systematic way possible (which we are given in detail) but have found nothing. Dupin jests 'Perhaps the mystery is a little *too* plain.' Accordingly he goes to D—'s apartment and sees the letter hanging from the mantelpiece, barely disguised with D—'s cipher or seal. Contriving the momentary distraction of D—'s attention, he takes the letter and substitutes another with D—'s seal upon it. Then he presents the Queen's letter to the Prefect of Police and gains his 50,000-franc reward. He then proceeds to describe to the narrator how he did it, and outlines two theories: one of a system for second-guessing an opponent, the other a theory of what might be called concealment by exposure. His final triumph over D—, who once, he says, 'did him an evil turn', adds the element of revenge (so frequent in Poe) by writing some lines in the letter in handwriting D—— would recognize.

The story illustrates a system of detection, and also the way in which a crime is solved by repeating the mental processes of the criminal. Its pattern of repetition has lent itself to allegorical interpretation: Jacques Lacan has famously seen it as a diagram of the 'the agency of the [alphabetic] letter in the unconscious'. The unconscious for Lacan is 'structured like a language'.[19] The letter (alphabetic or, in the story, epistolary) remains in the same place in the structure of relationships in the story, and in the psychoanalytic process. It stands for a recurring element, a hidden object of desire, around which the relationships are structured. The letter in this story also represents some clandestine sexual transgression (one infers – though it could be some other state secret) which is never revealed. The story itself illustrates a motif which could be called that of 'the analyst analysed'. The minister D— sees the letter hidden 'openly' on the Queen's desk, steals it from under her eyes, and hides it himself in a similar way; Dupin sees it hidden openly on D—'s mantelpiece and takes it while D— is still in the room. It is a quintessentially Poean form of revenge: the man of wit outwitted, the analyst analysed, the biter bit (and 'the interpreter interpreted': the pattern has been applied to interpretation itself).[20]

Science, horror and comedy

Poe's short stories cover an extraordinary range: horror of various kinds, revenge, fantastic farce, the 'scientific' romance (or what has come to be known as science fiction), hoax, criminal detection, philosophical fantasy, satire and comedy. The science fiction stories include 'The Facts in the Case of M. Valdemar' (1845) (about a case of hypnosis and communication with a dead man); 'The Balloon-Hoax' (1844, about a trans-Atlantic balloon voyage, a story which actually fooled the public); and the satiric 'Mellonta Tauta' (1849), a letter written from 'Pundita' who is on a 'pleasure excursion' in a balloon some thousand years in the future with satirical reflections on aspects of history. Aristotelian scientific method (that of 'a Turkish philosopher' – or 'Hindoo possibly' – called Aries Tottle) is ridiculed, as is the absurd 'Amriccan' idea of self-government and human equality, and women's fashions.

This piece is more of a satirical sketch than a short story, though there is still the vestige of a narrative element (the balloon journey) to create the fictional premise. But the element of satirical humour is more characteristic of Poe than is often thought, and we find it in unexpected places. For a master of the horror story, for instance, he was surprisingly satirical about the genre. In 'How to Write a Blackwood Article' he parodies the fashion for 'personal experience' horror in the British magazine (pieces like Henry Thomson's 'Le Revenant' of 1827, which recounts the experience of a man who was hanged),[21] with a piece by one Psyche Zenobia (there is a dig at women writers here, too), who recounts in minute detail the experience of being decapitated by the hand of a giant clock. In the story 'Premature Burial' (another essay which develops into a narrative), the narrator begins with several ghastly instances of the phenomenon and discusses his own fears and precautions against the eventuality but then modulates into an anecdote about his own experience, when he awakes from one of the cataleptic trances he is subject to, to the horrific realization of premature burial. He minutely details his sensations of terror, his struggles, his 'long, wild, continuous shriek, or yell of agony'. But at this point the mood switches suddenly to farce: he is roused by gruff voices, and he discovers he has gone to sleep in the narrow berth of a small sloop carrying garden mould and the burial binding around his jaws is a handkerchief used as a nightcap. A revulsion against his fears ensues: 'I thought upon subjects other than Death. I discarded my medical books . . . I read no *Night Thoughts* – no fustian about churchyards – no bugaboo tales – *such as this*.' Horror is suddenly mocked: the story turns upon itself.

The satiric turn prompts reflections about Poe's work in general. Even in his most horrific stories the extremity of the fantasy often teeters on the edge of absurdity, and with a writer as self-consciously aware as Poe one feels this must be deliberate. In 'The Cask of Amontillado' the fiendish revenge of Montresor on Fortunato (in which he bricks him up in his wine vault) is touched by black farce: Fortunato's absurd Carnival Fool's costume and Montresor's manic jesting (as when he suddenly produces a trowel to prove he is a member of the brotherhood of Masons) make this the story of a malign practical joke. And Poe's notorious style – full of the most outrageous mannerism, exaggeration and melodrama – is throughout his work the source of a kind of irony – the irony of the showman who knows he can grip the listener with the mere mesmerism of his technique. Horror, revenge, murder, cruelty are all treated with this intense mannerism, which keeps us guessing as to whether horror or comic showmanship has the upper hand.

In 'A Descent into the Maelström' (one of Poe's stories of fantastic travel, like 'MS Found in a Bottle' or his one novel *The Adventures of Arthur Gordon Pym*) the narrator survives by holding on to a light spar of wood which through a complicatedly explained (but implausible) process of physics whirls back to the surface of the maelstrom rather than being sucked down with the boat. This last process might even be seen as emblematic of the processes of Poe's art: by the fantasies of fictional terror presented with a highly conscious self-awareness, and carried deliberately to the edge of absurdity and beyond – by what is essentially a technique of 'lightness' – Poe can survive his own inner mental maelstroms.[22] He explores and fantasticates genuine terrors as a way both of indulging and of controlling them. It was, perhaps, a dangerous game: the imp of the perverse is mischievously comic, but it is also perverse, and Poe's often tormented life – his unhappy relationships, his bitter literary quarrels, and his alcoholism, particularly after the onset of his wife's consumption – testify to devils not subdued. Whatever the moral bearing of his art (and very distinguished critics – among them Henry James, T. S. Eliot and Yvor Winters – have had serious reservations about Poe), it is undoubtedly the case that the short story was the perfect form for it: intense, unified in effect, enabling an idiosyncratic narrative voice, holding its reader in the grip of a single sitting, and building, at its most characteristic, to climactic closures.

Chapter 5

Herman Melville

The majority of Herman Melville's short stories form a distinct group in his *oeuvre* and a distinct moment in his literary career. As a writer he is best known for his epic novel *Moby Dick* (1851) the story of the heroic and obsessed Captain Ahab's search for the great white whale. He also published the novels *Typee* (1846), *Omoo* (1847) and *Mardi* (1849), all based on his experiences in the Polynesian Islands; *Redburn* (1849), based on his voyage as a seaman to Liverpool in 1839; and *White-Jacket* (1850), an account of life as a sailor aboard a British man-of-war. *Moby Dick*, despite its great later reputation, received mixed reviews when it came out and sold badly. Another novel, *Pierre* (1852), was very harshly reviewed, and a recent critic describes it as 'a work of moral and metaphysical nihilism that estranged him from his readership'.[1] In the early 1850s Melville also suffered from family sorrows: his third child died in 1853 and his fourth in 1854. The new decade was therefore a time of doubt and self-searching for Melville.

At the beginning of that same decade, however, he wrote the essay 'Hawthorne and his Mosses' already cited above, a review of Hawthorne's collection of tales, *Mosses from an Old Manse.* Melville discusses 'Young Goodman Brown', 'Egotism, or the Bosom Serpent', and 'Earth's Holocaust', as well as a number of sketches and stories which are less often read today, and praises Hawthorne for his 'tenderness', but above all for 'his great deep intellect, which drops down into the Universe like a plummet'. And it is notable that, as well as finding 'the power of blackness' that has been discussed above, he is sure that this volume of short stories – rather than, say, *The Scarlet Letter*, which he also mentions – 'will ultimately be accounted his masterpiece'. It appears, then, that Melville's mind was already turning towards the idea of the power of short fiction, perhaps in response to Hawthorne's example, perhaps in reaction against the reception of *Moby Dick*, and moving in a literary direction that would find its fruit in the fourteen stories and sketches he wrote and published between 1853 and 1856, six of which he collected in *The Piazza* (1856).

The six pieces published in *The Piazza* are 'Bartleby', 'The Encantadas, or Enchanted Isles' (a series of short sketches or stories), 'The Lightning-Rod Man', 'The Bell-Tower', 'Benito Cereno' and 'The Piazza'. The last named, written specially for this volume, is not in itself one of the best, but it does present certain recurring preoccupations in the other stories, and sets the tone for them all. It begins by describing the piazza of the narrator's new farmhouse (Melville had moved into a farmhouse in the Berkshires, Massachusetts in 1850, and this setting for the telling of the stories in the collection probably owed something to the example of Hawthorne's 'Old Manse'). From it the narrator sees one evening a solitary spot of sunlight on the northwestern hills. 'Signal as a candle. One spot of radiance, where all else was shade. Fairies there, thought I.' His imagination is kindled by the spot, and he goes in search of it. He finds a solitary girl, who tells how she often looks down from her cottage into the valley and sees a particular marble house; and the narrator realizes it is his own abode 'glimmering much like this mountain one from the piazza'. The girl says: 'I have often wondered who lives there; but it must be some happy one.' The story is a kind of parable of the workings of the imagination and the longing for the ideal. Both narrator and girl see their ideal place in the far-off sunny spot, while in their own place they are only aware of shadows and gloom; and this gives us what is the dominant symbolism of the story, and to a great extent for the volume, that of light and dark. For both the narrator and the girl the gleaming light in the distance is in one way delusive, and the narrator resolves to give up his quest for 'fairy-land' and to be content with the beauty of the view from his piazza – but also with its shadows. For 'every night, when the curtain falls, truth comes in with darkness. No light shows from the mountain. To and fro I walk the piazza deck, haunted by Marianna's face, and many as real a story.'

'Truth comes in with darkness.' It could almost be an epigraph for the volume as a whole. The other stories, too, are often, and more harrowingly, concerned with isolation, sorrow, the threats to domestic contentment, and the ambiguities of perception between good and evil. At the same time they are sometimes alleviated by Melville's ever-present humour, sometimes grotesque, sometimes genial and domestic.

'Bartleby, the Scrivener: a Story of Wall Street' was probably the first to be written. This powerful and haunting story, which appeared in *Putnam's Magazine* in 1853, is the best in the volume and seems to be a turning point for Melville's art. The central figure of the lawyer's clerk who gradually withdraws from his work and the society of others into a kind of solipsistic isolation has been variously interpreted, but it is as well to begin with the art of Melville's telling. The key to this is the narrator, a lawyer and (as he boasts)

'Master in Chancery', whose character and voice gives us whatever bearings we have. The narrator is, in his own words, 'an eminently *safe* man', good-natured but highly conventional, and (initially at least) complacent. The genial pomposity of his tone, and his worldly values, are given early in his self-description: 'I do not speak it in vanity, but simply record the fact, that I was not unemployed in my profession by the late John Jacob Astor [a legendarily rich New York businessman]; a name which, I admit, I love to repeat, for it hath a rounded and orbicular sound to it, and rings like unto bullion.' While we are clearly led to be critical of him we are aware of his basic humanity, he is our 'focalizer' for the story (the eyes through which we see), and our general point of view is also to a great extent his.

The employees in his office – Turkey, Nippers and Ginger Nut – are drawn, as their names suggest, in sharp Dickensian caricature, and they also have their part in the pattern of the whole. Turkey's face, by twelve o'clock, blazes 'like a grate full of Christmas coals' (we infer the effect of drink), and although he is a faithful and hard-working employee, his behaviour in the afternoons becomes strangely reckless and 'altogether too energetic'. Nippers, by contrast, is the sallow victim of 'two evil powers – ambition and indigestion', which lead him to grind his teeth and become obsessed with trivial adjustments to his working conditions, like changing the height of his table. Ginger Nut, a lad of twelve, is named after the nutshells in his desk, and the cake which he is sent out to purchase by the other two. These three present various contrasts to Bartleby, the withdrawn and increasingly work-shy scrivener: the first by his erratic and frequently destructive energy, the second by his dyspeptic ambition, the third by his youthful appetite.

Bartleby gradually withdraws from all work, meeting his employer's requests with the mild reply 'I would prefer not to.' The wording and tone are important: formal (not 'I'd rather not') and polite (not 'I won't'). The suggestion is he would *prefer* not to, but if his employer insists . . . This throws the responsibility on to the narrator, who is not a tyrant, and is strangely impressed by Bartleby's tone, though increasingly exasperated. The question of human coercion and human responsibility is raised. The narrator cannot force Bartleby, and is too kindly to dismiss him. But in the end, when Bartleby takes up residence in the office, the narrator feels himself forced to move his chambers to another location. Bartleby continues to haunt the building, but is eventually removed by the police as a vagrant and taken to 'the Tombs', the New York prison. The narrator visits him there but he refuses to eat, and soon he dies. The narrator adds an epilogue about how he discovers that Bartleby's previous employment was in a 'dead letter' office, where letters are sent which do not reach their destinations. The narrator's concluding comment is: 'On errands of life, these letters speed to death. Ah Bartleby! Ah humanity!'

This parable of human isolation has been variously interpreted. The story is subtitled 'A Story of Wall-Street' (New York's financial district), and it is that in several senses. It has been seen as a commentary on the dehumanizing effects of bureaucracy and capitalism. At the same time the narrator's chambers look out at both ends on two blank walls, Bartleby also stares out of his side-window in 'dead-wall reveries at a wall three feet away': a more universal image of human enclosure. Bartleby is a scrivener or copyist – that is, a kind of writer – and the story can be read as a parable of a writer's quiet rebellion against his 'employers', his publishers and readers who expect him to follow conventional modes (Melville's own experience of the reception of *Moby Dick* is relevant here).[2] He has been seen as a kind of religious recluse: his section of the office is twice described as his 'hermitage'. He can be seen as a kind of hero of existential independence ('he was more a man of preferences than assumptions') – like Henry David Thoreau in *Walden*, published a few years earlier in 1846, who withdrew from society 'because I wished to live deliberately, to front only the essential facts of life'.[3] 'If a man does not keep pace with his companions,' Thoreau wrote 'perhaps it is because he hears a different drummer. Let him step to the music which he hears, however measured or far away.' Bartleby steps to his own distant music; but it has to be said, too, that unlike the hero of Walden he does not provide for himself, and we get no account of Bartleby's philosophical motives or view of society. Is this a story of romantic rebellion or one of psychological withdrawal? (Bartleby's case has echoes of anorexic pathology: the other members of the office are obsessed with food, from which Bartleby gradually withdraws; the only other prisoner who takes an interest in him in the Tombs is 'the grub-man'.)

Perhaps the question cannot be finally answered. Rather the story seems to be a kind of parable of the mystery of human isolation. For the modern reader, Bartleby has a kinship with Kafka's K. in *Metamorphosis*, or with 'The Hunger Artist'. The epilogue about the dead-letter office has sometimes been criticized as unnecessary, but it adds a final emblematic representation to the everyday tragedy of failed relationship, failed communication. The narrator's persistent sense of responsibility for Bartleby, and a grudging respect for him in spite of all, suggests that Bartleby stands for something positive as well as negative. The beautiful passage describing the yard in the heart of the Tombs, where the narrator finds Bartleby in his final sleep, suggests emblematically a delicate and secluded life hidden from common perception:

> The yard was entirely quiet. It was not accessible to the common prisoners. The surrounding walls, of amazing thickness, kept off all sounds behind them. The Egyptian character of the masonry weighed upon me with its gloom. But a soft imprisoned turf grew under foot. The heart of the eternal pyramids, it seemed, wherein, by some strange magic, through the clefts, grass-seed, dropped by birds, had sprung.

'Bartleby' is one of the greatest short stories in English, and one of the greatest short stories in any language.

In 'Benito Cereno', the longest of the *Piazza* tales, Melville explores, through a gripping story of rebellion at sea, the ambiguities of the perception of good and evil and the labyrinthine ironies of contemporary racial attitudes. But its length (some eighty pages or 32,000 words) and its bi-partite structure (consisting of the story of a Yankee captain's mysterious encounter with a slave ship where the crew of slaves have covertly taken control followed by the twenty-page trial transcripts which reveal what had really happened) qualifies 'Benito Cereno' as a novella rather than a short story, and so in accord with the boundaries of this study it will not be discussed in detail here. This will, however, allow a focus on a group of remarkable short stories in *The Piazza* which have not always obtained the attention which they deserve.

'The Encantadas' ('the Enchanted Isles') is a series of ten, mostly very short, sketches and stories of about the weird group of volcanic islands some five hundred miles off the coast of Ecuador. These barren 'heaps of cinders', with their 'woe-begone' pelicans and their giant tortoises with their 'strange infatuation of hopeless toil' call up all of Melville's feeling for the dark, the lost, the deserted and the strange. The few stories are very short (more like anecdotes) but the most memorable are, 'Charles' Isle and the Dog-King', about a sailor who buys one of the islands and peoples it with subjects over whom he and his dogs tyrannize; 'Hood's Isle and the Hermit Oberlus', whose titular figure, asleep in his cave, is like 'a heaped drift of withered leaves', who avoids strangers 'like a stealthy bear' and whose 'sole superiority . . . over the tortoises was his possession of a larger capacity of degradation'; and the longest piece, 'Norfolk Island and the Chola Widow'. This last is a story of abandonment and suffering: as Melville is again moved by human isolation, whether self-inflicted as in 'Bartleby' or inflicted by the cruelty of others as here: 'Humanity, thou strong one, I worship thee, not in the laurelled victor, but in this abandoned one.'

'The Lightning-Rod Man' and 'The Bell-Tower' are both parables of human presumption. In the former a travelling salesman tries to sell the narrator a device to protect him from lightning, and the story becomes a comic satire on types of human fear and superstitious placebos, encompassing Puritan hell-fire theology, Catholic 'indulgences' and modern insurance companies. 'The Bell-Tower' is more ambitious, and although it has been criticized for its schematism, it is a strongly told allegory which mocks human pride, modern science and notions of racial superiority. The protagonist Bannadonna (his name suggests a misogyny which is part of his masculine pride) builds a huge tower with a clock-bell struck by a giant 'domino' or masked figure – whether robotic or human is left ambiguous – 'clad', it is eventually revealed, 'in scaly mail, lustrous as a dragon-beetle's'. The crowning moment of Bannadonna's achievement is meant to come when the figure strikes the hands of the allegorical female 'hours' Una and Dua and severs them (the destruction of female companionship); but when the moment comes there is no bell-note, and the assembled dignitaries find Bannadonna dead, with the domino standing above him, 'manacled, and its clubbed arms uplifted, as if, with its manacles, once more to strike its already smitten victim'. The allegory is not precise – this is an essential part of its effect of mystery – but the suggestions of slave rebellion (in a story written only six years before the outbreak of the Civil War) are clear; as are the Hawthornean implications of the overweening ambitions of technology. Bannadonna is 'a practical materialist', determined to 'solve Nature, to steal into her . . . to rival her, outstrip her and rule her'. For him 'common sense was theurgy; Prometheus, the heroic name for machinist; man, the true God'. But in pointing to the meaning of the story we should not forget its atmosphere: the setting of Renaissance Italy, the dark malignity of the grandee Bannadonna, the drama of the casting of the bell ('the unleashed metal bayed like hounds') and the Frankensteinian mystery of the scaly 'domino'.

There was clearly a side of Melville's imagination strongly drawn to the symbolic possibilities of the short 'Romance' story, and two further tales from the 1850s, 'Paradise of Bachelors and Tartarus of Maids' and 'I and My Chimney', are, respectively, powerful and whimsically humorous illustrations of this. 'I and My Chimney' is more a sketch than a story – that is, it is mainly the description of a situation or state of affairs – though it has narrative elements. It concerns the narrator's relationship with his fireside and in particular his chimney, which becomes a kind of symbol of his fundamental values. He is a man who likes all old things ('old Montaigne, and old cheese, and old wine'), and his chimney represents various aspects of his conservative traditions. It is associated with hospitality, 'back-bone', royalty (to take it down would be 'a regicidal act'), 'ivied old England', both native America (the camp-fire of 'Iroquois Indians') and the English aristocracy, the unity of the state and the heart of his own lineage (the chimney was built by his kinsman and 'To break into that wall would be to break into his breast'). It is also associated (as we might guess) with the narrator's sense of virility. When a neighbour interrupts him exploring its foundations with a spade he is embarrassed, and when the neighbour suggests that perhaps he regards it as 'too small' he is offended ('"Sir!" said I, throwing down the spade, "do not be too personal".'). The element of narrative tension in the piece comes from the threats of the narrator's wife to have the chimney taken down to make more space in the house. She is a 'natural projector', and her maxim is 'Whatever is, is wrong; and what is more, must be altered.' Clearly the issue is one of patriarchal authority. (The narrator is among other things a kind of successor to Irving's Rip Van Winkle, a 'dozy old dreamer' with 'a horror of industry', hen-pecked by his wife.) It is also a matter of his sanity and mental independence: a local architect called Scribe (cf. 'writer') informs him of a 'secret closet' in the chimney, with what it contains 'hid, with itself, in darkness' which increases his wife's and daughter's desire to explore the chimney. There is some evidence that Melville's family once asked the local doctor and noted writer Oliver Wendell Holmes to examine Melville for signs of mental illness.[4] But even without this information it is clear that the chimney with its secret closet comes to represent the narrator's psyche, and his determination to keep its secrets hidden is a kind of allegory for a writer's determination to avoid the intrusions of analysis. These darker matters, and the whole sense of personal beliefs that the story embodies, are handled with a light and playful humour. The essential thing in the story is its wonderfully judged tone: comic and serious, genial and critical, self-ironic and nevertheless suggesting deliberate and fundamental values.

'The Paradise of Bachelors and the Tartarus of Maids', also first published in *Putnam's Magazine*, is a kind of diptych, or pair of contrasting sketches or portraits (like the less vividly imagined and more straightforwardly didactic 'Rich Man's Pudding and Poor Man's Crumbs' and 'The Two Temples' of 1854 and 1855), which again exemplifies Melville's ability to raise social, political and psychological issues in the form of intriguing allegorical romance. 'The Paradise of Bachelors' is about a dining-club in one of the inns of court near Temple Bar in London (and based on the memory of dinners with the brother of his publisher John Murray, which Melville recorded enjoying during his visit to England in 1849–50). 'The Tartarus of Maids' is about a New England paper-mill the employees of which are all female. The atmosphere of the 'paradise' is masculine, convivial, self-indulgent and somewhat decadent. The modern descendants of the romantic old Knights

Templar have become sybaritic. There is an analogy here with Melville's ambiguous attitude towards the 'romantic chivalry' of the American South: as the narrator thinks of the genial hospitality he has received in the 'paradise', he finds himself softly singing 'Carry me back to old Virginny!' His attitude is admiring, and while there is irony in the portrait – the opening description of the Knights Templar records their decline as 'the worm of luxury crawled beneath their guard' and the dinner the narrator attends is described in military metaphors which recall the departed heroism of the old Knights – the main feeling is one of fraternal or collegiate good cheer. The civilized decorum of the bachelors is stressed and the contrast with the succeeding sketch comes as a deliberate shock. This causes the reader to look back over the first story and question his original reaction, since the luxury depicted there can be seen to depend, economically and psychologically, on the suffering in the second story.

'The Tartarus of Maids' is a strange and vividly drawn allegory of social and sexual oppression. Near a pass in New England called, because of its winds, the Mad Maid's Bellow's-pipe, lies the Devil's Dungeon, a hollow through which flows the 'strange-colored torrent Blood River'. Here is situated a paper-mill 'like some great whited sepulchre', in which the labour force is made up entirely of women. The only males in the establishment are Old Bach, the boss, and a kind of errand-boy called Cupid. The narrator (who is a 'seedsman') is shown round the factory by Cupid. In a corner of the factory he sees a huge frame of iron 'with a vertical thing like a piston periodically rising and falling upon a heavy wooden block', with a tall and pallid girl, 'its tame minister', feeding rose-hued paper into it, upon the corner of which it places 'the impress of a wreath of roses'. He sees the machinery for making pulp rags: long, glittering scythes, 'vertically thrust up' before each girl, against whose edges they 'forever dragged long strips of rags . . . converting the tatters almost into lint'; and the vats for the pulp 'full of a white, wet woolly-looking stuff, not unlike the albuminous parts of an egg, soft-boiled'. In a room 'stifling with a strange, blood-like, abdominal heat', the 'germinous particles' are rolled out into paper, a process that takes 'nine minutes'. The description of the factory is realistic enough to convey a real place, but the accumulating details gradually impress themselves on the reader as an allegory of the process of childbirth; and the Lockean idea of human beings as sheets of blank paper ready for the impress of experience is explicitly alluded to at one point. The whole piece amounts to a parable about both industrial exploitation (particularly of women) and about sexual exploitation: either the denial of female sexuality by the enforced 'maidenhood' of the factory system with the production of the paper a grotesque parody of childbirth; or perhaps, more deeply, a satire on human sexuality itself, in which childbirth becomes a mechanical process controlled by men, a mechanism which the maids serve 'as the slave serves the Sultan'. When paraphrased the story may sound schematic, but the piece has a poetic force: the description of the place and inmates has a strange pictorial actuality, and a penumbra of suggestiveness which gives the images a charge beyond any single allegorical correspondence. Melville writes here in the tradition of Hawthornean allegorical Romance (just as the guardian of 'the mossy old chimney' in the last-discussed story and the similar allegorical sketch 'The Apple-Tree Table, or Original Spiritual Manifestations' of 1856 recall Hawthorne's sketches), in which the idea is hero, but vividly embodied in a poetic symbol.

Melville wrote five other short pieces in the 1850s in addition to those already mentioned and discussed, the most interesting of which is 'Cock-A-Doodle-Doo'. In this energetically and darkly comic parable the narrator is roused from a mood of deep gloom by the crowing of a splendid cock. He tracks down its owner, Merrymusk, a wood-sawyer, who lives with his family in extreme poverty beside a railroad track which carries trainloads of the wealthy (a location and contrast to become almost archetypal in subsequent American popular culture and folklore), but whose life is irradiated by the splendour of his prize possession. On subsequent visits the narrator witnesses the death of Merrymusk's wife and children, the man himself, and finally the cock. But he buries them, and the cock, and raises a gravestone inscribed with the words from Corinthians 15: 55: 'Oh! death, where is thy sting? / Oh! grave, where is thy victory?' On the face of it the tale could be seen as a parable of the persistence of artistic faith and its triumph over death (the theme, structure and a parodic 'quotation' suggest a deliberate reference to Wordsworth's poem 'Resolution and Independence'), but there is a tone of irony which complicates this interpretation. The initial pungent sourness (finely and comically done) of the narrator's mood and his gloomy grumbling against modern life are dispelled by the end; but the successive deaths of the family and the cock have a farcical abruptness which almost undermines the optimism, and the optimism itself comes to have a kind of willed stridency, as in the narrator's final exultant crowing: '[N]ever since then have I felt the doleful dumps, but under all circumstances crow late and early with a continual crow. COCK-A-DOODLE-DOO!–OO!–OO!–OO!–OO!' If this is the narrator's resolution and independence it has a desperately forced gaiety about it.

The pieces of the 1850s constitute a remarkable and coherent portion of Melville's *oeuvre*, and 'Bartleby' is among his finest achievements. While he will always doubtless be remembered by the epic sprawl of his masterpiece and most ambitious work, *Moby Dick*, these stories have an art and unified force of lasting, and for some readers even equal, value. There is an analogy here to the relation of Keats's short odes to his epic *Hyperion*, or Kafka's short stories to his novels: the shorter pieces often capturing the essence of the vision in a finished and concentrated form.

Chapter 6

New territories: Bret Harte and Mark Twain

Bret Harte

Until the second half of the nineteenth century, and even beyond, the cultural identity of the United States was dominated by the East Coast. Hawthorne was part (albeit a detached part) of the Boston literary society which constituted the most powerful cultural grouping. Irving was a New York writer whose chosen literary territory was the Hudson valley, while Melville was born in New York City, settled for a time in Massachusetts and then moved again in 1863 to New York City, where he stayed for the rest of his life. Poe spent most of his early life in Richmond, Virginia, adopted something of the style and social aspirations of a Southern gentleman, and later lived in Philadelphia and New York City.

But from the middle decades of the century the West, hitherto mainly populated by Native Americans and immigrant Spanish colonialists, began to be opened up by Americans of English origin. In 1848 gold was discovered in California, and the gold-rush began that increased the non-Native population of California from around 14,000 to over 250,000 by 1852.[1] In 1860, a young staff writer on the San Francisco newspaper the *Golden Era*, Francis Brett Hart, using his newly adopted *nom de plume* Bret Harte, published his first short story, 'The Work on Red Mountain' (later entitled 'Mliss'). In 1864 he became a contributor and occasional editor of the weekly *Californian*, and in 1868 the founding editor of the *Overland Monthly.* In that year he published his most famous story. 'The Luck of Roaring Camp', and then in the following year 'The Outcasts of Poker Flat', 'Miggles', 'Tennessee's Partner' and 'The Idyl of Red Gulch'. *The Luck of Roaring Camp and Other Sketches* was published in 1870, and the volume created what can fairly be called a literary sensation in American literary circles. In the same year Bret Harte was offered a professorship of recent literature at the University of California,

Berkeley (which he declined), and signed a $10,000 contract to contribute pieces for a year to *Every Saturday* and the prestigious *Atlantic Monthly* (edited from 1871 by William Dean Howells), whose editors wrote asking for a story 'similar to the "Luck"'.

The story tells of how the miners of the camp bring up a baby, when the mother, Cherokee Sal (the only woman in the camp), dies in childbirth. The baby is suckled by the camp's mule, and all the miner's chip in to contribute to the expenses of its chief protector, Kentuck, who – much to his own embarrassment – is won over by the charms of the infant ('"He rastled with my finger . . . the d—d little cuss"'). The child has a dramatically civilizing effect on the rough miners, who, with unaccustomed solemnity, christen it 'Thomas Luck', and vote, after discussion, not to introduce a female nurse into the camp. Next spring they decide to build a hotel in the camp, and to introduce 'one or two decent families' to reside there to give 'the Luck' the benefit of female companionship. Many, however, hope something will turn up to prevent this. 'And it did.' In the winter of 1851 a flood sweeps into the town, and Kentuck is found washed up downstream, dying, with Luck in his arms ('he's a taking me with him, – tell the boys I've got the Luck with me now').

It is difficult today to recapture the impact of 'The Luck of Roaring Camp'. The story strikes the modern reader as quaint and sentimental, with its idealized miners with hearts of gold and its all too abrupt and conventional (one might say 'Victorian') death-scene ending. Perhaps part of the novelty was the treatment of this rough new world by a writer who was clearly educated and literate (the suckling by the ass is described as 'the ancient treatment of Romulus and Remus', the 'greatest scamp' in the camp has 'a Raphael face', and Oakhurst the gambler 'the melancholy air and intellectual abstraction of a Hamlet'), but who also knew the mining camp world at first hand. The literary feel of the piece suggested that here was a Washington Irving for the Sacramento rather than the Hudson valley, and the effect is as much that of Romance as of realism. But perhaps too it suggested, in the manner of a founding myth, that this violent, masculine world could be sensitive and domestic – and, curiously, without the intervention of women. The story is thus a kind of masculinist 'idyll' which maintains that strain of all-male camaraderie which we have seen, in a very different context, in 'Rip Van Winkle'.

The other sketches ('The Luck . . .' is listed as a sketch, suggesting brevity, and an emphasis on mood rather than plot) and stories in the 1870 volume mostly retain the combination of realism (the stories have settings from 'ordinary' life in the West) and Romance (their characters are generally idealized or sentimentalized and their plots are contrived). 'The Outcasts of Poker Flat' tells the story of a gambler (John Oakhurst, as in other stories), a drunkard and two whores (or 'ladies' whose 'impropriety was professional' as Harte puts it), who are banished from town and meet up with two 'innocents', a newly eloped young couple. They take refuge from the winter in a mountain cabin, in which they become snowed up; the drunkard escapes with the mules, the young husband leaves on foot for help, the women die (the 'maiden', as Harte calls her, asleep on the breast of one of the 'ladies') and Oakhurst is found 'still calm as in life', with his own bullet in his heart. Once again the 'unrespectable' life of the West is romanticized and sentimentalized with a literary stylishness that clearly won the hearts of its readers. And the other stories repeat a similar formula in different ways. 'Miggles' – a combination of brisk comedy and, mostly, maudlin sentiment – tells the story of a fine young woman, once rich and popular ('gentlemen like yourself, sir, came to see me'), who dedicates her life to looking after her 'baby', a man who once 'spent a heap of money on me' and who is now struck down by disease. 'Mliss' has a sharply observed young girl, outcast and delinquent, who insists that the local schoolteacher allow her to come to school. The story then turns into a wish-fulfilling romance (Harte was once a schoolteacher himself in a small Californian town): the two fall in love with each other and the schoolmaster takes her away with him. In 'Tennessee's Partner' – one of the earliest 'buddy' stories in American fiction – Tennessee takes his partner's wife, is abandoned by her, returns to his partner, is defended by him unsuccessfully in a murder trial, and is hanged. His partner brings along an old horse to 'bring him home' (just as he has done so many times when Tennessee was drunk); and not long after the partner dies too, imagining Tennessee is once again coming home 'all by himself, sober, and his face a-shining. Tennessee! Pardner! And so they met.'

In all this it is clear, again, that sentimentalism predominates. But there is also a certain humorous detachment and irony that saves the stories from complete mawkishness. In that last story, for example, the members of Tennessee's funeral wake (drummed up in an *ad hoc* fashion by his partner) think, as they leave the town, they see Tennessee's partner sitting on the grave, 'his face buried in his red bandanna handkerchief. But it was argued by others that you couldn't tell his face from his handkerchief at that distance; and this point remained undecided.' The red handkerchief has been earlier described as 'a shade lighter than his complexion', and the comment could be seen to undercut the appeal to our sentiments. But it can also confirm it by allowing humour to mitigate the nakedness of the appeal. As David Wyatt writes, 'A master of affective stylistics, Harte writes for a reader in whom he can provoke, more or less simultaneously, a sentimental response and its critique.'[2]

The Luck of Roaring Camp and Other Sketches has one further romance or 'idyll' (to use Hart's term). In 'The Idyl of Red Gulch', a virtuous schoolmistress in a mining town inspires the love and reformation of a beautiful but dissolute drunkard, but then discovers he has fathered an illegitimate child to a 'dubious mother'. She abandons him saving the child in response to the mother's pleas. By contrast, the most interesting aspects of the book's other sketches or 'Bohemian Papers' are their power of evoking place, as in the description of Dedlow Marsh in 'High-Water Mark', and more importantly, their feeling for 'minority groups' in the society of the American West – whether that of the older Spanish inhabitants in a story like 'Notes by Flood and Field' (a story about a conflict between an older Spanish and a newer Anglo-Saxon landowner) or in the short sketch of 'The Mission Dolores'; or the new Chinese immigrants to California in 'John Chinaman', later echoed and amplified in a piece like 'Wan Lee, Pagan' (1874). These are picturesque and sympathetic sketches. It must be admitted that their tone is condescending and their picturesqueness contains no small degree of 'exotic' stereotyping and 'quaintness'. But viewed historically these seem small faults at a time when there was a considerable amount of vicious racial prejudice against such immigrants. Basically Harte's attitude to the men combines a recognition of their shared humanity with a sense of their intriguing 'otherness'; any lingering condescension in this seems a small price to pay for the underlying sense of human equality which, at the end of 'John Chinaman', speaks out firmly against 'the conscious hate and fear with which inferiority [i.e. the moral inferiority of 'a certain class' of white men] always regards the possibility of even-handed justice, and which is the key-note to the vulgar clamor about servile and degraded races'.

Between 1870 and 1903 Harte published over twenty volumes of short stories and sketches, in addition to two volumes of 'condensed novels', highly concentrated pastiche-parodies of a range of writers from Fenimore Cooper, Dickens and Kipling, to a number of French authors including Alexandre Dumas and Victor Hugo. There are more stories about cool-handed, philosophically detached and morally noble gamblers, such as 'A Passage in the Life of Mr John Oakhurst' (1874), in which Oakhurst fights a duel with another gambler over a mistress, again to save the honour of the husband; or 'A Protegee of Jack Hamlin's' (1893), in which Jack saves a young, abandoned woman (Sophy) from suicide, and sets her up as a portrait artist in the house of his old black servants. In a highly contrived piece of plotting, Jack's mistress (whom he has been trying to avoid) sees a portrait of him and discovers the studio, discovering also that Sophy is her long-lost sister – whereupon Jack beats a convenient retreat. (This kind of over-complex plot seems to have been a snare during the period, and is satirized by Mark Twain in stories like 'A Medieval Romance' (1870), in which the plot gets so contorted that the storyteller literally gives it up and leaves the heroine 'to get out the best way that offers'.[3]) Bret Harte wrote over a hundred and fifty short stories and sketches, but very few of these remain in print. He is remembered today as the author of the still anthologized 'The Luck of Roaring Camp' and 'The Outcasts of Poker Flat', those highly romanticised stories of the mining West which emphasized, as he said in his essay 'The Rise of the "Short Story"' (1899), 'the treatment of characteristic American life, with absolute knowledge of its peculiarities and sympathy with its methods; with no fastidious ignoring of its habitual expression, or the inchoate poetry which may be found even hidden in its slang'.[4]

The aspect of this new literature that Harte stressed above all others in his essay was '*Humour* – of a quality as distinct and original as the country and civilization in which it was developed'. Like Raymond Carver, he linked it to the anecdote or 'story' which was 'orally transmitted'.

> It was common in the barrooms, the gatherings in the 'country store', and finally at public meetings in the mouths of 'stump orators'. Arguments were clenched, and political principles illustrated, by a 'funny story'. It invaded even the camp meeting and pulpit. It at last received the currency of the public press. But wherever met it was so distinctively original and novel, so individual and characteristic, that it was at once known and appreciated abroad as 'an American story.'[5]

And in the line of the American humorous story, a writer even more influential than Harte himself was Mark Twain.

Mark Twain

Mark Twain (real name Samuel Clemens, 1835–1910) met Harte in San Francisco in 1864 and they later collaborated on several literary ventures, including a jointly authored play. Though they fell out later, in 1866 Twain generously said that 'though I am generally placed at the head of my breed of scribblers in this part of the country, the place properly belongs to Bret Harte'.[6] But in 1865 Twain published 'Jim Smiley and his Jumping Frog', first in New York and then, as 'The Celebrated Jumping Frog of Calaveras County', in Bret Harte's San Francisco magazine, the *Californian*. And this story, together with a number of subsequent stories by Twain, has come to represent the classic American 'humorous story' or 'tall tale', in subsequent tradition. It has its rough forebears in the anonymous tales and legends about Davy Crockett in *The Crockett Almanacs* from 1836, in the *Sut Lovingood Yarns* of George Washington Harris (1867) or *Georgia Scenes* (1835) by Augustus Baldwin Longstreet (whose 'The Horse Swap'[7] is also a forerunner of Faulkner's great 'tall tale', 'Spotted Horses').

'The Celebrated Jumping Frog' is a story, told to a visitor (the primary narrator) from the Eastern States, by Simon Wheeler, a garrulous old goldminer from Angel's camp. (Angel's camp was a real Californian location, and Wheeler was based on a miner Twain knew, called Ben Coon.) The story, of a bet between Jim Smiley and a visiting stranger over whose frog can jump highest, a bet which Smiley wins by filling his opponent's frog with 'quail-shot' (gun pellets), is 'tall' (outlandish) and humorous enough in itself: but the art of the story lies in its rambling, colloquial delivery, one of the first instances of vernacular 'voice' in American literature. The frog is called Daniel Webster (a hit at a pompous Whiggish senator and congressman of the 1830s and 1840s with a protuberant belly and an oratorical style Twain found 'diffuse, conceited, eloquent and bathetic').[8]

> Why, I've seen him set Dan'l Webster down there on this floor . . . and sing out, 'Flies, Dan'l, flies!' and quicker'n you could wink he'd spring straight up and snake a fly off'n the counter there, and flop down on the floor ag'in as solid as a gob of mud, and fall to scratching the side of his head with his hind foot as indifferent as if he hadn't no idea he'd been doin' more'n any frog might do.

The striking thing about Wheeler's 'interminable narrative', says the Narrator, is the 'vein of impressive earnestness and sincerity' which runs through it. Wheeler is one of the first examples of the 'dead-pan' humorist. Before the story of the frog he warms up with short accounts of Smiley's mare (the asthmatic, distempered, consumptive nag who always finishes races 'about a neck ahead, as near as you could cipher it down') and his bull-pup Andrew Jackson (the name of the famous Republican President whom Twain disliked), who never loses a dog fight until he is opposed by a dog with no hind legs to catch hold of. After the frog story he launches on another about Smiley's 'yaller one-eyed cow that didn't have no tail', but the Narrator has had enough and leaves.

The story is one of several in Twain in which a 'sophisticated' narrator who speaks in the language of the East Coast establishment is strung along by a simple-seeming but canny West Coast story-teller, often to the amusement of local bystanders, and it thus constitutes a kind of 'ragging' or tricking of East Coast sensibilities. In 'His Grandfather's Ram' (from *Roughing It*, 1872, a book about Twain's early adventures in the West) 'the boys' inveigle the Narrator into witnessing one of the narratives of the 'tranquilly, serenely, symmetrically drunk' Jim Blaine. The story starts off about the ram but digresses immediately into collateral matters, including, all in a matter of four or five pages, the story of Miss Wagner's glass eye, Jacops the coffin-peddler's marketing techniques, the fate of Maria Martin and her missionary husband ('biled' merely as a culinary experiment), Uncle Lem's dog, and William Wheeler (who died in a carpet factory accident and ended up woven into fourteen feet of carpet), brought to the funeral by his widow. All this is connected by a baffling network of relationships and happenstance typical of small town gossip, and marked by the narrator's eccentric sense of the inter-connectedness of things ('Prov'dence don't fire no blank ca'tridges, boys'). It is thus also a kind of parody of the way consciousness is made up of a mass of barely related stories, and of the human mind's need for stories. In 'Jim Baker's Blue-Jay Yarn' (from *A Tramp Abroad*, 1880) a garrulous old miner living alone in the woods tells the story of the blue-jay who tried to fill up a hole with acorns, but the 'hole' turned out to be a whole cabin. Again it is the narrator's character and delivery that is central: it has been suggested that in his solitude he fills his life with words and talking animals just as the blue-jay fills the cabin,[9] and it is his innocent earnestness that is the source of the humour, as in his insistence on a blue-jay's power of language ('Now I've never heard a blue-jay use bad grammar but very seldom; and when they do they are as ashamed as a human; they shut right down and leave'). And at the end of the story there is a dig at Canadians, with an owl 'come from Nova Scotia to visit the Yosemite', who is the only bird unable to see the joke.

Twain has such a variety of stories that it would be impossible to describe all his 'kinds' in a single chapter. They are mostly slight pieces, written 'on the run' (to use Twain's own phrase), many of them to keep the pot boiling or to fill a corner of a magazine. But their variety and inventiveness is impressive. 'The Story of the Bad Little Boy' (1865) and 'The Story of the Good Little Boy' (1870) satirize and turn upside down the clichés of children's conduct books. 'Journalism in Tennessee' (1869) and 'How I Edited an Agricultural Paper' (1870) make fun of backwoods journalism. 'Political Economy' (1869) and 'The Danger of Lying in Bed' (1871) are satires on the growing fashion for life-insurance (the former, like Melville's 'The Lightning-Rod Man', about a seller of lightning conductors, and the latter a farcical game with statistics). Three stories about 'the McWilliamses' find comedy in the domestic dis-agreements of wives and husbands (with the wife's fussing and anxiousness the main butt of the jokes) and satirize, variously, illness 'scares', insurance salesmen (lightning rods again) and burglar alarms. 'The Stolen White Elephant' (1882) and 'The Double-Barreled Detective Story' (1892) parody to the level of farce the genre of the detective story, and mock the so-called expertise of the 'great' detective. (In the latter Sherlock Holmes fails to solve a murder engineered in his presence.) 'The £1,000,000 Bank-Note' (1893) and 'The $30,000 Bequest' (1904) are stories satirizing the illusions and deceptions of capitalism, the first a rather laboured mixture of sardonic humour and love romance; and the second a darker piece about the 'castle in the air' fantasizing that takes over the lives of a married couple when promised a bequest that never materializes.

These stories and others, while not in the first rank as literary pieces (and not aiming at that), nevertheless give comic and satiric glimpses of various facets of American life and amount to a kind of varied and extempore critique of them. But one or two pieces stand out and deserve fuller discussion. In the sketch 'A True Story' (1874) Twain gives a voice, almost for the first time in American literature, to the experience of the African American ex-slave. Joel Chandler Harris's phenomenally popular Uncle Remus stories began to appear from 1876 (*Uncle Remus: His Songs and his Sayings* came out in 1880), with their ideologically complex combination of elements: children's tales, post-Civil War nostalgia and idealization, authentic (or semi-minstrel?) African American voice and the genuine folk-tale rebel and trickster Brer Rabbit.[10] But Twain's portrait in 'A True Story' of Aunt Rachel (based on a servant in Twain's family) and his ventriloquizing of her story is more complex as a literary piece. It deliberately challenges the stereotype of the 'happy Negro' (so often used by pro-slavery Southern apologists), and has her tell a story of varied suffering and happiness, which gives the lie to the narrator's opening question '"Aunt Rachel, how is it that you've lived sixty years and never had any trouble?"' In reply Aunt Rachel tells of her early life in Virginia, of going into slavery, of the brutal treatment by the slave owners, of the loss of her husband and her six sons. Twenty years later, left working as a cook for some officers of the by now victorious Union army, she finds her youngest son again in a scene of great joy.

The story is remarkable in its dramatization of African American speech, and together with the short and only recently republished sketch 'Sociable Jimmy' (1874), it was clearly crucial to Twain's literary development, anticipating his all-important mastery of 'voice' in *Huckleberry Finn*, begun two years later.[11] It is also remarkable for its dramatization of the story-telling situation. The narrator is sitting one summer evening 'on the porch of the farmhouse' with Aunt Rachel sitting 'respectfully below our level, on the steps'. Soon after she begins her story she 'had gradually risen, while she warmed to her subject, and now she towered above us, black against the stars' (117), an image which makes her heroic. And at the very end of the story Aunt Rachel physically enacts her meeting with her youngest son, her enthusiasm quite overcoming the boundaries of 'respect' and deference in her physical contact with the narrator. She tells how she was carrying a pan of hot biscuits when she recognized her son:

> 'De pan drop' on de flo' an' I grab his lef' han' an' shove back his sleeve – jist so, as I's doin' to you – an' den I goes for his forehead an' push de hair back so, an' "Boy!" I says, if you an't my Henry, what is you doin' wid dis welt on yo' wris' an' dat sk-yar on yo' forehead? De lord God ob heaven be praise', I go my own ag'in!'

And her last line repudiates with vehement irony the oversimplifying black stereotypes both of suffering and of contentment: 'Oh no, Misto C—, *I* hain't had no trouble. An' no *joy!*'

Two stories by Twain explore a theme which has a persistent significance in nineteenth-century American culture – the theme of conscience. The idea of conscience as the voice of God is crucial in Puritan theology: it lies behind the original seventeenth-century emigrations, and the subsequent clashes of ideology between Puritans and Quakers. Conscience is central to many of Hawthorne's stories ('Egotism; or the Bosom-Serpent', 'The Minister's Black Veil', 'Ethan Brand') and in a very different way to many of Poe's ('William Wilson', 'The Tell-Tale Heart', 'The Black Cat'). In Twain the issue of conscience is most powerfully treated in his greatest novel *Huckleberry Finn* (1884), in which Huck's decision to rebel against his 'conscience' (here almost exactly what Freud would later call the super-ego, which represents the moral conventions of the adult world) comes in Chapter 31, where he tears up his letter to Miss Watson telling her he has got her runaway slave Jim and is ready to give him up. But in the story 'The Facts Concerning the Recent Carnival of Crime in Connecticut' (1876) the subject is treated in a more personal and ambiguous way, and with a comedy which is both savage and farcical.

The first-person narrator is congratulating himself that he has finally managed to ignore his Aunt Mary's admonitions to stop smoking, when he opens the door to find 'a shriveled, shabby dwarf', some two feet high and about forty years old, covered in 'a fuzzy, greenish mould', with a cunning, alert and malicious expression, 'a sort of remote and ill-defined resemblance to me', and 'an exasperating drawl that had the seeming of a deliberate travesty of my style' (shades of the double in Poe's 'William Wilson' in this last detail). 'I am your Conscience!' it eventually announces. The narrator tries to catch it but his 'cheerful' eagerness makes it too light and it 'darts' up to the top of a high bookcase. From there it holds forth on the duties of consciences: they are appointed by a higher authority, but it admits, 'we *do* crowd the orders a trifle when we get the chance, which is most of the time. We enjoy it.' It tells, for example, how it once tortured a man who 'had accidentally crippled a mulatto baby': the baby recovered completely in three weeks, but the man 'blew his brains out' after forty-eight hours of agony. The narrator complains that his conscience torments him about his treatment of tramps, both when he helps them and when he refuses to, and the dwarf exults that 'It is my *business* – and my joy – to make you repent of *every*thing you do.'

It is clear that Twain is exploring through comedy the dilemma of distinguishing between moral conscience and neurotic guilt. The horrible green dwarf is a kind of travesty of conscience, a distorted psychological obsession. Other people have either fine upstanding consciences or almost none at all (Aunt Mary's is so large that it lives always in the open air, whereas one of the narrator's publishers has one so small it takes a microscope to see it). In a showdown with Aunt Mary, the narrator swears he will smoke, and the dwarf gets so heavy and depressed that the narrator is able to catch it – whereupon he tears it to shreds and throws it on the fire. The brief concluding paragraphs describe the exultant freedom and 'bliss' he indulges in, the 'carnival of crime' of the title: he kills thirty-eight persons in two weeks, swindles a widow, and places an advertisement to sell 'assorted tramps' to medical colleges. The wild comic violence of the conclusion suggests a hysterical liberation and makes the tale's drift ambiguous: is the narrator's conscience a neurotic disease, or the only thing that stands between him and moral anarchy? Is the ending a kind of wild wish-fulfilling comic fantasy that simply celebrates through comic exaggeration, or a warning that undercuts our endorsement of the narrator? The answer is that it is both. The dilemma of conscience remains, but we have been allowed a hilarious but also disturbing holiday from moral claims.

Twain was a kind of anti-moralistic moralist – deeply sceptical of conventional moral claims, but also aware, sometimes painfully, of the psychological labyrinths of internal moral processes. The most complex and powerful example is Twain's greatest short story, 'The Man Who Corrupted Hadleyburg' (1899). In this story Twain's capacity for ingenious plotting (sometimes a weakness in his stories, sometimes a source of parody), his acute sense of moral complexity, his genius for broad farce and a certain dark and tragic pessimism about human weakness, all here achieve their most concentrated expression.

Mr and Mrs Richards are among the leading citizens of Hadleyburg, a town that takes great pride in its honesty and uprightness. One day they discover, left in their house, a sack containing forty thousand dollars worth of gold. With it is a letter, which they are to place in the local paper, that promises the sack to the benefactor who once helped the writer of the letter in a time of need, by giving him $20 and a particular piece of advice – which the benefactor will of course remember. That person should prove his identity by leaving a note of the words of advice with the Rev. Burgess, who in a month's time will reveal the benefactor at a meeting in the town hall. The advertisement is placed, and soon after the Richardses receive another letter from one 'Howard L. Stephenson' telling them that the benefactor was Goodson, now dead, and that the piece of advice was: 'You are far from being a bad man: go, and reform.' In addition, Goodson had apparently told 'Stephenson' that he was indebted to Edward Richards for an unspecified 'very great service', and had made Richards his legitimate heir. Unknown to the Richardses, eighteen other leading townspeople have received this same letter. The story focuses on the dilemma of the Richardses, but the upshot is that all the citizens contrive to 'remember' the gift to the stranger and the advice they gave him. So they all come to the town hall thirty days later, with the words written on a piece of paper, which they hand to the Rev. Burgess. Burgess then takes the pieces of paper out one by one and reads them out, repeating each time the claim and the words of advice. So the deceit and hypocrisy of the town's leading families is exposed, much to the delight of its ordinary folk who join in the pantomimic farce of the proceedings by chanting the fatal phrase to a tune from the 'Mikado' as Burgess reads it out. There is more complexity regarding the fate of the Richardses (of which more below), but the story concludes with the words: 'It is an honest town once more, and the man will have to rise early that catches it napping again'; and a pictorial emblem of the town's old and new motto, 'Lead us not into temptation', is changed to 'Lead us into temptation'.

There are two initial 'morals' to this parable, one clear and the other ambiguous. 'I cannot praise a fugitive and cloistered virtue', wrote Milton in the *Areopagitica*: the moral of the changed motto suggests that Hadleyburg fell because it had never been tested. The other one is potentially more cynical: Hadleyburg may have reformed or it may simply have become more canny, as the last sentence of the story could imply.

There is also a broad satire against upper-class respectability in the story: the culprits are the first nineteen families, and the common townspeople (represented in particular by the joker and layabout Jack Halliday) have an uproarious time seeing them brought low. But in the complexities of the

Richardses' dilemma, there is a darker note which suggests the painful inadequacy of all human morality.

Twain's extraordinarily precise and complicated plot is, as well as being a satire on small-town hypocrisy, a kind of mechanism for subjecting the Richardses to a series of moral tests, each one more difficult to pass than the last. In spite of their meaning well, and their insight into what is happening to them, they are not strong enough to overcome firstly their longing for money and secondly their desire to keep their good name. Mary Richards has a penetrating sense of where they and the town have gone wrong. When Edward speaks of their training in honesty she replies: 'Oh, I know it, I know it – it's been one everlasting training and training and training in honesty – honesty shielded, from the very cradle, against every possible temptation, and so it's *artificial* honesty, and weak as water when temptation comes . . .' When Edward himself has to lie to Mary by pretending that he promised Goodman not to tell her about his good deed, he at first feels pangs of conscience, but then rationalizes: '[S]uppose it *was* a lie, what then? Was it such a great matter? Aren't we always *acting* lies? Then why not *tell* them.' Twain captures the processes of self-deception with great psychological precision. And the torment of the Richardses' agonized conscience becomes dark and painful towards the end. The reader is led – however unwillingly – to identify with them, and so their struggle becomes a matter of pathos, and even tragedy in so far as we feel they are 'good' people forced by circumstances into guilt. Beneath the public satire there is a darker and more painful story of the moral weakness of the well-meaning.

It might be argued that the story is overloaded with plot complexity (particularly with the financial machinations by the stranger, to further trap the Richardses, at the end). But its intricacy is brilliantly worked, and becomes itself a kind of correlative of the Richardses' guilt. Complex plot (often hitherto used by Twain for comic purposes) here becomes a kind of tortuous symbol of moral entrapment and self-entrapment. And the short story form, with its compression of effect, is the ideal medium for this. The moral idea, or perhaps even more the moral structure, is the hero: a structure which, like much in Twain's later work (for instance his late novella, *The Mysterious Stranger*), tends towards a deep pessimism about human fate. Ordinary human goodness is seen as inadequate to the trials which fate or circumstance put upon it.

Chapter 7

Realism, the grotesque and impressionism: Hamlin Garland, Ambrose Bierce and Stephen Crane

William Dean Howells, realism and Hamlin Garland

William Dean Howells, novelist, short story writer, editor of the prestigious *Atlantic Monthly* from 1871 to 1881 and one of the most influential critics of the period, was a significant influence in the movement towards literary realism towards the end of the nineteenth century, and in his critical advocacy of the short story form. In 'The Editor's Study' (1887) he wrote of 'the foolish old superstition that literature and art are anything but the expression of life, and are to be judged by any other test than that of their fidelity to it'.[1] Howells's own best short story, 'Editha' (1905), is a sharply anti-idealistic story about war and conceptions of honour. In *Criticism and Fiction* (1891) he also advances the possibility that American writers in particular have 'brought the short story nearer perfection in the all-round sense than almost any other people' and ranks them only below Russian writers. And he singles out innovations of language, particularly the use of dialect, as among the writers' primary means for re-invigorating literature. American writers, he says, should 'go into the shops and fields' for their subjects and language, and 'when their characters speak, I should like to hear them speak true American, with all the varying Tennessean, Philadelphian, Bostonian and New York accents'. And the ultimate motivation for this movement was democratic: 'The arts must become democratic, and then we shall have the expression of America in art.'[2]

Howells was also a generous promoter of the work of other writers, and he wrote an Introduction for *Main Travelled Roads* (1891), a volume of stories by Hamlin Garland (1860–1940), a young writer brought up in the rural areas of Wisconsin, Dakota and Iowa. Howells praised Garland's book as a true portrait of rural conditions, of characters 'whom our satirists find so easy to caricature as Hayseeds', but whose lives are often tragic in their suffering. 'The type caught in Mr Garland's book is not pretty, it is ugly and often ridiculous; but it is heartbreaking in its rude despair.'[3] Howells also notes the recent success of published volumes of short stories, and suggests the powerful influence of Kipling's and Maupassant's popularity and (albeit in something of a *non-sequitur*) 'the critical recognition of the American supremacy in this sort'.

Garland's stories are told plainly and without any attempt to heighten their literary impact by complex plotting or figurative or symbolic language. Above all they use the dialect of the country people who are their subject. The focus on the elemental facts of love and hate, survival and death, prosperity and poverty, peace and war: the relationships and struggles of men and women enacted in a setting of natural harshness and beauty. The original volume of *Main Travelled Roads* (1891) was made up of six stories ('Under the Lion's Paw', 'The Return of a Private', 'Up the Coolly', 'Among the Corn Rows', 'Mrs Ripley's Trip', 'A Branch Road'), and six more were added in later editions.

The best of the stories are the bitterest. In 'Up the Coolly' Howard, a successful actor and playwright, returns to the little country town in Wisconsin where he grew up and where his mother and brother still live. He finds they have moved to a smaller house 'up the coolly' (or 'coulé', small valley). His mother is sick and ageing, and his brother Grant is full of resentment at his own lack of success and his inability to keep up the mortgage on their old house. Howard's nostalgic memories of his childhood and his pleasure in the beauty of the surrounding country jars harshly with his realization of his mother's illness, his brother's resentment and the poverty of the household. He compares his city apartment with its Millet reproduction on the wall – 'A farm in the valley!' (the conventional pastoral of art) – with his present room, 'the assertive odor of stagnant air, laden with camphor . . . the springless bed under him . . . a few soap-advertising lithographs on the walls'. Howard is moved by their poverty and guilty about his own neglect, and decides to buy back the old house for his brother and mother. But though Grant softens towards him he refuses the offer. The story avoids any superficially consoling ending, and Grant speaks with a harsh sense of closed possibilities: 'I mean life ain't worth very much to me. I'm too old to take a new start. I'm a dead failure. I've come to the conclusion that life's a failure for ninety-nine per cent of us. You can't help me now. It's too late.' There is a measure, though, of Garland's recognition of a kind of heroism in the farming brother, in the concluding sentence, which sees Grant as 'tragic, sombre in his softened mood, his large, long, rugged Scotch face bronzed with sun and scarred with wrinkles that had histories, like sabre-cuts on a veteran, the record of his battles'.

That last image has in it an element of idealization: but even if so, it is a generous gesture. Even 'Realism' must acknowledge certain kinds of heroism. 'Under the Lion's Paw', on the other hand, gains its power from its refusal of even that kind of interpretation of rural poverty, and from its recognition of individual human greed and malevolence as part of the forces that make up rural conditions. The Haskins family are travelling through Wisconsin in the dead of winter, forced to leave their land in Kansas by a four-year scourge of grasshoppers ('"Eat! They wiped us out. They chawed everything that was green. They just set around waitin' f'r us to die t'eat us too. My God! I ust t'dream of 'em sitt'n' 'round on the bedpost, six feet long, workin' their jaws. They eet the fork handles. They got worse 'n' worse, till they jest rolled on one another, piled up like snow in winter."'). The Council family give them food and shelter, and Stephen Council introduces Haskins to the land speculator Jim Butler. Butler rents Haskins a farm for three years, with the chance of buying it at the end of the term. Haskins and his whole family work ferociously hard on the land, and when summer comes 'the wide field of wheat began to wave and rustle and swirl in the winds of July'. Haskins proudly takes his wife out to look at it. 'It was grand. Level, russet here and there, heavy-headed, wide as a lake, and full of multitudinous whispers and gleams of wealth, it stretched away before the gazers like the fabled field of the cloth of gold.' Two years of good harvests later Haskins approaches Butler with an offer to buy: but Butler has doubled the price, cynically arguing that the farm and land have been improved – as they have, through Haskins's work and money. In a climactic confrontation Haskins threatens Butler with his pitchfork but is brought to his sense by the sight of his daughter. Butler retires shaking with fear, but he has won. The story is the most tightly organized of the original six, moving through four vividly seen separate episodes (the exhausted Haskins family arriving in the bitter winter at the Councils'; their revival in the warmth of the latter's generosity; the deal with Butler and their hard work and success; the meeting with Butler three years later) to its dramatic climax. The tragic bitterness of the individual case is also an indictment of a whole economic ethos. As Butler says: 'Don't take me for a thief. It's the law. The reg'lar thing. Everybody does it.'

Garland also wrote several novels and, at the end of his life a successful trilogy of autobiographical works, but it is generally agreed that *Main Travelled Roads* is his most significant achievement. The short story form allowed the focus on individual predicaments which would not, in their simplicity, sustain the length of a novel, but which are powerful in their vividness and sense of human suffering, and which put together as a collection give us a portrait of a whole region, economic class and human type, so that they are both local (examples of 'local colour', but with more human engagement which that detached and aestheticizing term suggests) and general in their application. They open up a new tract of America for literature, and a new mode of literature for America.

Ambrose Bierce

The achievement of Ambrose Bierce (1842–?1914) is more a matter of psychological than topographical space, and while 'realism' is an element of some of his short stories (particularly those about the Civil War) the term is of limited use in relation to his wayward and often fantastical imagination. In his essay 'The Short Story' he writes: 'Probability? Nothing so improbable as what is true. It is the unexpected that occurs . . . Everything being so unearthly improbable, I wonder that novelists of the Howells school have the audacity to relate anything all.'[4]

Born in Ohio, the son of a farmer, he enlisted in the ninth Indiana regiment in 1861 and fought on the side of the Union right through the Civil War. He had worked on an anti-slavery paper while at school in Kentucky, and began his professional writing career in 1867 when he submitted poems and prose to the *Californian* in San Francisco. He published his first short story, 'The Haunted Valley', in *The Overland Monthly* in 1871; and he travelled to England between 1872 and 1875. Thereafter he lived mainly in San Francisco, and became the city's leading literary figure. While in England he published three collections of essays, epigrams and other short pieces, under the pseudonym 'Dod Grile': *The Fiend's Delight*, *Nuggets and Dust* (both 1873) and *Cobwebs from an Empty Skull* (1874). Back in America various other book publications followed, but Bierce's most important collections of short stories were *Tales of Soldiers and Civilians* (1892, published simultaneously in England with the title *In the Midst of Life*) and *Can Such Things Be?* (1893).

Bierce's stories can be roughly divided into those about the Civil War, stories of horror and the supernatural, and comic or 'tall' stories, though the categories sometimes overlap. His plots are often subtly contrived; he writes with great economy and visual vividness, and his stories often have a caustic and satiric, sometimes misanthropic edge. The short story was clearly the ideal medium for him; and he was noted also for even shorter forms like the fable (as in *Fantastic Fables*, 1899) and the epigram (as in his best-known book, *The Devil's Dictionary*, first published as *The Cynic's Word Book* in 1906). In his impressionistic accounts of war, his love of the outrageously tall story and his predilection for horror he clearly has affinities with his younger contemporary Crane, and with his forebears Hawthorne (whom he admired), Poe and Twain. At the same time, in his contrivances of plot (which include frequent use of analepsis or flashback, prolepsis ('flashforward') and other re-orderings of the time-scheme, his constant preoccupation with the vagaries and fallibilities of perspective, his exploration of dreams and the surreal and his acute awareness of the processes of fiction itself, he has been likened to postmodernist writers like Borges, Cortazar and Akutagawa.[5]

Bierce's stories about war, like most of his other stories, focus not only on violence, but also on the uncanny, the strange and the macabre. He has an extraordinary ability to record how perception reacts to experience before organizing it conceptually – a kind of 'impressionism' or phenomenological awareness of the world, often achieved by sudden shifts of point of view. It is a technique of moral and emotional detachment, which lends itself at once to a precise rendering of sense perceptions and to a sardonic sense of the absurdity and inhumanity of war. No writer (with the possible exception of Crane) has conveyed so vividly the heightened sense-awareness of the mind in close proximity to death, and of its passionate self-deceptions in its hunger for life.

Bierce's most famous story, 'An Occurrence at Owl Creek Bridge', details the perceptions of a man who is being hanged from a railway bridge by a company of soldiers. In the first section of the story the exact technical process is given with minute precision, and at the end of it his body falls down between the cross-ties of the bridge. Part 2 goes back in space and time to a picture of his home life, his enlistment, and the activities as a spy which have brought him to where he is. Part 3 returns to the present and to a microscopic focus on the man's physical sensations: 'the pain of a sharp pressure upon his throat', followed by a succession of sensations which modulate from the physical to the imagined as he feels the rope break and his body plunging deep into the water. In his experience of escape down-stream his awareness of the physical world is heightened to a preternatural, a visionary clarity ('He looked at the forest on the bank of the stream, saw the individual trees, the leaves, the veining of each leaf – he saw the very insects upon them'); and his swift journey, to the very gate of his home and vision of his waiting wife, is exhilaratingly done. The end of the story (which may be guessed, but which need not be precisely revealed here) comes as a sharp perceptual shock of reversal to the reader, and transposes what has gone before into a new perspective which seems to preserve and heighten its vividness in the memory: we have been taken through a process which makes us acutely aware of the power of human delusion and of literary imagination, and perhaps of the disturbing closeness of the two. There is some critical debate about how far the story is also an exposure of the false perceptions of heroism.[6] It is true that Bierce is ironically detached from the protagonist's Southern values and military aspirations, but while he obviously does not endorse them, he does not condemn them either, regarding them as natural and not at all despicable, and only registering his sardonic scepticism in his comment that Farquhar was 'at heart a soldier,' and 'in good faith and without too much qualification assented to at least a part of the frankly villainous dictum that all is fair in love and war'. But the main impulse of the story seems visceral rather than moral, and the writer's compulsion is not a hatred of war so much as a fascination with (in Dr Johnson's phrase) the imagination 'hungering for life'.

In another case of perspectival shift, war turns things literally back to front. Bierce's precise rendering of topography (that of a military man) is also a metaphor for broader perceptual changes. In his most horrifying war story, 'Chickamauga', a deaf-mute child witnesses the retreat of the Confederate troops after the battle of that name. The child wanders out towards the battle and encounters 'a strange moving object which he took to be some large animal,' and then several others. 'They were men' – stumbling, crawling, dragging themselves away from battle, 'in silence, profound, absolute'. In his incomprehension the child thinks they are playing a game, and tries to ride on the back of one of them, as he had done on the backs of his father's 'Negroes'. But the man flings him to the ground and then

> turned upon him a face that lacked a lower jaw – from the upper teeth to the throat was a great red gap fringed with hanging shreds of flesh and splinters of bone. The unnatural prominence of the nose, the absence of chin, the fierce eyes, gave this man the appearance of a great bird of prey crimsoned in throat and breast by the blood of its quarry.

The child retreats and watches the silent mass of men, and then drawn by the glow of a great fire, in his innocent exhilaration, he leads them as if into battle, waving his toy sword in front of him. He reaches the scene of the fire and looking about him slowly, 'when suddenly the entire plantation, with its enclosing forest, seemed to turn as on a pivot. His little world swung half around; the points of the compass were reversed. He recognized the blazing building as his own home!' His mother lies dead before him, and he utters 'a series of inarticulate and indescribable cries – something between the chattering of an ape and the gobbling of a turkey – a startling, soulless, unholy sound, the language of a devil. The child was a deaf mute.'

Here the reversal of physical orientation (the confusion of which the reader has shared) is both instance and emblem of the larger reversals of the story: war as a matter of youthful enthusiasm and heroism is revealed as bloody horror; the child's innocent game of war is in fact a terrible scene of carnage; the childhood game with the African American slaves (to free whom this war is being fought) becomes a hellishly parodic instance of misplaced triumphalism. The dead and dishonoured mother seems for a moment – in the reversal of perspective – to be the victim of her son (war as a perversion of natural bonds). And the final detail of the child's deaf-mute condition both explains in retrospect the uncanny silence of the scene we have witnessed and symbolizes the child's incapacity to understand and express the horror he has witnessed. The pathos of the child's innocence is accentuated, but at the same time, in the absence of understanding, experience can never be redeemed and controlled, and language becomes not a means of revelation or explanation but the inarticulate 'language of a devil'.

The subject matter of the comic tales is often concerned with violence and transgression: the tone is usually ironically (or sometimes pathologically) detached. 'An Imperfect Conflagration', the story of a murderer who fails to remove by fire the traces of his crime because he hides the bodies in a fireproof bookcase, begins: 'Early one morning in 1872 I murdered my father – an act which made a deep impression on me at the time.' In another story, 'My Favourite Murder', the narrator tells how he defended himself against the charge of murdering his mother by arguing that the murder was relatively trivial in comparison with his murder of his grandfather, which was accomplished by tying him in a sack and having him butted by an angry ram. The sadistic violence is slightly, but not entirely, offset by the cartoon, 'Tom and Jerry' quality of the violence: in its charges the ram is 'a prolonging white streak with monstrous undulations, and it delivers the coup de grace by flying some forty or fifty feet into the air like 'some great white bird' so that the narrator is 'lost in admiration of its grace'. But in Tom and Jerry cartoons nobody really gets hurt or dies: here the humour has a brutal edge.

In stories like this the nineteenth-century tall tale reaches a violent apogee (to be followed in the twentieth century by the strip cartoon and the spoof horror film). What readers make of it will depend on their threshold of tolerance for violence in humour (although there remains, perhaps, a psychoanalytic interest in these stories which lies partly outside a purely literary one). Bierce combined a reactionary temperament, a caustic wit, a cynical disposition, a philosophically critical mind and a fantastic imagination in equal measure. There is a genuine element of satiric force in his wit and – against war-madness, say, and commercial greed, and simply against human blindness and folly; there is a striking resourcefulness and modernity in his literary technique and a fascination with the possibilities of the short story form; and there is in addition the exhilarating and disturbing note of a writer not entirely in control of his own impulses. Trying to discriminate between these powerful elements and determine the proper interest and literary status of Bierce is not least among the pleasures of reading him.

Stephen Crane

Stephen Crane (1871–1900), like Ambrose Bierce, was drawn to short forms. His longest and best-known work, *The Red Badge of Courage* (1895), runs to 131 pages in the Library of America edition, or about 52,000 words, and is usually thought of as a short novel; *Maggie, A Girl of the Streets* (1893), at 71 pages or 28,000 words, is the second longest and would be described by most critics as a novella or long story. And it is notable that Crane came to regard *The Red Badge* as 'too long'.[7] Both works operate in a mode which focuses on vivid, self-contained chapters – scenes or pictures (of battle in the former work and the life of Maggie or her family in the latter). But in *Maggie* the chapters are shorter, and if anything there is less reflection and more concentration. Crane wrote three other significant novellas: *George's Mother* (1896), *The Monster* (1899) and *The Third Violet* (1897, about a young artist's love affair). But his most achieved work apart from *The Red Badge* lies in the realm of the short story proper: *The Little Regiment* (1896; stories and sketches about the Civil War); *Wounds in the Rain* (1900; about the Graeco-Turkish and the American-Cuban wars) *Whilomville Stories* (1900; about the comic mock-heroics of childhood); various tales of cowboys and the West; and particularly the three stories 'The Open Boat' (1897), 'The Bride Comes to Yellow Sky' (1898) and 'The Blue Hotel' (1898), the first of which challenges *The Red Badge of Courage* for the place of Crane's masterpiece.

Crane saw himself as aiming at a goal 'particularly described by that misunderstood and abused word, realism', and added that 'Tolstoy is the writer I admire most of all'.[8] He meant by realism a mode which gets 'nearer . . . to life', and which avoids romanticization and idealization. More specifically, contemporaries like Conrad (and subsequent critics) were inclined to describe him as an 'impressionist', indicating by that a mode which focuses on the phenomenological, or the precise way events strike the perceiving mind.[9] W. D. Howells, with what seems like an example from Bierce's 'One of the Missing' in mind, put it that 'You must render, never report. You must never write "He saw a man point a gun at him". You must put it: "He saw a steel ring directed at him".'[10] And the emphasis on subjective perception opens the way, paradoxically, for a kind of writing which is far from 'realist' in the sense of journalistically explanatory or photographically descriptive. In the end, Crane should be seen as a markedly poetic writer who uses the full poetic resources of tone, irony, stylization, hyperbole (including 'the grotesque'), metaphor and symbol to achieve his effects. The concentrated intensity of this kind of writing led again to the concision of the short story and the novella.

Paradoxically too (for a 'realist'), among Crane's most persistent preoccupations were the ideas and facts of innocence and heroism: concepts which he approached with a unique combination of romantic enthusiasm and coolly (even coldly) detached irony. His first major work *Maggie, A Girl of the Streets*, finds both qualities in the squalid conditions of New York's Bowery district. The highly wrought intensity of Crane's prose in *Maggie* would be oppressive in a long novel, but in the short scenes of this novella it works with impressive effect. And in the short stories similar, though often somewhat more subdued, qualities are combined with even greater compression and the possibilities of more formal shaping of narrative structure. Crane wrote a number of stories about cowboys and the Far West, usually involving an ironic examination of the nature of Western naivety, bravery and the gunslinger ethic. In 'Twelve O'Clock' the arrival of a cuckoo-clock in Placer's bar leads to incredulity, bets, challenges and the absurdity of irrational violence (Crane's cowboys are often very like the children of the *Whilomville* stories, and vice versa: part of Crane's enduring preoccupation with the heroisms of childhood and the childishness of the heroic posture).

In 'The Bride Comes to Yellow Sky' (1898) Crane fashions a miniature myth of the civilizing (or Easternizing) of the West (there are interesting similarities of theme with Harte's 'The Luck of Roaring Camp', though a great difference in style). The story is also almost a copy-book tragi-comedy (and theatrical into the bargain): the marriage happens (it is true) just before the story begins, but there is the threat of death, subverted by comedy, before the marriage can be finally confirmed. Texan Sheriff Jack Potter makes the train journey westward from San Antonio to Yellow Sky with his new bride, and the opening paragraph of the story is a precise phenomenological and symbolic description of the West moving East: 'a glance from the window seemed simply to prove that the plains of Texas were pouring eastward. Vast flats of green grass, dull-hued spaces of mesquite and cactus, little groups of frame houses, woods of light and tender trees, all were sweeping into the east, sweeping over the horizon, a precipice.' Potter is apprehensive of the town's reaction to his marriage; but the first call on him when he arrives is to deal with the trigger-happy Scratchy Wilson who is – verbally at any rate – terrorizing the town. The theatricality of the situation and setting is underlined by Crane's imagery (the 'vivid green grass plots' on the main street 'resembled the grass mats used to represent lawns on the stage'); and Scratchy's posturing and childish bravado is caught by his cheap, decorative shirt, made 'on the east side of New York', and his boots with red tops and gilded imprints 'of the kind beloved in winter by little sledding boys on the hillsides of new England'. Finally confronted by Potter without a gun and with his wife at his side, Scratchy finds himself 'in the presence of this foreign condition, a simpler child of the earlier plains', and can only say, slowly: 'Well . . . I s'ppose it's all off now.' It is, as they say, the end of an era. The last line of the story suggests (as a number of critics have pointed out) a dinosaur lumbering to extinction: 'His feet made funnel-shaped tracks in the heavy sand' – an image which also balances nicely, tragi-comically, with the opening sentence of the second paragraph ('A newly married pair. . .'): this opening sentence speaks of things new-born, the later one of things dying. It illustrates once again (like 'My Kinsman Major Molineux' or 'Rip Van Winkle') the power of the short story to encapsulate a moment of personal and cultural crisis.

'The Blue Hotel' is more enigmatic, another study of innocence (or naivety) and experience, bravery and fear, heroism and posturing heroics, but this time curiously multiple in its significance. A Swede comes to the Blue Hotel in the small Western town of Romper, and seems fearful and suspicious of those around him. He plays cards with the owner's son Johnnie and two other guests, a cowboy and a man from the East; accuses Johnnie of cheating and fights him; goes off into the town in the midst of a violent snow-storm and ends up in a bar where he tries to force the local gambler (an exemplary citizen with 'a real wife and two children and a neat cottage in a suburb') to have a drink with him, and gets shot. In the last section of the story the cowboy and the Easterner discuss the affair; the Easterner admits that Johnnie was cheating and concludes that 'We, five of us, have collaborated in the murder of this Swede. . . and that fool of an unfortunate gambler came merely as a culmination, the apex of a human movement.' But the cowboy protests rebelliously (unwittingly confirming the Easterner's point): '"Well, I didn't do anythin', did I?"'

The story has been seen as a 'study of fear' or paranoia[11] – fear bringing on its own nemesis as in Poe's 'Usher' – but it can also be read as a study of fate as circumstance (or environment), and a story of neurotic or infantile 'heroism' or the delusions of wild-west fantasy. The Palace Hotel, with its shade of light blue, stands out from all the other buildings of Romper, and with its stage-Irish owner Scully, its enormous stove 'humming with a godlike violence', and its stock guests ('the cowboy', 'the Easterner') it seems like a kind of technicolour or film version of the West, a stage set or 'dime novel' (as the Easterner says) where, the Swede thinks, the hotel-keeper is liable to poison him with his whiskey and the son to cheat him at cards. The Swede is on the one hand a posturer who, as his confidence grows, adopts the cowboy's card-playing habit of 'board-whacking'; on the other, drinking Scully's whiskey, he is like a kind of furious infant at the breast: 'as his lips curled absurdly around the opening and his throat worked, he kept his glance, burning with hatred, upon the old man's face'. One irony of the outcome is that it is the respected, cultivated and suburban gambler who kills the Swede, not the colourful inmates of the Blue Hotel: another is that a kind of impersonal mechanism seems to lead to the Swede's death – as impersonal as the cash-machine that in the final film-like 'shot' of the murder scene shows to the dead, staring eyes of the Swede the legend '"This registers the amount of your purchase."' But perhaps the most persistent impression left by the story is of men roused to absurd violence by their mixture of pride and fear, overweening pretensions which are put into perspective by the extreme violence of the snow-storm that rages outside during the fight and the Swede's departure into town. Men's 'conceit' in the face of the terrific power of inhuman nature is caught in a passage of extraordinary rhetorical intensity:

> He might have been in a deserted village. We picture the world as thick with conquering and elate humanity, but here, with the bugles of the tempest pealing, it was hard to imagine a peopled earth. One viewed the existence of man then as a marvel, and conceded a glamor of wonder to these lice which were caused to cling to a whirling, fire-smitten, ice-locked, disease-stricken, space-lost bulb. The conceit of man was explained by this storm to be the very engine of life. One was a coxcomb not to die in it.

The power and beauty of non-human nature are also at the heart of Crane's greatest story, 'The Open Boat' (1897). Based on a real incident in which Crane was involved while sailing to cover the revolution in Cuba as a journalist, it tells of four men, 'a captain, an oiler, a cook and a correspondent' at sea for thirty hours in a small boat after the wreck of their ship. The bare bones of the real-life story of the voyage and shipwreck are given in a newspaper piece, 'Stephen Crane's Own Story', published a few months before; but the account in 'The Open Boat' lifts the matter from journalistic record into art. Crane's prose is extraordinarily alive to the beauty and terror of the sea, and the beauty and terror is heightened rather than undermined by the persistent tone of wondering irony that runs through the whole. The irony serves as a means of controlling emotion – both at the time and in the telling – but for the reader it makes the emotion all the more powerful.

> A singular disadvantage of the sea lies in the fact that after successfully surmounting one wave you discover that there is another behind it just as important and just as nervously anxious to do something effective in the way of swamping boats . . . As each slaty wall of water approached, it shut all else from the view of the men in the boat, and it was not difficult to imagine that this particular wave was the final outburst of the ocean, the last effort of the grim water. There was a terrible grace in the move of the waves, and they came in silence, save for the snarling of the crests.

I stress below the human dimension of the correspondent's experience, but it is debatable whether that or the story's sheer sense of poetic wonder should receive the final emphasis. The poet John Berryman, at any rate, in what is surely the best book on Stephen Crane, feels that the story's realization of comradeship is a fine thing, but the beauty and terror of that last sentence is even finer.[12] The story records the quiet stoicism and humour and constant wakefulness of the wounded captain (his chuckle can express 'humor, contempt, tragedy all in one'), the occasional absurd conversations between the men (the argument about whether houses of refuge have lifeboats, the cook's attempt to start a conversation about pies), the oiler's quiet realism and his adroitness and practicality as a rower. There are moments of horror in the close '*whirroo*' of a shark's dark fin through the water, or of grim comedy in the 'unblinking scrutiny' of the seagulls and the attempt of one to land on the captain's head. And as they near the shore, separated from it by the murderous surf, the correspondent's head is filled with the near delirium of this mock-philosophic refrain (like an irritating tune you can't get out of your head): 'If I am going to be drowned – if I am going to be drowned – if I am going to be drowned, why, in the name of the seven mad gods who rule the sea, was I allowed to come thus far and contemplate sand and trees?'

The close rendering of physical and mental impressions builds to an intense, slow-motion climax in the description of the men being finally washed ashore as their boat breaks up on the incoming waves. The correspondent's detailed perceptions – of the cook in his cork lifejacket paddling himself like a canoe with a loose oar, of the captain clinging with one hand to the keel, almost like 'a man raising himself to look over a board fence', and the strange clarity of the houses on the shore, as if appearing to 'one who in a gallery looks at a scene from Brittany or Holland' – and the final moments of urgent action as a helper from the beach runs to the captain then to the correspondent and then to the oiler, are followed by the almost unbearably quiet single paragraph (like a dramatic musical *pianissimo* after a *forte*), which lets the fact of the oiler's death be registered through the impression: 'In the shallows, face downward, lay the oiler. His forehead touched the sand that was periodically, between each wave, clear of the sea.'

But as well as the poetry of immediate impressions the story carries a moral significance which cannot be separated but may be distinguished from them (and without which the death of the oiler would not be so poignant). The correspondent 'who had been taught to be cynical of men' is aware, even at the time, that the comradeship developed among the men 'was the best experience of his life'. Or, in a mode of understatement even more characteristic of Crane's quizzical irony: 'They were a captain, a cook, an oiler and a correspondent, and they were friends – friends in a more curiously ironbound degree than may be common.' The other, contrasting thing learned is that metaphysical solace is absent. The universe 'did not seem cruel to him then, nor beneficent, nor treacherous nor wise. But she was indifferent, flatly indifferent.' What remains is a remarkably complex sense of the primacy of moral obligation:

> It is, perhaps, plausible that a man in this situation, impressed with the unconcern of the universe, should see the innumerable flaws of his life and have them taste wickedly in his mind and wish for another chance. A distinction between right and wrong seems absurdly clear to him, then, in this new ignorance of the grave-edge, and he understands that if he were given another opportunity he would mend his conduct and his words, and be better and brighter during an introduction, or at a tea.

The complexity lies, again, in the Cranean irony, which sees simultaneously a moral truth and the difficulty of holding on to it, a moral conviction gained in the face of death and a scepticism which can also see it as a 'new ignorance of the grave-edge' (merely a new kind of ignorance, or a new ignorance of death itself?), the self-importance of men's moral tenets and the trivial conditions, for the most part, of their realization. This is the correspondent's interpretation of his experience, and it this interpretation which is alluded to in the solemn coda of the last paragraph of the story: 'When it came night, the white waves paced to and fro in the moonlight, and the wind brought the sound of the great sea's voice to the men on the shore, and they felt that they could then be interpreters.'

Chapter 8

Henry James

In his extraordinarily sustained and productive literary career, Henry James (1843–1916) published fifteen novels, as well as travel books, criticism and essays, and a collection of short stories and 'nouvelles' which runs to 111 stories in Leon Edel's twelve-volume edition. He was undoubtedly the literary master of his age, both in America and in England (where he spent much of his life, settling there in 1898), and brought to fiction a searching inwardness of perception and a refinement of style that are unique. His greatest novels, like *Portrait of a Lady* (1881), *The Bostonians* (1886) and *The Ambassadors* (1903), will doubtless always command the most widespread literary attention, but his achievement in the short and long story is itself a major one, and would assure his classic status even without the novels. He himself wrote in a letter of 1871: 'To write a series of good little tales I deem ample work for a lifetime. I dream that my lifetime shall have done it.'[1] And it did.

What James found in the short story form was the possibility for mobility of 'point of view' and variety of attack. A conversation with the French critic Hippolyte Taine in 1889 had the effect, he wrote in his Notebooks,

> of reviving, refreshing, confirming, consecrating, as it were, the wish and the dream that have lately grown stronger than ever in me – the desire that the literary heritage, such as it is, poor thing, that I may leave, shall consist of a large number of perfect *short* things, *nouvelles* and tales, illustrative of ever so many things in life – in the life I see and know and feel – and of all the deep and delicate – and of London, and of art, and of everything: and that they shall be fine, rare, strong, wise – eventually perhaps even recognized.[2]

The artistic reason for choosing the short forms, he wrote a few years later, was '*par excellence*. . . simply the consideration that by doing short things I can do so many, touch so may subjects, break out in so many places, handle so many of the threads of life'.[3] And James's stories do, indeed, cover a wide range of experience – mainly, that is, within the world he knew, that of the rich and cultivated upper class of his time in America and Europe. He wrote of Americans travelling in Europe, of businessmen, of counts and countesses, of painters, writers and actors, of governesses and tutors, of students and professors, of journalists and editors; and his settings range from Boston and New York to London, Paris and Rome, the country houses of England and the *palazzi* of Italy. Everywhere he evokes the colours and tones of places, the accents of educated speech and thought, and above all the finer shades of feeling and the intricacies of emotional life and moral decision.

There is, however, a certain paradox in James's ambition to write 'perfect *short* things'. He was not a writer whose expression tended naturally towards anecdotal concision (unlike, say, his French contemporary Maupassant, whose short stories he greatly admired, though with reservations).[4] This is not to say that he is always long-winded and over-elaborate (though the charge has often been brought against his later works). He writes with unusual exactness, and the length of his sentences and the qualifications of his subordinate clauses are, at his best, always impelled by precision of thought and suggestion. But his search for the inner qualities of character and situation often needs more space than the 'very short tales – things of 7,000 to 10,000 words' of which he spoke when writing of his story 'The Real Thing' (which is about 7,500 words in length) in 1891. Consequently, his stories tend to be long stories, or – to use the term James preferred – *nouvelles*. Looking back on the composition of his stories, James wrote in one of the Prefaces to the New York Edition (1909–11) of 'our ideal, the beautiful, the blest *nouvelle*', which allowed for 'shades and differences, varieties and styles, the value above all of the idea happily *developed*', and where 'the hard and fast rule of the "from six to eight thousand words" . . . was a little relaxed'. And relaxed it often was: to about 23,000 words in the case, say, of *Daisy Miller* (1878) – which still has essentially the feel of a 'story' – and as much as 35,000 words in the case of *The Aspern Papers* (1888) or *The Turn of the Screw* (1898), a length which is probably around the upper limit for a *nouvelle* in most estimations. In line with the boundaries set for this study I shall, with some reluctance, ignore the *nouvelles*, but with the hope that some of the less noticed qualities of the shorter stories will be given their due.

Portraits of ladies: 'new' and old

One of James's recurring and persistent interests, one might almost say curiosities, throughout his career, was the changing nature of the modern (usually American) woman and the social attitudes that surrounded her. *The Portrait of a Lady* and *The Bostonians* are perhaps his greatest and most sustained explorations of this topic, but the short story allowed him briefer, more concentrated and specific treatments of particular types and problems. In *nouvelles* like *Daisy Miller: a Study* (1878) and *In the Cage* (1898) James explores, at the length he preferred, the lives of modern young women who were, in different ways, the victims of social conditions: the former of society's restrictive notions of propriety, and the latter (who triumphs over them) of the economic condition of the single woman. In his short stories proper he explores more particular, and generally less romantic, examples of women's experience. The women are often more calculating, and also often older. The youthful romantic idealism of Daisy Miller and the more complex mixture of romantic fantasy and disinterested benevolence in the heroine of *In the Cage* are replaced by more ironic portraits, either of heroines who are spurred by unmistakably worldly motives, or ones who are of a more 'special type', achieving a certain distinction through their unconventionality. Here, the 'new' woman tends to be resilient and independent (though almost always aiming pertinaciously for a socially 'good' – or otherwise remunerative – marriage).

In 'Miss Gunton of Poughkeepsie' the 'charming' and 'pretty' American heroine of the title is wooed, for love and her grandfather's money, by an Italian prince, but she resolutely ensures that he makes the running, by moving successively to Paris and to London and expecting him to follow her. He does, and proposes, but he is anxious that she should write to pay her respects to 'the Princess', his mother. Lily Gunton, however, feels that the Princess should make the overture by writing to *her*. Their confrontation over the matter is mediated by an older lady (Lady Champer), fully versed in the ways of Europe, baffled by the young lady's stubborn expectations, but shrewdly amused at the Prince's subjection to his mother. Miss Gunton holds out; the Princess's letter is finally sent but crosses with one to the Prince from Miss Gunton breaking off the engagement. The Prince says tearfully to Lady Champer '"And I believed she loved me!"' '"*I* didn't"', Lady Champer replies. American toughness confronts European protocol: America wins. The relative brevity (for James) of this story points up the contrast of the two worlds. Miss Gunton is a kind of tougher Daisy Miller who has already passed from innocence to experience.

After 1890 James attempted more short stories than before (while continuing to write extremely successful *nouvelles* like *The Turn of the Screw*, and *In the Cage*, both of 1898), stories which lent themselves to the study of different types of women. In 'The Special Type' (1900) an artist's model, Mrs Dundene, acts as the third party in a divorce case where the husband does not want to 'besmirch' the reputation of the woman he plans to make his second wife. Told by an artist narrator – a friend of the husband who suggests the model to him – the story treads a careful path through a morally ambiguous terrain (the kind of terrain in which James most likes to find himself in his stories): the surrogate co-respondent is, of course, 'not a lady', but neither is she socially or morally condemned by the narrator. And when the husband offers her (as well as payment) a gift of 'anything in the world' she most desires, she asks for the portrait of him, by the narrator, which had been destined for the new wife. The new wife-to-be is indignant, but the husband can hardly refuse, and the narrator feels the choice 'the key to his freedom' since it enables him to repay the model for involving her in a shady business. It is apt repayment, too, he tells the new wife, since 'they [he uses the new wife's euphemism for the surrogate 'lover'] never saw him alone'. (635). It could be said of this story that the character of Mrs Dundene, the 'special type', could come more sharply into focus; but James at least suggests a woman (significantly from the art world) who though 'not a lady' is serious, self-aware and at least as worthy of respect as the husband and the new wife, perhaps more so. And in James's world and time this is a distinct readjustment of the social and moral boundaries.

In a very late story, 'Julia Bride' (1908), the moral boundaries are further questioned, if not clearly readjusted. James here is clearly intrigued by the changing social mores whereby young ladies could have before marriage a number of close relations with men, leading very often to formal engagements, without forfeiting social respectability (though some effort had to be made to repair the slightly misted, if not tarnished, image). Like many of James's stories it is, in a small compass, revelatory of the complex social manoeuvring and jockeying for position that went on in the marriage market (and, increasingly, in the second-marriage market) of the upper classes in *fin de siècle* and *nouvelle siècle* London. Julia Bride, with six or seven young gentlemen in her past and a twice-divorced mother as a millstone round her neck, wants her stepfather (the second husband) to admit, socially, that he was the 'guilty' party in his divorce, to help her marriage chances. But he in turn appears with a new lady, Miss Drack, for whom he wants Julia to perform exactly the same function for *him*. Julia rises to the occasion with 'splendour'; but it leaves her with only her most recent gentleman, Murray

Brush (James's names usually give out various signals – here of a kind of grocerly smartness, perhaps), now engaged to someone else, to vouch for her respectability to the world and in particular to Basil French, the extremely rich bachelor who is Julia's latest – and perhaps for the first time deadly serious – marital target. Murray and his fiancée grasp at the chance to 'get at' the rich and socially elevated Frenches, and Julia realizes with bitterness that they will make their connection, through her, but that she will not. The story is satisfying in its formal mirrorings and rich in the nuances of social behaviour in a changing age. Its subject is slight but intense (Julia Bride's situation is complex but she is not a morally complex heroine) and the dilemma it encapsulates would hardly stretch to a novel but ideally fits the short story. James, with his 'small circular frame, has 'snapshotted' one small but vivid corner of the social scene. Though '"foreshortened" to within an inch of her life', as James himself put it in his Preface, '[w]hat if [she] were the silver key, tiny in itself, that would unlock a treasure – the treasure of a whole view of manners and morals, a whole range of American social aspects?'

Lessons of the Master

One group of James's stories holds a particular interest, representing as it does a sustained exploration (hardly paralleled in his novels) of the nature of art and the predicament of the writer or, sometimes, painter or 'thinker'. One of them, 'The Special Type', has been discussed above. The others, written in the decade of James's own 'middle years', include two *nouvelles*, *The Lesson of the Master* (1888) and *The Coxon Fund* (1894), and the short (and long) stories 'The Private Life' (1892), 'The Real Thing' (1892), 'The Middle Years' (1893), 'The Death of the Lion' (1894), 'The Next Time' (1895), 'The Figure in the Carpet' (1896) and 'The Real Right Thing' (1899). These stories are often concerned with the perils, for a writer, of social success – James was already widely known by the 1890s – and the acute sense of what he felt he still had to achieve.

'The Real Thing', altogether more compact and concentrated than the *nouvelles* mentioned above, gives a penetrating insight into the nature of art and its relation to 'real' life. It is also a telling critique of the nineteenth-century ideal of the English gentleman and gentlewoman. The narrator is an artist, a book illustrator who takes on as models for illustrations of upper-class life – to do them a good turn since they are out of funds – the splendidly named Major Monarch and his wife. But the stately pair are too much (yet also not enough) 'the real thing'. Their looks ('It was in their faces, the blankness, the deep intellectual repose, of twenty years of country-house visiting'), their voices and behaviour are impeccable, but there is a fatal stiffness of manner, a lack of plasticity ('even the highest respectability may fail of being plastic', the narrator eventually concludes). The little cockney artist's model Miss Churm, and even an Italian ice-cream seller, Oronte, have more talent for their roles. The major and his wife are perfect examples of their type: they 'didn't do anything' but their manner and accoutrements were perfect and they 'could have been counted on for cheerfulness' which always makes them welcome at the country-house weekends. But for the illustrator (and, one takes it, for the writer) 'the defect of the real [subject] was so apt to be a lack of representation'. The position reminds one of Flaubert's contempt for mere 'realism' in the sense of servile copying. The two professionals can, like actors, 'represent' their characters, and above all *give* them character, personality, individuality, which Major and Mrs Monarch, simply being themselves, so signally lack. ('"Oh, I'm not a Russian Princess" Mrs Monarch protested [when asked to 'do' one], a little coldly. I could see that she had known some and didn't like them.') The illustrator and the illustrator's model, like the novelist, have to *represent*, to throw into relief, to dramatize and pictorialize. The poor Monarchs, who are reduced in their tactful embarrassment to clearing up the studio to make themselves useful, are too much their own stereotypes to be anything else.

The other stories of literary life take various aspects of that life and hold them up to ironic and critical, and sometimes a kind of elegiac, scrutiny. 'The Middle Years' tells of the eminent novelist, 'poor Dencombe' (James is curiously fond of the affectionately patronizing adjective for his elderly writers), who, while convalescing in Bournemouth, encounters a young admirer who has just read his latest novel. Dr Hugh reassures him of its great artistic success, and spends much time with him. But Dr Hugh's wealthy employer, 'the Countess', 'opulent', 'massive' and saved from vulgarity by an 'agreeable off-hand tone', becomes jealous of the time the young doctor spends with the novelist, and Dencombe urges him to return to her. She dies, however, and leaves nothing to Dr Hugh; while Dencombe, suddenly aware of his own missed chances and failures, longs himself for 'a second chance', to do now what he feels he had only just learned to do. But he is too ill, and just before he dies, he comes to the realization (in one of James's most famous passages, deeply felt, and saved, in context, from the flourish of melodrama by the gently valetudinarian character of 'poor Dencombe'): 'A second chance – *that's* the delusion. There never was to be but one. We work in the dark – we do what we can – we give what we have. Our doubt is our passion, and our passion is our task. The rest is the madness of art.'

'The Figure in the Carpet' is a piece of teasingly humorous irony about James's own craft. The narrator, a young literary reviewer, is urged by his friend to capture on paper the 'pleasure so rare' the 'sense of . . . something or other' of the novels of Hugh Vereker. He tries and (according to the friend) fails, but his piece is bandied about by Lady Jane, and comes to the attention of Vereker. The great man unintentionally snubs the young reviewer and in kindly remorse reveals in conversation, that no-one has *ever* found his 'little point', 'the particular thing I've most written my books *for*', or what he later calls his 'little trick', his 'exquisite scheme', and later 'the very string . . . my pearls are strung on'. But he will not, cannot – of course – say what it *is:* the books are there; he *has* said it. 'It governs every line, it chooses every word, it dots every i, it places every comma.' The comedy of the story comes from the narrator's baffled pursuit, Vereker's enthusiastic metaphors and weary despair of the narrator's questions, the collaboration of an earnest young lady, and so on. The idea, the quarry, that the narrator tracks down and which Vereker approves, is 'something like a complex figure in a Persian carpet': and it has, of course, become a household word among critics of Modernism for that pattern beneath surface complexity without which many an article on the modernist poem or novel would be at a loss. The critic of this story or any other of James's – armed only with the narrator's own helpless terms of 'style' and 'thought', 'form' and 'feeling' (Vereker finds the distinctions pitiful) – should perhaps be wise enough to be deterred by James's irony from himself identifying the 'figure'. And perhaps (once we have ruled out, as the narrator does, the awful possibility that this is all a *pose*) that is the point. But something Vereker says while questioning the narrator's distinctions of form and content is worth recalling: 'He hesitated: "Well, you've got a heart in your body. Is that an element of form or an element of feeling? What I contend that nobody has ever mentioned in my work is the organ of life.'" Nothing can be more well-worn by now, as a critical term, than the idea of 'life': but nothing as a literary quality is more important, and great writers have been able to use the term convincingly (see D. H. Lawrence, *passim*). It is not so much a 'figure in the carpet' as a quality in the vision and in the prose. But at the end of the story the narrator is no wiser, and the critic had better remain at least tactfully hesitant where James refuses to tread.

The story does, however, raise important questions about the relation of literature to ideas, and metaphor to truth. In its own time James's story (and much else in his criticism and practice) can be seen as an implicit rebuke to what might be called the 'Browning Society' view of literature: the urge to find a coherent 'philosophy' beneath the *oeuvre.* Fiction is not ideas so much as the embodiment of ideas and what matters in it is as much truth to feeling as the truth of concepts. Philosophers have often been (at least until recently) suspicious of metaphor, which has been seen as a disguising and distorting of the truth. But perhaps certain kinds of truth (particularly truth to feeling) can only be caught in metaphor: there are matters that cannot be put in any other way. And it may be that one of the special values of the short story (over against the rambling discursiveness of the novel) is that it is compelled to remain within the realm of dramatization, embodiment and metaphor, and cannot afford to 'digress' into philosophical modes, as the greatest novelists – a Proust, a Tolstoy or a Lawrence – are prone to do.

Metaphor and the ghostly

One group of stories that James accumulated over the years raises the principle of metaphor to the level of a separate genre. The 'ghost story' was not, James said, 'a *class* of fiction' that he was especially 'disposed to cherish', being drawn more towards 'a close connotation, or close observation, of the real'.[5] But he was nevertheless drawn in several instances towards what his admired predecessor, Hawthorne, called Romance.[6] So in ten stories James uses actual 'ghosts' or apparitions as part of the plot, and in a number of others events take on a ghostly tinge.[7] In all these cases one can read the stories as employing a means of intensifying metaphor into the literal or the figurative into a ghostly 'figure'. As a rule, ghosts in James appear not merely for the sake of the *frisson* they arouse (though they can certainly do that), but also for some psychological point or human case that they bring to light.

In 'The Private Life', for instance, an idea of the nature of the successful writer (illustrated in other ways in the stories discussed above), and also a broader idea of the divided nature of the personality, is explored in a story of high social comedy in which the idea of a 'divided self' becomes literalized. The narrator, on holiday in the Alps with a group of fashionable Londoners, is struck by the banality of the public *persona* of the eminent writer Clare Vawdrey (James revealed later that his model here was the poet Robert Browning). How could 'this particular sound, loud, hearty presence', as he puts it in his Preface, have written 'the immortal things'? The answer is mysteriously revealed when one evening, while Vawdrey is holding forth to the company, the narrator goes to Vawdrey's study to fetch a manuscript, and glimpses through the door a figure bent over the desk. It is Vawdrey the writer, 'the one who does it' as Mrs Adney the famous actress puts it later. Conversely, another of the party, the majestic Lord Mellifont ('the host, the patron, the moderator at every board'), is revealed to be 'all public and had no corresponding private life', and when Mrs Adney (on a sketching outing for which the lord's equipment is, of course, of the finest type) returns to the spot at which they left him sketching, 'the place was utterly empty', and Lord Mellifont only reappears to the view at the sound of her voice. There is a chilling element in this idea of Mellifont's hollowness (Lady Mellifont evinces intense anxiety when the subject is approached and they cannot speak to her of it), but the main mood is comic, with Mrs Adney girlishly gay at the end, having met the 'real' Vawdrey and got 'her part' (the role she wants him to write), though with a final ironic comment from the narrator that Vawdrey and Mrs Adney seemed to have quarrelled, and it wasn't, in the end, 'the great part'. The ghostly element here both heightens the entertainment and extends the metaphors of divided selves and hollow men into 'literal' figures.

Other 'ghost' stories literalize the figurative to bring home other moral preoccupations. In 'Owen Wingrave' (1892) the young son of a military family, a 'conscientious objector', meets his fate encountering a family ghost in order to prove his courage: the struggle between ancient aggressive atavisms and modern civilized conscience is embodied in the ghostly figure. In 'The Real Right Thing' (1899) the narrator is employed by a great writer's widow to write his biography, but becomes gradually aware of the writer's haunting and restraining presence, by subtle shifts from metaphoric to literal (he hears 'documents on the table behind him shifted and stirred'); and (though 'haunted' too by the living widow) he finally abandons the project. 'The Friends of the Friends' (1896) explores how despite their friends' efforts to introduce them, a man and a woman who in the past have had similar ghostly premonitions uncannily fail to meet until shortly before (or is it after?) the death of the woman. The distinction matters particularly to the narrator, the bosom friend of the woman and also the fiancée of the man, who is now unable to suppress her jealousy. The story is at once a subtle study of what Goethe called 'elective affinities', those special qualities of sympathy and shared experience which draw two people together, a comic tale of social manoeuvring, and at the end a surprisingly moving account of mutual loss. The 'ghostly' simply raises to the literal level those invisible ties of spiritual sympathy (and their entwining with the physical) which bind two people together. There is also great psychological interest, as well as compelling atmosphere and narrative tension, in one of James's last and best ghost stories, 'The Jolly Corner' (1908), in which Spencer Brydon, returning to New York after thirty-three years in Europe, encounters a mysterious presence in his unoccupied house in Irving Place, which he comes to realize is his 'other' self, the man he should have been had he stayed in New York. The story has an obviously personal resonance – James himself returned to New

York in 1905 after twenty years spent mainly in Europe – and there is a final revelation of the ominous 'other', 'the dark stranger', 'evil, odious, blatant, vulgar' in impeccable evening dress (but with the curious detail, as his hands at first cover his face, of two fingers missing 'as if shot away' from his right hand), advancing finally 'as for aggression'. Brydon's horror is finally that this figure – its identity fitting his, he inwardly protests, 'at no point' – could be, or could have been, himself.

Chapter 9

Rebecca Harding Davis, Sarah Orne Jewett and Mary Wilkins Freeman

From its earliest years in the United States, the short story was a form which attracted a growing number of women writers. Magazine publication, which did so much to foster the short story form, was from the first often aimed at women readers. *Godey's Lady's Book*, first published in Philadelphia in 1830, grew out of the fashion for annuals, and was a monthly volume containing articles, tales and sketches, engravings of fashionable ladies and landscapes, and colour fashion plates.[1] A rival magazine from Boston, *The American Ladies' Magazine and Literary Gazette*, appeared in 1837, and its editor Sarah Joseph Hale announced: 'We have the assistance of many of our best female writers. We offer a field where female genius may find scope; where the female mind may engage its appropriate work – that of benefiting the female sex.'[2] Nathaniel Hawthorne, notoriously, dismissed women writers of his day as that 'damned mob of scribbling women'[3], but nineteenth-century women writers have recently begun to regain critical attention; republication of the main authors, together with a number of anthologies, has helped to rediscover an important strand of literary tradition.[4] This chapter and the next will focus on seven writers who have come to be seen as especially significant: Rebecca Harding Davis (1831–1910), Sarah Orne Jewett (1849–1909), Mary E. Wilkins Freeman (1852–1930), Charlotte Perkins Gilman (1860–1935), Kate Chopin (1851–1904), Edith Wharton (1862–1937) and Willa Cather (1873–1947).

But there are other women writers who wrote at least one outstanding short story: like Catherine Sedgwick's 'Cacoethes Scribendi' ('the itch of writing') (1830) – a witty and self-mocking tale of early American bluestockings – or Harriet Prescott Spofford's 'Circumstance', a strange, poetically powerful Romance (much admired by Emily Dickinson) about a woman who is captured by an 'Indian Devil' or jaguar, in which the central image becomes a kind of metaphor for sexual captivity.[5]

Rebecca Harding Davis

Rebecca Harding Davis was born in Washington, Pennsylvania and studied at the Washington Female Seminary. She published her best-known work, 'Life in the Iron Mills', in 1861 in *Atlantic Monthly.* The story is about Hugh Wolfe, a furnace-tender who sculpts figures out of korl (slag or iron residue), who is imprisoned for stealing from a visiting gentleman (in place of Wolfe's wife, the real thief) and who dies in prison. It conveys a powerful sense of the bleak industrial setting, though it is marred by a rhetorical and didactic tone which addresses the reader directly with a hectoring earnestness. There is a lengthy debate between the mill-owner, a critical but cynical visiting stranger, and a kindly philanthropic doctor, which raises questions of political action (the stranger says that change will only come from below, not *via* philanthropy from above), though the conclusion of the story tends towards a Christian quietism. The central and most memorable image is Wolfe's sculpted korl figure of a powerful nude woman, crouching on the ground, 'her arms flung out in some wild gesture of warning' – at once a symbol of working-class and feminist protest and a symptom of the thwarted creativity of Wolfe himself.

In 'Marcia', another currently accessible story of Davis's, the narrator, who is a writer, tells the story of a small, vivacious, 'ugly'-faced ('I believe other women would have called it') woman from Mississippi, who has come to the North and who visits the narrator, having sent her some writing to look at.[6] She tells of the difficulty of her life back home, where she is the only white child on a poor plantation, and of her family's hostility to her writing. The story is written in a plain, direct style, which gives a vivid portrait of the outspoken protagonist and a lively rendering of her speech and ultimately of her fate in all its pathos. She continues to be rebuffed by editors, falls into poverty and ends up going to prison for stealing; and in a sad final triumph for conventional values, she is taken home by her prospective husband, the well-meaning, brash and authoritarian son of the overseer, to whom she has been promised as a bride. Like many women's stories of this period, this one focuses on the difficulties of the woman writer, but in a way that distances it from the author herself and avoids any hint of self-pity. Davis herself had a breakdown brought on by the conflict of her duties as a wife and her literary aspirations, which she recorded in 'The Wife's Story' (1864) in *Atlantic Monthly*, but she went on writing throughout her life, producing among other works a study of ex-slaves and mulattos after the Civil War (*Waiting for the Verdict*, 1868), another example of the way women writers were often drawn to social questions.

Most critics feel she did not live up to the potential of 'Life in the Iron Mills', but 'Marcia' shows that she did develop as a writer, and could command a terser and plainer prose and a lively realism.

Sarah Orne Jewett

Sarah Orne Jewett was born in South Berwick, Maine in 1849, the daughter of a country doctor. From 1869 she published stories in the *Atlantic Monthly*, and her first collection of stories and sketches, *Deephaven*, set in a coastal town, was published in 1877. She published further volumes in the late 1870s and early 1880s, but the work with which she established her lasting reputation is *The Country of the Pointed Firs* (1896). Set in the maritime village of Dunnet, on the coast of Maine, the book is a sequence of stories and sketches told by a female narrator (clearly a persona for the author herself) about the people of this seaport. Dunnet, in the story, has long since declined from its great days as a trading and whaling port and embarkation point for Northern exploration; most of the inhabitants seem to be women, and the surviving men are either old eccentric seafarers regretting the loss of past times (like Captain Littlepage) or young-old men like the sixty-year-old William Todd, the brother of the narrator's hostess, Mrs Almira Todd. It is, in fact, very much a matriarchal society, and the large, earth-mother figure of Mrs Todd, with her esoteric knowledge of herbs and remedies, dominates it like some ancient sibyl.

The Country of the Pointed Firs is perhaps better seen as a collection of sketches rather than stories, although some of the chapters have a significant narrative element – such as Captain Littlepage's rapt tale of his friend Gaffett's voyage to the far North, filled with images of fantasy and Miltonic poetry somewhat like an abbreviated and naturalized version of Poe's *Arthur Pym*, carefully restrained by the slightly patronizing (or matronizing) narrator. The most telling story in the sequence (in three short parts, 'Poor Joanna', 'The Hermitage' and 'On Shell-heap Island') is about a hermit woman who lives alone on a remote island. She has retreated there after an unhappy love affair, and lives a life of extreme quietness and simplicity, visited only very rarely by passing fishermen, who may bring her hens or other provisions; though her friends keep watch through their spy-glasses to see if there are signs of life on the tiny island. Mrs Todd tells of a visit to Joanna with the Reverend Mr Dimmock ('"pompous enough"', says Mrs Fosdick, '"but I never could remember a word he said"'), and of Joanna's troubled preoccupation – that typical Puritan preoccupation, reminiscent of

Hawthorne's Ethan Brand – with secret guilt for having committed 'the unpardonable sin' ('"We don't seem to hear nothing about the unpardonable sin now"', Mrs Fosdick comments, '"but you may say 'twas not uncommon then"'). The tale is sad and elegiac with a note of 'lacrimae rerum' – like much else in the book – and poor Joanna clearly touches a chord of sympathy in the narrator, as she looks across to the mainland, 'which lay dim and dreamlike in the August haze, as Joanna must have watched it many a day':

> There was the world, and here was she with eternity well begun. In the life of each of us, I said to myself, there is a place remote and islanded, and given to endless regret or secret happiness; we are each the uncompanioned hermit and recluse of an hour or a day; we understand our fellows of the cell to whatever age of history they may belong.

The Country of the Pointed Firs has the added interest of being the first significant example in the American short story tradition of the short story cycle – a collection of pieces linked by their setting in the same location or by the recurrence of the same characters; it thus looks forward to Sherwood Anderson's *Winesburg, Ohio* or Eudora Welty's *The Golden Apples.* But Jowett also wrote many free-standing stories, of which perhaps the best known is 'A White Heron' (1886). In this 'Romance' story a shy nine-year-old country girl is enraptured by the beauty of a white heron in the woods near her village, but her childhood life and feelings are disrupted by the arrival of a vigorous young hunter. She is romantically struck by him, and promises to take him to where he can find the heron; but in the end her love for the bird leads her to keep her secret and reject the young man. The story can be read as a 'green' tale of the protection of the natural world, and also (as it has by feminist critics like Elizabeth Ammons)[7] as a story in which a young girl rejects the male world of guns, power and heterosexuality; an 'anti-bildungsroman' (as Ammons puts it) in which Sylvia decides not to step over the threshold of adult life and remains in the world of her grandmother. It does indeed seem to represent a view of life which attempts to preserve a world of innocence and ideal beauty by rejecting the male world; but whether it can be made to bear the weight of a serious feminist ideology is more doubtful: any such ideology which attempts to preserve certain values by refusing the entry into an adult world of full experience (however this may be reconceived) is open to the criticism that it endorses a Victorian sentimentalism which idealizes childhood to the point of evasion and denial of life.

Mary Wilkins Freeman

Mary Wilkins Freeman also tends towards an emphasis on the pathos of women's lives, though perhaps with a greater variety of types and situations. 'A New England Nun' (1891) – her best-known story, though not necessarily her best – tells of the cloistered Louisa Ellis, who waits fourteen years for her betrothed, Joe Dagget, to return from making his fortune in Australia. In the course of that time she has developed a love of her own privacy and orderly ways; and on Dagget's return she also overhears a conversation he has with another village girl, Lily, expressing strong feelings for her but renouncing her so he may keep his word to Louisa. At the end of the story she decides against marriage with Joe (though she never mentions Lily), and is left, after a little sadness, in happy possession of her life of cloistered simplicity. The world Freeman depicts here is delicate and 'feminine', but in the restricted sense of that term which tended to prevail at the time.

In other stories, however, Freeman shows a more problematic sense of women's identity in mid-nineteenth-century America, and a more general preoccupation with what became of the tradition of Puritanism in its heartlands of Massachusetts and Vermont. One of her critics has strikingly called her 'the anatomist of the latter-day Puritan will', that strong sense of individual relation to God, with its strenuous Calvinistic responsibilities and its frequent contortions into wilfulness and eccentricity, particularly in a society which had dwindled economically since colonial times.[8] In 'A Conflict Ended' (1886) a man sits every Sunday on the steps of the Congregational Church in his village, because of a vow he has taken never to enter the church after a doctrinal objection to the appointment of a new minister, while his beloved, the local milliner, refuses to marry him because she cannot bear the way he has become the laughing-stock of the village. Only when she has been inspired by the actions of a young employee of hers who finally agrees to let her fiancé's mother live with them after their marriage does the milliner decide to sit with her man; but moved from his stubbornness, he rises and enters the church with her. In 'A Village Singer' (1889) an elderly woman, embittered by being retired from her post as principal singer in the church, plays her parlour organ loudly in her nearby cottage, drowning the solos of the new singer; and cuts her nephew, engaged to the new singer, from her will. But on her deathbed she relents, and asks the new singer to come and sing to her. She listens to the performance with 'a radiant expression'; while the story is saved from too mawkish a sentimentalism by her final flicker of professional dignity: '"You flattened a little on – soul."'

Freeman's stories usually contrive to end happily: her undoubted feeling for realism – for the impoverished lives and constricted souls of these latter-day Puritans – is tempered by the element of popular Romance, which usually brings reconciliation between her feuding relatives and neighbours. These endings often strike the modern reader as sentimental, though they are not always implausible. But in the body of the stories there is often a powerful insight into the workings of over-developed conscience (as in 'An Honest Soul', 1884), or sibling resentment ('The Reign of the Doll', 1904), or stubborn independence. In 'A Church Mouse' (1889) a village woman suddenly made homeless decides to fill the vacant post of sexton and to move in to the meeting house with her bed and stove, since the village has no poor-house and the Deacon will not take her in. There is a foretaste here of Eudora Welty's 'Why I Live at the P. O.', and the assertive country-wit of the woman is nicely caught: 'Men git in a good many places where they don't belong, an' where they set as awkward as a cow on a hen-roost, jest because they push ahead of women.' Freeman's work has a predominant focus on women's lives and a frequently witty feminism which rarely if ever gets preachy or strident. One of her best-known stories, 'The Revolt of "Mother"' (1890), tells of a wife's rebellion against her husband's obsession with his farm, when she moves herself and her family into the new barn which he has built for the animals in spite of the meagreness and poverty of the family dwelling. At the same time her championing of women's rights does not preclude a sly irony about female vanity. 'The Old-Maid Aunt' (1908), told in the first person, is primarily an amusing refutation of conventional wisdom about 'old maids' (this aunt is attractive, romantic, mischievous and manipulative); but in her loquacious and self-regarding narrative there is surely more than a hint of an alternative reading in which the aunt becomes an unreliable narrator, so full of her romantic attachments and successes – she is convinced, for instance, that she has inspired a passion in her much younger niece's fiancé – that the reader becomes suspicious.

In 'Old Woman Magoun' there is a more desperate rejection of a male world of corruption and violence, in the story of an old woman who lets her fourteen-year-old granddaughter die (by letting her eat deadly nightshade berries), rather than be given by her father to a stranger in payment of a gambling debt. The story is told for the most part with a plain realism which makes no attempt to gloss over the unpleasant facts and gives a convincing portrait of the male characters; but it also makes a great deal of the pathos of Lily's death and the grandmother's attempt to prepare her for death with a sentimental fantasy of how she will 'come to a gate with all the colours of the rainbow' and 'walk up a gold street' and 'cross the field where the blue flowers come up to your knees', until she finds her dead mother. There is a stronger justification (in the facts of Lily's father's abuse) for her escape into death than there is in many examples of nineteenth-century stories of the deaths of innocent children,[9] and the uncomfortably sentimental pathos of the grandmother's words of consolation is mitigated elsewhere by the plain, matter-of-fact narration and absence of moralistic or sentimentalist rhetoric. But it is difficult to escape the feeling, nevertheless, that the death of the child is being used for the indulgence of sentimental feelings which collude subtly with the status quo.

But Freeman's talents do not always tend towards effects of pathos, and she can also demonstrate how the genre of non-realism, or Romance, particularly of the supernatural, can be an effective vehicle for psychological insight. 'Luella Miller', which begins with the conventional ghost story opening of a house abandoned and untenanted and regarded in the village as fearful and malign, is the story of a softly beautiful but intensely manipulative young woman whose relatives and friends all die after getting lured into attending to her every whim. After the descriptive opening, the story is told in a convincing New England vernacular by a vigorous old woman who had known Luella as a neighbour, but who had resisted her manipulations until the very end of Luella's life when she is drawn out of compassion to attend her deathbed. She too begins to feel ill and crosses the street for her medicine; but on her return she sees 'Luella Miller and Erastus Miller, and Lily, and Aunt Abby, and Maria, and the doctor, and Sarah, all goin' out of her door, and all but Luella shone white in the moon-light, and they were all helpin' her along until she seemed fairly to fly in the midst of them'. Even Luella's ghost seems to command the help and attention of the victims of her selfishness. The ending gives the story its ghost-story status, but as in many good ghost stories (particularly of the more modern variety) its strength lies in its convincing psychological element: the way in which Luella's egotistical manipulations seem to prey on the ordinary human goodwill of her relatives and friends. To carry this to the point of supernatural malignity and posthumous blight is only to follow the fears and bafflements of the situation of ordinary life, helped by incomprehension and superstition towards the irrational, a few steps over the threshold of the supernatural domain. The conviction of the story is ensured by the strong, humorous, no-nonsense character and authentic speech of the narrator, Lydia Anderson, and her mixture of fascination and exasperation.

> 'Luella Miller used to sit in a way nobody else could if they sat up and studied a week of Sundays . . . and it was a sight to see her walk. If one of

> them willows over there on the edge of the brook could start up and get its roots free of the ground, and move off, it would go just the way Luella Miller used to.

Or when she tells of Luella's marriage to a man called Hill, her disparaging sense of Luella's oddity comes out comically – in the way such things do – in an irrelevant aside: 'There was always a sight of 'l's in her name, married or single.' What gives this story its edge is the style of the narrator: as often in Freeman, and with the American short story in general, the quality of voice (often involving regional dialect) is essential to its effect.

Chapter 10

Charlotte Perkins Gilman, Kate Chopin, Edith Wharton and Willa Cather

Charlotte Perkins Gilman

In the last quarter of the twentieth century, Charlotte Perkins Gilman's 'The Yellow Wall-Paper' (1890) became perhaps the most famous nineteenth-century story by an American woman, and an icon for American feminist criticism. Like Freeman's 'Luella Miller', it achieves its extraordinary impact by means of the narrator's individual voice. The narrator is the wife of a doctor: according to her husband, she is suffering from a 'temporary nervous depression' and must avoid all work, particularly her writing, while she herself believes she needs 'congenial work, excitement and change'. She is confined to a bedroom at the top of the colonial mansion they have recently rented, a sinister room that has bars on the windows and rings in the walls (it was once a nursery and a gymnasium), and a wallpaper with a colour 'repellent, almost revolting; a smouldering unclean yellow, strangely faded by the slow-turning sunlight' and a dull confusing pattern which irritates and provokes: 'when you follow the lame uncertain curves a little distance, they suddenly commit suicide – plunge off at outrageous angles, destroy themselves in unheard of contradictions'.[1] The narrator writes her account in the room itself, talking directly to the reader in the present tense, or perhaps, more disturbingly, talking to herself. Gradually she becomes obsessed with the idea that she sees the figure of a woman, trapped in the yellow wallpaper, trying to get out. She becomes aware of an unpleasant smell ('a yellow smell') and notices a mark low down on the wall, 'a long, straight, even *smooch*, as if it had been rubbed over and over'. She thinks she sees the figure of a woman creeping about in the garden (and we have learned that she herself was at first allowed to take exercise there). And gradually her identification with the woman in the wallpaper becomes complete: she begins to tear off pieces of the paper, and to 'creep smoothly on the floor': 'my shoulder just fits in that long smooch around the wall'. She locks her husband out and throws the key from the window, and when he retrieves it and opens the door the story reaches its shocking last sentence: 'Now why should that man have fainted? But he did, and right across my path by the wall, so that I had to creep over him every time!'

The story achieves its compelling effect because of the subtle technique of first-person, present-tense narration, virtually of dramatic monologue (one might compare Poe's 'The Tell-Tale Heart') – short, staccato paragraphs of a lively but increasingly disturbed mind. Clues are dropped in the woman's monologue that gradually suggest the blurring of inner and outer states, the uncanny ambiguity between things perceived as external and deriving from the past, and things effected by the woman herself. 'How those children did tear about here. The bedstead is fairly gnawed', she says; but then a few lines later: 'This bed will *not* move!' (it is bolted to the floor). 'I tried to lift and push it until I was lame, and then I got so angry I bit off a little piece at one corner – but it hurt my teeth.' The technique conveys the woman's initially sane attitudes towards her own condition mixed with a lively excitability, gradually deteriorating into a kind of 'reasoned' or logically argued madness, and it is the latter which makes the story so disturbing.

It is also, of course, more than a tale of one woman's psychological delusions, but stands as a representative symbol of the oppression of nineteenth-century women – and in particular women's writing – by male authority. The doctor husband's well-meaning but sinisterly repressive regimen for his wife is chillingly done. As Elizabeth Ammons points out,[2] there are shades of Poe's 'The Cask of Amontillado' – albeit redone in the quite different mode of psychological realism – in the moment when she asks if she may go downstairs, and he says he will 'go down cellar, if I wished, and have it whitewashed into the bargain'. Indeed, it is as if one of Poe's female victims (say from 'Ligeia' or 'The Black Cat') were at last given her own voice. Gilman herself made clear that the story was a parable of her own situation. In a short, revelatory article of 1913 ('Why I wrote "The Yellow Wall-Paper"') she tells how for many years she 'suffered from a severe and continuous nervous breakdown, tending to melancholia', and how her physician advised her to live 'as domestic a life as possible', and 'never to touch pen, brush or pencil again, as long as I lived'. She later wrote that her purpose was to 'reach Dr S. Weir Mitchell [the specialist in nervous diseases] and teach him the error of his ways'. The first readers of the story were horrified by its direct presentation of a disturbed mind (One letter to *The Boston Evening Transcript*, headed 'Perilous Stuff' doubted whether 'such literature should be permitted in print'.) But Gilman records that she was told that her doctor had admitted to changing his treatment for neurasthenia after reading her story; and she concludes her article: '[The story] was not intended to drive people crazy, but to save people from being crazy, and it worked.'

Gilman's later career and writing was mainly in the field of social and political reform (she was related on her father's side to Harriet Beecher Stowe): a volume of satirical poetry, *This Our World* (1894); *Women and Economics* (1898); *The Home: its Work and Influence*; *Human Work* (1904). And although she published a number of other stories, none of them are a match for the power and immediacy of 'The Yellow Wall-Paper'. Indeed the great majority of them are little didactic stories, almost anecdotes, or moral *exempla* of a new secular creed, ranging from four to ten pages long, marked by a relentlessly vigorous optimism, and illustrating the possibilities of a reassessed idea of women's social and familial roles. They are exemplary of a certain strain of late nineteenth- and early twentieth-century feminism, and many of them are remarkably prescient of later twentieth-century social developments. In 'Deserted' (1893) a despotic husband makes over his property to his wife to avoid his creditors, whereupon she leaves him, sets up in business with great success, and agrees to have him back on her own terms ('It made a new man of him' (65)). In 'The Widow's Might' published in 1911 in *The Forerunner*, a monthly magazine which Gilman herself owned, wrote and published between 1909 and 1916, a recently widowed mother reveals to her adult children that (contrary to their half-rueful expectations) she has no wish to live with any of them; that her husband's will has been superseded by a deed to her of all his property, that she has been running a small hospital and keeping cows, and that she has accumulated enough money to travel and, at last, 'to live'.

Kate Chopin

Kate Chopin is best known for her novel about female sexual self-discovery, *The Awakening* (1899), but her usually brief short stories also explore the social and sexual mores of her particular region, Louisiana. The emotional liberation of women is a persistent theme and she writes about it with a certain lightness and picturesque feeling for place, but without much attempt to explore any great complexity of feeling or moral dilemma. One of her characteristic tones is a kind of light, brisk and essentially optimistic irony. 'At the 'Cadian Ball' (Acadians were descendants of Nova Scotia living in Louisiana) tells of the wooing of the fiery Calixte by the mild and good-natured Bobinot, and the latter's rivalry for her affections with the more dominating and imperious Alcée. In an ironic turn of events at the ball Alcée is summoned home by his other lover, Clarisse, whose declaration of love as they ride home transforms his feelings; while Bobinot is left to ride home with Calixte who sulkily says he can marry her if he wants. In a sequel to the story, 'The Storm', Alcée takes refuge in Bobinot and Calixte's house during a storm, while Bobinot is sheltering at the store with his small son Bibi: a chinaberry tree is struck by lightning and Alcée's comforting Calixte leads to their making love. Chopin's description of sex and the body is bold and sensuous for its day: 'Her firm, elastic flesh, that was knowing for the first time its birthright, was like a creamy lily that the sun invites to contribute its breath and perfume to the undying life of the world.' Bobinot returns with shrimps for his wife, who greets him affectionately, while Alcée writes a loving letter to his wife Clarisse who is staying with her babies in her old home-town of Biloxi, suggesting she stay a few days longer if she is enjoying it. Clarisse for her part is quite contented where she is ('their intimate conjugal life was something which she was more than willing to forego for a while'), and the story concludes 'So the storm passed and everyone was happy.'

Darker notes are struck in a story like 'Desirée's Baby', in which a young white woman becomes aware of a fact that has already been growing apparent to her husband Amand and her mother-in-law, that her baby is dark-skinned, and that somewhere in her ancestry there is slave blood. In despair she walks of into the bayou (a Louisianian creek or swamp) and disappears, while her husband burns all her baby's clothes and his wife's letters. But among the latter is one from his mother to his father which thanks God that Amand will never know that 'his mother belongs to the race that is cursed with the brand of slavery'. Chopin does not offer any comment, but the implicit effect of the story is to call attention to the tragedy, and the ironies, of racial prejudice.

Chopin's feeling for the Louisiana landscape of bayous and levees, magnolia trees and summer storms, her sensuous feeling for women's experience of sexual love together with her economy of fictional form and her ability to capture in writing the local French inflected patois, give her a firm place both in the tradition of American women's writing and in the tradition of 'local colour' literature (as it was known in its day and for some time after) which opened up new regions of the United States to fictional treatment and mainstream cultural awareness. Her use of the short story form (ranging from five to a dozen pages) enables her to treat a number of themes and predicaments, small local tragedies and ironic comedies, or mild satires like 'A Pair of Silk Stockings', which gently mocks the fantasy world that its heroine builds out of a small spending spree on clothes, cosmetics and an expensive meal.

Edith Wharton

The world of Edith Wharton's fiction is by contrast, for the most part, that of the life of the rich East Coast establishment in America and Europe; and while her literary reputation rests mainly on novels like *The House of Mirth* (1905) and *The Age of Innocence* (1920), she was prolific in the writing of short fiction, producing some eighty-six short stories and eleven novellas, which enabled her to explore a wide range of human problems and aspects of modern American experience. She also felt a particular affinity with the short story as a form. In a letter of 1907 she spoke of doubts about her ability as a novelist, her tendency to try to cover too much ground at the expense of 'the smaller realism that I arrive at, I think, better in my short stories', and 'the sense of authority with which I take hold of the short story'.[3]

In the second chapter of her book *The Writing of Fiction* (1925), entitled 'Telling A Short Story', she also has a number of suggestive remarks about the form. She saw it as having been moulded by the great nineteenth-century French and Russian practitioners, in whose hands it became, she wrote, 'a shaft driven straight to the heart of human experience'. Whereas the novel can explore and develop 'character' over a period of time, the short story focuses on 'the dramatic rendering of a situation' and 'the impression of vividness, of *presentness*' is even more important than in the novel.[4] The short story should observe the unities of time, and of 'point of view' (here Wharton develops the idea which Henry James originated). This last is especially important:

> The short story writer must not only know from what angle to present his anecdote if it is to give out all its fires, but must understand *why* that particular angle and no other is the right one.[5]

Wharton also saw the crucial importance of beginnings and endings in the short story, but above all of beginnings:

> The rule that the first page of a novel ought to contain the germ of the whole is even more applicable to the short story, because in the latter case the trajectory is so short that flash and sound nearly coincide.[6]

The ending should be, as she put it, '*ab ovo*', or implicit in the germ of the story, and 'in accordance with its own deepest sense', and she would doubtless have strongly endorsed R. L. Stevenson's striking formulation that 'the body and end of the short story is bone of the bone and blood of the blood of the beginning'.[7] So the beginning of 'The Reckoning' (1902), one of Wharton's best stories, in which a wife discovers that she has come to hate the principles of sexual freedom on which her marriage was founded, has the 'attack', the establishment of point of view, and the germ of the story in its first two sentences.

> 'The marriage law of the new dispensation will be: *Thou shalt not be unfaithful – to thyself*.'
>
> A discreet murmur of approval filled the studio, and through the haze of cigarette smoke Mrs Clement Westall, as her husband descended from his improvised platform, saw him merged in a congratulatory group of ladies.[8]

The subject of the story – modern liberal attitudes to marriage – is presented with dramatized immediacy in the line from Mr Westall's lecture; the 'haze' of cigarette smoke has a symbolic as well as literal function; and Mrs Westall's point of view gives a particular, ominous significance to the 'congratulatory group of ladies'. The last paragraph of the story correspondingly rounds off the themes of the pressure of social convention and the imagery of clarity, haziness and darkness, and Mrs Westall's realization of her moral and emotional situation.

In her treatment of divorce and broken marriage Wharton shows a canny worldly awareness of the pressures of society and the facts of human weakness and compromise. She does not, it becomes clear, have either a tragic sense of these forces (like that of, say, Tolstoy in *Anna Karenina*), where passion and convention are locked in a struggle to the death, or the boldness to take her characters beyond the threshold of convention into the real experiment of alternative ways of living and of conceiving the moral issues of relationship, as in D. H. Lawrence. Her *forte* is a kind of social comedy of manners in which for the most part ordinary people engineer compromises between desire and convention. One of Wharton's wittiest and pithiest treatments of divorce is contained in 'The Other Two', where the protagonist and 'point of view', Waythorn, is forced to meet and have dealings with his wife Alice's first and second husbands, and becomes aware, with a disconcerting simile, how easy it is for his wife to accommodate herself to meeting them again:

> With sudden vividness Waythorn saw how the instinct had developed. She was 'as easy as an old shoe' – a shoe that too many feet had worn. Her elasticity was the result of tension in too many different directions.

But at the end of the story it is Waythorn who is left ruefully conscious of the slightly comical figure he cuts, as, at an afternoon tea meeting of the three husbands, Alice hands him the third cup of tea.

A large number of Wharton's stories deal in some way or other with the problems of modern marriage, but she has also a wide range of other topics, usually tackling a contemporary issue of manners or morals: the adoption of what turns out to be a dauntingly pedantic and demanding young girl in 'The Mission of Jane' illegitimacy in 'Roman Fever', 'His Father's Son' and 'Her Son' the social survivals of 'Old New York' in 'Autres Temps' and 'After Holbein' (a comic macabre study of old age which could be seen as a kind of realist version of Hawthorne's 'Dr Heidegger's Experiment'); the pretensions of modern cultural theory in the comic study of a ladies' reading group in 'Xingu'.

Wharton also experimented in the remarkably persistent and ubiquitous genre of the ghost story (for another contemporary instance see Henry James pp. 85–7 above), which in its turn-of-the-century practitioners becomes more and more a vehicle for the exploration of psychological states. In 'All Souls'' she achieves a remarkable effect of the uncanny in a modern setting (first mocking the notion that the ghost story was no longer possible in the age of the electric light): the protagonist meets an unknown woman visiting her servants on a snowy All Souls' Night and confined to bed that night with a fractured ankle after slipping on a frozen puddle, wakes the next morning to find the house (normally alive at that time with the activities of the maids and menservants) utterly silent, cold and deserted. Her struggling progress through the empty house is tensely done, the uncanniest moment occurring when she is about to reach the kitchen, and hears a voice, speaking fluently and insistently in low tones as if explaining something. The fact that this voice turns out to be coming from a radio is prosaic enough and not central to the plot explanation (which turns out to involve a midnight 'Coven' – the world of 'Young Goodman Brown' surviving into a modern setting), but the shock of our realization plays on the potential uncanniness of a very modern version of 'ethereal' voices. In 'Bewitched' (1926) a remote New England village in the grip of winter is the scene of the tale of a man's haunting by a young girl, dead a year since – a tale which, as several of its commentators have noted, plays on the ambiguity between supernatural and sexual possession.[9] The story contains the powerful portrait of a cold, puritanical wife, whose religious vehemence mingles chillingly with her sexual jealousy. After the dead girl's father encounters the 'ghost' – or is it her wild and equally handsome sister? – in the icy abandoned house, the sister dies of pneumonia; and after the funeral the puritanical wife seems to revive, the story's last line being her suggestively brisk remark: '" 'S long as we're down here I don't know but what I'll just call round and get a box of soap at Hiram Pringle's." '

That last example of the clinching yet spontaneous and fully dramatic close suggests Wharton's general mastery of the short story form. She has a lively command of dialogue which can suggest nuances of feeling and turning-points of consciousness, and she has a sure sense of narrative structure, above all of the balance between past and present, and between the general situation of a story and the 'vividness' and '*presentness*' (as she called it) of the immediate drama. In some of this (particularly in the mastery of nuanced dialogue, the suggestion of states of mind, and, of course, the use of 'point of view') she was greatly influenced by the master writer of the age, Henry James. But though she never attains James's subtlety of feeling and fineness of moral perception she possesses a power of concision (which notoriously tended to elude James), a certain practicality of common sense towards certain modern social problems, and a power of invention (that urge for 'making up' which possessed her from childhood) which gives her short stories an unusual range and force. That 'sense of authority' with which she felt she '[took] hold of the short story' was undoubtedly justified.

Willa Cather

The relation of Willa Cather to the short story form is perhaps more problematic, and certainly her reputation rests mainly on her novels, particularly *My Antonía* (1918) and *Death Comes for the Archbishop* (1927). But she published three collections of stories in her lifetime (*The Troll Garden*, 1907; *Youth and the Bright Medusa*, 1920; and *Obscure Destinies*, 1942) and one collection, *The Old Beauty and Others* (1948), was published the year after her death. And her stories explore a wide range of subjects: opposing the new fictional terrain of the immigrant communities in Nebraska and the Mid-west, in stories like 'Peter' (1892; retold in *My Antonía*), 'Eric Hermannson's Soul' (1900), 'The Bohemian Girl' (1912) and 'Neighbour Rosicky' (1928), with the life of artists and musicians (or would-be artists and musicians) and their conflict with the life of an uncultivated middle class, as in 'The

Sculptor's Funeral' (1905), 'A Wagner Matinée' (1904), 'Paul's Case' (1905) and 'Uncle Valentine' (1925), or – in a sharper and more satirical vein – in 'The Diamond Mine' (1916) 'A Gold Slipper' (1916) and 'Scandal' (1916). There are also one or two stories that stand outside these categories, like 'Behind the Singer Tower' (1912) and 'Coming, Aphrodite!' (1920), which nevertheless have an odd and distinctive interest.

Of the stories of immigrant communities, 'Neighbour Rosicky' is the most successful. It is a rich portrait of the life of a Czech immigrant who has settled in Nebraska, and a kind of Wordsworthian pastoral (though without the darker elements of a poem like 'Michael'), with a distinctly elegiac feeling at the close. What clearly impresses the narrator about Rosicky is his vitality, his love of life and a kind of instinctive wisdom. The stories about the life of artists are also at their strongest when they keep their focus on a single character or situation. 'Paul's Case' is the story of a troubled adolescent with a passion for opera and theatre who rebels against his parents' stultifying bourgeois life, steals money from his employer, and goes to New York to enjoy a life of culture, elegance and refinement; but his motives are mixed and confused (elegance and riches lure him as much as or more than any real artistic impulse) and, faced with the shame of his actions, he ends up jumping under a train. The narrative is well organized, and the story combines sympathy for his rebellion and irony towards his inner confusions. 'The Sculptor's Funeral' has a strong central focus on the return of a famous composer's body for burial in his home town, the town's vulgarity and incomprehension of his genius and the local lawyer's denunciation of the inhabitants in his final speech. 'Uncle Valentine', on the other hand, runs to some 18,000 words and seems to attempt to deal with a breadth of material which needs the scope of a novel: the narrator's memories of his life with his aunt and uncle, their relations with the eccentric Ramsay family (father and two sons), and in particular his awareness of the life of one of the sons, Uncle Valentine, his love affairs and his artistic talent. A lot of characters and their stories are packed in here, and the story's focus suffers, without being allowed the length (as in a novel) to develop a number of stories in successive chapters and hold them together through the narrator's consciousness.

Cather's most successful short stories are those in which she does not attempt to achieve in little the rich reflective and descriptive strengths of novels like *My Antonía*, but goes for the sharper focus of the more traditional tale or *conte*, where the emphasis is on a drama or irony of situation. 'Coming, Aphrodite!' is a comic and off-beat story about an opera singer, Eden Bower, later famous and popular, who moves in to an apartment next to that of the austerely principled artist, Don Hedger (the relation between the names seems suggestive). After she has complained about finding the hairs of his dog, Caesar, in their shared bath, and he has spied on her nakedness through a peephole in his closet, he invites her out and they have an affair. But they part after the incompatibility between their views of artistic success seems insuperable. Embedded in the story is a mythic tale Hedger tells his lover about an amorous princess, later a queen, whose chastity has to be preserved to ensure rain in the kingdom; when the King discovers her with her lover they are both put to death and a great drought comes upon the land. Bower leaves Hedger for more glittering companions, but years later, out of curiosity, asks a famous dealer about him and learns he is 'one of the first men among the moderns'. She is pleased: ' "One doesn't like to have been an utter fool, even at twenty." ' The story, in its odd way, makes its moral (and mythic) point, but lightly, and without moralism against 'Aphrodite', sexual passion. ('Coming, Aphrodite!' – the slyly punning title of the story – is the legend in electric lights above the Lexington Opera house before Eden Bower's triumphant return from Paris.)

The success of this emblematic or parabolic story – more successful as a short story, I suggest, than Cather's better-known realist pieces of life on the Nebraskan plains – is an instance of how often in the American tradition the strongest short stories have taken non-realist, or Romance, forms. But the brilliant if 'uncharacteristic' story (as one editor of her stories calls it)[10] 'Behind the Singer Tower' is both realist in procedure and emblematic of the whole predicament of race and class in American capitalist society, and in its analysis of civic pride and tragic disaster as timely today as in 1912. A group of businessmen and journalists are taking a trip on a private launch on the East River, the day after the notorious Mont Blanc Hotel fire in which three hundred died. The engineer Hallet tells the group the story of how he worked 'with a gang of twenty dagos' in the foundations of the Mont Blanc Hotel building project one blisteringly hot summer some years before. He got to know a little, eager, frightened Italian immigrant, Caesarino; and when Caesarino was crushed to death by a falling earthmover Hallet took up his cause and promised to expose the employer of negligence if he did not compensate Caesarino's family in Ischia. He got his way and sent the money. And in his telling of the story Hallet recalls the phrase with which he first made friends with Caesarino – 'Buono soldato', said as reassurance in a moment of stress, and said again to the dying little Italian, to calm him; and his reply, 'Buono soldato – ma perché?' ('Good soldier – but why?'). The phrase is taken up again in Hallet's reflections after the story:

> Here we are, six men, with our pitiful few years to live and our one little chance of happiness, throwing everything we have into that conflagration on Manhattan Island, helping, with every nerve in us, with everything our brain cells can generate, with our very creature heat, to swell its glare, its noise, its luxury, and its power. Why do we do it? And why, in heaven's name do *they* do it? *Ma perché*? as Caesarino said that night in the hole.

'*They*' are the immigrants whose labour makes New York possible; and Hallet's answer to the question is that 'we', and 'they', are all 'the slaves of an 'Idea' – an idea of civilization. The story is Conradian in its reach and suggestiveness (not least because of its Conradian method of narrative frame – the East River makes us think of the Thames in *Heart of Darkness*, and Hallet of Marlow); and its main theme is counterpointed by a subtle intermittent argument between the men on the launch about national purpose and identity and its relation to different ethnic groups. At least the 'Idea' 'will be ours' says one of Hallet's listeners. But what is 'ours'? 'Hallet laughed "Don't call anything ours, Johnson, while Zablowski is around."' But their mild-mannered, well-liked Jewish colleague (who has already countered the suggestion that the Singer Tower is 'Jewy-looking' with the idea that it could be Persian, or 'like a Buddha') makes no reply. '"Zablowski", Johnson said irritably, "why don't you *ever* hit back?"' And so the story ends – a small masterpiece of actuality, as immediate as a newspaper report but as universal as a philosophical meditation; vivid in its quiet conversational drama and profound in its epitomization of society's tragic ambition.

Chapter 11

Growth, fragmentation, new aesthetics and new voices in the early twentieth century

The beginning of the twentieth century saw a huge growth in the popularity and sales of the short story, and at the same time important changes in its form and preoccupations, particularly among serious practitioners. In 1885 there were around 3,300 magazines in the United States which published short stories. By 1905 this figure had risen to 10,800.[1] The short story was seen as the ideal popular form because of its easily assimilable length, and its frequent preoccupation (inherited originally from Poe) with the sensational, the strange and the dramatic. As Andrew Levy has pointed out, it also appealed to an age which was beginning to value the virtues of efficient mass production, the 'machine aesthetic' which lauded the well-made, the conventional and the easily used, 'maximal efficiency and minimum waste'.[2] The first twenty years of the century also saw the appearance of handbooks on how to write short stories, which were popular to well into the mid-century (and still persist): those guides to commercially successful writing which laid down 'rules' of plot structure, character presentation, the creation of atmosphere and the like.[3] Needless to say, these books tended actively to discourage innovation – 'Don't stray from the norm' one publication of 1957 was still advising – and appealed to writers very different from the ones discussed in this book. But the latter certainly influenced the handbooks: and Jack London's adventure stories and the contrived plots of O. Henry (rather than his exuberant rhetoric and stylistic parody) spawned a host of imitators.

Among the most serious practitioners of the short story as an art, however, there was a tendency away from plotted stories and towards a more oblique and more fragmentary style learned primarily from Maupassant in France and Turgenev and Chekhov in Russia. Sherwood Anderson denounced the artificial constrictions of the 'poison plot', and Willa Cather wrote of 'The Novel *Démeublé*' – disencumbered of the unnecessary furniture of much nineteenth-century realism – an aesthetic even more applicable to the short story.[4] The new pressures of the age – the accelerating growth of cities, the

Great War of 1914–18, the financial boom and consequent slump, the Wall Street Crash of 1929 – led to a fiction which reflected the breakdown of older certainties: the loss of the solidarity of small, cohesive communities, and increasing social mobility among the middle and working class. The intellectual changes of the period also led to a sense of human nature and society cut off from its older roots. Nietzsche had proclaimed the 'death of God', and by the second decade of the century, the works of Freud began to destabilize the notion of a unified self.[5] Sherwood Anderson's story sequence, *Winesburg, Ohio* (1919), is the portrait of a small rural town peopled with lonely, repressed characters, whose buried lives often erupt in surprising and grotesque ways. Hemingway's stories and sketches in *In Our Time* (1925) offer public and private facets of individual lives spiritually deracinated by war and the false gods of its aimless aftermath. In 1922 the central voice in T. S. Eliot's poem *The Waste Land* ruefully closes the last section of the poem with a stanza of fragments from European and Eastern culture and the statement 'These fragments I have shored against my ruins'; another American, Ezra Pound, in his poem *Hugh Selwyn Mauberley*, quoted Heraclitus on how 'All things are a flowing' and saw the art of the miniaturist as Mauberley's sole stay against the cultural flux.

But the aesthetic of fragments and short pieces was not only a negative or despairing one. In Russia, Anton Chekhov (1860–1904) had focused his literary vision in shorter works – plays and stories: as Raymond Carver pointed out, Chekhov liked beginnings and endings and got bored with the length of the novel. Chekhov's short stories frequently focus on moments of loss and tragedy and the breaking points of human life. But the short story was also for him an essentially democratic form, which allowed him to explore a great range of 'ordinary' human lives. 'In my head', he wrote in a letter of 1888, 'there is a whole army of people asking to be let out, and waiting for the word of command.' These people are often unhappy, but they are also frequently resilient in their search for happiness. One of the offspring of modernism, with its generally anxious sense of dislocation and deracination, was a feeling too for the possibilities of building up a sense of life from the grass roots of day-to-day impressions, the small incidents which the short story was ideally suited to record and explore. If there was a growing scepticism about the ability of ancient structures (whether of Faith or Enlightenment) to sustain coherent and adequate systems of belief, there was a recognition of the possibilities of a role for art in building a strength of consciousness from an examination of small particulars. The English poet Thomas Hardy described his *Poems of the Past and the Present* (1901) as

> a series of feelings and fancies written down in widely differing moods and circumstances and at various dates. It will therefore be found to contain little cohesion of thought or harmony of colouring. I do not greatly regret this. Undigested impressions have their value, and the road to a true philosophy of life seems to lie in humbly recording diverse readings of its phenomena, as they are forced upon us by time and change.

Hardy was writing of lyric poems, but his remarks also provided a possible aesthetic for the new short story.

Developments in the visual arts also provide suggestive analogies for the development of the short story. The term 'impressionism' was, as we have seen, taken over from the French movement in painting which dated from the 1870s, and applied, by Joseph Conrad and others, to the writings of Stephen Crane and Ambrose Bierce, to describe their method of focusing on perceptual phenomena at a point before these are organized into meaning. Crane's symbolic or emotive use of colour in description, and his focus (in stories like 'The Blue Hotel' and 'The Open Boat') on extreme states of emotion like fear and wonder and horror, can also be compared to Expressionist painting, like that of Edvard Munch and Soutine.

More closely relevant to the American short story are the enigmatic and haunting realist paintings of Edward Hopper (1882–1967). In paintings like 'Night Windows' (1928),'New York Movie' (1939) and 'Sunday' (1926) he created a world of urban loneliness inhabited by solitary, introspective figures. And while he said that his paintings did not aim to tell a story, they often seem to present scenes in which some hidden drama of everyday life is being enacted. 'Summer in the City' (1949) shows a man lying naked on a bed, his face pressed into the pillow, with a woman in a red dress sitting beside him staring into space. And the ironically titled 'Excursion into Philosophy' (1959) reverses the positions: a pale, fully clothed man with a book on his knee stares hopelessly at the floor, while behind him a half-naked woman lies with her face turned away to the wall. Such paintings, through an aesthetic of 'the glimpse',[6] present images of isolation and lack of communication and rootlessness (Hopper is fond of the anonymous locations of hotel lobbies, offices and cafeterias) which evoke the fragmented world of Ernest Hemingway's stories from the 1920s or Raymond Carver's in the 1970s. The famous image of the city bar in 'Nighthawks' (1942) could be an illustration for a story like Hemingway's 'A Clean, Well-Lighted Place' (1933), with its island of light in the middle of darkened streets, or a depiction of the bar in 'The Killers'; the couple in 'Hotel By a Railroad' (1952) could be posing for Hemingway's 'Cat in the Rain'. All these paintings are scenes which evoke a mood of isolation or non-communication; they tell no explicit story but they imply the unseen presence of one, suggesting states of being, unspoken tensions, subtexts of enigmatic dramas.

The growth of photography and film also has parallels with the growth of the short story. Photography had from the 1820s onwards been gradually supplementing or even replacing the cultural role of realist or documentary painting, and its aesthetic of revealing a world through the catching and framing of a transient moment also suggests the short story writer's focus on a scene or a moment to evoke a larger and more general condition. And by 1900, photography was an established part of American culture and sensibility. Henry James's remarks on his short stories as 'a multitude of pictures' taken with his 'small circular frame' have already been quoted, and T. W. Higginson had noted, in an essay of 1892 on 'The Local Short-story', that 'the rapid growth of the portable kodak has scarcely surpassed the swift growth of local writers, each having apparently the same equipment of directness and vigour'.[7] Sherwood Anderson said that the artist's aim was to 'fix the moment, in a painting, in a tale, in a poem'. And his idea of the visual glimpse suggests the instantaneous capturing by a photograph:

> There was a suggestion, a hint given. In a crowd of faces in a crowded street one face suddenly jumped out. It had a tale to tell, was crying its tale to the streets but at best one only got a fragment of it.[8]

One thinks of the faces in the New York Street photographs of Weegee (Arthur Fellig, 1899–1968) or Helen Levitt (b. 1913). Later in the century, Diane Arbus's quintessential images of suburban life, like 'A Family on Their Lawn One Sunday in Westchester, New York' (with its bleak tokens of middle-class pleasure, the drinks, the sunbeds, the child with the small inflatable pool, the stark expanse of empty lawn with the dark trees at its end), seem to come from one of the more disenchanted stories of John Cheever or John Updike. The Argentinian writer Julio Cortázar has enlarged on the analogies between short story and photograph:

> Photographers like Cartier-Bresson or Brassaï define their art as an apparent paradox: that of cutting off a fragment of reality, giving it certain limits, but in such a way that this segment acts like an explosion which fully opens a much more ample reality, like a dynamic vision which spiritually transcends the space reached by the camera . . . the photographer or the story writer finds himself obliged to choose or delimit an image or an event which must be meaningful, which is meaningful not only in itself, but rather is capable of acting on the viewer or the reader as a kind of opening, an impetus which projects the

> intelligence and the sensibility toward something which goes well beyond the visual or literary anecdote contained in the photograph or the story.[9]

A new poetic sensibility was also to have its effect on the short story in the first three decades of the twentieth century. Edgar Lee Masters's *Spoon River Anthology* (1915) was a collection of short, free verse poems in which the inhabitants of a small Midwestern cemetery look back on their lives and reveal their essential lineaments (often hidden during their lifetimes). This disenchanted revelation of small-town ills, and the voices of its characters – sometimes colloquial, sometimes elevated in their rhetoric – are a precedent for, possibly an influence on, the series of portraits in Sherwood Anderson's *Winesburg, Ohio.* The Imagist movement in poetry – led by Ezra Pound and Amy Lowell – had an influence which extended well beyond its own poetic achievements. In the short story, Ernest Hemingway's *In Our Time*, with its brief narratives of episodes in individual lives, and its even shorter sketches of war and bullfighting, reflected the influence of an Imagist aesthetic, and Hemingway associated for a time with Gertrude Stein and Pound in Paris. Pound's 'manifesto', 'A Few Don'ts By an Imagiste' ('Use no superfluous word, no adjective, which does not reveal something.' 'Go in fear of abstractions.' 'Use either no ornament or good ornament'), has a remarkable similarity to the precepts that Hemingway said he learned from his time as a newspaper reporter.

Gertrude Stein, a highly cultivated American Jewish expatriate living in Paris, herself began her literary career with *Three Lives* (1909), three short fictions, 'The Good Anna' 'The Gentle Lena' and 'Melanctha', which depicted the lives of two German servant women and one black American woman. The third story is more a novella in length and scope, and the other two are long ones: Stein did not aim here at concision. But her techniques of colloquial language and poetic 'repetition with variation' and her focus on lower-class lives were an influence on Sherwood Anderson and Hemingway, and 'Melanctha' was praised by the African American writers later in the century, like Jean Toomer and Richard Wright.

Another short story writer who was impressed by Stein and who as a poet shared a similar aesthetic to the Imagists, was William Carlos Williams. Williams developed a distinctively American modernism in poetry, and his achievement and influence in the short story are also significant. His stories, written mostly in the 1930s and collected in *The Farmers' Daughters* (1961), are vivid objective records, in a direct plain style, of his life in New Jersey, mainly drawing on his experience as a local doctor working among the poorest parts of the community. The best of these present memorable portraits of the ordinary people in the cities of Rutherford and Paterson. In 'The Girl with a Pimply Face' he meets a fifteen-year-old girl in a poverty-stricken household where he is visiting a sick baby. The girl impresses him with her directness, her strength and attractiveness of body and character, surviving in the midst of depression and demoralization. Other doctors gossip cynically that they have encountered her all over the place 'on the street', but the narrator is non-judgemental and gives her ointment to cure her acne. That is about all there is to the story, but it stays in the mind as a photographically vivid documentary account. 'The Use of Force' tells of a more psychologically disturbing episode in which the doctor is exasperated into using brute force to examine the throat of a stubbornly uncooperative little girl who he suspects may have life-threatening diphtheria. 'But the worst of it was that I too had got beyond reason. I could have torn the child apart in my own fury and enjoyed it.' The story runs to a mere four pages and ends with his discovery of the disease and the child turning on him: 'Now truly she *was* furious . . . Tried to get off her father's lap and fly at me while tears of defeat blinded her eyes.' No unnecessary further reflection, no artful closure: just the physical and emotional facts. Other stories are more expansive and more humorous, but always straight from life, raw and unmediated. 'Pink and Blue' tells the story of a woman who uses her money as a 'kept' mistress to advertise for husbands in a lonely hearts column; finds one, turns up at his house dressed entirely in pink, marries him, instals her relatives in her house and spends all his money. Returned to her former lover after the marriage quickly breaks down, she soon after falls ill and dies, having insisted that for her funeral she be dressed entirely in blue. It is simply a little anecdote, but it is finely shaped and told, and stays in the mind as an example of a comic and touching human determination to succeed, to impose one's will on life. Many of Williams's stories, simply by recording facts of human experience without prejudice or moralizing judgement, extend the boundaries of human sympathy in a way that was remarkably advanced for his time. 'The Knife of the Times' tells of a woman's perplexity, embarrassment and growing sense of sympathy and emotional uncertainty when an old childhood girl-friend suddenly, in middle age, makes passionate sexual advances towards her.

In all these stories Williams follows an aesthetic of the plainest, most direct statement, and succeeds in exactly catching colloquial tone in dialogue. In his 'Notes' on 'A Beginning on the Short Story', he gives a suggestive account of the reasons, human and technical, for his choice of the short story form. Why the short story?

> Answer: The character of the evidence: to accommodate itself to the heterogeneous character of the people, the elements involved, the situation in hand. In other words, the materials and the temporal situation dictated the terms.[10]

Williams acknowledged that his kind of story did not 'sell', but argued that it was all the more important on that account: 'Nobody was writing about [such people], anywhere, as they ought to be written about.'

Another very different kind of writer, Ring Lardner, writing a little earlier in the 1910s and 1920s, approached the terrain of rather better-heeled but still very ordinary middle- and lower-middle-class life from a more popular, humorous angle, but at his best wrote stories whose comedy laid bare banalities, self-deceptions and everyday cruelties, in a style that specialized in catching the nuances of dialect and group jargon. Lardner was a newspaper man, and his highly popular stories for *The Saturday Evening Post* initially aimed simply at creating comic characters – like Alibi Ike, the hero of his baseball stories, who never ceased to amaze his managers and team-mates by the baroque elaboration of his excuses (for failing to turn up, playing badly, not marrying, or whatever). 'His right name was Frank X. Farrell, and I guess the X. stood for "Excuse me."'[11]

But his later stories achieved a bleaker and more penetrating satiric comedy of common life. 'The Haircut', narrated (as if to a barbershop client) by the most unreliable of narrators, a garrulous, crude-minded and impercipient barber, tells of a local joker whose jokes – like his baiting of the brain-damaged Paul – were clearly a lot less funny than the barber thinks them, and whose 'accidental' death while boating with Paul was obviously not quite as the barber understands it. In 'I Can't Breathe' a silly upper-class girl tells, in diary mode, of her passionate attachments and engagements to a series of hapless young men, to each of whom she makes eternal promises without disabusing the previous one. Her comical refrain ('I can't stand it. I can't breathe, life is impossible') reveals the growing panic mingled with her delight, and she finally decides to invite Frank, Walter and Gordon to meet Merle (boy number four), since Frank 'will guess when he sees me with Merle,' and with Walter and Gordon both there 'it will only hurt each one half as much as if they were alone . . . I can't wait.' 'Who Dealt?' is a brilliant dramatic monologue, in which the speaker is the chattering, fluff-headed bridge partner of a silent husband (a writer). Her every word – about the game, their friends, Tom's editors, his drink problem – digs deeper the hole of social embarrassment in which we see her blithely descending, reaching its nadir (the point at which Tom's forbearance clearly breaks) at the conclusion of the story, when she reads a sentimental love poem he had written for her:

> Isn't that pretty? He wrote it four years ago. Why, Helen, you revoked! And, Tom, do you know that's Scotch you're drinking. You said – *Why Tom!*

Edmund Wilson compared Lardner at his best with Sherwood Anderson and Sinclair Lewis, but he suggests that as well as being funnier Lardner never loses sight of actual human beings through getting immersed in their spiritual sensations like Anderson, and that in comparison with Lewis he is 'less likely . . . to falsify and caricature because he is primarily interested in studying a person than in drawing up an indictment'.[12] The story he had in mind was one of Lardner's finest and most bleakly comic, 'The Golden Honeymoon': an elderly middle-class American tells of his trip with his wife to Tampa, Florida, for the Golden Wedding anniversary, in a narrative full of drab, repetitious jokes, and a tired and somewhat desperate gaiety and *bonhomie.* His retailing of the train timetable speaks of a life consumed by trivia; his pride in his son (who 'made $12,000 one year'; and 'The Rotarians was after him a long time to join') suggests a horizon of values bounded by parochial respectability. His conversations with his wife (whom he calls Mother) are piquantly banal ('You can't get ahead of Mother'), and they put this story in an American tradition of hen-pecked husband stories that goes back through Twain and Melville to Irving's 'Rip Van Winkle'. Lardner's comedy of bourgeois boredom becomes satiric in this story, or in a story like 'Ex Parte', where another browbeaten husband finally blows his cool over his wife's fussy demands about interior decoration, and takes an axe to the family house. H. L. Mencken wondered if academic criticism would attempt to convert Lardner into something he is not, 'as they have converted Swift, Smollett and Sterne'.[13] Lardner is not quite in this league, but one of his strengths is that he never took himself too seriously. As Mencken himself concluded in the same article, the professors would not make him respectable for at least fifty years. 'He is doomed to stay outside, where the gang is.' And perhaps Lardner is still refreshing because he stays outside.

The increasing popularity of the short story in the first decades of the twentieth century led to new voices and new techniques which drew less on the literary experiment of Crane and the high literary refinements and elaborations of Henry James and more on the semi-popular tradition deriving from Bierce and Twain. The magazine adventure story and the story of humour and sentiment, in particular, provided a powerful generic mode between 1900 and 1920, and this enjoins a closer look at their most outstanding practitioners, Jack London and O. Henry.

Chapter 12

O. Henry and Jack London

O. Henry

Two writers who particularly represent the growth of the popular short story at the beginning of the twentieth century are O. Henry and Jack London, the first capturing the public taste through cleverly plotted comic stories and the second through stories of adventure and travel. Born in 1862 in Greensboro, North Carolina, William Sydney Porter, who took 'O. Henry' as his *nom-de-plume,* began publication of his own humorous weekly magazine, *The Rolling Stone,* which ran for a year in 1894. In 1898 he was tried for and found guilty of embezzling public funds from his job at the First National Bank in Austin, Texas, sentenced to five years in prison, and released after three years for good behaviour. While in prison he wrote several stories which were published in national magazines. During the remaining twelve years of his life he published stories in a number of magazines (*Dispatch* in Pittsburgh, and *Ainslee's* and *Sunday World in New York,* among others), and in twelve books, including *Cabbages and Kings* (1904, his first book) and *The Four Million* (1908, a collection of twenty-five new York stories which brought him international fame and popularity).[1]

O. Henry's popularity and his literary reputation have fluctuated considerably. By 1920 nearly five million copies of his books had been sold in the United States, and he was widely read in England and Europe. Nearly a million copies were sold in Russia between 1924 and 1927. He became known as 'the Yankee Maupassant', and there are a few superficial points of similarity: the cleverly structured plots, the demotic subject matter, the man-of-the-world attitudes. But Maupassant is fundamentally and subtly realist, tougher, more cynical and less humorous, and above all not a practitioner of the 'comic Romance' which, it will be argued below, is O. Henry's distinctive mode.

But there was also a strong critical reaction against O. Henry's work from an early date. H. L. Mencken in 1920 wrote of his 'smoke-room and variety show smartness,' and F. L. Pattee in 1923, who conceded that 'his swift rise to dominance has been one of the sensations of the new century', concluded that despite his brilliant verbal facility he sacrificed everything for entertainment and finally 'worked without truth, without moral consciousness and without a philosophy of life. He created no characters, he worked with puppets, lay figures without souls . . .'[2] However, there are different approaches to truth in fiction than through the mode of literary realism. The creation of 'character' in the nineteenth-century sense is no longer seen as a *sine qua non* even in the novel, and in the short story it has always been a less central element. More recently there have been reassessments of O. Henry which show him as a highly self-aware artist of parody and literary play, whose stories embody a comic critique of genre and convention.[3]

There is also one penetrating piece of early criticism that sees him in just this way. Boris Eichenbaum's essay 'O. Henry and the Theory of the Short Story' was published in Russia in 1925.[4] Russian critics had praised O. Henry's treatment of working-class life, seeing him as a critic of capitalism, but Eichenbaum, as a 'formalist' critic, concentrated on him as a literary artist and craftsman with 'a keen feeling for form and tradition':

> The genuine, original O. Henry is found in his comic, picaresque, and parodic stories, stories with surprise endings, with clever dialogue and ironic author commentary. They are the ones brimful of literary irony, resulting as a consequence of his sensitivity to clichés both of language and of story structure.[5]

Eichenbaum makes a comparison with the Sterne of *Tristram Shandy*, and from our present vantage point we may see him as the precursor of post-modern experimentation with form and genre. O. Henry can be seen to have more in common with Robert Coover and Donald Barthelme than with the more closely contemporary Anderson and Hemingway.

Rhetoric is a crucial element in all O. Henry's stories. And the range of his rhetorical effects is dazzling: mixed metaphor for effects of false eloquence ('"Let me tell you first about these barnacles that clog the wheels of society by poisoning the springs of rectitude with their upas-like eye", said Jeff, with the pure gleam of the muck-raker in his own' – 'The Man Higher Up'); puns and word-play where it makes little difference whether we think the puns 'good' or 'bad', since if they are bad we can blame them on the speaker ('"It's part of my business", says Bill Bassett [a robber in the aforementioned story], "to play up the ruffles when I want to make a riffle as Raffles . . . I first make an impression on the girl", says Bill, "and when she lets me inside I make an impression on the locks"'); malapropism ('"Aren't you ashamed of yourself, you whited sculpture?"') and deflationary burlesque ('a young man in a lavender necktie, whose grandfather had been the Exalted High-pillowslip of the Ku-Klux-Klan' – 'The Rose of Dixie'); frequent quotation and parodied quotation from the Bible, Greek and Roman classics and above all Shakespeare ('"'[T]will serve – 'tis not so deep as a lobster à la Newburgh, nor so wide as a church festival doughnut; but 'twill serve"' – on a beef stew without vegetables in 'The Third Ingredient'); or mock-erudition upset by puns:

> Sam Galloway was the last of the Troubadours. Of course you know about the troubadours. The encyclopaedia says they flourished between the eleventh and the thirteenth centuries. What they flourished doesn't seem clear – you may be pretty sure it wasn't a sword; maybe it was a fiddlebow, or a forkful of spaghetti, or a lady's scarf. ('The Last of the Troubadours')

O. Henry's linguistic fooling, its tone and delivery, can often remind us of Groucho Marx.

The subject-matter of O. Henry's stories, which the varieties of rhetoric serve to present and explore, covers a wide area: city life (shop girls, cops, vaudeville artistes, hobos, bank clerks and bank managers), South American political shenanigans, the wild west, the Deep South. Recurring preoccupations are the lives of the poor and the corruptions of the rich, and the universal practice of 'hustling', whether by small town cardsharpers or big-time businessmen. And frequently the point of a story is driven home by what has become O. Henry's trademark, the surprise ending, the 'snapper' or twist in the tail. The technique was certainly worn to death by O. Henry's imitators in countless magazine stories in the first twenty or thirty years of the new century (and some would say by O. Henry himself), but it has its own particular satisfactions. It is also in many ways a paradigmatic element of the short story as a genre, where the importance of the end has often been pointed out.[6] The short story is characteristically an 'end-directed' form: it typically leads to a climax which involves a moment of revelation, either to the central character or to the reader or to both. It also often involves the element of mystery or 'riddle': a situation is set up which is in some way baffling or obscure, and the story proceeds to solve it or sometimes simply to dissolve it, often at the last possible moment. The element can be found in writers as far apart in other ways as Poe, Hawthorne, Twain, James and Edith Wharton: in fact there are few short story writers who are not touched by it at some point in their work. It speaks to one of the most primitive desires which narrative satisfies: the twin desire for mystery and revelation. In this sense O. Henry, with his carefully crafted if often simple plots, is a paradigmatic storyteller.

O. Henry's most famous story, 'The Gifts of the Magi', will illustrate his use of plot in relation to the lives of the poor of the big city. It also illustrates his general democratic attitudes, his warm-hearted sympathies for those at the bottom end of the economic system. Whether or not it is true that President Franklin Roosevelt once said that his sympathy for working-class suffering and his policy of the new Deal in the 1930s was influenced by O. Henry's stories, it is certainly plausible. Behind the wisecracking showman's style there is a genuine sympathy. If it frequently takes the form of sentimentality (which we might define as exaggerated emotion and the calculated appeal to the reader's shallower feelings) then perhaps that is a venial fault: it could be said that it is something to arouse feelings of sympathy at all.

In 'The Gift of the Magi' a young New York couple, both earning very little, sell their dearest possession to buy a Christmas present for the other. Jim sells his gold watch in order to buy a set of tortoiseshell combs for Della's hair; while Della, unknowing, sells her hair to buy a platinum fob watch-chain for Jim's watch. The concluding paragraph about the magi past and present ('Of all who give and receive gifts, such as they are the wisest. Everywhere they are the wisest. They are the magi') is an unusually solemn piece of moral-pointing for O. Henry. But even here the sententious note is modified by an interpolated aside about the original Biblical magi ('Being wise, their gifts were no doubt wise ones, possibly bearing the privilege of exchange in case of duplication'): even where he is being earnest O. Henry cannot resist being entertaining.

O. Henry's view of working-class life often has a strong moralizing element, but he is essentially conservative in his appeal to 'the way things are': human reformation, if possible at all, is to be found in individual charity and sympathy, not in any vision of political change. There are also elements of satire, but rarely of that searching kind that is motivated by a real anger at human folly. It is characteristic of him that most of his stories of poverty and urban distress focus on women, and bring out in him a kind of chivalrous, sentimental romanticism which, despite elements of real shrewdness, leads him to pity working women but rarely to consider that their fate could be bettered by other means than merely changed attitudes in their fathers, lovers or husbands. Nevertheless his women characters are not just helpless damsels in distress, and some of his stories open up new possibilities for attitudes to gender.

'The Trimmed Lamp' (*The Trimmed Lamp*, 1907), compares the attitudes of two working girls, Lou and Nancy. Lou works in a laundry and makes $18.50 in a week, buys smart clothes and is looking for a millionaire to marry. Nancy works in a clothing store for $5 but is proud of her contact with fashionable ladies like the legendary Mrs Van Alstyne Fisher. O. Henry resists stereotypes here, saying at the outset that he refuses to call them 'shop-girls' ('But why turn their occupation into an adjective. Let us be fair. We do not refer to the girls who live on Fifth Avenue as "marriage-girls" ' – which is also, of course, a shrewd hit at upper class women). The upshot of the story is conventional enough (with a slight twist): Lou finds a nice but poor young man, but holds out for her millionaire and is unhappy. Nancy gradually modifies her snobbish beliefs and marries the nice but poor young man and is happy. But the story is more than a magazine romance: O. Henry has a detailed sense of the girls' economic conditions, their sense of style, their aspirations, and manages to give an insight into the real conditions of their lives, how they talk and how they dress. And the picture is enlivened by a sharp visual sense, moments closely observed and caught, as when the two girls meet in the park some time after their respective marriages: 'After the first embrace they drew their heads back as serpents do, ready to attack or to charm, with a thousand questions trembling on their swift tongues.'

A large number of O. Henry's stories explore trickery or deception, often involving revenge, whether they are dealing with urban poverty, South American gunrunning or wild-west adventure. There is a long tradition of this in American literature in the nineteenth century, and particularly in the American short story, from Native American and African American stories of trickster figures to Poe's stories of revenge trickery ('The Cask of Amontillado, 'Hop Frog', 'X-ing a Paragrab' to name but a few), and Melville's novel *The Confidence Man*; to Twain's 'Hadleyburg', and 'Jumping Frog' and other 'tall stories', and Louisa M. Alcott's novella *Behind A Mask; or A Woman's Power.* It tends to die out in the twentieth century, but survives in such different examples as Scott Fitzgerald's 'Bernice Bobs Her Hair' or Flannery O'Connor's 'Good Country People'. It is doubtless connected to the conditions of a swiftly changing society made up of a wide-ranging mixture of social and ethnic groups, in which the less privileged try to outwit the more privileged: the frontiersman delights to outwit the East-coast dude, countryman to outwit urban intellectual, worker to outwit capitalist, women to outwit men, and one ethnic group to outwit another. In O. Henry the genre lends itself, of course, to his predilection for clever reversals of plot; but it also continues to be a way of exploring and celebrating the rich diversity of cultural conflict.

O. Henry's Jeff Peters stories celebrate the comic adventures of the traditional conman, and are also ways of pointing up, even at times satirizing, the mutual antagonisms between different classes. 'Jeff Peters as a Personal Magnet' is a relatively simple story of the duping of pompous authority, in which a Mayor thinks he is tricking the charlatan medicine-man Peters into being arrested, while we learn finally that the arresting policeman is Jeff's buddy and the trick has been capped by a more elaborate one. 'The Man Higher Up' turns on the relative powers of trickery of a burglar, a con-man salesman (Jeff Peters) and a capitalist businessman: Peters dupes the burglar out of his loot with rigged cards, but 'the man higher up' dupes the con-man with fake bonds: capitalist fraud is always the biggest winner.

Some of the most interesting of O. Henry's stories are those which deal with relations between different ethnic groups, and with the conflict between the Northern and Southern States. O. Henry was a Southerner, and although his attitudes became mainly Yankee by adoption, he retained an ironic and irreverent sympathy for the stereotypical Southern values of conservatism, chivalry and romantic love, and he had an ambiguously tolerant (not inclined to disturb the prejudices of many of his readers) yet sceptical attitude towards racism. In one of his most famous stories, 'Thimble, Thimble', an old African American retainer, Uncle Jake, visits the New York office of two cousins, one from a family who settled long ago in the North and the other from the South, to deliver an ancestral watch bequeathed to the Southern cousin. The cousins decide to test him to see if he can identify the Southerner. While he is there a young lady comes into the office to hold the Southern cousin to his promise to marry her – or she will sue him for $10,000; the Northerner offers the $10,000, the Southerner chivalrously offers his hand in marriage; the lady pockets the cheque ('a girl has feelings you know'); and in the closing paragraph Uncle Jake gives the watch to its rightful recipient. The story mocks the stock ideas of the old romantic South and the new business-oriented North (and the 'new woman'), but in a gentle way that heals rifts and encourages mutual self-irony on both sides. On the other hand it also introduces the stock figure of the loyal 'Negro' retainer, a half-comic half-sentimental stereotype which, from its association with racism, has become highly questionable and problematic for modern readers.

Like Twain in 'A True Story' – and indeed like most authors, black and white, who present old-style Southern African Americans – O. Henry attempts to reproduce African American dialect in his syntax and orthography. Imitative dialogue is a problematic device, since it can be associated with the stock 'Negro' figure, who was often seen seen as intrinsically comic. But if we can certainly exculpate Twain from any crude racist denigration (in, say, 'A True Story'), it is not clear why we cannot do the same with O. Henry. One might reflect, indeed, on the whole process of 'imitation' in this area, tainted as it is by its associations with minstrelsy (the performance of popular black song and dance by white entertainers). A white writer who tries to imitate the cadences and rhythms of African American – or Native American, or working-class – speech could be seen (as with Twain) to be assaying a process of empathy which allows him or her to enter the mind and feelings of someone from another social group. Mimicry, and even minstrelsy, has recently been seen as having been a potential means of understanding and celebrating as well as ridicule.[7]

'The Duplicity of Hargreaves' is one of O. Henry's most comically successful explorations of stereotyping, role-play and mimicry. John Hargreaves, a vaudeville actor, makes a great hit playing an old-time Southern general by modelling his performance closely on the style and mannerisms of his landlord, the proud but impoverished Major Pendleton Talbot, even down to a lovingly detailed (and vividly described) reproduction of his making of mint juleps. But the Major, who sees the play, is mortally offended by the imitation, and Hargreaves has to leave his lodgings. In the last part of the story an old 'Negro' comes to see the Major, claiming he has returned to pay a longstanding debt (which the Major has forgotten about); and the Major is touched by his loyalty. At the end of the story the Major's daughter gets a letter from Hargreaves revealing he was blacked up as the old Negro. Hargreaves' mimicry has enacted two stereotypes, the first for comic yet sympathetic portrayal (as a newspaper review of Hargreaves' performance makes clear) of a stage character, the second to do good by covert means. O. Henry raises in this story, as in 'Thimble, Thimble', the whole question of the value and validity of literary stereotypes. As a writer of comic romance, his tendency is to view the topic benignly and optimistically. The corollary of this is, however, a sentimental glossing over of racial problems. The modern reader has to take due note of that fact.

Jack London

Jack London began his literary career as a writer of short stories at the very beginning of the twentieth century: his first volume, *The Sons of the Wolf*, was published in 1900. While he is perhaps best known for the novellas set in Alaska which have dogs as their protagonists – *The Call of the Wild* (1903) and *White Fang* (1906) – he wrote about two hundred short stories, some of which, like the extraordinarily successful and widely published and translated story 'To Build a Fire' (1902 and 1908), are among his most significant and highly regarded work. The short story was an ideal form for London, since his major preoccupations – above all the preoccupation with human crisis, particularly with crises of survival – lent themselves to short and concentrated treatment. Writing to a fellow author in 1904, he showed his grasp (partly instinctive, partly learned from a careful study of magazine stories and in all likelihood some of the increasing number of short story handbooks) of the principles of short story writing:

> Remember this – confine a short story within the shortest possible time-limit – a day, an hour, if possible – or, if, as sometimes with the best of short stories, a long period of time must be covered, – months – merely hint or sketch (incidentally) the passage of time, and tell the story only in its crucial moments.
>
> Really, you know, development does not belong in the short story, but in the novel.
>
> The short story is a rounded fragment from life, a single mood, situation, or action.[8]

London also continues the American tradition of the short story as a means of making sorties into new territory. Just as Mark Twain and Bret Harte opened up the far West as a topic for serious literary writing, so London pushed the boundaries further into Alaska and the Klondike (with his 'Northland' stories), and into the Pacific with his stories of the South Seas. He also extended the social boundaries of the short story, with his tales (influenced by socialist theories) of urban poverty and social division. In 1893 he served abroad a sealing schooner on an eight-month voyage to the Baring Sea and to Japan: his first short story, 'Story of a Typhoon off the Coast of Japan', was published in the same year. In the following years he worked in a jute-mill and as a coal-heaver in an electric power-plant. In 1896 he joined the Socialist Labour party, and spent two semesters at the University of California at Berkeley. And in 1897–8, in a journey that was crucially formative for him as a man and a writer, he joined the Klondike Gold Rush to Alaska, returning with a profit of $4.50, after a hazardous journey rafting over a thousand miles from Dawson to St Michael on the Baring Sea. Intellectually he was also formed by his reading in Nietzsche, Darwin, Marx, Ernst Haeckel and Herbert Spencer. From Darwin and Haeckel he inherited a view of 'the survival of the fittest', which profoundly influenced his sense, compounded by first-hand experience, of the relentlessness of evolution and the nature of human survival in harsh conditions. At the same time he learned from Spencer's *Philosophy of Style* (a literary application of ideas of force and conservation of energy in the notion of 'the causes of force in language'), which London later claimed influenced his attempts to forge a style of directness and simplicity.[9]

London's short stories can be divided into three main groups: the Northland stories, written for the most part in the years 1899–1902, after his Klondike journey; his South Sea tales, written after his tour of the South Pacific (including Hawaii, the Marquesas Islands and Tahiti) in 1907 and collected in book form from 1910; and his stories and parables of social development and deprivation written at various times throughout his career.

The Northland stories are above all concerned with the laws of physical survival. And London's greatest Northland story is at the same time one of his simplest and most direct. The first (shorter and in terms of achievement much lesser) version of 'To Build a Fire' was published in 1902 and aimed at younger readers. In that version Tom Vincent, travelling in the Yukon and forced to build a fire to prevent himself freezing to death after getting soaked in a stream hidden under the snow, builds his fire and survives, the story concluding with the simple and trite moral '"*Never travel alone!*"' In the second version, which is more than twice as long, the man (this time he is not given a name, emphasizing the general and impersonal) builds his fire, but it is extinguished by a fall of melting snow from an overhanging branch, and he dies in the wilderness, leaving his dog (who was not in the first version) to watch him nervously for a time and then to head along the trail to the next camp. The story, which according to one of its editors has been translated into more languages than any other single piece of American literature,[10] is a masterpiece of the presentation of man's physical struggle against the elements. It focuses on facts and sensations, with the minimum recourse to general reflection needed to put the struggle into some kind of philosophical context. It is not a psychologically complex story, and the plot is of the simplest. What then accounts for its extraordinary power and critical as well as popular success?

The answer, I believe, is its representation of physical conditions and its concentration on survival. London has an extraordinary ability, by focusing only on what he knows and on essentials, to convey the feeling of a place and the sensations of a man battling for his life; and he does this in a plain prose which delivers action rather than reflection. Man's material existence at its most elemental level, and its close kinship with that of animals, is here given a sustained dramatization. And the drama engages the reader so that he feels his own physical life with a renewed imaginative keenness. The change from the 'happy ending' of the first version is crucial; but what is most significant and perhaps surprising about it is that the conclusion of the story leaves the reader with a feeling of intense aliveness rather than the melancholy of defeat and death.

There has been some debate among critics about the true significance of the story: it has been seen as a parable about imagination and its lack, about man's arrogance towards the natural world, and even as having the structure and effect of a Greek tragedy.[11] But while there may be some element of truth in all these, they seem for the most part to invest the story with too 'literary' a significance. London is not in the main a symbolic writer, nor one who structures his stories with an eye to literary tradition and allusion. The power of this story comes from London's close knowledge of the extreme conditions he is writing about (he wrote to his first editor insisting that he himself had lit a fire at 74 degrees below zero, and that it could not be done wearing mittens)[12] and his focus on the plain facts. Then there is the precision of action: of every detail of the man's preparing his first fire after his soaking, then his second, and his attempt to hold his matches in his freezing fingers. But there is also the constant emphasis on the relation between thought and action, between what the man knows (or does not know) and what he does. The phrases 'he knew', 'he did not know', he was 'keenly aware', 'he realized' run through the story almost like a refrain. And the contrast between the dog's instinctive knowledge and the man's learned or calculating knowledge is also central: 'This man did not know cold . . . But the dog knew.' The story could almost be called a study in cognition, human and animal, not in the spirit of drawing any exhortatory moral about man's loss of instinctive imagination or the limitations of his over-confident calculations (as some critical views would have it) but simply in the spirit of presenting his condition as it is, in its existential strength and limitation.

The drama of the battle between man and nature is charged with acute suspense, and becomes in the end an elemental battle between warm blood and cold ice. We feel the physical, bodily quality of life with an extraordinary intensity; so much so that at the very end of the story we empathize as much with the survival of the dog as with the death of the man. As the man's predicament becomes more desperate in the course of the story, the bodily life he shares with the dog becomes more apparent: 'The blood was alive, like the dog, and like the dog it wanted to hide away and cover itself up from the fearful cold.' In the story's last paragraph the focus (and at moments the point of view, though without any anthropomorphism) is that of the dog:

> And still later it crept close to the man and caught the scent of death. This made the animal bristle and back away. A little longer it delayed, howling under the stars that leaped and danced and shone brightly in the cold sky. Then it turned and trotted up the trail in the direction of the camp it knew, where there were other food-providers and fire-providers.

Whatever else human life is, it is inescapably bodily, and shares with animal life the necessity of food and warmth. In this last paragraph life has left the man, but remains with the dog, and (in one single and inspired touch of metaphoric imagination) with the entirely other 'life' of the cosmos, with 'the stars that leaped and danced and shone brightly in the cold sky'.

In other stories there is more emphasis on social and political conditions: in 'The Apostate' young Johnny, the protagonist, after a life from childhood of working in a factory, rebels against the creed of work and leaves home and mother to head on west in the box-car of a freight-train. The story emphasizes the machine-like nature of his work, and contrasts it with his visionary awareness of a tree which grows across the road from his house, which seems to 'lurk just under his eyelids', implicitly an image of natural freedom. But his calculating powers also play a part in his rebellion: he gets to 'figurin'' the number of physical movements he makes each day in the factory (twenty-five million a year in his present job at the looms), and decides he simply wants to 'set' (sit) and 'rest'. In the story's last sentence; 'Johnny was lying down in the box-car, and in the darkness he smiled.' The theme of the industrial mechanization of human life is treated here with a close attention to primary physical need.

London's South Sea stories, drawing on his own experiences in his South Pacific tour of 1907 and mostly published in *South Sea Tales* (1911), mark a new direction for his writing in more than just location, and are a good example of how the short story is the ideal medium for looking at various facets of a society new to the writer. According to his biographer Andrew Sinclair, London's explorations of South Sea societies, together with his new reading of Freud and Jung (replacing Darwin, Nietzsche and Marx), 'show a writer moving away from the harsh vision of the shortcomings of mankind and society into a quest after psychological depth and truth'. More particularly, 'What the reading of Jung had done was to begin to separate in his mind the validity of ancient myths that illuminated the best of his later work about Hawaii from the racial prejudice that darkened the worst.'[13] However this may be, it is certainly true that the short story offered a mobility and variety of approach for the exploration of his changing ideas in the last nine years of his life, before his untimely death at the age of forty.

London's psychological response to race (which can also be illustrated from stories about Native Americans like 'The Wit of Porpotuk' and 'The God of His Fathers') is complex and paradoxical. In 'The Chinago', the story of a Chinese worker recruited to work for an English company on French-governed Tahiti, the emphasis is on racist brutality and cultural misunderstanding. Ah Cho is wrongly convicted of the murder of a white overseer, because of a clerical mistake in the spelling of his name. The regime under which Ah Cho works is starkly exposed, focusing on the brutality of the German overseer Karl Schemmer. The story is told from the point of view of Ah Cho, and his sense of the incomprehensibility and ruthlessness of the 'English devils' is sympathetically done. There is also an inward sense of his satisfaction at earning ten or twenty times more in a year that he could earn in his home village, and of his aspirations to return home after five years, to a house, and wife and children and 'a small garden, a place of meditation and repose, with goldfish in a tiny lakelet, and wind bells tinkling in the several trees'. But at the same time his own cruelty is not glossed over: he regards the Frenchmen as fools for not torturing suspects to find out who committed the murder. The story is given a conventional 'sensation story' twist (the tradition of Poe and *Blackwood's Magazine* is persistent) in Ah Cho's conversation with the French gendarme Cruchot about whether a guillotined man feels the knife merely 'tickle' in the split second before his death, and his discovery 'for one great, fleeting instant' that 'The knife did not tickle. That much he knew before he ceased to know' (London's preoccupation with physical knowledge is involved here too). But the strength of the story lies in its harsh insight into cultural difference and racial intolerance.

London's racial attitudes, and his preoccupation with disease, are more ambiguous in 'Koolau the Leper'. It is clearly relevant that London himself suffered on his Pacific journey from a skin disease which seemed very like leprosy, but the preoccupation with disease is also a development of London's abiding concern with man's bodily condition. Koolau is a member of a society of lepers on the island of Kauai, whom the white authorities want to move to the leper colony on the island of Molokai, but who are determined to resist and retain their independence. London seems to have felt that their aspirations are doomed, but the story is told from Koolau's point of view ('It is the will of the white men who rule the land. And who are these white men?') and he is given certain dignity in defeat ('I have lived free and I shall die free'), and an inner life of memory and reflection (he remembers his vigorous youthful days of horse-breaking and bull-hunting). But at the same time there is a fascination with the horrifying details of leprosy itself, and its bizarre conjunctions with the beautiful setting of the island. Here the point of view is clearly external to Koolau:

> They were monsters . . . They mowed and gibbered in the moonlight, under crowns of drooping, golden blossoms. One, whose bloated ear-lobe flapped like a fan upon his shoulder, caught up a gorgeous flower of orange and scarlet and with it decorated the monstrous ear that flip-flapped with his every movement.

Clearly London's compassion for the lepers and respect for their freedom is mingled with a fascination with physical decay which seems to be a morbid development of his powerful sense of the bodily.

Jack London's short stories are undoubtedly the best way into his work and mind, and the best of them are as significant as anything he wrote. His most famous work, the novella or short novel *The Call of the Wild*, the story of the wolf-dog Buck, is a sustained feat of imagination and certainly of central importance in understanding his sense of life. But its treatment of animal consciousness makes an interesting comparison with the treatment of the dog in 'To Build a Fire'. In the novella London, by choosing to tell the whole story from Buck's point of view, cannot avoid the (for some readers) uncomfortable problems of anthropomorphism, the problem of giving human thoughts to the animal. It can be accepted as a convention, but the implied equivalences between animal and human become sometimes questionable. In 'To Build a Fire' the short story form enjoins not only concision, but also a focus on what can properly be said.

Chapter 13

Sherwood Anderson

Whereas London and O. Henry were best-selling popular writers whose choice of the short story genre made their work widely disseminated through the magazines, as well as in books, Sherwood Anderson (1876–1941) was more experimental in his use of the form, and more self-consciously dedicated to it as a means of opening up new creative ground. A number of his critics have also seen the short story as focusing his distinctive strengths and avoiding the tendency to preaching and essayistic digression which sometimes mars his novels.[1] His great literary breakthrough into the form came with the short story cycle *Winesburg, Ohio* (1919), and it is this volume on which his reputation today mainly rests. But he published three further volumes of individual stories, *The Triumph of the Egg* (1921), *Horses and Men* (1923) and *Death in the Woods* (1933), and it is arguable that the best of the stories in these collections achieve qualities – or what might be called 'short story values' – which are even more suited to the form, and push its possibilities into even newer territory.

In terms of technique, Anderson above all reacted against the emphasis on plot to be found in O. Henry and his host of imitators as well as in Maupassant, and also against the moralizing tendency of many of the magazine stories. As he says in his autobiography, *A Story Teller's Story*,

> There was a notion that ran through all story telling in America, that stories must be built about a plot and that absurd Anglo-Saxon notion that they must point a moral, uplift the people, make better citizens, etc., etc. The magazines were filled with these plot stories, and most of the plays on our stage were plot plays. 'The Poison Plot' I called it in conversation with my friends as the plot notion did seem to poison all story telling. What was wanted was form, not plot, an altogether more elusive and difficult thing to come at.[2]

Form for Anderson had elements of the organic, the lyric and the kinetic, and he saw the writing of a story as an action or a completed movement:

> The short story is the result of a sudden passion. It is an idea grasped whole as one would grasp an apple in an orchard. All my own short stories have been written at one sitting.[3]

The last sentence resituates from the point of view of writing Poe's idea about reading at a single sitting; and the metaphor of grasping the apple echoes Anderson's metaphor for Doctor Reefy's story in 'Paper Pills' in *Winesburg, Ohio:* 'It is delicious, like the twisted little apples that grow in the orchards of Winesburg.'[4] As John Updike observed, this is a poignant image for the gnarled, abandoned and overlooked lives which Anderson savours in *Winesburg*, where the best stories focus their condition in a single representative act, the form of which is replicated by the writer's act of writing at a single sitting.[5]

It is also particularly fitting that Anderson's stories should frequently focus on a single action which can be seen as the culmination of a process, as a turning point or crisis and an expression of an underlying condition. The writing of *Winesburg, Ohio* itself came about as the result of one such dramatic turning point in Anderson's own life, and one which he came to see as emblematic of the writer's rebellion against conventional values.

He began his working life as an advertising salesman and writer in 1900, in 1906 became the president of the United Factories Company, and in 1907 went to work in his own business in Elyria, Ohio. He had married in 1904, and settled down to a conventional businessman's life, joining the Country Club (that badge of middle-class orthodoxy and respectability), contributing to the magazine *Agricultural Advertising* and preaching the gospel of business in classic American fashion. Then one afternoon in November 1912 (as he himself relates in *A Story Teller's Story*) in the middle of dictating a letter to his secretary, he suddenly left his desk and walked out of town along the railway track towards Cleveland, and was found a few days later, 'wandering around aimlessly and talking incoherently'.[6] He had had what was diagnosed as a nervous breakdown, but after it he never went back to the business world, dedicating his life to writing. It was a story he told many times over the coming years (during which process it doubtless acquired mythical accretions), and it serves as a real-life instance of the classic short story situation: the crisis, the life-changing turning point. It may not be too speculative to surmise that in its dramatic decisiveness, as well as serving as a classic *topos* for the idea of the rebellious, anti-bourgeois writer for both Anderson and later writers, the experience was itself an influence on the form which so many of Anderson's fictions subsequently took.

Winesburg, Ohio is, at any rate, a collection of stories which focuses on repressed and lonely lives which at decisive moments break out into passionate expression. Based on Anderson's own experience in his home town of Clyde, Ohio, mingled with his later experience as a novice writer living in rooming-houses in Chicago, the book centres on the experience of George Willard, a young journalist who works for the local paper, and whose position in the town gives him knowledge of many hidden lives, and makes him the recipient of many confidences and confessions. From one point of view the book can be seen as a kind of fragmented novel, a *Bildungsroman*, or Portrait of the Artist as a Young Man. There are separate stories about Willard's mother, Elizabeth, and her relations with her son (in 'Mother'); about George's first sexual experiences (callow and selfish in 'Nobody Knows', humiliated by a rival in 'An Awakening' and touched with a first glimmering of mature tenderness in 'Sophistication'); about his relations with his schoolteacher, Kate Swift ('The Teacher'), and her encouragement and advice to him about his writing ('You must not become a mere peddler of words. The thing to learn is to know what people are thinking about, not what they say'); and about his leaving Winesburg ('Departure'). In most of the other stories, each of which focuses on a particular member of the town, George is also present at certain moments as a listener or interlocutor or just observer. (Only 'Godliness', the longest story, does not feature George at all, and it may not be coincidence that it is the least successful.)

The originality and the significance of *Winesburg, Ohio* lie in both its subject matter and its form. Its focus on obscure and misshapen small-town lives, and particularly on sexuality, was undoubtedly new in American fiction and shocked many contemporaries: one review, headed 'Sordid Tales', made the time-honoured objection that over half of the stories 'are of a character which no man would wish to see in the hands of a daughter or a sister' and spoke of its 'total disregard' for 'that kindlier, humaner, cleaner side of small town life, which not only exists but is the larger and dominant side'. The latter view is not without its *descriptive* validity (there are all kinds of aspects of small-town life which the book ignores), but as a value judgement it misses Anderson's aim entirely. This is a book about repressed lives and about 'the grotesque' in human experience. It bears witness to a side of life which is undeniably there, and it treats it with sympathy and humanity. '[I]t does treat their lives with respect,' Anderson insisted: 'What the book says to people is this – "Here it is. It is like this. This is what the life in America out of which men and women come is like." '[7]

The form, that of the short story cycle, has precedents in American literature, as we have seen in works like Sarah Orne Jewett's *Country of the*

Pointed Firs, or (to some degree) Crane's *Whilomeville Stories*. And critics have also drawn attention to its similarities with Edgar Lee Masters' volume of part-ironic, part-satirical verse portraits and sketches, *Spoon River Anthology* (1915). It allows a subtle interlinking of characters, preoccupations and imagery. Each story can stand by itself (though as we shall see, some do so more successfully than others), and at the same time stories can throw light on each other. The form suits particularly the treatment of the limited individual lives of a small town, where the individual characters' stories would scarcely sustain a whole novel, but where lives are interconnected, sometimes only momentarily, in ways that show the combined proximity and isolation of those individuals.

The book begins with a kind of overture – the chapter 'The Book of the Grotesque' – that sounds a central theme of the whole. An old man (a kind of *persona* of the author) lies in bed dreaming of a procession of figures, and he decides to write 'The Book of the Grotesque'. What had made these people grotesques was their clinging to a single truth ('the truth of virginity and the truth of passion, the truth of wealth and poverty') out of a host of many possibilities: 'the moment one of the people took one of the truths to himself, called it his truth, and tried to live his life by it, he became a grotesque and the truth he embraced became a falsehood'. The idea expresses a recurring theme, though not all the characters and stories illustrate it. Alice Hindman in 'Adventure' clings to an ideal of fidelity to the man who has abandoned her, but becomes trapped in a sad and sterile old-maidhood as a result, her repressed emotions breaking out suddenly in the climax of her story. Jesse Bentley in 'Godliness' pursues his belief in his God-chosen destiny to succeed as a farmer and patriarch (an illustration of the classic association of Protestantism with the work ethic) to the point of an eccentric authoritarianism that terrifies his young grandson. In 'The Strength of God' the Reverend Hartman clings to his belief in a sexual purity in the face of voyeuristic temptation, and smashes a window to remove the temptation, running with his bleeding hand into George Willard's office proclaiming 'The strength of God was in me and I broke it with my fist.' On the other hand, as Irving Howe points out,[8] many of the characters are as much victims of others and of their environment as of their own beliefs: Wing Biddlebaum in 'Hands', for example, does pursue an ideal of helping the young boys he teaches, but he is also the victim of homophobic prejudice and suspicion. Anderson's sense of realities is too strong to allow the stories to be entirely dictated to by the theme announced in his first chapter.

As well as occasionally having characters in common, the stories are given a powerful unifying tone and atmosphere by the recurrence of certain images and motifs. Howe has pointed out how many of the stories take place, or at least have central scenes, at night or in the half-light of evening, and many are located in confined spaces, single rooms which partly constitute and partly symbolize the characters' trapped existences.[9] The image of hands is recurring, variably expressive of feelings and desires which cannot be articulated in speech or action, and repression of which often propels the outcome of the stories. One story is actually entitled 'Hands': here a reference to the hands of its protagonist, Wing Biddlebaum, who has been nicknamed after them because of their 'restless activity'. His hands betray him by caressing the heads and shoulders of the boys he teaches, which leads to his being driven from his home town; later, when passionately telling Willard his story, his hands 'stole forth and lay upon George Willard's shoulders'. And in the final striking image that closes the story, Biddlebaum's yearning for love is given a religious connotation as he picks up bread crumbs from his floor: 'The nervous expressive fingers, flashing in and out of the light, might well have been mistaken for the fingers of the devotee going swiftly through decade after decade of his rosary.' In other stories, too, hands are often expressive of a hidden physical strength or passion: the hands of Dr Reefy, the secret and unfulfilled lover of Elizabeth Willard, are 'extraordinarily large': 'When the hands were closed they looked like clusters of unpainted wooden balls as large as walnuts fastened together with steel rods.' A few lines later they are like the 'twisted apples' that are also an emblem of the lives of the inhabitants of Winesburg. The saloon-owner Tom Willy has a deep red birthmark on his hands, and '[a]s he grew more excited, the red of his fingers deepened'. Ed Handby's fists 'were large . . . but his voice, as though trying to conceal the power back of his fists, was soft and quiet'.

The book, then, is convincingly held together by a number of elements that might well be characterized as poetic, depending as they do on subtle suggestions of language and imagery, as well as by its theme of the coming of age of George Willard, and the persistent preoccupation with loneliness and thwarted relationships. A 'purist' aesthetic, however (like that, say, of Brander Matthews in his 1885 essay 'The Philosophy of the Short Story'),[10] would dictate that the short story does not gain from being placed in a larger group and should essentially stand alone; and from this point of view the individual stories vary in success. The best are those which focus on a central scene or incident (– like 'Adventure' (the old-maid Alice Hindman's story), or 'The Strength of God' or 'Hands'. One of the best is 'The Untold Lie'. Ray Pearson, a farmworker, is confronted in a field by Hal Peters's demand for advice about whether to marry the girl he has got pregnant. Ray thinks of his entrapment by his own early marriage and is filled with sudden anger at what he sees as a wasted life of work, poverty and the demands of his wife and many children. Why should Hal submit to the same yoke? He must warn him. But when Hal returns he tells Ray he has made up his mind to marry his girl. Ray 'felt like laughing at himself and all the world', and as he goes home

> some memory of pleasant evenings spent with the thin-legged children in the tumble-down house by the creek must have come to his mind, for he muttered words. 'It's just as well. Whatever I told him would have been a lie', he said softly, and then his form also disappeared into the darkness of the fields.

The story works so well because it focuses on a single scene ('a picture' as Anderson calls it, of the two men, Hal's hands on Ray's shoulders 'in the big empty field with the quiet corn shocks standing in rows behind them and the red and yellow hills in the distance'), a single dilemma and a culminating realization. It also, one might add, gives the lie to those critics who have felt that Anderson's view of life in the book is entirely obsessed with the negative and the distorted. This story (like 'Sophistication', which tells of a touching and genuine moment of communion between George Willard and Helen White) suggests the presence in Anderson of a humane sense of the creative possibilities of life.

The less successful individual stories tend either to be those which try to include too much plot detail, or those which depend entirely on the voicing of a particular philosophy. 'Godliness', the longest story in the book, is in four parts, and tries to encompass a span of material – three generations of the same family – which would not be ill-suited to a 'saga' novel. The most coherent part is probably Part 4, which concentrates on the confrontation between the religious patriarch farmer Jesse and his grandson David, in which Jesse in an impromptu ceremony involving a sacrificial lamb tries to dedicate David to continuing the traditional life of farming and religious observance, while the terrified David runs from him, felling him with a stone (there are Biblical shades both of Abraham and Isaac and of David and Goliath here). The other parts, particularly the story of Jesse's daughter Louise and her marriage to John Hardy, suffer from an overload of what narratologists call 'accelerated' narrative detail, in which a large period of time is covered in a short space of text.[11] The story 'The Philosopher', about the persecuted (or paranoid?) Dr Percival, also suffers structurally from an overload of disparate details from Dr Percival's life (like his relations with his brothers), before focusing on the incident with the injured girl that confirms his feelings of persecution by the townspeople.

The prime example of a sententious or 'message'-dominated story is 'Tandy', which also illustrates a tendency towards sentimental philosophizing that is one of Anderson's weaknesses as a writer. A drunken stranger in a bar regales a five-year-old girl with his philosophy of womanhood. 'Be Tandy', he exhorts – Tandy being his name for the quality in woman that 'Perhaps of all men I alone understand'. Part of his advice is unexceptionable as long as we forget the drunkenness of the man and the age of his listener ('Dare to be strong and courageous . . . Be brave enough to dare to be loved'). But some of it seems vacuous and whimsical ('Be something more than man or woman. Be Tandy'). 'Tandy' is also all too patently an ideal of womanhood tailored to meet the self-serving needs of men ('It is something men need from women and they do not get'). It could be argued that the context 'places' the man as a maudlin drunk whose ideas are seen above all ironically: but some of Anderson's attitudes elsewhere, and here the little girl's tearful plea at the end of the story that she wants to be called Tandy, make one suspect that the arguments are being endorsed by the author.

Anderson's current reputation, both as a short story writer and in general, is sustained above all by *Winesburg, Ohio*. A number of his later stories, however, show a different kind of art and arguably a deepening of his achievement. One of the stylistic problems of *Winesburg* is a tendency towards a certain literariness or affectation. In his remarks on style Anderson seemed to endorse a use of vernacular words and plain straightforward sentence structure. 'How little native American words have been used by American writers', he wrote.[12] And in his *Memoirs* he claimed that under the influence of Gertrude Stein he had consciously attempted to capture the colour and cadence of his own Midwestern speech, by laying word against word 'in just a certain way in order to convey the feelings . . . a kind of word colour, a march of simple words, simple sentence structure'.[13] But these qualities are not especially characteristic of *Winesburg*, the style of which is often marked by metaphor, archaism and poeticism. Of Wing Biddlebaum he writes that in the presence of Willard, 'his shadowy personality, submerged in a sea of doubts, came forth to look at the world', and the activity of his hands is 'like unto the beating of the wings of an imprisoned bird'. The syntax is Biblical, again, when he writes of Willard 'He was perplexed and knew not what to do.' Dialogue, clearly the place for the vernacular, is relatively infrequent in *Winesburg* in contrast to many of Anderson's other stories, and (as in the speech of the drunk in 'Tandy') it often has a formal quality that seems to come more from the author that from the speakers: '"You must begin to dream"', says Wing Biddlebaum to Willard. '"From this time on you must shut your ears to the roaring of the voices."' The woman-hater Wash

Williams, a telegraph-operator, telling his philosophy to Willard, says: '"I would like to see men a little begin to understand women. They are sent to prevent men making the world worth while. It is a trick of Nature."' But perhaps it is misguided to expect colloquial realism in *Winesburg*: the book is not so much a realist study of small town life, but a poetic vision of distorted lives. Its characters are eccentrics, and a kind of stylization or caricature is part of Anderson's technique.

The stories in Anderson's three later volumes, on the other hand, often do show a commitment to psychological and linguistic realism. Above all, many of them explore the possibilities of first-person narrative and the development of a distinctive vernacular narrative voice. In 'I Want to Know Why' (in *The Triumph of the Egg*, 1921) a teenage boy tells of his life as a 'swipe' or groom on racetracks around the country of the Midwest, of his love of the horses and hero-worship of one of the trainers; and his voice is heard distinctly, as here for instance, where the prose is sharply alive to physical sensation (a quality less characteristic of *Winesburg*):

> Well, out of the stables they come and the boys are on their backs and it's lovely to be there. You hunch down on top of the fence and itch inside you. Over in the sheds the niggers giggle and sing. Bacon is being fried and coffee made. Everything smells lovely. Nothing smells better than coffee and manure and horses and niggers and bacon frying and pipes being smoked out of doors on a morning like that. It just gets you, that's what it does.[14]

This authentic voice later brings home the crisis and discovery in the story, the boy's first baffled awareness of sexuality. After his hero's victory on the boy's favourite horse, the boy sees him with a prostitute in local brothel, and his idealism and belief in the 'pure' and heroic world of men and horses is irrevocably shaken:

> Darn him, what did he want to do like that for? I keep thinking about it and it spoils looking at horses and smelling things and hearing niggers laugh and everything. Sometimes I'm so mad about it I want to fight someone. It gives me the fantods. What did he do it for? I want to know why.

An exploration of sexuality, through various narrators and situations, is typical of many of Anderson's free-standing stories; and what distinguishes them from the treatment of sexuality in *Winesburg, Ohio* is frequently their exploratory nature and the tone of questioning and uncertainty. In *Winesburg* the characters are presented, albeit sympathetically, as a kind of gallery of grotesques. In other stories the narrator himself is often the protagonist, and himself undergoes perplexity and bafflement, as in 'I Want To Know Why'. 'The Man Who Became a Woman' (*Horses and Men*) explores sexual and emotional ambiguity: another racetrack groom tells of his life on the track, his feelings for one of his buddies ('I suppose I got to love Tom Means . . . although I wouldn't have dared say so then. Americans are shy and timid of saying things like that . . . I guess they're afraid it may be taken to mean something it don't need to at all'). One night in a bar he sees his face in the mirror as that of a girl; and later, sleeping in his stables, he is the near-victim of a sexual assault by two drunken black men who in the dark mistake him for a girl. The story breaks new ground for its time, and is sensitive and subtle in its presentation of emotional complexity. As well as raising difficult issues of sexuality, it also explores interracial friendship: in the narrator's friendship with the African American groom Burt his consciousness of race inhibits him but does not prevent a special kind of intimacy (though not a sexual one in any conscious way).

The stories discussed above share similar preoccupations, but there is a wide range to Anderson's explorations of sexuality. Once again we can see the short story collection as the ideal way of examining a variety of ideas and situations from a variety of angles. The strikingly titled 'There She Is – She Is Taking her Bath' is a dramatic monologue about paranoid jealousy, in which the distinctly unreliable speaker (one might compare Poe's narrators here) tells how he employs a private detective to spy on his wife, and then using another name gets another detective from the same firm to fake a report which shows his wife is completely innocent. The story makes its distinctive impact by means of the monologue technique which arrests our attention through the man's edgy, over-excited tone and the small quirks of his neurotic imagination.

These stories and others are marked by a kind of philosophical reflectiveness about the use of stories to explore particular human problems. This reflective quality also explains their frequent reliance on primary and secondary narrators, and their generalized observations: on human behaviour, on its need to explain itself in narrative, and on the way narrative is sometimes the only means of getting inside an ethical problem. The reflectively humorous story 'The Flood' is about a college professor of philosophy who is writing a book about values. His wife is unintellectual, 'a light-hearted little woman, fond of frills'. When he was writing, he tells the narrator after her death, she 'would come in, put one arm around his neck, lean over him, kiss him, and with the other would punch him in the stomach'. He adored his wife, he says, and yet 'sometimes, often, he said he hated her'. The professor's book is trying to develop an idea of a balance between material and spiritual values: but he also has another idea about the 'flood' of experience – external events in particular – which frequently drowns the individual. After his wife's death he struggles with his book for a number of years, and then his wife's sister (who is also frivolous, 'a new printing, one might say, of his dead wife') visits him, and fills his house with visitors and parties. He is exasperated and attracted and finally marries her. The story ends with an exchange that charmingly sums up the different balances of narrative, philosophy and life:

> 'Kiss me quick while I feel that way', she said.
> That, at least gets a certain balance to my tale.
> The scholar, however, says there is no balance.
> 'There are only floods, one flood following another', he says.
> When I talked to him of all this he was a bit discouraged.
> However, he seemed cheerful enough.

There is great variety among Anderson's free-standing stories. Several tell of symbolic moments which come to typify a life. In 'The Egg' the narrator tells of his comically bleak childhood on a chicken farm, of 'the many and tragic things that can happen to a chicken', and of his father's desperate ambition to run a popular, successful restaurant ('The American passion for getting up in the world took possession of [his parents]'). The effort culminates in his father's grotesque and doomed attempt to entertain a solitary client with 'Columbus's egg-trick' (standing the egg on its end without cracking it). That night the son awakes at dawn and looks at the egg on the table and wonders 'why eggs had to be and why from the egg came the hen that again laid the egg. The question got into my blood.' The question is, of course, in ironic and bathetic form, the writer's question about the meaning of life itself; and 'the triumph of the egg' of which the narrator speaks in his closing sentence is nothing less than the Triumph of Life, relentless and implacable as in Shelley's poem.

The triumph of life, in both a positive and a negative sense, is the subject of one of Anderson's most powerful, searching (and oddly neglected) stories, 'Brother Death', which explores the life and death of the body and spirit. The eleven-year-old Ted Grey suffers from heart disease, and his parents (a tough, landowning father and a loving mother) are anxiously solicitous of him, curbing his adventures and pleasures to the point of stifling his life. His older sister Mary stands up for him, and in a moving scene confronts her mother with a prohibition: 'Her lips trembled: "You mustn't do it anymore. Don't you ever do it again."' And the mother accepts the rebuke: 'There were values in life, implied by a child's words: "Life, what is it worth? Is death the most terrible thing?"' In a parallel but reversed second plot, the father wants to cut down two beautiful and venerable trees, planted by his father-in-law, but his older son, Don, resists his order. The mother intervenes and the son has to capitulate to power and authority: something in him has to die before he himself inherits that same power and authority. The younger son, we are briefly told, eventually dies in his bed, but his sister reflects that he 'would never have to face the more subtle and terrible death that had come to his older brother'. The story is told with a quietly reflective intensity, and is given a poetic resonance by the symbol of the stumps of the two trees which dominate the opening and are returned to in the penultimate paragraph. Ted, at the beginning, wonders whether the stumps will bleed like those of men in war, and insists that men's suffering is of a more tragic kind than women's. There is a wealth of suggestiveness in this central symbol, evoking as it does man's ruthless domination over natural life, his masculinist pre-emption of tragic experience, and below all this the raw facts of suffering, untimely death and the breaking of continuities of inheritance. It is a classic example of how the short story form can, in its own way, achieve the power and resonance of a lyric poem.

Chapter 14

Ernest Hemingway

Ernest Hemingway is the foremost American writer of the short story in the first half of the twentieth century, and while he is also a novelist of repute with some four major novels to his name, many critics have felt that as an artist and innovator his most outstanding work lies in his short stories. His famous prose style – plain words, simple but artfully structured syntax, the direct presentation of the object – lends itself particularly to small-scale, concentrated effects. And his subject matter – the fragmentary nature of modern life, with its small local victories and defeats, its focus on the present moment and its prevailing mood of disillusion – also seems to fall naturally into those short forms which deal with glimpse, crisis, turning point and representative episode. If O. Henry is an American vaudeville version of Maupassant, Hemingway can be seen as the successor of Chekhov and Turgenev: he much admired the stories and sketches of the latter, as did Sherwood Anderson. But he was a more disciplined stylist than Anderson, and in his short stories can also be seen as the prose equivalent of Imagist poetry, of which he became aware in the 1920s through his association with modernists like Ezra Pound and Gertrude Stein. At the same time the personal experience on which he frequently drew directly in his writing was full of confusing tension and conflict – between masculine and feminine elements in his personality, between admiration for physical courage and a growing disillusion with violence, and between the optimism of youth and physical energy, and the inevitable depredations of old age and death. In his short stories we see vividly developed snapshots of turmoil, precise delineations of individual fragments of disparate experience.

Hemingway, who spent his childhood in Illinois and Michigan, began his writing career as a newspaper reporter on *The Kansas City Star*, and the precepts he learned on that paper he described as 'the best rules I ever learned for the business of writing'.[1] Among the 110 rules in the paper's style-sheet were the following:

(1) Use short sentences. Use short first paragraphs. Use vigorous English.
(9) Eliminate every superfluous word.
(21) Avoid the use of adjectives, especially such extravagant ones as splendid, gorgeous, grand, magnificent etc.
(64) Try to preserve the atmosphere of speech in your quotation.

The rules about brevity and concision are particularly germane to the short story, and the emphasis on anti-adjectival plainness and colloquial dialogue is also abundantly borne out in Hemingway's writing. He later spoke of how Pound also 'taught me to distrust adjectives', and said that his ambition was 'to eliminate everything unnecessary to conveying experience to the reader'.[2] In his book on bullfighting, *Death in the Afternoon* (1932), he has various reflections on the art of prose, one of which is of particular relevance to the short story:

> If a writer of prose knows enough of what he is writing about he may omit things that he knows and the reader, if the writer is writing truly enough, will have the feeling of those things as strongly as though the writer had stated them. The dignity of the movement of an iceberg is due to only one eighth of it being above water.[3]

The art of writing was, for Hemingway, the art of implication; and implication is at the heart of the modernist short story.[4]

The directness, the artful simplicity, of Hemingway's' style, his unmistakable individual voice, is central to the extraordinary impact his writing has had on American literature, and it is a quality which is seen at its most powerful in the short stories, since it lends itself to a careful focus on precise objects and places and particular situations. It is particularly good at conveying physical sensation, but the physical sensation is also the pointer to a state of mind. At the beginning of 'Big Two-Hearted River: Part I' (from *In Our Time*, 1925) Nick Adams is looking at trout in a river:

> Nick looked down into the pool from the bridge. It was a hot day. A kingfisher flew up the stream. It was a long time since Nick had looked into a stream and seen trout. They were very satisfactory. As the shadow of the kingfisher moved up the stream, a big trout shot up the stream in a long angle, only his shadow marking the angle, then lost his shadow as he came through the surface of the water, caught the sun, and then, as he went back into the stream under the surface, his shadow seemed to float down the stream with the current, unresisting, to his post under the bridge where he tightened up facing into the current.
>
> Nick's heart tightened as the trout moved. He felt all the old feeling.

Phrases relating directly to feeling are deliberately vague ('They were very satisfactory'; 'all the old feeling'): but the feeling is given precision by the close observation of the trout, observation which itself conveys feeling to the reader, and indeed becomes a kind of 'objective correlative' of the feeling. It is an essentially poetic technique.

Hemingway once wrote of war that the language of feeling and evaluation (words like 'glory', 'sacrifice' and 'honour') had become so hackneyed and debased that it sometimes seemed best simply to record 'the concrete names of villages, the numbers of roads, the names of rivers, the numbers of regiments and the dates'.[5] Literary language tends always towards elaboration: from time to time in the history of literature it has to be pulled back towards direct presentation and focus on the object. But there are features of Hemingway's style which also show a deliberate rhetoric in pursuit of this aim. One central feature is repetition, the repetition of basic nouns and simple phrases. In the seventeen-line first paragraph of 'Cat in the Rain', a description of the scene in front of a hotel in a seaside town, a picture is woven out of the syntactically varied repetition of key objects: 'sea', 'palms' or 'palm trees', 'war monument', 'public garden' or 'gardens' (each three times), and 'rain' or 'raining' (four times). It is a rhetoric which works musically (on the principle of repetition with variation) and visually to impress the scene and its distinctive monotony on the mind. Such effects are rarely used mechanically or over-insistently – the variety of Hemingway's 'simplicity' should be stressed – but these examples illustrate some of the key principles. They are at work throughout his fiction, but because of the concentration of focus they can often be seen most memorably in his short stories.

Hemingway's first major volume of short stories, *In Our Time* (1925), consists of a series of stories, many of them about the childhood and youth of the recurring figure of Nick Adams, interspersed with very short *vignettes* or sketches in fifteen numbered 'chapters', mainly of First World War scenes and bullfights with one or two other aspects of modern life. As well as suggesting a portrait of an age, the title – given the context of the aftermath of the Great War – probably alludes to the Episcopalian prayer, 'Give peace in our time, O Lord'; and the strategy of putting together stories and sketches seems to be a way of setting private, individual experience (in the stories) against glimpses of the largely anonymous life of the public world. How far the work makes a unified whole is a question to which critics of the 1950–80s turned their attention; certainly they identified hints of an overall structure and juxtapositions that establish various ironies and contrasts. For example 'Chapter VI' shows two soldiers, Nick and Rinaldi, lying in the street of a town shattered by war. Nick is wounded and says ironically to Rinaldi: 'You and me we've made a separate peace . . . Not patriots.' (Hemingway himself, fighting in Italy for another country, withdrew from the war soon after being wounded by a fragment of shrapnel.) The sketch comes almost halfway through the volume, and together with the stories of defeat and disillusion on either side of it ('The Battler' and 'A Very Short Story') seems to mark a turning point from stories of youth and sketches where the war is seen as a largely uproarious adventure to sketches and stories of adulthood and post-war modern life. But there is no absolute division: the sketch in 'Chapter V' of 'six cabinet ministers' (country unnamed) being shot at 6.30 a.m. in the rain is as bleak and disillusioned as any. The sense of fragmentariness, the random juxtaposition of sketches and stories, with the chance contrasts and parallels that these throw up, may be as important for the volume as any more structured 'unity' discerned by critics. Such putting together of fragments certainly constituted a large part of the work's newness in its day; indeed, this aspect of *In Our Time* – which it shares with T. S. Eliot's *The Waste Land* (1922) – reflects the spirit of the age.

One group of seven stories (and one *vignette*, as we have seen) in *In Our Time*, with four additional stories from other volumes, which can conveniently be looked at together, are those about Nick Adams. Adams, the son of a doctor and a devout Christian mother, is seen during childhood in Michigan and later as a soldier during the Great War. Clearly, then, he is a *persona* for Hemingway himself, who shared all these biographical elements. The Adams stories in *In Our Time* find Nick in various situations in childhood, adolescence and young manhood, and constitute a kind of fragmentary *Bildungsroman* or 'novel of growing up'. There are clear parallels here with Anderson's *Winesburg, Ohio*, but in the latter the protagonist in his role as writer is as much an observer as an agent, and the stories together form a picture of a community. Only towards the end of the book, and in passing, is Nick Adams referred to as a writer, and the focus is more exclusively on him as a representative young American from the country, his conflicts with his parents, his early love affairs, his encounters with the world of experience, failure, death and war. There is also less of an attempt than in *Winesburg* to link his stories together, so that the effect is more of independent episodes from the same life, snapshots of representative experience.

In 'Indian Camp' the young Nick (he cannot be much more than seven or eight) accompanies his father to the camp to witness the delivery of an Indian woman's baby. The birth is harrowing, and the father toughly, indeed ruthlessly, 'professional' ('But her screams are not important'). Under the emotional strain of the delivery (it seems) the Indian father, taking refuge in a bunk behind a blanket, cuts his own throat. As Nick and his father row back over the lake the sun is coming up, a bass jumps, Nick trails his hand in the water which feels 'warm in the sharp chill of the morning'. The last sentence is: 'In the early morning on the lake sitting in the stern of the boat with his father rowing, he felt quite sure that he would never die.'[6] This strong positive sense of life in the last sentences seems to survive the shocking experience of the almost simultaneous birth and death. The story is a resonant image both of life's pain and cruelty and of its resilience. Critics have also pointed to the sceptical treatment of the father, and have suggested that there is significance in the absence of the accompanying uncle from the end of the story (he leaves because he is disgusted with his brother's callousness). But the main point seems to be to convey the boy's unevaluated raw experience of the events: he turns away from watching his father, but makes no conscious criticism of him (though our attitude may, importantly, be different).

'The Doctor and the Doctor's Wife', on the other hand, is a small incident which epitomizes the tensions between father and mother, and of the son with both, and makes clear the son's allegiance to the father. 'The End of Something' and 'The Three-Day Blow' relate the end of Nick's relationship with a girlfriend and the subsequent comfort of male camaraderie: both stories are done with fine economy to suggest the element of callowness in the hero, the strength of the girl and the comic over-seriousness of Nick with his friend as they sit drinking whisky and talking about books they've read ('They were conducting the conversation on a high plane') – there is an element of humour and self-criticism which is sometimes overlooked in accounts of Hemingway.

The rest of the Adams stories are about a grown-up Nick. In 'The Battler' he has a disturbing encounter with a slightly mad ex-boxer and his African American minder in a remote wood by a rail-track: Nick's first encounter with old age and failure. The two-part 'Big Two-Hearted River' simply recounts a fishing trip, but its steady gaze and sure-handed grasp of detail embody an attitude to experience in the plainly recounted facts: the war is not mentioned, but there is a feeling of therapeutic solidity in this post-war episode, a getting back into touch with elemental things, and even of a recovering soldier's overactive awareness of the 'tragic' in simple moods and experiences, as in his decision not to fish in the deeper, darker water of the swamp.

The Nick Adams stories outside *In Our Time* are 'The Killers' and 'Ten Indians' from *Men Without Women* (1927) and 'A Way You'll Never Be' and 'Fathers and Sons' in *Winner Take Nothing* (1933). 'The Killers', one of Hemingway's best-known stories, is memorable above all because of the ground-breaking – and now classic – hoodlum dialogue of the killers in the lunch-room, the forerunner of low-life dialogue from Raymond Chandler to David Mamet.

> 'What do you do here nights?' Al asked
> 'They eat the big dinner', his friend said. 'They all come here and eat the big dinner.'
> 'That's right', George said
> 'So you think that's right?' Al asked George
> 'Sure.'
> 'You're a pretty bright boy, aren't you?'
> 'Sure', said George.
> 'Well, you're not', said the other little man. 'Is he Al?'
> 'He's dumb', said Al. (p. 268)

'The Killers' is also – but almost as it were in passing – about Nick's growing awareness of the nature of city life. At the end of the story, appalled in particular by the passive fatalism and despair of the killers' intended victim, Nick decides he is going to get out of town. This is just thrown in at the end, there is no big point made of the moral discovery. Like the fleeting and fortuitous appearance of a Mrs Bell – not even the victim's landlady but a *stand-in* for the landlady[7] – Hemingway's art moves with the appearance of randomness and contingency. Although they are in fact carefully chosen and plotted, this and many other stories seem like unorganized bits of experience, which is what gives them their freshness and spontaneity.

'Fathers and Sons', the concluding story of *Winner Take Nothing*, describes a journey Nick Adams takes with his son – now about the same age as Nick was in 'Indian Camp' – back to Michigan, giving the opportunity, rooted in the present moment, for a meditation on past (his own), present and future (his son's). While its experimental lyrical writing about Nick's first sexual experience with the Indian girl Trudy does not (most critics agree) really work, his recollections of his father and his thoughts about time and his son contribute to a ruminative story (one could compare Coleridge's poem 'Frost At Midnight') which satisfyingly closes the volume and the whole Nick Adams sequence.

The title of Hemingway's next volume of stories, *Men Without Women* (1927), sums up a whole area of experience with which the writer was preoccupied throughout his career, the experience of men in the world of exclusively male pursuits: on one hand war, which he had known at first hand in Italy in 1917–18, and on the other the world of male sports – bullfighting, boxing, big-game hunting – which in many ways channels the impulses of aggression and combat and to reproduce those challenges to courage and survival which are found in war. What became known as the Hemingway 'code' – honourable behaviour in situations of physical or other danger, fair play, courage and dignity in defeat – was exemplified above all in his short stories, the brevity and intensity of which provided a formal analogy to the brief but intense periods of time in battle or sport. The confrontation, for example, between matador and bull is an extreme moment of crisis, and hence especially suited to the short story form. 'The Undefeated' presents an ageing matador, Manuel, who persuades the agent Retana to give him a mere $300 for one last fight (the popular matador Villalta gets $7,000). The story focuses on bullfighting as a prosaic, unglamorous job for the unsuccessful matador; the bored cynicism of the newspaper bullfight correspondent; the harsh unforgivingness of the crowd; and centrally on the fight itself – Manuel's state of mind, and the instinctive action without thought which Hemingway particularly admires. Manuel kills the bull, messily, and is jeered by the crowd and badly wounded. He is 'undefeated' but the tone of the story is far from heroic, and ends with a curious lack of closure, as Manuel's friend Zurito (who has in a strange 'joke' pretended to cut off Manuel's *coleta* or pigtail, a mock ritual of defeat and superannuation) stands over Manuel's body while he is given an anaesthetic for the operation. The story is an ironic tale of dogged victory in the midst of cynical indifference and hostility. The only other major 'bullfight' short story is even more disenchanted. 'The Capital of the World' (1936) is about a young waiter who is killed accidentally when taking part in a mock-bullfight with a friend pushing a chair with knives strapped to it for horns. The keynote of the story is struck at the end, where the narrator comments that Paco died 'full of illusions', having had no real experience of life, and without even, he sardonically concludes, having had time 'to be disappointed at the Garbo picture which had been disappointing Madrid all week' (p. 48). Edmund Wilson comments that Hemingway the artist 'registers in this very fine piece the discrepancy between the fantasies of boyhood and the realities of the adult world', just at a time when Hemingway 'the war correspondent is making himself ridiculous by trying to hang on to' those fantasies.[8]

Many of Hemingway's stories, though ostensibly 'without women', gain their significance and point from the fact that women's presence is still felt significantly in the background. In 'In Another Country' the narrator, convalescing from a war-wound in a North Italian hospital, meets a major who 'angrily' insists a man 'must not marry'. '"He should find things he cannot lose."' He later reveals that his wife has just died, and '"I cannot resign myself."' The sudden outburst of feeling from the 'straight and soldierly' major is very movingly done. In its brevity and restraint it is perhaps more telling than the longer-drawn-out and more romantic grief of the hero Robert Henry, in a similar situation, in *A Farewell To Arms.* As Edmund Wilson says, Hemingway does not show a novelist's 'solid sense of character': 'the people in his short stories are satisfactory because he only has to hit them off: the point of the story does not lie in personalities, but in the emotion to which a situation gives rise'.[9]

The major's grief at his wife's death, in a story about war, prompts a critical paradox: Hemingway's art, so often associated with his public persona as above all the masculine, indeed 'macho' writer (bullfight *aficionado*, big-game hunter, deep-sea fisherman etc.), may perhaps be at its finest and least complacent when it is dealing about men *with* women, and about the ambiguities of sexual experience. And in this area too, the short story, with its mobility of experimentation and its ability to focus on new areas of experience in ways that epitomize large problems, was particularly important to Hemingway. The early story 'Up In Michigan' was omitted from *In Our Time* because the publisher, Liveright, objected to its explicit sexual content.[10] But from today's perspective it strikes one as a sensitive treatment of a youthful sexual encounter, in which the man's clumsiness and callousness is contrasted with the girl's deeper emotional involvement and tenderness. The story is told in the third person, but its point of view and style is primarily that of the girl, Liz: Hemingway uses a kind of free indirect discourse, which describes Liz's feelings by using her own style of language, but without quotation marks (e.g. 'When she saw the wagon coming down the road she felt weak and sick sort of inside').[11] 'Cat in the Rain' (from *In Our Time*), about a bored American couple in an Italian hotel, is also told mainly from the woman's point of view. Focusing on the briefest and slightest of incidents (the woman's sudden desire to rescue the cat from the rain), it evokes the whole world of the relationship: the rainy Italian town, the rootless hotel existence, the woman's frustrated desire for children and her responsiveness to the hotel *padrone*'s old-world courtesy, the man's terse boredom. The story works poetically – a case of the short story as lyric poem – but without poeticizing, to suggest a whole condition through simple, concrete details and snatches of banal conversation.

The woman's point of view is again central to one of Hemingway's most famous stories about men and women (and also his own favourite story), 'Hills Like White Elephants'. This is another episode-story, presenting simply a couple's forty-minute wait at a small Spanish railway station and their conversation about (it is implicitly clear but never stated) the woman's proposed abortion. The story is almost entirely made up of simple dialogue, and its success lies in the way this dialogue is charged with tone and implication. The man's detachment and the woman's deeper emotional involvement and anxiety emerge sharply in their tense exchanges. When at the end of the story the man asks the woman 'Do you feel better?' and she replies 'I feel fine . . . . There's nothing wrong with me, I feel fine', we know that her tone is charged with a variety of possible inflections: sarcasm, irritation, or a brisk rousing of herself and repression of feeling. Exactly how we hear the tone depends on our own creative engagement with the story. The brevity of the story and the absence of tonal markers (adverbs, for instance) make for an active participation by the reader. In a similar way the title's relation to the story prompts our imaginative response: it is both a sharp visual image of the landscape and an instance, since it is her phrase, of the woman's greater liveliness of apprehension. It evokes both the place and her response to it.[12]

If these stories are striking for their empathy with female experience, a larger group are notable for their exploration of failed or ambiguous sexual experience. In 'Mr and Mrs Elliot' the tone is marred by a kind of sneering contempt towards the hapless protagonists' unsuccessful attempts to have a child, but the portrait of an arid marriage has (it has convincingly been suggested) a wider application than the real-life minor writer whom Hemingway had most directly in mind, and may allude to the marriage of T. S. Eliot and his wife Vivienne.[13] It also hints at a lesbian relationship between Mrs Elliot and her female friend. A more subtle treatment of lesbianism can be found in 'The Sea-Change,' where a young man in a café breaks with his girlfriend because of her relationship with another woman. The man is pompously censorious (without, it seems, being emotionally very engaged), and the point of the story would seem to be its ironic view of him. There is some finely understated comedy in the counterpoint of the couple's conversation with that of two clients at the bar, and in the man's recourse to a rather self-satisfied conversation with the barman at the end of the story (though there seems no reason to press the story for further ironies about the man's own covert homosexuality).[14]

'The Light of the World' is another story which gives an evocative glimpse of attitudes to love and sexuality, this time in a low-life setting. It centres on a discussion in a station waiting-room between two whores, witnessed by a homosexual cook and the two young men who are the nominal protagonists of the story. The two whores, Alice and 'the peroxide blonde', get to arguing about the late Steve Ketchel (a famous real-life boxer), and which of them loved him more. 'Peroxide' is sentimental and idealizing about their relationship, whereas Alice's feelings, and her account of the man, are clearly more heartfelt and authentic. Meanwhile some of the other men in the room taunt the cook about his homosexuality. The story has been described by Carlos Baker as 'a complicated defence of the normal [presumably represented by Alice] against the abnormal': but this (while having an aspect of truth) conventionalizes and in one respect distorts the story, which may rather be raising the whole question 'What *is* "normal"?' Alice's love for Ketchel is certainly authentic but there seems no need to raise it to the status of a 'norm'; and Baker contrasts 'the raucous play of human emotions' with 'the furtive yearnings of the homosexual cook', whereas the story rather shows the cook responding with dignity to the taunts ('"Can't you stop that sort of thing," the cook asked. "Can't we speak decently?"'). If at the end of the story the young men give him the cold shoulder, that just registers, neutrally, the facts of the case. The title 'The Light of the World' is Jesus' phrase from John 8:12 and elsewhere in the New Testament (and it is also known that Hemingway's mother donated a copy of Holman Hunt's famous painting of that name to her local church). If the Light of the World is Christ, or love, the title is both ironic and not so ironic: love does not confine itself to the respectable and the conventional, and its nature is everywhere mysterious.

Hemingway's stories are reports from the front, the vanguard of early twentieth-century experience in all its new complexities of class and gender. Arguably they are at their best when they are at their shortest and most suggestive. Two of his longer stories, despite their power, seem to suffer from a certain laboured quality and, in part, from a loss of moral clarity. 'The Short Happy Life of Francis Macomber' (1936) is a memorable treatment of the psychological effects of physical courage, and a disenchanted portrait of a certain type of rich, ruthless American woman. But in so far as the English safari guide, Wilson, seems to be the repository of the values Hemingway most admired – physical courage, fair play (in sport if not relationships), professionalism and carelessness of death – it is disconcerting to find him so savagely persecuting Margot Macomber at the end with the sarcastic suggestion that she shot her husband deliberately. Critics have argued about the validity of this suggestion, but it is belied in the text ('Mrs Macomber, in the car, had shot at the buffalo'), and it is a more subtle reading to see Wilson as simply capitalizing on the accident for his own purposes of domination. The story typifies the later 'tough-guy' Hemingway, but it suggests a limitation in his positive values. As Frank O'Connor said, it is difficult to see the ability to face a charging lion or buffalo as the paradigm of all human value. 'The Snows of Kilimanjaro', on the other hand, loses itself in a quagmire of retrospection, and one is suspicious – given the obvious closeness of the dying writer Harry to Hemingway himself – of the tortuous combination of self-criticism, self-pity and self-justification in which those retrospections indulge. The one thing that saves the story is the vision at the end, as the dying man hallucinates an escape from his confinement and a plane journey over the brilliant snows of the mountain. Criticisms of the plausibility of this rather miss the point. It is both a breathtaking narrative device, reminiscent of the *coup de théâtre* of Bierce's 'Occurrence at Owl Creek Bridge', and a poetic symbol of the triumph of writing, the beautiful vision rising above and lasting beyond 'the fury and the mire of human veins'. As such it combines two strands of the American short story: narrative artifice (in Hawthorne, in Twain, in Bierce, in O. Henry) and the modernist tradition of poetic symbolism (in Joyce, in Hemingway, in Flannery O'Connor).

But the brilliant symbol of the snows of Kilimanjaro may be too flamboyant a note on which to close this account of Hemingway's short stories. Nor are his greatest strengths shown by the later long story *The Old Man and the Sea* of 1954 (for all that it was probably decisive in his winning the Nobel prize). Depite passages of epic simplicity and power, it becomes somewhat ponderous in the execution of its humanistic and tragic intent. In particular, the old man's running monologue (silent and voiced) does not always ring true: too much of Hemingway himself creeps in. A better place to end would be back with the altogether admirable and representative short story of 1933, 'A Clean Well-Lighted Place'. This story about an old man and two waiters in a café is a kind of emblem of the human need for order and community at its most basic level. In its precise observation and delicate physical awareness, its unpretentious humanity and its unsentimental sense of human vulnerability it stands for a sense of life which lies deeper than the flourishes of the Hemingway masculinist 'code'.

> It was late and everyone had left the café except an old man who sat in the shadow the leaves of the tree made against the electric light. In the day time the street was dusty, but at night the dew settled the dust and the old man liked to sit late because he was deaf and now at night it was quiet and he felt the difference.

Chapter 15

F. Scott Fitzgerald

The great popularity and at the same time the critical esteem of the short story in the early part of the twentieth century is nowhere more evident than in the short stories of F. Scott Fitzgerald (1896–1940), and the tension between the popular and the estimable – the two not always at odds, but often pulling in different directions – is at the heart of his work. Fitzgerald published four major volumes of short stories during his lifetime: *Flappers and Philosophers* (1920), *Tales of the Jazz Age* (1922), *All the Sad Young Men* (1926) and *Taps at Reveille* (1935). Most of these stories, together with many others, were also published initially in the magazines – most notably the popular *Saturday Evening Post* and the more seriously literary *Scribner's*. None of his short story collections as a whole is as significant as his achievement in the genre of the novel, particularly his masterpiece *The Great Gatsby* (1925), but the best of them, which would include 'The Diamond as Big as the Ritz', 'The Rich Boy', 'May Day', 'Absolution' and 'Babylon Revisited', show both the romantic verve and *élan* and the counter-romantic critical edge of his best writing and gave him the opportunity to add a number of brilliant facets to his treatment of the American scene.

Fitzgerald rarely had anything good to say on behalf of his short stories. 'I hate writing short stories', he wrote in 1926, '. . . and only do my six a year to have leisure to write my novels'; and writing of *The Great Gatsby* he spoke of 'the sustained imagination of a sincere and yet radiant world' in contrast to 'trashy imaginings as in my stories'.[1] And it is true that the economic incentive to publishing short stories was a powerful one: between 1919 and 1940 Fitzgerald made well over twice as much money from his short stories as from his novels.[2] Yet his ambitions as a serious writer led him also to write: 'The necessity of the artist in every generation has been to give his work permanence in every way by a safe shaping and a constant pruning, lest he be confused with the journalistic material that has attracted lesser men.'[3] And this sense of craft, of 'shaping' and 'pruning', is as evident in his best short stories as in his best novels. One opportunity the short story form gave him was to focus on specific moral issues as well as specific aspects of modern life. There is a tendency to diffuseness in all his novels except *The Great Gatsby.* He once complained that in his novel-writing he had not reached the stage of 'ruthless artistry which would let me cut out an exquisite bit that had no place in the context'.[4] This lack of discipline is necessarily checked in the short story, which must be shaped to a certain limit and can hardly allow digression, however exquisite.

In terms of subject-matter and treatment alike, there is an abiding conflict in Fitzgerald's writing between a romanticism that was drawn to youthful exuberance, gaiety and the *dolce vita*, and an adult scepticism which saw through the frequent semblances of these qualities in actual experience. His short stories can be seen as vivid flash-photographs of a stylish world which capture its glitter and its glamour but also, in those 'shots' which go behind the scenes to the private rooms and solitary moments of its protagonists, the pallor and the strain on the faces of the fashionable in their unguarded moments.

Fitzgerald is both the celebrant and the critic of the 'Jazz Age' whose name he invented. In and of that world as he was, there is always the question (perhaps even more in his stories than in his novels) whether its specious allure dazzled his vision. On the whole, however, the stories which were reprinted in the book collections maintain a fine balance between the enjoyment of upper-class life and a clear-sighted perspective on it. Two stories from *Flappers and Philosophers* show contrasting tendencies towards a comic and a tragic sense of life. 'Bernice Bobs Her Hair', set in the 1920s, is a light but sharp-witted story of two girls, 'sophisticated' Marjorie, the star of her set, the lure of all its young men and the envy of all its young women, and her pretty but awkward cousin Bernice who comes to stay with her. Bernice is the despair of her cousin until she decides to accept the latter's advice and become deliberately and wittily outrageous in manner and conversation, and finally to 'bob her hair' – to have it cut in that boyish way which so typified the smart and daring new young woman of the 1920s and so shocked her parents' generation. The story has been seen as a kind of sharp modern rebuttal of Louisa M. Alcott's famous novel *Little Women* (1868–9), which for the previous two generations of American womanhood had provided an attractively presented, traditional model of 'the womanly woman' for female readers.[5] Marjorie certainly has some good hits at this ideal. 'You little nut!', she says to Bernice:

> Girls like you are responsible for all the tiresome colourless marriages: all those ghastly inefficiencies that pass as feminine qualities. What a

> blow it must be when a man of imagination marries the beautiful bundle of clothes that he's been building ideals around, and finds that she's just a weak, whining, cowardly mass of affectations.[6]

The result of Bernice's education is some wonderfully funny comedy (as when Bernice greets the earnest theology student Draycott Deyo with 'Hello, Shell Shock!' and asks him his views on female bathing and dressing), and a nice reversal – the novice outdoing the teacher – when Bernice, in a final 'rape of the lock', cuts off Marjorie's blonde braids ('"Huh!" she giggled wildly, "Scalp the selfish thing!"'). Having taken her revenge, Bernice is ready to face the modern world as a New Woman.

'The Cut-glass Bowl' is set in the previous generation (the 1890s and early 1900s), 'the cut-glass age' as Fitzgerald calls it in a mock historical opening, and its sense of the world of wealth is altogether harsher. The bowl of the title is given as an ill-fated wedding present to the heroine Evylyn by a former spurned admirer, who calls it an emblem of herself, 'as hard as you are and as beautiful and as empty and as easy to see through'. Its large, glittering presence presides over and is involved in three dark scenes in Evylyn's subsequent life – her husband's discovery of a love affair (her lover's arm strikes the bowl as he is trying to escape), her daughter's blood-poisoning (from a cut from the bowl) and the news of her son's death in the Great War (the letter is left in the bowl). The story has been criticized for its highly schematic plot and symbolism, but this may be a prejudice of realist expectation. It should be seen as an emblematic story, in which the bowl functions as a central symbol of a malign fate, which expands to represent the overarching sphere of the heavens, and which delivers its final taunting 'moral' just before the heroine falls to her death while trying to destroy it. As such it looks back to the parabolic stories of Hawthorne, with a touch of the melodrama of Poe. In its crafted structure and glittering texture it stays in the mind as a symbol of a dark view of a fateful universe.

Tales of the Jazz Age contains two stories which perhaps more brilliantly than any others highlight the elements of fantasy and farce in Fitzgerald's imagination. At the same time, his ambivalent attitude to wealth and luxury, and his sense of the exhilarating but sometimes tragic confusions of his age are revealed. 'The Diamond as Big as the Ritz' lives up to its *bravura* title: the young John Unger from the town of Hades, South Carolina, goes to visit the family of his friend from St Midas School, Percy Washington, who live in a fabulous mansion on a mountain which consists of a single gigantic diamond. He falls in love with Percy's sister Kismine, but then discovers he is trapped because the father Braddock Washington cannot allow him to escape to give away the secret of his diamond mountain. The satirical elements in the fairy-tale are clear: if Hades is like hell (a hell of petty respectability as well as Southern heat), Washington's estate is a false heaven; John's school is named after the king (changed ironically to a saint) whose touch turned everything to gold; Washington bears the name of the first American president; his Negro slaves do not know that the Civil War has ended and Emancipation has been gained; the airmen he has imprisoned because they had the misfortune to fly over his territory are all of Chinese or Irish or Italian extraction, suggesting the fate of poor immigrants in an America dominated by a white Anglo-Saxon ascendancy. In the climax of the story, when the outside world is about to invade his world, Braddock Washington offers a bribe to God of his fabulous diamond mountain. American materialism, its worship of fabulous wealth and its inversion of religious values, is here lampooned by means of the grandest of hyperbolic fantasies. One of the most effective scenes in the story is the beginning of the second section, where the spectacle of the trans-continental train that deposits John and Percy and the buggy that comes to collect them from the station is witnessed in a state of stunned wonder by the twelve inhabitants of the village of Fish. The number of villagers, the name of the place and the language generally suggest a striking parody of some religious sect. But (like the crowds who go to gawp at movie-stars)

> the men of Fish were beyond all religion – the barest and most savage tenets of even Christianity could gain no foothold on that barren rock – so there was no altar, no priest, no sacrifice; only each night at seven a silent concourse by the shanty depot, a congregation who lifted up a prayer of dim, anaemic wonder.

But the satiric impact of the story is mitigated in part by the sheer luxury of the fantasy. Fitzgerald himself commented on his state of mind when he composed the story: 'I was in that familiar mood characterized by a perfect craving for luxury, and the story began as an attempt to feed that craving on imaginary foods.' No doubt a satirist may often be secretly drawn to the excesses he is satirizing, or a moralist attracted by the luxury he condemns (one might think of Spenser and the Bower of Bliss). But in this story one wonders if the fantasy has seduced the author to fall in love with his machinery. The long descriptions of the fairy-tale château (an uncanny foreshadowing of Disneyland) or of the elaborate mechanism which wakes John and tips him gently into a body-temperature crystal bath in a blue aquarium are indulged for their own sake. One could argue that this tension is what gives the story its entertaining vitality. It is notable that Braddock

Washington's architect and interior designer was, he tells John, 'a moving-picture fella', and the tinsel luxury of his domain is pure Hollywood. There is a certain irony in the fact that Fitzgerald was to became a scriptwriter in Hollywood in 1931, and there is already a touch of Hollywood (a hard-bitten scriptwriter's bravado) in the dialogue at the end of the story. John says to Kismine as they escape the exploding mountain: 'At any rate let us love for a while, for a year or so, you and me. That's a form of divine drunkenness that we can all try. There are only diamonds in the whole world, diamonds and perhaps the shabby gift of disillusion.' One almost hears the voice of Humphrey Bogart.

'May Day' is a bleaker and in many ways sharper account of social confusion (mainly that of the upper class, but less usually for Fitzgerald giving a glimpse of working-class life too) in the New York of the immediate post-First-World-War period. The opening paragraphs are a bravura parodic flourish in the style of ancient legend or history, ironically giving the kind of grand synoptic view of the movement of civilizations (useful for propaganda) which obscures the reality of the individual lives to be explored by the story. In the successive parts of an artfully constructed plot we follow the fortunes of three main groups of characters in the twenty-four hours from 9 a.m. on 1 May 1919 until the next morning. Gordon Sterrett is an upper-class young man down on his luck, who has to beg a loan from his contemptuous former friend Philip Dean. Dean is in love with the beautiful Edith Bradin, whom Sterrett has also worshipped from a distance. Gus Rose and Carrol Key are two demobbed soldiers whose wanderings through the city take them to a Socialist rally, the kitchens of Delmonico's (where the rich characters are at a ball), and finally to an attack on the office of a left-wing newspaper, in which Key is pushed from a window and killed. Dean goes off on a drinking spree with his friend Himmel; Sterrett drunkenly proposes marriage to his chorus-girl friend Jewel; Rose drifts along the streets of New York. All five end up at 8.00 a.m. in Child's restaurant on Columbus Circle, among a 'noisy medley of chorus girls, college boys, debutantes, rakes, *filles de joie*', where, with 'a prolonged and involuntary "Oh-h-h" ', they all witness a transformation scene:

> The great plate-glass front had turned to a deep creamy blue, the colour of a Maxfield Parrish moonlight . . . Dawn had come up in Columbus Circle, magical breathless dawn, silhouetting the great statue of the immortal Christopher, and mingling in a curious and uncanny manner with the fading yellow electric light inside.

It is a small epiphany of America, its ambiguous splendour caught in that final detail of the mingling of the dawn with the tawdry electric light. In the final two scenes of the story Dean and Himmel, drunkenly masquerading with two door-signs as 'Mr In' and 'Mr Out', ascend in a hotel elevator ('"Higher" said Mr In. "Heaven" said Mr Out); and Gordon Sterrett, waking to realize he has no money and has just married a chorus-girl, shoots himself.

The story works as a kind of tragicomic farce, the author positioning himself just close enough to his subjects to preclude hostility but far enough away for ironic detachment. It captures brilliantly the chaos and gaiety and despair of post-war New York. As in 'The Diamond as Big as the Ritz', Fitzgerald is not finally a satirist – he is as much indulgent as critical – but a dazzling critic, commentator and fabulist of the social scene and the tendencies of his time. If he is a romantic, he is an elegiac rather than a revolutionary one, and his romanticism is held in tension with a disenchanted realism tending to cynicism or a sentimental sadness.

Fitzgerald once said that his earliest public saw him above all as the chronicler of 'young love', but that as time went on he found 'young love' more and more difficult to treat with sincerity. Examples of early and relatively successful stories on this subject, already touched by the elegiac note, are 'Winter Dreams' (from *All the Sad Young Men* of 1926), in which the lovelorn hero is left lamenting the loss of 'the country of illusion, of youth, of the richness of life, where his winter dreams had flourished', and '"The Sensible Thing"' (from the same volume), in which a nervously apprehensive girl calls off her wedding, deciding it is 'the sensible thing' to do. There is a rather weak and unsatisfactory ambiguity at the end of the story (will the relationship continue or is the last scene just a sentimental final farewell?), but the elegiac note can be fitted to either reading: 'Well, let it pass, he thought: April is over. April is over. There are all kinds of love in the world, but never the same love twice.'

One other story in the 1922 collection is a rather more bitter and thoughtful rendering – perhaps owing to a greater authorial detachment from the protagonists – of the elegiac note. 'The Lees of Happiness' is a remarkably melancholy story for an early collection. It tells of the marriage of Jeffrey Curtain, a minor novelist, and Roxanne Milbank, a transitory star of the stage; of their friendship with Harry, unhappily married to Kitty; of Jeffrey's startlingly sudden blood-clot on the brain and his early death; and of Harry's and Roxanne's saddened but persisting friendship. There is a memorable scene early in the story in which Roxanne, in youthful high spirits, nails some rock-hard, overcooked biscuits to the wall – which are still there when Harry visits after the onset of Jeffrey's illness: a striking image of comic craziness turning into one of painful grotesquerie. There is also a powerful portrait of Harry's petulant and tyrannical wife, wrapped in self-pity, and dirty pink 'mules' and housecoat, in an apartment with dirty pink walls. But the final note is again the elegiac – tending to the sentimental, the author of twenty-three or twenty-four enjoying the sadness a little too much: 'To these two life had come quickly and gone, leaving not bitterness, but pity; not disillusion, but only pain. There was already enough moonlight when they shook hands for each to see the gathered kindness in the other's eyes.' As well as the moonlight we see the arc-lights: Hollywood is not far away.

Fitzgerald has been praised as the recorder of young love and romantic regret, but perhaps he is at his best when he is most detached, or when his protagonists are not too close to himself (as they clearly are in stories like 'Winter Dreams' and 'The Sensible Thing', or in 'Two Wrongs', which attempts, not entirely successfully, to show a brashly successful theatre producer learning to atone for thoughtless neglect of his wife).[7] One of the best stories from *All the Sad Young Men* (1926) and one of Fitzgerald's most famous, 'The Rich Boy', uses the device of a narrator within the story who is not the protagonist, rather as Fitzgerald does with Nick Carraway in *The Great Gatsby.* The device enables the narrator to treat the protagonist as a phenomenon, difficult to assess – a specimen of that class which so fascinated Fitzgerald, the rich (or in this case the very rich indeed): 'The only way I can describe young Anson Hunter is to approach him as if he were a foreigner and cling stubbornly to my point of view. If I accept his for a moment I am lost – I have nothing to show but a preposterous movie.'

Anson has inherited his wealth from an old New York family, and he manages his life, both work and play, with an effortless superiority. But it is a superiority which leads him to a supercilious carelessness about relationships, even his relationship to the one woman her really loves. After getting badly drunk not long before he is due to be married and shocking his fiancée and her family, he 'apologized with sincerity and dignity', but 'He made no promises, showed no humility, only delivered a few serious comments on life which brought him off with rather a moral superiority at the end.' When he and Paula meet again six weeks later neither realizes that 'the psychological moment had passed forever'. As time goes on Anson assumes an elegant but prematurely middle-aged role among his friends: he advises the slightly younger ones in their affairs and becomes an authority for his younger relations. But his fundamental egoism persists. He has an affair with the daughter of a nouveau-riche 'publicist': when she shows signs of tiring of him he decides to show her 'to whom she belonged' and takes her to his country estate in a show of intimacy and commitment, and callously drops her. In another episode he officiously and ultimately rather brutally intervenes in an affair between his aunt (the wife of the head of the family) and her lover. The upshot is that the lover commits suicide. Anson's life progresses to a stage of empty, efficient dutifulness at work and expensive casual pleasures. There is a good scene where, discovering that all his friends are out of town and he has no desire to join them or go down to his family in the country ('for almost the first time in his life he had nothing whatever to do'), he is reduced to going to his favourite hotel bar and reminiscing with the barman, who responds doubtfully to his memories and is clearly awkward about being cast in the role of 'old family servant'. (Disenchanted exchanges with barmen are almost archetypal in American short stories and films: one thinks of Fitzgerald's own 'Babylon Revisited' (see below, pp. 158–9), the conversation in Hemingway's 'The Sea-Change' or the chilling episode in Stanley Kubrick's film *The Shining*). In the last scene the narrator travels with Anson on a ship to Europe, 'glad he was himself again, or at least the self I knew, and with which I felt at home', and marvelling at his continuing charm, and success with women. 'Perhaps they promised that there would always be women in the world who would spend their brightest, freshest, rarest hours to nurse and protect that superiority he cherished in his heart.' This, the last sentence of the story, could be seen as a fairly damning indictment of Anson's pride; but in the context it comes across merely as admiring irony: the narrator is clearly still fascinated and seduced by Anson, who has nevertheless in the course of the story (if we attend to the facts) been shown as calculating, snobbish, officious and bullying. The story has been much admired as one of Fitzgerald's best, and there is considerable subtlety in the portrait of Anson. But structurally it is somewhat diffuse and episodic, there are clumsinesses of construction, and in the end one feels that despite the detachment of the narrator he is too enamoured of Anson to present his cold, wealth-sustained pride with a proper decisiveness. Anson's great difference from the Gatsby of Fitzgerald's masterpiece is his traditional social position and lack of mystery: Gatsby is a more successful study than Anson because no-one quite knows where he comes from: he represents an incalculable and mysterious element in the story of American wealth.

F. Scott Fitzgerald wrote one hundred and seventy-eight short stories in all. Forty-two of these are published in the most recent standard anthology,[8] and the nine so far discussed are among the few that have over the years, through frequent republication and critical attention, come to be regarded as of lasting value. It is, indeed, difficult to know where to lay the final emphasis, for there are signs that a wider range of stories is beginning to reclaim critical attention.[9] It may be that Fitzgerald's best short stories are not his longer and more characterologically ambitious pieces (like 'The Rich Boy') – which may be rather too like foreshortened novels – but his shorter, terser, more sharply witty pieces which focus on smaller fragments of contemporary life: the infantile fight between two fathers in 'The Baby Party'; the crisp, sardonic study of emotional confusion in Hollywood in 'Magnetism' (better than the genial but more simply farcical and slight series of Pat Hobby stories about Hollywood); or an over-romantic young man's sudden access to a new maturity in 'The Bridal Party'.

One comes back to the question of Fitzgerald's reputed 'romanticism'. It comes to seem that the romanticism of his stories is sometimes rather a shallow one (too much a matter of fleeting party-induced 'romances' and too ready to yield to an elegiac 'despair'). Perhaps his strength should be seen in those places where he is most aware of this, places where a critical counter-romanticism and a disenchanted clear-sighted realism come into play. One of the finest examples of this is 'Babylon Revisited', first published in 1931, in which Fitzgerald works into fiction a story very close to his own most painful memories of his marriage to Zelda and his relations with his young daughter Scottie. It is also a story that writes the epitaph of the Jazz Age. Charlie Wales is in Paris visiting his sister-in-law and her husband, who are guardians to his nine-year-old daughter. His purpose is to try to persuade them that his days of extravagance and alcoholic excess are behind him and that he is now fit to look after the child. Wales has a sharp insight into his own former folly, above all the way he and other Americans had only a few years before overbearingly and arrogantly colonized Paris as a kind of personal terrain of pleasure. 'We were a sort of royalty', says Charlie. But now in the Ritz bar, 'he felt polite in it, not as if he owned it'. But it is not so easy to change, and part of the strength of the story is the sense that he is trapped in the character he has made for himself, as opposed to 'character' in the moral sense. ('[He] wanted to jump back a whole generation and trust in character again as the eternally valuable element.') His attempt to convince his daughter's guardians of his new reformation is completely scuppered when two drunken friends from the old days descend on Charlie in the guardians' home. The story resists self-pity and concentrates rather on the bitter ironies of his moral condition. Among other things it is a culminating testament, more telling perhaps even than 'The Rich Boy', to the illusions of money. When a friend says to him: 'I hear you lost a lot in the crash' (the Wall Street crash of 1929), he replies, 'I did . . . but I lost everything I wanted in the boom.' His worst memory is of once locking his wife out in the snow: but back in 1929 'the snow . . . wasn't real snow. If you didn't want it to be snow you just paid some money.' But even this sardonic insight cannot entirely free him from the sense we have of his continuing entanglement in the world of money and 'payment' in another sense. Even in a brief encounter with a prostitute in a *brasserie* he exercises some of his 'old world' patronage by buying her some eggs and coffee. And at very the end of the story, in the Ritz bar again, he says to a waiter 'What do I owe you?' and then reflects: 'He would come back some day. They couldn't make him pay for ever.' There is 'paying', and then there is 'paying' in another sense. The story shows Fitzgerald's subtle fictional awareness of how the ability to do one does not preclude the other. One final critical question remains: the story clearly shows strength in its great effort at clear-sightedness, its resistance to self-pity. Does it finally achieve this? The last two sentences read: 'He wasn't young any more, with a lot of nice thoughts and dreams to have by himself. He was absolutely sure Helen [his estranged wife] wouldn't have wanted him to be so alone.' The first of these sentences has a marked sardonic tone. The second could be read two ways: either as Fitzgerald's desperate lapse into pathos, or as Charlie's final bitter moment of self-delusion. Perhaps Fitzgerald can be given the credit, at the clinching moment of this painfully honest story, of the latter interpretation.

Chapter 16

William Faulkner

As a writer of short stories William Faulkner (1896–1962) presents a paradox. His reputation as the greatest American writer of the first half of the twentieth century rests above all on his novels, particularly those written between 1929 and 1936: *The Sound and the Fury* (1929), *As I Lay Dying* (1930), *Sanctuary* (1931), *Light in August* (1932) and *Absalom! Absalom!* (1936). And his most characteristic narrative style, expansive, repetitive, circling on itself, incorporating wide-ranging, multifarious material in long, sustained, heavily loaded sentences, would seem to lend itself above all to the longer form. But he also wrote a large number of short stories or longer tales which, in the eyes of many critics, contain some of his finest achievements. There are forty-two stories in the *Collected Stories* which came out in 1950; in 1979 there appeared a further volume, *Uncollected Stories*, containing several early versions of stories later revised, twelve uncollected stories, and thirteen stories never previously published.[1] In addition there are the stories in *Go Down, Moses* (1942), sometimes seen as a novel but better treated as a cycle of related stories, mainly about the McCaslin family and their neighbours in Jefferson, Yoknapatawpha county, Mississippi, that semi-mythical area in which a great part of Faulkner's fiction is set. Malcolm Cowley, one of Faulkner's most noted critics, has compiled *The Portable Faulkner* (1946), which sets out chronologically some of the most important episodes – short and long stories and parts of novels – from what Cowley calls the Yoknapatawpha 'saga'.

Cowley has argued that Faulkner is 'best . . . and most nearly himself either in long stories like "The Bear" . . . and "Spotted Horses" . . . or else in the Yoknapatawpha saga as a whole. That is, he has beeen most effective in dealing with the total situation always present in his mind as a pattern of the South, or else in short units which . . . have still been shaped by a single conception.'[2] And Irving Howe in his influential study of the writer, quoting the above view, comments that despite its exaggerations Cowley's statement contains the valid insight that 'Faulkner has shown himself master of a certain kind of narrative which lies somewhere between the short story and the novel in length and approach. (He mentions D. H. Lawrence's novellas as a comparison, and had he gone back in time he might have added Henry James).[3] Another critic has rated the stories even more highly, without the proviso that it is the novellas or longer stories that count most. Michael Millgate writes:

> Faulkner is perhaps more consistently at his best in his short stories than he is in the novels, and in his most successful stories we find an intensity of effect, allied with a directness of style and firmness of thematic treatment, which puts them indisputably among his greatest achievements.[4]

The *Collected Stories* of 1950 are divided into six sections: 'I. The Country' (that is, the country round about Jefferson – a fictional town but based closely on Oxford, Mississippi, where Faulkner was brought up); 'II. The Village' (Jefferson itself, in reality a village in the nineteenth century and still small in the first thirty years of the twentieth century, when these stories are mostly set); 'III. The Wilderness', in which the stories go back to the nineteenth century, the time of the Indians and gradual encroachment of white settlers and cotton planters with their African American slaves; 'IV. The Wasteland', stories set in England and France during the First World War; 'V. The Middle Ground', an assortment of stories, mostly set in Mississippi but also elsewhere in the States, ranging in time from the 1860s Jefferson in 'Wash' and 'My Grandmother Millard' to Beverley Hills in the 1940s in 'Golden Land'; and 'VI. Beyond', stories set in various parts of Europe and America, but all dealing in some way with the supernatural or the mysterious. This chapter on Faulkner will use that division as a structure for a consideration of the stories, also drawing on examples from *The Unvanquished* (1938) and *The Hamlet* (1940), two loosely episodic novels which could be regarded as short story cycles, and the already mentioned cycle *Go Down, Moses.*

In the first section of *Collected Stories*, 'The Country', one story stands out. In 'Barn Burning' Abner Snopes, a member of the poor white family which features in a number of Faulkner's stories and novels, sets fire to the barn of the landowner Major de Spain as a revenge for de Spain's threat to dock his wages for dirtying a fine carpet in his house and then failing to get it cleaned properly. The story is told from the point of view of Abner's son, and is an example of a frequent theme in Faulkner's stories, the rebellion against authority. Abner rebels against Major de Spain (as he has already done against a previous employer), and his son rebels against him by warning de Spain against the arson. The story's opening places us immediately in a world dense with strong sense impressions and powerful feelings, with the son sitting in the store in which a justice of the peace is hearing a complaint against Snopes, amidst the tin cans and the smell of cheese:

> this, the cheese which he knew he smelled and the hermetic meat which his intestines believed he smelled coming in intermittent gusts momentary and brief between the other constant one, the smell and sense of just a little fear because mostly of despair and grief, the old fierce pull of blood.

The involved syntax of this is deeply characteristic of Faulkner, in whose writing sense impressions, thoughts and feelings crowd together, mixed with memories and associations that seem to carry with them a whole history – of self, family and larger society – which is present in every moment. 'The old, fierce pull of blood' here is also a presiding image in this story and others, the 'blood' of family and race which pulls the protagonists to their various dooms like a tidal undertow. 'Fire' is another central image, that of the barn burning itself but also carrying a metaphorical charge: 'the element of fire spoke to some deep mainspring of his father's being, as the element of steel or of powder spoke to other men, as the one weapon for the preservation of integrity'. The story focuses on a moment of crisis for Abner which is an even greater crisis for his son – the moment at which he denies his father (another recurrent motif in Faulkner). It builds to a climax of typically Faulknerian power, in which long sentences full of present-tense subordinate clauses ('and he springing up and into the road again, running again, knowing it was too late and yet still running . . .') as the son escapes into the woods thinking his father has been killed give way to the final decisive statement: 'He did not look back.'

Pride – personal, familial, social and racial – that great sin and virtue of the American South and of mankind, is a subject at the core of a number of stories from 'The Village' section in *Collected Stories.* One of the most famous, and notorious, of these is 'A Rose for Emily', a story perhaps all too readily assimilable into the category of 'Southern Gothic'. For although it culminates in a revelation of horror, it does not exist simply for the sake of that horror. Aunt Emily is a revered old lady of Jefferson, and the story is told by an anonymous member of the town, a kind of choric figure who represents its conventional prejudices and respectabilities. In a narrative that moves between present and near-past in section 1, more distant past (Emily's youth and middle age) in sections 2–4 and back to the present in 5, he recalls how Emily became 'a tradition, a duty and a care' for the town after her domineering father died; how she refused to pay taxes and the town authorities could not bring themselves to force her to do so; how a strange smell around her house assumed to be rats had to be dealt with covertly and surreptitiously because, as Judge Stevens said, '"Dammit, sir, will you accuse a lady to her face of smelling bad?"'; and how she had been wooed by a Northern businessman who suddenly disappeared, leaving her looking like 'those angels in coloured church windows, sort of tragic and serene'. The power of the story comes from the contrast between the bland respectfulness of the narrator's tone and the gradual revelation – disguised by the ordering of the narrative – of Aunt Emily's murder of her unfaithful lover, which does not become fully apparent until the last scene in which his decomposing body is found in a bed in her house; the full moral horror of it is withheld until the very last sentence. The story is an emblem of the corruption of Southern pride – the pride of a lady and the pride of the men who helplessly uphold a corrupted code of male chivalry – into a mad obsession of privacy and possessiveness.[5]

Faulkner seems to have used the short story form for episodes from his rich experience of the South which did not find a place in one of his novels but which often contribute to the overall picture of Yoknapatawpha County. The experience of African Americans is a central theme in his novels, and is also the subject of two of the most significant stories from 'The Village'. In 'Dry September' the black Will Mayes is accused, on very little evidence, of the rape of the middle-aged white spinster Minnie Hughes. It is clear from the outset that at least one sympathetic character, the barber Hawkshaw (whose quiet independence and integrity have been established in the otherwise unrelated story 'Hair'), is convinced he did not do it. The crucial elements in the story (what really happened to Minnie, the final lynching of Will) are not presented in the narrative, which proceeds in separate glimpses of the collateral events, and carries all the more weight and horror from this oblique mode of inference, implication and rumour which 'had gone like a fire in dry grass'. The atmosphere of the parched September permeates the story: as the barber leaves to follow the lynching party 'the sparse lights, insect-swirled, glared in rigid and violent suspension in the lifeless air'. On the journey in the car 'they seemed to breathe, live in a bowl of molten lead', and 'where their bodies touched one another they seemed to sweat dryly, for no moisture came'. The final scene finds the lynch-party leader at home, angry with his wife for waiting up, striking her, sweating and panting in the heat, staring out from his porch: 'The dark world seemed to lie stricken beneath the cold moon and the lidless stars.' The last sentence, with its touch of cosmic cold after the persistent heat, clinches both mood and theme of this powerful story, in which the white men are presented as in the grip of a great irrational hatred: the world is 'stricken' with that.

In 'That Evening Sun' (or, in its original version with different character names, 'That Evening Sun Go Down', alluding to the blues song 'I hate to see that evening sun go down') the subject of relations between black and white is less stark, more understated, complicated by the violence of black against black. The story is told by Quentin Compson, a younger member of that family who feature centrally in a number of Faulkner's novels (particularly *The Sound and the Fury* and *Absalom! Absalom!*). He looks back fifteen years to the time he was nine years old, with his sister Caddy (7) and Jason (5). Their Negro cook Nancy is terrified of her husband Jesus, thinks he is going to kill her, and wants to stay at the Compsons' house. Mr Compson is kindly and tries to reassure her but is firm that she should go home. Without telling him Nancy persuades the children to go with her, and at home she tells them stories or sits fearfully 'making that sound again' which is 'singing and not singing'.

The story counterpoints the innocent incomprehension or half-comprehension of the children (together with the incipient racism of the youngest, Jason, who is concerned to make clear to everyone just who is a 'nigger' and the fact that 'I ain't a nigger') with the background of violence – both the violence of Nancy's black husband, and that of the more incidental and casual violence of white against black in the background incident of Nancy's being knocked to the ground and kicked in the face by the bank-clerk because she harasses him for not paying her. It shows the closeness of the children to their black servants (a vitally important element of Southern experience, and a source of the deeply ambivalent combination of love and prejudice in many whites); the limited kindness of the master of the house and Mrs Compson's querulous lack of sympathy. It is a relatively sketch-like and unplotted story – what happens between Nancy and Jesus remains unresolved – but is somehow all the more authentic and vivid for that: a passing episode that impresses the reader with a sense of the complex mingling of elements in Southern life.

A story like 'That Evening Sun' achieves its success through a new mode of realism that in its focus on small detailed scenes and use of dialogue may owe something to Hemingway. But a number of Faulkner's stories derive from a tradition that goes back through Crane and Bierce to Twain and the frontier story-tellers, the tradition of the tall tale, which uses comedy, farce and outrageous incident to make its point. At the same time the tall tale in Faulkner is almost never totally divorced from the realistic (though it may be from formal realism), and the tension between the two is a measure of the nature of the experience of the deep South. Two other stories from 'The Village' illustrate this. In 'Death Drag' a team of daredevil stunt airmen appear out of the sky in Jefferson, and proceed to enthral the town as much by their desperate bid for money and their crazily self-destructive quarrelling as by their daredevil skill. 'Mule in the Yard' is a cross between a one-act farce and a rococo sketch in which Mrs Hait and her black female servant old Het chase an escaped mule which proceeds to cause mayhem. The rococo element is there in the style, which adds to the chaos of the farce by loading it with grotesque or absurdly minute detail. As Mrs Hait runs out into the yard, the narrative suspends itself to note her physical appearance, 'calico wrapper', 'sweater coat', her deceased husband's felt hat, and even her man's 'high shoes which buttoned, with toes like small tulip bulbs, and in the town they knew she had bought them new for herself'.

The farce and tall tale are there in the action: the mule rushes round and round the house, each time chasing a rooster and eight chickens which run under the house from one side to another, colliding with the mule each time; finally it knocks over bucket of live coals which has been set in the entrance to the cellar. The house burns down; Mrs Hait shoots the mule; and then offers $10 to its owner, Flem Snopes: $10 being the difference between the $60 Snopes used to claim for mules killed on the railroad line and the $50 he used to give Mr Hait for helping him to drive them on to the line. The issue of money – usually made by nefarious means, but sometimes (as in 'Hair', also from section II) the measure of integrity – is central to the Southern idea of justice.

Flem Snopes is a recurring figure in Faulkner's world – a 'low born' horse-trader who stands for toughness, vulgarity, and a kind of mysterious anarchic ruthlessness. 'Mule in the Yard' is in fact a simpler version of one of Faulkner's short fiction masterpieces, 'Spotted Horses' (from *The Hamlet*),[6] in which Snopes and an unnamed Texan bring a herd of untameable, uncatchable wild ponies to Frenchman's Bend, and proceed to sell them, causing injury, one death and general chaos. The wild comedy of the story arises from the chaos caused by the horses, but also from the laconic ruthlessness of Snopes, the unfazeability of the Texan and bemusement of the townsmen, stirred to grudging defensive wit by the spectacle before them. The Texan seizes one horse by its neck and nostrils and says, 'veins standing white and rigid along his neck an across his jaw': 'See, all you got to do is handle them a little and work hell out of them for a couple of days', and then springs back:

> As he did so, a second horse slashed at his back, severing vest from collar to hem down the back, as exactly as the trick swordsman severs a floating veil with one stroke.
>
> 'Sho now,' Quick said. 'But suppose a man doesn't happen to own a vest.'

The story becomes an epic struggle between the forces of animal anarchy, silently overseen by the Machiavellian Snopes, and the town's vain attempts to salvage some sort of justice from the ensuing mayhem. What stays in the mind above all are Faulkner's descriptions, both realistic (he knows every technical detail of horses and horse-dealers)[7] and mythical, of the horses themselves. They are a sheer anarchic force, at one point 'gaudy and motionless and alert, wild as deer, deadly as rattlesnakes, quiet as doves', at another 'like phantom fish, suspended apparently without legs now in the brilliant treachery of the moon', at another surging 'in short, huddling rushes' and finally breaking out, 'a gaudy vomit of long wild faces and splotched chests which overtook and scattered [the men] and flung them sprawling aside'. Out of the struggle between man and this force of nature Faulkner has created, in startling and powerful prose, a small comic and epic masterpiece.

'The Wilderness' section in *Collected Stories* consists of four stories about the 'Indian' or Native American settlements in Yoknapatawpha County in the first half of the nineteenth century. It is significant however that Faulkner does not make the precise chronology clear (as Cowley does, as far as possible, in *The Portable Faulkner*). Time in Faulkner's world is fluid: names and situations repeat themselves from generation to generation; the present is often inextricable from the past and the future contained in both. In the Native American world in particular we seem to inhabit a different kind of time to that of modern civilization, a time which is governed by repetition and recurrence. As one of the Native Americans says in 'Red Leaves', 'Tomorrow is just another name for today.' The four stories are all concerned in some way with ritual or legal decision: turning points in the life of the community. In 'A Justice' Quentin Compson looks back across two generations, re-telling the story told to him by Sam Fathers (illegitimate son of a Chickasaw father and an African American mother). It is a complex chronicle which relates the conflict between Sam's Native American father and his mother's African American husband, the coming of the steamboat which, run aground, becomes the tribal chiefs' house, and the poisoning of the chief Old Issetibbeha. As a 'short story' it cannot be called successful: rather, it is like a confused but suggestive piece of oral history, full of vivid glimpses of a complex world. The most successful and powerful Native American story is 'Red Leaves', the tale of the burial rites of the dead chief Issetibbeha and the hunt for the black slave who is to be sacrificed, according to custom, with the dead chief. This drama occupies the foreground in sections I, III, V and VI; sections II and IV go back in time to Issetibbeha's earlier history (with glimpses of odd details – like the clothes and red shoes he brings back from Paris – which evoke the cultural complexity of the Native American community) and the scene of his death. The primary drama, however, is a tragic study of the fate of the Native Americans' black slave. The oppression and squalor of the slave quarters in the camp is powerfully evoked (the slaves in their dark cabin are 'like the roots of a huge tree uncovered, the earth broken momentarily upon the writhen, thick, fetid tangle of its lightless and outraged life'), but at the same time the presentation is impartial, not condemning the Native American oppressors. And the half-hearted attempt of the doomed slave to escape is given all the more pathos – even a sense of tragedy – by the grotesque terror of the slave and the calm dignity of the Native Americans. In the final scene they catch up with him, give him water, and wait while he drinks: 'They waited, patient, grave, decorous, implacable. Then the water ceased, though the still empty gourd tilted higher and higher, and still his black throat aped the vain motion of his frustrated swallowing.' Faulkner's attitude to the social question of race is a matter of controversy (he has been criticized for his explicit public stance of gradualism: the feeling that integration should be taken slowly and left to the Southern community). But his presentation as an artist of the complexity of racial issues, his sense of history and his intense feeling for the life of those characters he depicts (whether Native American, African American or white), is both powerful and humane.

The most notable stories in the fifth section of *Collected Stories* are all concerned in different ways with extremes of behaviour driven by the sense of personal or family honour. (The section's title is somewhat obscure, but seems to refer to the 'middle ground' between North and South, between classes, and between masculinity and femininity.) In 'Mountain Victory' a Confederate officer and his black servant, on their way home at the end of the Civil War, ask for refuge in a Yankee household. The owner gives them food and whisky but says they must move on. The officer insists on staying in the barn because his servant gets too drunk to travel, and the young son of the household (in a rebellion against his father and the ethic of violence and revenge which is reminiscent of the son's actions in 'Barn Burning') tries to warn the officer of a coming ambush when they leave, but the officer refuses to turn back. He is killed, and in the last sentence the black servant is at bay, facing death: 'The Negro's eyes rushed wild and steady and red, like those of a cornered animal.' The theme of the younger generation turning against the culture of violence of their elders is also central to a story from *The Unvanquished*, 'An Odor of Verbena'. The young Bayard Sartoris is called upon to avenge his father's murder by J. B. Redmond, a political and business rival. His stepmother Drusilla gives him a sprig of verbena (which she says is 'the only scent you could smell above the smell of horses and courage') as a token of honour, but becomes hysterical when she senses he is not going to kill Redmond. The next day he walks into Redmond's office unarmed and lets Redmond fire at him twice: Redmond misses (deliberately) and leaves Jefferson never to return. Drusilla has also left town, but before he too leaves Bayard finds on his pillow a sprig of verbena, implicit token of Drusilla's recognition of his courage. The story is dense with the physical atmosphere of the South, but also with the oppressive weight of the past and the names and events of family history. As with Joyce's Stephen Daedalus, history for Faulkner's younger heroes (and frequently one feels for Faulkner himself) is a nightmare from which they are trying to awake.

One final group of stories which deserves more attention than it usually gets is section VI of *Collected Stories*, 'Beyond'. The title points to the 'beyond' of the abnormal and the supernatural, which figures in the stories in a variety of ways (including one comic story, 'Divorce in Naples', about the 'marriage' relationship of two sailors). In 'Mistral' a pair of young American men on a walking holiday in Northern Italy become aware of a strange drama of murder and forbidden love taking place in the village where they stop for the night. A young girl, the ward of the local priest – about whose relationship with her there are dark rumours – was about to get married, but her rich, respectable fiancé has been murdered. Her former lover has just been demobbed and has returned to the village, and the priest (in whose house the young men stay) is disturbed and agitated. When they leave the village the next night they hear a whimpering sound, and over a stone wall in a field they see the priest, lying on the ground with his robes over his head, talking to himself and '[s]huddering, writhing, twisting from side to side'; beyond they see a copse, and the young lover's bicycle. There is a subtle tension in the story between the sharp, flippant exchanges of the two Americans and the dark atmosphere of windy cold ('the unimpeded rush of the mistral, that black chill wind full of dust like sparks of ice') and the secret drama in the town, an atmosphere quite different from anything in Faulkner's American stories. And the tension conveys not only the violent mystery of the plot, but also the keen apprehension of the protagonists and the way the mind is drawn towards horror and passion, 'the secret nostalgic sense of frustration, and objectless and unappeasable desire'.

'The Leg' is an even stranger story, this time overtly supernatural, and one about which critical disagreement is likely to be marked. The story involves the friendship of two young men in Oxford (England) just before and during the first world war, the murder of a Thames lock-keeper's daughter whom they once met in a comic and idyllic scene early in the action, and the strange irrational guilt that comes to haunt the narrator. The latter loses a leg during the war; and the lost leg becomes the focus of a bizarre sexual obsession, in which it is associated with the seduction and murder of the young woman. Clearly, it becomes a kind of Freudian substitution for the phallus, a metonymy for murderous sexual desire. Extraordinarily (given this weird plot) the story, in Faulkner's telling, achieves a powerful psychological charge. In a field hospital, the narrator is shown a photograph of himself at a place near the scene of the crime – marked with a dedication to the murdered girl, 'an unprintable phrase', and a date on which he was in fact in France. He comes to see the lost leg as representing a kind of *alter ego*, the alien murderer who appears as 'vicious and outrageous and unappalled' in the photograph; and he tells his friend 'to find [the leg] and kill it'. In the closing paragraphs of realization, guilt and resolve, Faulkner's prose has a remarkable intensity:

> [Y]et it was my own face, and I sat holding the picture quietly in my hand while the candle flame stood high and steady above the wick and on the wall my shadow held the motionless photograph. In slow and gradual diminishment of cold tears the candle appeared to sink, as though burying itself in its own grief. But even before this came about, it began to pale and fade until only the tranquil husk of the small flame stood unwinded as a feather above the wax, leaving upon the wall the motionless husk of my own shadow.

A few lines later the last paragraph reads:

> I told him to find it and kill it. The dawn was cold; on these mornings the butt of the leg felt as though it were made of ice. I told him to. I told him.

'The Leg' must be one of the strangest and most powerful supernatural stories ever written, a kind of Freudian dream-narrative, with its symbolic substitutions; and the quality of the writing (as in that penultimate paragraph) ensures that the bizarre plot carries conviction. Its mingling of romantic idyll and horror, sexual desire and the violence and mental disturbance of war, touches on deep psychological fears and compulsions.

These final stories in Faulkner's *Collected Stories* testify to the extraordinary range and power of his imagination. As a chronicler of the American South alone his achievement would be secure, even if one confined oneself to the novels. But the overflow of his creativity into the prolific and protean intensities of the tales confirms our sense of his variety and fecundity, and confirms his classic status in twentieth-century American literature.

Chapter 17

Katherine Anne Porter, Eudora Welty and Flannery O'Connor

Katherine Anne Porter

From the 1920s to the 1950s there was a remarkable flowering of the Southern short story in the work of three writers: Katherine Anne Porter (1890–1980), Eudora Welty (1909–) and Flannery O'Connor (1925–64). Katherine Anne Porter came originally from Texas, from a family with illustrious Southern roots. She saw herself above all as a writer of short stories, publishing five main volumes: *Flowering Judas* (1930), *Flowering Judas and Other Stories* (1935), *Pale Horse, Pale Rider* (1939, three longer stories or novellas, comprising the title story, 'Old Mortality' and 'Noon Wine'), *The Leaning Tower and Other Stories* (1944) and *The Old Order.* Her *Collected Stories* were published in 1964. Her single novel, *The Ship of Fools*, by contrast took her over twenty-five years to write, and did not appear until 1965.

In *Flowering Judas* the title story draws on Porter's experience of Mexican revolutionaries in the 1920s. It is a portrait of a chaste young woman (based on an Irish girl Porter knew) who dutifully helps with the revolution but is averse to the blandishments of the overweight, self-indulgent leader Braggioni (who sings to her, excruciatingly, accompanying himself on his guitar) and holds herself conscientiously aloof from him. The predominant tone seems to be sardonic, but it is complicated by a strain of romantic longing in the heroine who at the end dreams of escaping with a young prisoner she has been visiting in the local jail: the dream turns into a nightmare of death and sacramental murder, as she eats the petals of the Judas tree outside her window and the young prisoner calls her 'murderer' and 'cannibal'. Ultimately the effect of the story seems uncertain, since the irony is not marked enough for satire and at the same time neither the girl's revolutionary idealism nor her suppressed passions are ever made very substantial. A more successful story from this collection is 'The Jilting of Granny Weatherall', which with sharp humour and sense of tragedy gives us the stream of consciousness of an old woman nearing death, whose memories of marriage and her several children are ultimately overridden by the painful memory of being jilted on her wedding day by her first lover, and whose last moments of consciousness are also denied any word or sign: 'Again no bridegroom, and the priest in the house.' The other stories in this collection are notable for their variety, but the shorter ones are more successful than the longer. 'The Martyr' is a light but nicely judged satire on Rubén, 'the most illustrious painter in Mexico'; 'Virgin Violeta', a brief but subtle study of a young girl's first sexual encounter (a kiss) with an overbearing older cousin; and 'He', the sad story of woman's love for her retarded son. This last story, like the very different 'Rope', is notable for its use of free indirect discourse (see p. 146 above), which allows for a combination of the points of view of the character (s) and the narrator, comic in the case of 'Rope' and full of pathos in 'He'.

Porter's arguably most successful volume of stories is *Pale Horse, Pale Rider*, which consists of three long stories (Porter herself called them short novels), the title story, 'Noon Wine' and 'Old Mortality'. The first is a study of a young woman's experience, in a New York setting of wartime love and loss: a presentation of consciousness and impressions reminiscent of Virginia Woolf. The young woman just escapes death from influenza, but her lover succumbs to it. The title comes from a Negro spiritual about death, a song that the woman and her lover sing together at one point in the story, and the motif broods over the whole. There is a use of dream sequences and fleeting impressions, and the story achieves an atmosphere of youth, buoyant and doomed. But despite its celebrity (due no doubt partly to the strong title) and its modernist technique, it is finally less memorable than the other two in the collection.

'Noon Wine' is a powerful and haunting story of the mystery of sanity and insanity, tolerance and intolerance, banality and crime, in a mode close to what was soon to be identified (though often misleadingly) as 'Southern Gothic'. A farmer's fortunes improve substantially when he takes on a Swedish farmhand: the latter works hard, speaks scarcely at all, and in his rare moments of rest plays a single tune on one of his prized harmonicas. After nine years the farmer's new life of prosperity is shattered when a man arrives claiming that the Swede is an escaped lunatic who has murdered his own brother, and who should be returned to the asylum. This man, Mr Hatch, is a powerful study of evil disguised as law-abiding orthodoxy: his brutal aggressiveness, masked by a hard, relentless, wisecracking bonhomie, is brilliantly done (one memorable touch is his habit of congratulatorily shaking hands with himself when he has made a joke). In the climactic scene the farmer, thinking Mr Hatch is going to stab the Swede, kills him with the blow of an axe. He is acquitted, but his guilt compels him to travel round the country trying to justify himself to his neighbours; his sons finally turn against him when they think he is threatening their mother; and the story ends with his suicide. In her essay '"Noon Wine": the Sources' Porter relates how the story began from her experience of three unrelated scenes. As a small child, she heard the cry of a man being murdered, a sound which was never explained to her. Some years later, there was a couple sitting in a buggy outside her house; she heard the man say '"I swear, it was in self-defence! His life or mine! If you don't believe me ask my wife here. She saw it. My wife won't lie!"', to which the wife, 'without lifting her head or moving', had replied 'in a low voice, "Yes, that's right I saw it."' Another day, she saw 'a bony, awkward, tired-looking man' with 'bleached hair' sitting with his back against a run-down shack, playing the harmonica, 'the very living image of loneliness'. It is a good example both of how the short story writer frequently starts from suggestive images or scenes, and how fiction can combine unrelated experiences into a new whole.

The third long story in this collection, 'Old Mortality', deals with the childhood and youth of its protagonist Miranda, and the complex set of Southern family relations in which she is enmeshed. The most striking things about the story are its power to evoke memory and past time, and its range of human sympathy. In the third and last part the now adult Miranda is journeying back by train for an uncle's funeral, and she meets Cousin Eva, an 'old maid' and active suffragette who has previously been regarded during Miranda's childhood as a figure of fun though also of pathos, 'shy and chinless, straining her upper lip over two enormous teeth'. Now in the train conversation we see things from Cousin Eva's point of view; Miranda too sees her afresh as a vigorous, witty, sharp-tongued middle-aged woman, and realizes the justice of her mastered but still intensely felt bitterness at the unthinking cruelty of her parents and siblings. The story covers some twenty-seven years, but succeeds as a novella because of its focus on three quite separate time periods specified in the titles to each section: 1885–1902, 1904 and 1912. The close focus on particular moments gives a vivid sense of each, and the connection and contrast between them gives us a sharp perspective on the passing of time.

Porter's last volume of stories, *The Leaning Tower*, is perhaps less notable overall than the others, though the title story shows something of her variety and range, with its treatment of the youthful aspirations, high spirits and gloomy forebodings of a male student protagonist and his German and

Polish fellow lodgers in a *pension* in Berlin. The sequence of stories entitled 'The Old Order' has been praised, particularly the final story, 'The Grave', in which a young girl first experiences birth and death when she and her brother find a silver coffin-ornament and a dead rabbit with unborn baby rabbits inside it, in the now unoccupied family graveyard.[1] Porter's acute sensitivity to the dramatic moments in a child's life, however outwardly slight, and her power of symbolic suggestion are both illustrated here. The memory is brought back one day years later by seeing some confectionery animals in an Indian market, and, in a Proustian moment, the past is redeemed:

> Instantly upon this thought the dreadful vision faded, and she saw clearly her brother, whose childhood face she had forgotten, standing again in the blazing sunshine, again twelve years old, a pleased sober smile in his eyes, turning the silver dove over and over in his hands.

Eudora Welty

Eudora Welty was a great admirer of the short stories of Katherine Anne Porter, and what she saw as Porter's power of inner vision or 'the eye of the story'.[2] She herself is a writer who begins perhaps even more than Porter from the visual sense. She was also a professional photographer, and worked for the US government's Works Progress Administration, documenting poverty, mainly among the black population, in Mississippi.[3] In interviews she spoke of how her stories often began with her vision of particular scenes: of the station waiting-room in 'The Key' or the garden in 'A Curtain of Green'. She told how 'A Worn Path' took its inspiration from a moment on a journey with a landscape painter, watching an old African American woman walk slowly across her line of vision from one side of the landscape to the other: 'I knew she was bent on an errand, even at that distance. It was not anything casual. It was a purposeful, measured journey that she was making.' From this grew the story of an old woman making the long journey to town on foot to buy medicine for her sick grandson. Once again, the short story writer begins from one suggestive image. In *One Writer's Beginnings* Welty also tells of her acute responsiveness to sounds and smells (the ticking and chiming clocks in her parents' house, the 'sharpened yellow pencil and the cup of the daffodil' giving off 'whiffs just alike' in the schoolroom).[4] Along with this went a distinctive feeling for the physical quality of individual words: watching the moon as a small child, at the moment in the evening when it changed from 'flat' to 'round', 'The word "moon" came into my mouth as though fed to me out of a silver spoon. Held in my mouth, the moon became a word.'[5] More than any other American short story writer of the twentieth century, Welty's sensibility is that of a poet.

Across her career, Eudora Welty published three collections of individual stories – *A Curtain of Green and Other Stories* (1941), *The Wide Net and Other Stories* (1943) and *The Bride of the Innisfallen* (1955) – and a sequence of related stories, *The Golden Apples* (1949). The latter is an interesting experiment in the genre of short story cycle that includes Jewett's *The Country of the Pointed Firs* and Anderson's *Winesburg, Ohio*, but her most distinctive contribution to the short story probably lies in the other three volumes.

A Curtain of Green is a remarkable first collection, and in its intensity and variety arguably her best. Particularly characteristic of her stories is her feeling for the odd and the outlandish within ordinary settings (village, town and family life), where the oddity is revelatory of some central human impulse or condition. So, for example, she can deal memorably with the experience of violence or near-violence in ways that reveal its psychological workings from within. In 'A Piece of News' Ruby Fisher, drying herself in front of the fire of her cabin after being out in a storm, becomes dreamily fascinated by a newspaper story about another Ruby Fisher who was shot in the leg by her husband. The identity of the two names leads her to a kind of romantically masochistic wish-fulfilling dream that her own husband Clyde (who does indeed 'slap' her for going with other men) had shot her, and the newspaper story is about her. When Clyde returns, their bemusement at the idea causes them both to flush 'as though with a double shame and a double pleasure'. And the poetic consonance of inner and outer worlds – with the storm and its languorous aftermath mirroring the internal passion of the protagonist – is finely done, as in the final evocative image: Ruby stands by the window 'until everything, outside and in, was quieted . . . It was dark and vague outside. The storm had rolled away to faintness like a wagon crossing a bridge.' In 'Petrified Man' a woman's hairdressing salon is the setting for a raucously vulgar conversation about a wanted rapist discovered hiding as a 'petrified man' (his bones supposedly turning to stone) in a circus freak-show. The bizarre central image is symbolic of the inhumanity of rape itself, of the henpecked husbands of the speakers, and perhaps of the callousness (though they have a wonderful energy, too) of the scandalized women. In 'Flowers for Marjorie' (another story of deep sexual conflict) an unemployed man is driven to mania by his desperate state, and kills his pregnant wife out of a kind of mad hatred of her sheer physical, mindless fecundity. The man's state of mind, especially his dislocated sense of time, is conveyed through his vivid sensory impressions which also carry symbolic suggestions, like the objects in the shop windows – the slowly made doughnuts, the coloured prints of the virgin Mary, the imitation heart – and above all the flowers that recur in the story, which come to suggest his wife's body and sexual attraction itself. (In the last lines of the story he drops the roses he has been carrying home, and 'little girls ran up and put them stealthily in their hair'.) In 'A Curtain of Green', on the other hand, nature prevents rather than prompts a murder, when the coming of rain gently stops Mrs Larkin from killing her young black gardener in a fit of mad depression or despair after husband's accidental death.

Welty's sense of human strangeness also emerges in a recurring element of sly humour. In 'Lily Daw and the Three Ladies' Mrs Watts, Mrs Carson (with her 'sad voice, sad as the soft noises in the hen house at twilight') and Mrs Slocum are anxious to get simple-minded Lily Daw sent to the Institute for the Feeble-Minded at Ellisville, though at her best she 'can be a lady' (at the local tent show, says one, 'She was a perfect lady – just set [sat] in her seat and stared'). They are scandalized to discover she has been walking out with a xylophone player from a visiting band and says she is going to marry him, and they lure her with gifts to persuade her to go to the institute ('"What if I was to give you a pink crepe de Chine brassière with adjustable shoulder straps" asked Mrs Watts grimly'). But at the train station the xylophone player appears, and in an inspired change of tactics the ladies decide to make him meet his responsibilities. The mixture of mild pathos and comedy (with an emphasis on the latter, since the story ends with a marriage and we feel Lily has got her way) is typical of Welty's sense of life, and the short story form is perfect for its glancing but penetrating insight. The story is also typical of her preoccupation with the relation between eccentric outsiders and conventional society.

In 'Why I live at the P. O.', one of her most comic stories, the narrator is a forceful and garrulous young woman, Sister, who earns the money and does most of the work in a eccentric and bickering family: a family made up of a spoiled unmarried sister (Stella-Rondo), abandoned by her lover Mr Whitaker and left with a young child, a self-pitying mother, an ageing 'Papa-Daddy' and Uncle Rondo, who dresses up in Stella-Rondo's 'flesh-coloured kimono'. The comedy comes from the bickering, mainly between the narrator and the others (and largely about the origin of Stella-Rondo's baby, whom she and her mother insist is adopted, while the narrator has other very plausible ideas about Mr Whitaker), and from the robustly practical tone of the narrator in the midst of her eccentric relatives. Katherine Anne Porter, in a review of *A Curtain of Green*, oddly sees the narrator as 'a terrifying case of dementia praecox', presumably misled by her headlong, 'one-sided' self-justifications and drastic actions and the bitter arguments she stirs up in the family.[6] And although several commentators have persisted in stressing Sister's unreliability or mental instability, Eudora Welty herself commented: 'It never occurred to me while I was writing the story (and it still doesn't) that I was writing about someone in serious mental trouble.' It can be argued that Sister is actually the sanest character in the story, and that her refuge in the post office gives her a justified independence, and a satisfying comic victory over her censorious family.[7]

Welty's sympathies are evenly balanced between the eccentric and the conventional (she once wrote that of all literary virtues she most valued the 'act of a writer's imagination' in trying to enter 'the mind, heart, and skin of a human being who is not myself') but in these two stories and elsewhere her sympathies tend to be with the social outsider. In 'Clytie' she focuses on the state of mind of a dreamy, father- and sister-dominated old maid, who looks in vain at other faces to find some echo of her feelings and ends by staring at her own in a water-butt, falling in and drowning. In 'Keela, the Outcast Indian Maiden' she tells the horrifying story of a little black man who was cruelly used in a circus freak-show and now, though prevented by his embarrassed children, seems cheerfully ready to talk about his ordeal. The focus of this story, however, is the mind of the 'poor white' who is trying to make clear to himself, and get across to a friend, the enormity of the black man's ordeal. It is, therefore, as much a study of the struggle between reason and prejudice as a story of bizarre cruelty.

Another highly original study of racial perception is 'Powerhouse', the story of a black jazz singer reputedly based on the real-life Fats Waller. It is perhaps the best fictional study of a jazz artist by a white writer: what is so striking about it is its sense of vitality and energy, and the mixture of common humanity and strangeness. The narrator (by implication white) is amazed and enthralled by the otherness of Powerhouse, in a portrait that might seem to steer close to the wind of racism ('"Negro man"? – he looks more Asiatic, monkey, Jewish, Babylonian, Peruvian, fanatic, devil') but triumphantly avoids it. The point is that Powerhouse *is* strange to the white onlooker, strange and wonderful. The combination of animal power and witty humanity in his performance is a new phenomenon for the white audience. At the same time we see Powerhouse slyly constructing his own image both for his white audience and for his black colleagues: in the performance interval we see him concocting a humorous anecdote about his private life which keeps us and them guessing about its relation to reality. As well as evoking the effect of his music, the story is a study of life as performance, and the ambiguous complications of entrapment and empowerment that involves.

Flannery O'Connor

If the short story is above all the narrative genre of turning point, Flannery O'Connor (1925–64) has a claim to be the exemplary American short story writer of the twentieth century. Her vision is a religious one and her stories deal almost exclusively with spiritual crisis. Two statements she made about her writing may serve to indicate two important aspects of its nature. In relation to the idea of vision, she wrote: 'For the writer of fiction everything has its turning point in the eye, and the eyes are the organ that eventually involves the whole personality.'[8] And on the topic of religion: 'The idea that reality is something we must be returned to at considerable cost . . . is implicit in the Christian view of the world.'[9] So her subject is religious revelation and her method is precise visualization. Her mode is also predominantly that of 'romance' and the grotesque: she once said she felt more kinship with Nathaniel Hawthorne than with any other American writer (though she also admitted, with amused apology, the influence of Poe).[10] Strange and violent experience is central to her work, not for its own sake, but for the harsh and salutary spiritual lessons it can convey.

O'Connor published two volumes of short stories, *A Good Man Is Hard To Find* (1955) and *Everything That Rises Must Converge* (1965); *The Complete Stories* appeared in 1971. Nearly all her best stories appeared in the first two collections (included, of course, in the last). From the age of twenty-five she suffered from the wasting disease lupus, and she died at the age of thirty-nine; so her career was sadly a short one, and apart from a few apprentice-stage stories in the late 1940s her preoccupations and style show a strong consistency across the years.

O'Connor once said that her subject in fiction was 'the violent action of grace, in territory held largely by the devil',[11] and nowhere is this better exemplified than the title story from her first collection, 'A Good Man Is Hard To Find'. The story is also typical in its satirical treatment of modern family life and the conflict between generations. It describes a holiday car journey by the Bailey family from their home in Atlanta towards Florida; but they never reach their destination because the car runs into a ditch in dark and remote woods, and they encounter an escaped convict and his two sons, who shoot them dead because the grandmother recognizes the man as 'The Misfit' from a story she has read in the newspaper. There is sharp comedy in the treatment of banal family life (that familiar scene of tension, the car journey) in the early stages of the story – the dull Bailey, his wife with a face 'broad and innocent as a cabbage', the brattish, ill-behaved children, and the smartly dressed, bright and talkative grandmother who infuriates them all with her 'helpful' advice and observations along the way: she also insists on bringing her cat, whose antics cause the car accident. The Misfit is chillingly calm and philosophical and his thuggish sons are conveyed in a few telling details and lines of dialogue (O'Connor has a mastery of Southern dialect and an ear for the revelatory phrase). But the crux of the story lies in the final conversation between the grandmother and the Misfit: he tells of his experience in the penitentiary and his sense of injustice (he calls himself the Misfit 'because I can't make what all I done wrong fit what all I gone through in punishment'). He is also tormented by his lack of Christian belief, and by the idea that if he had only been able to witness the Resurrection he would not be like he is. Listening to him the grandmother, in spite of her terror, is moved to a sudden moment of compassion and reaches out to touch him; whereupon 'the Misfit sprang back as though a snake had bitten him and shot her three times through the chest'. His final comment on her is '"She would of been a good woman . . . if it had been somebody there to shoot her every minute of her life."' As O'Connor pointed out with mild reproach in a reply to a university professor who had written to her with his class's (wildly eccentric) reading of the story, the story 'is not meant to be realistic in the sense that it portrays the everyday doings of people in Georgia' and that 'It is stylized and its conventions are comic.' But even with the advent of the Misfit 'there is no lessening of reality'.[12] And perhaps the most striking thing about the story is the way it convinces us of its reality while giving us a powerful parable of good and evil, and of the 'action of grace' in a mode of the tragicomic grotesque.

The figure of the grandmother in 'A Good Man Is Hard To Find' is typical of a strikingly recurring theme in O'Connor's stories: the conflict between parents – usually mothers – and unmarried grown-up children (usually sons), often living at home. O'Connor herself lived with her mother in Milledgeville, Georgia, for most of her life: she seems to have kept a good and loving relationship with her, but the intergenerational tensions that run through her stories are doubtless closely related to her personal experience. And what is most notable about the treatment of this theme is the author's sympathy for the usually exasperating parental figures – for the most part old-fashioned and highly conservative – in their conflict with their more liberal and progressive offspring.

In 'Everything That Rises Must Converge' the grown-up Julian is exasperated by his mother's snobbery and reactionary views, particularly about race. But his own self-righteous liberalism is even less sympathetic. As he takes his mother on a bus to the local YMCA 'reducing class' his awkward attempts to talk to a middle-class African American are shown up as pretentious and condescending; and his vindictive delight when he sees a black woman wearing an identical hat to his mother's is short-lived when he realizes his mother is not discomfited but simply amused. And when the black woman (from the first seething with some unexplained anger) strikes his mother when she tries to give a coin to her child, the ensuing catastrophe brings him an intense and belated realization of love and remorse. In 'The Enduring Chill' the grown-up son Asbury, a would-be writer and intellectual, is contemptuous of his mother's attitudes to her religion and to her black farmhands. But his high-falutingly 'progressive' attitude to the first, and his childish rebellion in trying to fraternize with the second (encouraging them to smoke in the milk shed and drinking the unpasteurized milk against her rules), are taught a harsh lesson when he catches 'undulant fever', and in his fearful and debilitated state has one of those religious revelations characteristic of O'Connor's fictional climaxes. As he lies in bed, self-pityingly and mistakenly thinking he is going to die, the eagle-shaped mark on the wall above his bed, a source of fear in childhood, becomes to his feverish eye an image of the Holy Ghost. He realizes he will live 'frail, racked but enduring ... in the face of a purifying terror', as he watches 'the fierce bird': 'the Holy Ghost, emblazoned in ice instead of fire, continued, implacable, to descend'.

There are some wonderfully comic moments in the two stories just discussed – the business with the hat in the first, or the scenes between the pretentious Asbury and a down-to-earth Irish priest or the embarrassed and awkward farmhands in the second – but the comedy is always at the service of a penetrating moral vision. In 'Good Country People' there is again comedy of the grotesque in the situation of a farm-owning mother's intellectual grown-up daughter, who, having lost a leg after an illness, calculatingly decides to seduce a seemingly naive young Bible salesman but is outwitted by his streak of devilish anarchic humour. (He steals her artificial leg.) The reader may feel at first that the story's attitude to the daughter is uncomfortably harsh: but in the light of O'Connor's own experience as an intellectual invalid who has stayed at home with her mother, one realizes, with something of a shock, that the crippled daughter is a version of herself. O'Connor's comic and moral vision is here unsparingly, uncomfortably, self-critical.

One criticism that has sometimes been conceded even by O'Connor's admirers is that her stories all tend to have the same kind of subject and cover a limited range of experience. Indeed, to read several O'Connor stories in succession (particularly for the first time) is to experience a growing tension from about the middle of each story as one steels oneself for the almost inevitably violent climax. But her command of the short story form, her poetic eye for visual detail and ear for revelatory speech, and her powerful moral vision make her *oeuvre* one of the most remarkable of the twentieth century. And within the boundaries of her predominant concern with individual salvation she is also an astute commentator on some of the most pressing social issues of her time, particularly that of race, though in ways not always comforting to modern liberal sensibilities.

In 'Everything That Rises Must Converge' the title is a highly ironic application of a 'physical proposition' of the theologian Teilhard de Chardin:[13] in the story Julian's mother and the black woman converge in the most violent way. The story, as we have seen, also takes a satirical attitude towards Julian's self-righteous liberalism. In 'Judgment Day' Tanner, an old white man from Georgia who moves up to New York to live with his daughter, is unable to understand the cold, uncommunicative relations between white and black neighbours in the apartment block, and is set on the idea of being buried down South, when he dies, by his black friend Coleman. He is eventually attacked by a black neighbour when he addresses him, in old-style Southern mode, with would-be friendly racist banter. But perhaps the most subtle and revealing moment in the story is a flashback to the scene when, as a white farmer in Georgia, he first took on Coleman as a farmhand: a moment of potential violence is defused when he jokingly fashions a pair of steel spectacles for Coleman to wear, and Coleman plays along with the joke. Suddenly Tanner 'had an instant's sensation of seeing before him a negative image of himself, as if clownishness and captivity had been their common lot'. The motif of the double often arises in O'Connor's stories (the two identical hats in 'Everything That Rises' is another example), and as here it usually connotes a perception of similarity between opposites, a common fate shared between both sides of a political or social divide.

Because O'Connor's vision is above all a religious one, she sees political and social conflict in a larger (though some would say narrower) perspective of individual salvation. And this makes her treatment of racial conflict sometimes problematic, though always challenging. 'An Artificial Nigger', which she once said was her favourite story, tells of how Mr Head takes his grandson Nelson for a visit to the city, in the hope that once he had seen it he would never want to go again. On the train journey he mocks Nelson for not recognizing that one of the other passengers is 'a nigger'. In the city itself they get lost in a black district, and Nelson is fascinated by the half-maternal half-sexual allure of a big black woman in a doorway. Mr Head hides from Nelson as a practical joke, and when in his ensuing panic Nelson knocks over an elderly woman and is stopped by a policeman, Mr Head momentarily loses his nerve and denies any connection with him. In a moment he loses all authority over the boy and all his love and respect, and is reduced to despair. Trying to find the railway station, they suddenly find themselves face to face with the 'artificial nigger' itself: a garden statuette of a Negro (common in the racist South), its chipped face giving it 'a wild look of misery'. And the sight acts as a revelation:

> They stood gazing at the artificial Negro as if they were faced with some great mystery, some monument to another's victory that brought them together in their common defeat. They could both feel it dissolving their differences like an action of mercy.

They return home, and Mr Head 'feels the action of mercy touch him again'. 'He saw that no sin was too monstrous for him to claim as his own, and since God loved in proportion as he forgave, he felt ready at that instant to enter Paradise.' For his part, Nelson delivers his judgement on the city they have visited: 'I'm glad I've went once, but I'll never go back again.'

The story is a parable of religious salvation, a brilliant combination of realistic detail and symbolic suggestion. (The opening paragraph describing Mr Head's bedroom just before dawn is a typical example of O'Connor's power of charging precisely seen details with symbolic overtones.) But for interpretation and judgement the story presents a compelling problem. The figure of the artificial Negro is meant as a figure of universal suffering: O'Connor once wrote that she was trying to show, in this story, 'the redemptive quality of the Negro's suffering for us all'. And one might stress, in the quotation above, the phrase '*another's* victory': Mr Head and Nelson do not at this moment (one could argue) see the statue as a monument to their own social 'victory' over 'the Negro'; it is rather an emblem of 'their common defeat', the common defeat of all three of them. But Mr Head's joking reaction to the sight ('"They ain't got enough real ones here, they got to have an artificial one"') reasserts his authority for Nelson, and seems to confirm the solidarity of the two of them in the face of an alien 'other'. And the return of the pair to an Eden-like state in the country (the train glides away 'like a serpent') seems to enforce an idea of a primal innocence that turns its back on the city and the wider world of racial diversity. What Mr Head and Nelson learn does not change their view of African Americans, and a hostile critic might say that they gain their salvation at the expense of (or at least in collusion with) a social injustice. On the other hand it could be argued that O'Connor cannot be expected to show a redemption of the social problem in a story which focuses on Mr Head's and Nelson's personal redemption. A great deal depends on the phrases 'another's victory' and 'their common defeat': if we allow the first to mean the past 'victory' of white racism then Mr Head and Nelson, it is implied, are innocent of that; and the second phrase could include the two with the black race in a common suffering. Nevertheless, even if the meaning (and hence our ultimate evaluation) of the story is contestable, there is no doubt about the power of its artistry: the story holds the reader with the intense clarity of its vision.

Chapter 18

Charles Chesnutt, Richard Wright, James Baldwin and the African American short story to 1965

One strain of the African American short story has its pre-literary roots in a rich tradition of oral tales deriving from the earliest days of slavery. Humorous animal trickster fables about figures like Brer Rabbit, Brer Coon and Brer Terrapin, stories of magical Africans, of conjure figures (magicians who cast spells on others), or of clever slaves who tricked their masters, were all numerous in the Southern and South-Western states, and began to be collected by folklorists and historians towards the end of the nineteenth century.[1] 'When Brer Deer and Brer Terrapin Runned a Race', for example, tells of how Brer Terrapin despite his slowness wins the seven-mile race along the river bank to decide who will win the hand of Mr Coon's daughter. He puts one of his brothers at every mile-post and at the finishing post, and each time Brer Deer arrives at a post a brother puts his head out of the water and says 'Oho, here I is!' A conjure story from Eatonville, Florida, collected by the African American writer Zora Neale Hurston, tells of how Aunt Judy puts a particularly unpleasant spell on the dandy and womanizer Horace Carter to stop him chasing after women. In one very short example of the 'clever slave' stories about John and his Master, known as 'Baby in the Crib', John steals a pig and disguises it as a baby; and when 'Old Marsa' insists on seeing it John says: 'If that baby is turned into a pig now, don't blame me.'

Nearly all these stories celebrate in clever and comic ways the canniness of the slave, or the underdog in general, in outwitting the forces of greater power and authority. They have at their best a wonderful verve and sense of detail, and, as recorded by most of the collectors, a vivid sense of voice in the transcription of local dialect. One famous collection of animal fables was made by the white journalist Joel Chandler Harris and published in *Uncle*

Remus: His Songs and Sayings (1880), Uncle Remus being the kindly old slave who told the stories to the frame narrator when he was a little boy. The work has been criticized for its nostalgic sentimentalization of slavery (some of Harris's other stories, like those in *Free Joe and Other Sketches* (1887), also tend to argue that the 'Negro' was better off under slavery), but the portrait of the relationship between the old man and the boy is nevertheless a touching one. And as one of his recent commentators points out, Harris, with his sharp ear for African American narrative structure and dialect voice, recorded the rich humour of the antics of Brer Rabbit and his cronies in a form which brought the narrative genius of ante-bellum African American culture before a wider audience than would otherwise have been possible.[2]

Charles W. Chesnutt

One African American writer who perhaps did more than any other in the nineteenth century to develop the oral story tradition into a sophisticated literary form was Charles W. Chesnutt (1858–1932). Chesnutt, born in Cleveland, Ohio, was an educated man who returned south to his parents' home town of Fayetteville, North Carolina and in 1880 became principal of the State Normal School for African Americans there. Later, he moved back to Cleveland, passed the state bar examination and founded his own court-reporting firm. From his early twenties he declared his main ambition was to become an author, and by the late 1880s he was publishing stories in the prestigious *Atlantic Monthly*, alongside stories by Henry James. In 1899 his most successful and influential volume, *The Conjure Woman*, was published by the eminent house of Houghton Mifflin.

The Conjure Woman is a collection of stories in which Uncle Julius McAdoo, a former plantation slave and now a coachman in North Carolina, tells various stories to his employer John, a Northern white vineyard owner, who is the frame narrator. As well as giving the reader the conjure stories in the rich vernacular dialect of Uncle Julius, Chesnutt constructs a subtle interplay between Julius and his employer in the frames of the stories, in which the African American servant is often seen, obliquely, to outwit the courteous and educated employer. In 'The Goophered Grapevine', for example, Julius tells the story of his Aunt Peggy and how she put a spell (or 'goopher') on a field of grapevines to protect it from thieves. The story is vigorously comic, but Julius's possible ulterior motive in telling it – to discourage John from buying the field so that he can go on harvesting it himself – is gently implied by the narrator.

By constructing framed stories in which the narrator is a mild and civilized employer who writes in an educated way and is gently fooled by his black employee, Chesnutt contrives a subtle narrative not unlike the Twainian tradition of the tall story, where part of the humour comes from the conflict of sophisticated East Coast values with frontier canniness. Chesnutt's working of these oral tales into sophisticatedly ironic pieces is, as Richard Brodhead points out in his edition of *The Conjure Woman*, part of a cultural 'economy of exchange' in which each party gives something to the other, in a reciprocal process which is of course not equally balanced: Julius tells his stories to his employers in return for material favours, and Chesnutt, taking advantage of the current fashion for 'local colour' stories, passes them on to the dominant white literary establishment (*The Atlantic Monthly* and so on) in return for a measure of cultural acceptance by the mainstream.[3] It is another example of the way the genre of the short story, with its receptivity to the oral tradition, its circulation in magazines and its mobility of topic and approach, is especially suited to mediating between cultural groups. The mediation may not at first be an exchange between groups of equal power, but it promotes understanding and a shared (if wary) recognition and negotiation of mutual needs.

Chesnutt's other volume of stories, *The Wife of His Youth and Other Stories of the Color Line*, was published in 1899. Here he uses the more orthodox convention of third-person narrative and omniscient narrator to tell stories which question racial stereotypes in subtle ways. One aspect of race awareness that particularly preoccupied him was the prejudice existing between African Americans of different shades of skin colour. In 'The Wife of his Youth' Chesnutt gently mocks Mr Ryder, a light-skinned 'Negro' (like Chesnutt himself), for his pride in being president of the 'Blue Vein Society', so called by an envious detractor who suggests that 'no-one was eligible for membership that was not white enough to show blue veins'. The members themselves of course decry this idea, maintaining that character and cultivation are the only requisites for membership: it just so happens that those middle-class African Americans in the community who have these qualities tend to be lighter skinned. There are some nicely ironic moments when middle-aged Mr Ryder decides to present his new fiancée to the society at a ball: he looks for quotations from Tennyson's 'A Dream of Fair Women' to grace his speech ('O sweet pale Margaret, / O rare pale Margaret') but decides against them ('Mrs Dixon [his fiancée] was the palest lady he expected at the ball, and she was of a rather ruddy complexion, and of lively disposition and buxom build'). But the crux of the story comes when a little dark-skinned African American woman arrives at his door, who turns out to be 'the wife of his youth' when they were both still slaves. Like all marriages between slaves, this one was not legally binding and was dissolved at the whim of the slave owner. But Mr Ryder decides to honour his first love, and it is her that he presents at the ball, with a sententious little speech. The story is clearly a moralistic and slightly sentimental one, but it is done with a lightly humorous touch.

While the tone in this story is lightly comic, a story like 'The Sheriff's Children' presents the complexities of race in a tragic form. A black man wrongly accused of murder is protected from a lynching party by a white sheriff of bravery and integrity. But while in the local gaol the prisoner reveals himself as the sheriff's son by a black slave mother whom the sheriff subsequently sold: he threatens to kill the sheriff, but the latter's life is saved by his daughter, who wounds the son. The Sheriff spends a sleepless night debating whether to free his son, and decides he cannot do this but will employ counsel to get him acquitted and then try to make some reparation; but in the morning he discovers that the son has stripped off his bandages and let himself bleed to death. The story is told starkly, without any moralizing comment, and is notable for its narrative suspense and concision and its forceful weighting of different moral claims.

The early twentieth century and Richard Wright

Charles Chesnutt (who also wrote three novels) did not publish anything after 1905, perhaps (one of his editors suggests) 'because the ameliorating influence of a Booker T. Washington was being swept aside by a more militant faction of which he could never be a genuine compatriot'.[4] But the tradition of the African American short story in the first three decades of the twentieth century, while not necessarily marked by any great political militancy, was furthered by such writers as Paul Laurence Dunbar (1872–1906), Alice Dunbar-Nelson (1875–1935), Jean Toomer (1894–1967), Rudolph Fisher (1899–1934), Arna Bontemps (1902–), Langston Hughes (1902–67) and Zora Neale Hurston (1903–60). These writers are all represented by stories in Hughes's anthology of 1967, *The Best Short Stories by Negro Writers*.[5] Dunbar's story 'The Scapegoat' is a tale of political rivalry, duplicity and integrity among small-town black politicians. 'Miss Cynthie' by Rudolph Fisher is a lively, touching comic story about a black Southern grandmother who comes to New York to visit her grandson, whom she had hoped would become a doctor or 'at the very least an undertaker', and who is at first appalled by, then reconciled to, the fact that he is a successful tap dancer and singer on Broadway. Eric Walrond's 'The Wharf Rats' is a raw 'slice of life' story about the life of young blacks in Coco Té, a port near Cristobal at the northern end of the Panama Canal. Zora Neale Hurston's 'The Gilded Six-Bits' is a high-spirited and comic story about infidelity and reconciliation in the relationship of a young black couple. 'A Summer Tragedy' by Arna Bontemps is a bleak account of the suicide pact of an impoverished Southern farming couple, in which the purpose of their car journey is gradually and chillingly revealed with adept narrative obliqueness. Hughes's himself is represented by 'Thank You, M'am', a very short and slight comic piece about a young thief who is caught, lectured and (to his amazement) fed and rewarded by a brisk motherly woman.

It is notable that in his selection from this period, at any rate, Langston Hughes chooses stories which are mostly about relationships between African Americans exclusively, and not interracial relations. They are also mostly light and comic stories: Hurston's other best-known story, for example, which Hughes does not choose, is 'Sweat', a stark piece of realism about a violent husband and his wife's desperate revenge. And the chosen story by Jean Toomer is 'Fern', a lyrical descriptive sketch of a young girl. Toomer's *Cane* (1923), from which 'Fern' is taken, is one of the major works of a new black Modernism: a sequence of poems, sketches and stories exploring black consciousness from a variety of viewpoints. Among its other short stories are 'Blood Burning Moon', a powerful account of a Southern lynching and 'Box Seat', a comic and satirical account of a young African American's attempt to break out of the world of 'boxes' – literal (houses, grid plan streets, the theatre box to which he takes his girlfriend) and metaphorical – in which he finds his life encased. Violence and the interracial problem is not the exclusive focus of the work, but these elements are never far below the surface. Hughes's choice of a non-violent, 'non-racial' sketch from *Cane* may reflect his desire in his 1967 anthology to play down the emphasis on protest and racial injustice, and show a wider spectrum of African American life through the potentiality for variety and inclusiveness of the short story.

Hughes also includes in the anthology a story by his slightly younger contemporary Richard Wright (1908–60). 'Almos' a Man' begins his best-known collection of short stories, *Eight Men* (first published in 1961), and interestingly – given Hughes's other choices – involves no interracial element. Wright, mainly known and lauded for his novel *Native Son* (1940), was considered 'not only the leading black author of the US but also a major heir of the naturalistic tradition' (which included writers like Theodore Dreiser and John Dos Passos).[6] His two volumes of short stories are less well known, but are undoubtedly a major part of his *oeuvre*. And the first, *Uncle Tom's Children* (1938), is above all notable for the way it focuses attention on the terrible suffering of black people under the persistent racism of the early twentieth-century South. Its title alludes to the stock figure of the submissive Negro in Harriet Beecher Stowe's novel, but in a mode of irony: the 'children' of Uncle Tom are committed to violent rebellion, and one of the volume's epigraphs states unequivocally '"Uncle Tom is dead!"' In the expanded edition of 1940 there are, in addition to an autobiographical essay, five long stories, each of which presents a different kind of interracial violence in Mississippi. In 'Big Boy Leaves Home' the teenage central character and three friends are surprised while bathing in a local white landowner's pond by a young white woman, the fiancée of the landowner's son. As they try to get their clothes and escape, she panics: her fiancé shoots two of the boys, and a white posse tries to hunt down the other two. Big Boy escapes, but only after witnessing the burning of his surviving friend. 'Fire and Cloud' is about the struggle of a black minister, Reverend Taylor, to mediate between the different factions of the church, the local authorities, the local Communist group and the townspeople in a time of famine: he is whipped and humiliated by a group of white thugs, but the story ends with a rare moment of hope when he nevertheless joins a massive demonstration by blacks and poor whites, and comes to the conclusion that '"*Freedom belongs to the strong.*"'

The stories are all told in a direct plain style which focuses on action and dialogue, and they achieve an undeniable power. The suffering of black people and the brutal cruelty of white racism have rarely, if ever, been so starkly and harshly portrayed, and there are very few glimpses of hope to mitigate the sense of unremitting tragedy. Some of the stories also demonstrate Wright's serious engagement with the question of proper political action, and the element of Marxist analysis in his thinking, which sees the class struggle as of equal importance with the racial struggle. In 'Fire and Cloud' particularly, the Reverend Taylor's urgent discussions with the different factions in the town show a sharp sense of political awareness and Wright's ability to dramatize this in dialogue. Although Wright avoids any great psychological complexity in his characters, he nevertheless vividly conveys their pain, suffering and rebellion. His style equally eschews any elaboration of metaphor or symbol: its powerful narrative drive gives the stories those basic virtues of 'popular' literature, excitement and suspense, but also provokes reflection on 'what man has made of man'. The short story form, which can focus on one aspect of a human problem and one incident in which to dramatize it, and can create fast-moving narratives building to powerful climaxes, is here exactly the right medium for Wright's artistic purpose.

It is a measure of Wright's power of development as an artist that his next volume of stories, *Eight Men* (1961), is in a quite different mode. These eight portraits of black protagonists show Wright's ability to stand back somewhat from the mode of 'protest' writing of *Uncle Tom's Children* and his major novel *Native Son*, and to experiment with narratives that are often comic, satiric, critical (and self-critical). 'Big Black Good Man' comically upsets stereotypical expectations and gently mocks white paranoia in a story about a Norwegian hotel owner who is terrified of the big African American guest: when the latter's hands encircle his throat he does not realize that he is measuring his neck for his collar-size in order to buy him some shirts as a 'thank you' present. 'Man, God Ain't Like That. . .' tells the absurd 'tall story' of a white artist who brings a black Methodist-hymn-singing and ancestral-bone-worshipping African to Paris as a servant: the African becomes convinced the artist is God, and murders him so that when he rises again he will reward Africans with the big cities and great buildings which the Christian God has rewarded his followers. There is perhaps a mildly racist mockery of African 'primitivism' on Wright's own part here (one might contrast Baldwin's treatment of the Algerian Boona in 'This Morning, This Evening, So Soon', discussed below), but the main comic target of the story is the mutual incomprehension of other cultures' religious practices (the artist's wife is disgusted by the – polished and immaculate – ancestral bones). In 'Man of All Work' (which James Baldwin particularly admired)[7] the complicated inter-involvement of racial and sexual politics and prejudice is explored in an uncomfortably comic story about an impoverished young black man who dresses up in his wife's clothes in order to get a job as a housekeeper with a white couple. The farce that ensues when the male employer makes a pass at the man illustrates not only the demeaning nature of white attitudes to black women and male chauvinism in general but also the way racist attitudes and economic conditions 'feminized' blacks into positions of subservience.

The more tragic stories in *Eight Men* are perhaps less successful, although still interesting for their experimentation. 'The Man Who Lived Underground' is the semi-surreal parable of a black man wrongly charged with murder who escapes into the sewers of the big city and spies on white society (a church, a theatre, a store) through the walls and floors of city buildings, until he tries to rob a safe and kills another thief. He goes back to the police who first picked him up (who have already got another man convicted for the first murder), tries to take them to the places he has visited to prove the truth of his story, and ends up getting shot down the sewer manhole. As realism the story is hardly plausible, and it perhaps does not convey a clear enough message (beyond vague notions of the underground as the unconscious, or as a metaphor of black society in relation to white) to work as 'romance' or allegory. But it still has a kind of weird vividness. The final story, 'The Man Who Went to Chicago', is the only story in the collection told in the first person (by a character called Richard Wright), and is more episodic, autobiographical and at times essayistic in mode. It is less memorable as a unified story, but some of its individual parts show a new awareness of interracial relations and the nature of American society. In one part the narrator becomes shamefacedly aware of his own anti-Semitism towards a kindly Jewish employer; in another he realizes the way blacks as well as whites are trapped in a materialistic society, and that the 'real threat' to the social status quo is from those (both black and white) 'who do not dream of the prizes that the nation holds forth, for it is in them, though they may not know it, that a revolution has taken place, and is biding its time to translate itself into a new and strange way of life'. In the stories of *Eight Men*, despite their unevenness the genre shows itself as one responsive to experimentation with new ideas and new fictional modes.

James Baldwin

James Baldwin (1924–87) is, in the view of many critics, one of the finest African American writers of the twentieth century. While his reputation rests mainly on his novels (particularly *Go Tell It on the Mountain*, 1953; *Giovanni's Room*, 1956; and *Another Country*, 1962) and his essays (*Nobody Knows My Name*, 1961; and *The Fire Next Time*, 1963), his contribution to the tradition of the short story is undoubtedly significant, and his volume of eight stories, *Going to Meet the Man* (1965), shows him using the form with variety and incisiveness. One of the most striking things about Baldwin is his sophisticated artistry: his stories come, certainly, from his own deepest experience, but they are subjected to a refining process which results in a kind of artistic detachment and ability to explore that experience from different points of view and different centres of consciousness.

'Previous Condition' and 'Come Out the Wilderness' (first published in 1948 and 1958 respectively) both explore the problems of African Americans in New York. The title of the first story alludes to the wording of the fifteenth amendment of the United States constitution, which asserts that the right of citizens to vote 'shall not be denied or abridged . . . on account of race, colour or previous condition of servitude'. Peter, a black actor, has a white Jewish friend, Jules, and a white girlfriend; he gets turned out of his room (secured for him by Jules) by his landlady because 'I can't have no coloured people here'; he discusses the similarities and differences of anti-black and anti-Jewish prejudice; he remembers the first time he was called 'nigger' at the age of seven by a white girl in the South; he tells of the concerts he goes to with his girlfriend and the music he listens to (when he first heard Handel's *Messiah* 'My blood bubbled like fire and wine'). He has a violent argument with his girlfriend in a restaurant and they split up. He ends up drinking in an African American bar, feeling 'out of place'. The story is perhaps the least successful in the collection, too episodic and not focusing enough on any one incident to achieve any especial illumination: and yet in the various details of Peter's life there is an authenticity which conveys the lack of identity which is the story's theme. The story is not much of a story precisely because, as he says to a woman in the bar in the last line, '"I got no story, Ma."' 'Come Out the Wilderness' is about a similar unrootedness, and feels similarly episodic, but the authorial detachment and fresh angle given by the female protagonist seem to lead to a sharper vision. Ruth works in a typing pool with a progressive multiracial company where the 'atmosphere was so positively electric with interracial goodwill that no one ever dreamed of telling the truth about anything'. She is troubled by memories of her childhood, when her brother caught her with an older boy and called her 'black and dirty'; and she feels ashamed of her relationship with her white boyfriend because she does not love him, though she is drawn to 'lonely' white 'boys', the lost 'sons of the masters'. In her office, among a group of white secretaries, she is attracted to her black boss, a man whose easy courtesy and sense of humour remind her of the Southern 'Negroes' of her youth: her ease and enjoyment in this friendship – though we are left to wonder if it will develop into anything deeper – is warmly and sensitively done. The title of the story, from a Negro spiritual, is ironic: at the end of the story she leaves a restaurant, walks through the crowd and 'did not know where she was going'. The black race has, to some degree 'come out the wilderness', but like many in the city, black and white, she is still in it.

Music, and jazz in particular, was particularly important to Baldwin. He tells of how

> [i]t was Bessie Smith, through her tone and her cadence, who helped me to dig back to the way I must myself have spoken when I was a pickaninny, and to remember the things I had seen and felt. I had buried them very deep. I had never listened to Bessie Smith in America (in the same way that, for years, I would not touch watermelon), but in Europe she helped to reconcile me to being a 'nigger'.[8]

This feeling for blues music, and the sense of tension between the European influences on his sensibility and the traditions of the American South, is apparent in what is perhaps the finest story in *Going to Meet the Man*, 'Sonny's Blues'. It is also undoubtedly one of the best short stories ever written about jazz, its inward, tragic understanding contrasting strikingly with the sense of comic wonder in that other fine jazz story, Eudora Welty's 'Powerhouse'. A black middle-class schoolteacher tells of the relationship between himself and his brother Sonny, a jazz pianist. Sonny has had to fight against a drug addiction, and his more 'respectable' and conventional brother has difficulty in understanding the compulsions that drive him. The narrator and the rest of his family also have difficulty in approving of Sonny's jazz, a form they associate with loose living and crime. But in the course of renewed relations with his brother, and through his own suffering in the loss of a child, the narrator gradually retrieves a part of himself which has been deeply buried: his sense of his past, in particular the memory of the murder of his uncle (also a musician) by a gang of white youths in a car. He listens with fresh ears to the hymns of a revival meeting on the sidewalk ('the music seemed to soothe a poison out of them'). And in a powerfully moving final scene in the nightclub where Sonny performs, he feels for the first time the power of the blues to embody human suffering and to transform it. As well as being about jazz, the story, one feels, states Baldwin's own literary aesthetic. He speaks of how, in contrast to the 'personal, private, vanishing evocations' which most of us hear when we are opening ourselves to music, 'the man who creates the music is hearing something else, is dealing with the roar rising from the void and imposing order on it as it hits the air'; and of how '[Sonny] and his boys up there were keeping it new, at the risk of ruin, destruction, madness and death, in order to find new ways to make us listen.' These reflections are worked into a fine evocation of the performance: the conversation between the instruments, the achievement of unity, the transition into Sonny's own blues with the memories of suffering it evokes. At the end of the piece, and in the last sentences of the story, the narrator gives Sonny a glass of Scotch and milk.

> He didn't seem to notice it, but just before they started playing again, he sipped from it and looked toward me, and nodded. Then he put it back on the top of the piano. For me, then, as they began to play again, it glowed and shook above my brother's head like the very cup of trembling.

This fine ending beautifully infuses naturalistic detail with symbolic resonance. The delayed nod from Sonny marks the recognition of the new love and understanding between the brothers; the 'cup of trembling', mysteriously suggestive in itself, comes from the book of Isaiah, with its sublime promise of the end of suffering: 'Behold I have taken out of thine hand the cup of trembling, even the dregs of the cup of my fury; thou shalt no more drink of it again.'[9]

One of the central problems for the writer of prose fiction is the handling of time, and for the short story writer this problem has a particular aspect, that of the relationship between past and present within the confines of the form. The novelist can develop at length scenes and stories from different periods of time, and can more easily (though he does not, of course, have to) make the narrative order follow the chronological order of the events in the story. The short story writer has characteristically (at least in stories which maintain a conventionally realist sense of time) to compress elements from the past into a structure which focuses on the present incident and, above all, the crisis. As Frank O'Connor has put it, 'The short story represents a struggle with Time . . . it is an attempt to reach some point of vantage from which the past and the future are equally visible. The crisis of the short story *is* the short story.'[10] 'Going to Meet the Man' and 'This Morning, This Evening, So Soon' illustrate and (in the latter case) question this principle. The former takes as its 'present' time the night in which Jesse, a white prison officer, is trying to make love to his wife but finds himself impotent. The narrative then goes back (via Jesse's account to his wife) to the previous day when Jesse had a violent confrontation with a black prisoner involved in a prison protest (characteristically for Baldwin this involves constant singing, which particularly enrages Jesse); then revisits an incident between Jesse and the prisoner when the latter was a ten-year-old boy; then turns to general reflections on the black population of the town and the uneasy feeling among the prison officers (hardly articulated but expressed obliquely in uneasy jokes and remarks) of no longer being certain of their racial authority; and then finally recollects the memory from childhood of being taken on an 'outing' (the most terrible thing about it was the feeling of holiday) to witness the lynching of a Negro. And its recall – the recall of the primitive assertion of violent power – fires Jesse's sexual energy so he is able to make love to his wife ('Come on, sugar, I'm going to do you like a nigger'). This powerfully horrifying story has been criticized as an example of Baldwin's over-emphasis of the sexual element in race hatred; but it carries conviction. And it does so through a mastery of narrative time, in which the present 'crisis' provides a 'vantage point' from which to recall and understand the past; and the past horror (itself a crisis) in turn throws light on the present and on race relations in general.

In 'This Morning, This Evening, So Soon'[11] there is – in contravention of Frank O'Connor's principle – no real crisis, and the story lacks a certain impact as a result. But it does nevertheless attempt to get a 'vantage point' on past, present and future. The story's 'present' is a period of roughly twelve hours between one evening and the next morning, when the narrator, a celebrated black singer, living in Paris, is going out to dinner with the director of one of his films, prior to returning to live in the United States with his white Swedish wife and their seven-year-old son. The turning point in his life recalls other turning points – particularly his visit to the States eight years before, when he was confronted again with the racial attitudes he had escaped through exile; and an incident in which, working on the film, the director accused him of sentimentalizing his role (into a 'noble savage') and forgetting the reality of his experience: both these are given substantial narrative space. Some peaceful domestic scenes in the hotel and an incident with his black Algerian friend Boona at a café (which raises reflections on the relation between black Africans and black Americans), together with the flashbacks to the past, provide a sequence of 'ordinary' events which allow the past to fall into a new perspective. The story is quietly dramatized (though not 'dramatic' in the more popular sense) and allows essayistic reflections in the narrator which are full of Baldwin's keen and compassionate intelligence. And the 'future', too, gets a new perspective, as the narrator reflects on the more hopeful life which lies ahead for his son. The final quotidian detail concludes the story with a pleasantly casual symbolic suggestion of that future hope, however constrained by circumstance it may still be: '"What a journey!"' says a neighbour, as narrator and son, soon to leave for the States, enter the hotel lift.' "*Jusqu'au nouveau monde!*" I open the cage and we step inside. "Yes", I say, "all the way to the new world". I press the button, and the cage, holding my son and me, goes up.'

Chapter 19

Aspects of the American short story 1930–1980

Magazines, Jackson and Salinger

The heyday of the popular magazine short story in the United States was probably around the late 1930s just before the widespread adoption of television; and the king of all the popular story magazines was *The Saturday Evening Post.* Kurt Vonnegut has given an idyllic account of the role of the magazine short story in his own middle-class family: he comes home from school, picks up the *Saturday Evening Post,* thumbs through it, starts to read the story: 'My high school troubles drop away. I am in a pleasant state somewhere between sleep and restfulness.' A short while later his father comes home from work ('or more likely from no work') and picks up the same story: 'His pulse and breathing slow down. His troubles drop away, and so on.'[1]

But of all the mid-century magazines which published short stories (including *Atlantic Monthly, Harper's Magazine* and *Esquire,* among many others)[2] none was more sophisticated, successful and prestigious than that elegant mixture of seductive advertisements, metropolitan tabletalk, political commentary, witty cartoons and finely written fiction, *The New Yorker.* The magazine was founded in 1925 by Harold Ross, and in continuous publication since then it has featured among its contributors such fine short story writers as (in the mid-century) John O'Hara, Irwin Shaw, Shirley Jackson,

Eudora Welty, Peter Taylor, J. F. Powers, Truman Capote and J. D. Salinger; humorists like E. B. White, James Thurber and S. J. Perelman; Dorothy Parker, that queen of the one-liner and caustic recorder in very short, sharp stories (often dramatic monologues, as in 'A Telephone Call' or 'Just a Little One') of the lives of bright young things and bored married couples; and in subsequent years Bernard Malamud, Grace Paley, Donald Barthelme, Raymond Carver, Bobbie Ann Mason, Anne Beattie, Tobias Wolff and Richard Ford. The great variety among these writers belies the idea that there was any one style of 'New Yorker Story', even in the earlier years.[3] Shirley Jackson's famous – for some notorious – story 'The Lottery', published in 1948, provoked a larger volume of correspondence than any other single piece of writing in the history of the magazine, including several cancelled subscriptions. Beginning as a deceptively realist story of ordinary American small-town life, it develops gradually into a horrifying tale of the ritual murder of a human scapegoat. At a time when the first stories of the Jewish holocaust were reaching America, the story's bland narration and lack of explanation suggested an unidentifiable communal violence lurking below the surface of the most seemingly civilized society.

In the same year J. D. Salinger (b. 1919) began publishing stories, later collected in *Nine Stories* (in England entitled *For Esmé With Love and Squalor and Other Stories*) (1953) and *22 Stories* (1963), which more wittily and stylishly but no less edgily revealed the anxieties and neuroses, as well as a certain nostalgia for innocence and aspiration to spirituality, beneath the lives of its protagonists. One of Salinger's most persistent preoccupations is with encounters between a radical and sometimes doomed innocence and a society of disenchanted sophistication. In 'A Perfect Day for Bananafish' a young woman talks with her mother on the telephone about her brilliant but disturbed brother, with whom she is staying in a hotel by the sea; meanwhile her brother (Seymour Glass, a member of the precociously brilliant Glass family who are the subject of a number of Salinger's stories and novellas) has a long and playful conversation with a little girl on the beach; and in the last scene he returns to the hotel and shoots himself. In 'For Esmé With Love and Squalor' a world-weary American writer, stationed in England during the Second World War, encounters an English schoolgirl of startling candour – an intriguing mixture of naivety and precocity – who makes him promise to write her a story: 'Make it extremely squalid and moving. . . Are you at all acquainted with squalor?' Later in army camp in Germany, his nerves shot up and trying to cope with his earnestly dim-witted jeep-companion, Clay, the narrator receives a chatty letter and wristwatch (broken in the post) from

Esmé. We get the sense of the way the memory of the young girl's innocence sustains the narrator in what he calls 'the squalid part of the story', and her combination of naivety and sophistication, the comedy of the encounter and the disenchanted amusement of the narrator keep any potential sentimentality deftly at bay. Salinger's art clearly and deliberately walks a thin line between whimsy and profundity, and continually startles the reader with its fresh and unexpected combinations of tones and registers.

The rural West, Northern Catholic faith and Southern manners: John Steinbeck, J. F. Powers and Peter Taylor

It is always a difficult critical task, in a general introduction like the present study, to pick out, when it comes to the more recent past, those writers who seem to stand out from the mass of their contemporaries. But mention should undoubtedly be made of certain writers of the 1930s to 1950s whose work has sustained persistent critical interest over the years. John Steinbeck (1902–68), best known perhaps for his novel *The Grapes of Wrath* (1939), produced two outstanding collections of short stories, *The Pastures of Heaven* (1932) and *The Long Valley* (1938), mostly set in his native territory of Salinas Valley, California, and dealing, in both realist and mythical modes, with tales of isolation, violence and sexual repression against a vividly evoked pastoral setting of farming and rural life. It has been said that Steinbeck does for Salinas Valley what Faulkner did for Oxford County, Mississippi, or Anderson for small-town Ohio; and *The Pastures of Heaven*, like Anderson's collection, is also a cycle of linked stories. André Gide felt that Steinbeck never wrote anything 'more perfect, more accomplished, than certain of his short stories'.[4]

The stories of another distinguished mid-century writer, J. F. Powers (1917–99), mainly about the Catholic priesthood in small-town Michigan, give a vivid sense of the manners of their particular world, but also rise above their time and place in the artistry of their prose, and the unflinching clarity, humour and compassion of their moral vision. Powers published three major story collections – *The Prince of Darkness, and Other Stories*, 1947 (republished in 1948 as *Lions, Harts, Leaping Does, and Other Stories*); *The Presence of Grace*, 1956; and *Look How the Fish Live*, 1975 – and it is on these rather than his novels that his reputation rests.[5] The title story from the first volume is a sharply ironic study of a priest who despite his ambition fails to secure a parish of his own: Father Ernest 'Bloomer' Burner is frankly materialistic and unspiritual, though not entirely unconscientious in his duties. It seems a mistake to see him (as some commentators have done) as an evil man, despite one or two hints in that direction, and the force of the story comes from the way the reader is led to retain sympathy for him while seeing his faults, so that the ending produces both shock and a sense of justice. In 'Lions, Harts, Leaping Does', on the other hand, Powers writes a lyrical, Chekhovian story about the gently comic relationship of two elderly monks and the death of the older one. The quiet inner struggle of the dying Didymus (his sense of guilt at having not visited his older brother Seraphim on *his* deathbed, simply to punish his own hankering for earthly attachments); his unavailing attentiveness for a sign from God, and his admiration for the simple sanctity of Brother Titus; the atmosphere of the winter evening and the escape of the pet canary into the snow, which Titus touchingly attempts to hide from his friend: each detail with its unobtrusive symbolism contributes to an intense and poetic evocation of the interwoven nature of human and divine love, and the close achieves a rare poetry:

> The thought of being the cause of such elaborate dissimulation in so simple a soul made Didymus want to smile – or cry, he did not know which. . . and could do neither. Titus persisted. How long would it be, Didymus wondered faintly, before Titus ungrievingly gave the canary up for lost in the snowy arms of God? The snowflakes whirled at the window, for a moment for all their bright blue beauty as though struck still by lightning, and Didymus closed his eyes, only to find them there also, but darkly falling.

An almost exactly contemporary but very different writer, Peter Taylor (1917–94), explores the complex manners of 1930s Tennessee (mainly Nashville), in seven collections of stories which are remarkable for their Jamesian subtlety of tone and their critical stance towards the racism and other forms of reactionary conservatism that were still prevalent in white society. The long story or novella *The Old Forest* (1985) is perhaps Taylor's masterpiece, and explores with remarkable resonance and a feeling for the mysterious tensions of sexuality, history and tradition the changing attitude to the place of women in middle- and upper-class society. And one of his finest short stories, 'The Long Fourth' (1948), gives a portrait, through the experience of one day of inner drama, of a traditional Southern white lady of the upper class whose inherited racism is aroused but also challenged by a domestic incident with her black maidservant. Taylor's irony sharply illuminates the instinctive bigotry of the white woman but also gives a moving sense of its unconscious uncertainties and its capacity for change.

Extreme worlds: Truman Capote, Carson McCullers, Paul Bowles, Jane Bowles

Another celebrated Southern writer, Truman Capote (1924–84), published one volume of short stories, *A Tree of Night*, in 1949, and these and other stories have been collected in *The Complete Stories of Truman Capote* (2004). Capote was born in New Orleans and raised by relatives of his mother in Alabama, and many of his stories show a number of characteristics of what has come to be known as 'Southern Gothic': a preoccupation with the grotesque, the supernatural and the symbolic. In 'A Tree of Night', a young woman travels back home in a train after an uncle's funeral and encounters a strange couple who run a travelling 'freak-show' in which the man (who seems to be simple-minded) poses as the Biblical figure of Lazarus who rose from the dead. The girl is drawn hypnotically into their world, and the man comes to represent 'the wizard man', 'a childish memory of terrors that once, long ago, had hovered above her like haunted limbs on a tree of night'. Capote's 'Gothic' stories have perhaps dated in comparison with the intellectually tougher and altogether more demanding religious 'supernatural' of Flannery O'Connor, or the subtle explorations of eccentric states of consciousness in Eudora Welty. (One of Capote's more successful stories, 'My Side of the Matter', is a kind of reworking of the motif of the comic, ambiguously reliable narrator in Welty's 'Why I Live at the P.O.'.)

But perhaps the stories of Capote's that survive best are the three, close to memoir, which deal with his experiences as a child living with relatives in Alabama: 'A Christmas Memory', 'The Thanksgiving Visitor' and 'One Christmas'. The first two focus on the close personal relationship with Capote's elderly cousin, Sook – or 'my friend,' as he calls her – and the last describes an emotionally fraught Christmas with his estranged father in distant New Orleans. Capote can write with extraordinary accomplishment and vividness, and these stories movingly evoke the intense happiness and sadness of childhood experience, the pleasure in Christmas preparations with his childlike cousin, the mixed embarrassment and desire to please of his encounter with his father, and the unexpectedly bracing moral lesson (learned from his cousin) in a story of the wrongness of 'righteous' moral revenge in 'The Thanksgiving Visitor'. Much of Capote's writing deals with the extreme and the violent (like his most celebrated work the 'nonfiction novel', as he called it, *In Cold Blood*, the account of a real Kansas murder), and in later life Capote declined into drug-taking, backbiting gossip and mere celebrity. But in these stories we see a remarkably fresh and touching perception of innocence and fundamental human values.

Another southern writer of the mid-century, whose work was championed by Capote and who shares with some of his stories a taste for the strange or the 'Gothic', was Carson McCullers (1917–67). McCullers's best known story is 'The Ballad of the Sad Café' (1943) about an eccentric woman whiskey-store owner and her friendship and epic fight with an itinerant dwarf. Her other stories are generally less Gothic but focus on what she called 'spiritual isolation', youth, coming of age and unrequited love.

One of the major forebears of Capote's supernatural or grotesque stories – indeed the godfather of that whole tradition in American writing – is Poe; and Poe was particularly admired by another explorer of the strange, the uncanny and the horrific from the 1940s and 1950s, Paul Bowles (1917–99). Bowles writes in a style of cold elegance and clarity, evoking the world of the strange and the exotic in stories mainly set in North Africa (where he lived for much of his life) and the wilder parts of Central America. His main subject is the confrontation of American or Western values by the 'alien', 'primitive' world of African or indigenous Central American culture. His aesthetic is detached and his view of the world pessimistic, even fatalistic. He believed in the separation between (as T. S. Eliot put it) 'the man who suffers and the mind which creates', and once said enigmatically (anticipating a postmodernist perspective) that 'the writer does not exist'. But in one of his later stories, 'Unwelcome Words', a character whom he calls Paul Bowles speaks of his conviction that 'the human world has entered into a terminal period of disintegration and destruction', an idea which recalls D. H. Lawrence's remark about Poe's concern with the disintegration of 'the old white psyche'. His stories also in some ways recall Conrad's *Heart of Darkness*, but his protagonists are not idealistic like Kurtz and they drift to their (frequently horrific) ends in a kind of haze of intellectual detachment and capitulation. In 'A Distant Episode' (1947) an American professor of languages (the choice of profession is clearly significant) goes for a walk at night in a small North African town in search of the local 'little boxes made of camel udders' which he is collecting. He is captured by a Reguiba tribesman, who cuts out his tongue, dresses him in a costume made from tin cans, and keeps him as a kind of performing clown. He is sold to a Touareg man, but refuses to dance, and in a delirium of violence smashes up the room he is in and runs out into the desert as the chill night is coming on. In another story, 'Pastor Dowe at Tacaté' (1950), an American pastor fails to impress the Mexican Indians of the village with his stories of Don Jesucristo even when he tries substituting the names of their gods for the Biblical names. They only want him to play them 'Crazy Rhythm' on his gramophone and give them his store of salt. After a dreamlike journey downriver to Tacaté he finds himself in a local temple, himself praying to their god of 'elsewhere', Metzabok. And when back in his village he is offered as a wife a seven-year-old girl who carries a swaddled baby alligator as a doll he loses his nerve and leaves the village secretly at night. Another area which Bowles explores with uncanny clarity is that of extreme mental states and confusions of identity. In 'You Are Not I' the psychotically disturbed narrator tells, with complete 'logical' lucidity, of her escape from her 'Home' (or sanatorium) and her encounter with her sister, whose identity she in the course of the story assumes, referring to herself towards the end of the story in the third person.

Schizophrenic experience is also explored in the work of another outstanding short story writer, Paul Bowles's wife, Jane Bowles (1917–73), whose *Collected Works* (1966) were published with an introduction by Truman Capote. Her *oeuvre* may be a slender one, but her volume of stories *Plain Pleasures* (1966) is a brilliant collection of subtle, poetically suggestive pieces. In 'Plain Pleasures' a 'dignified and reserved' woman of Scottish and Spanish descent talks to her equally reserved neighbour for the first time after many years of living in the same apartment block, and accepts an invitation out to a dinner which leads her to a nervous, constrained but dangerously delirious revelation of buried feeling. But Jane Bowles's masterpiece is surely the longer story 'Camp Cataract', in which a woman, escaping to a North American summer camp from a psychologically claustrophobic household comprising herself, two sisters and a brother-in-law, is visited by the timid, unmarried sister who is herself desperate to escape. The sharp, painful comedy of neurotic sibling rivalry and identification ends in tragedy when the emotional pressure of the meeting drives the timid sister into psychotic fantasy. Like Paul Bowles in 'You Are Not I', but perhaps with a more moving sense of thwarted lives and the fear of independence, Jane Bowles evokes, with a surreal and imagistic precision, the pressures of love which lead to desperate emotional hallucination. Here, as in 'Plain Pleasures', Jane Bowles proves herself a striking poet of the psychology of the imagination and the desire for freedom.

The sorrows and consolations of suburbia: John Cheever and John Updike

One type of story that was representative of the period 1940–70 came from the terrain of East Coast urban and suburban life. The type was frequently elegant, eloquent, witty; often humorous, but equally often touched with a darker sense of anxiety and unease; and it analysed what might be called the sorrows and consolations of suburbia. Two writers, separated in age by twenty years, were outstanding examples of the genre: John Cheever and John Updike.

John Cheever (1912–82) published four novels and a novella, and six volumes of short stories, the best of which are collected in *The Stories of John Cheever* (1978). His novels (the best and best-known being *The Wapshot Chronicle*, 1957) have stood the test of time and are still in print, but it could be fairly suggested that his short stories are his most enduring legacy. Cheever was drawn to the short story form by a sense of its modernity, its suitedness to the fragmentary life of modern man. In a letter of 1935 he wrote:

> The powerful sense of passed and passing time that seems to be the one definable and commendable quality of the novel is not our property. Our lives are not long and well-told stories.[6]

Another aspect of the short story which has recurred in this study, the sense of crisis or turning point, is also marked in Cheever's stories. They frequently deal with a defining moment in a life. They also tend at times towards parable and even Romance in the mode of surrealism or allegory. In the title story of his first collection, *The Enormous Radio and Other Stories* (1953), Jim and Irene Westcott ('the kind of people who seem to strike that satisfactory average of income, endeavor, and respectability that is reached by statistical reports in college alumni bulletins') buy an enormous, ugly new radio, which begins, inexplicably, to pick up sounds and conversations from other apartments in the multi-storey block in which they live. At first these are benign (a nurse reading Edward Lear to a neighbour's child, a cocktail party, a bridge game) but gradually they become more ominous: when Jim comes home from work, Irene reports that Mr Melville is beating his wife, Mrs Hutchinson's mother is dying of cancer in Florida, the elevator man has tuberculosis. '"Everybody's been quarrelling. They're all worried about money."' And her new awareness of the proximity of suffering makes her acutely anxious about their own happiness: '"We're happy, aren't we, darling? We're happy, aren't we?"' she asks urgently. Jim gets the radio fixed, but the $400 bill makes him resentful, and he suddenly turns on Irene with a host of accusations and long-repressed resentments. The enormous radio (an enormity, as well as large) is the symbol and catalyst of human suffering, and also an instance of the weirdness of modern technology which both facilitates and disables. The surreal moment of its access to private lives is the one non-realist element in what is otherwise a realist story: a momentary flight into 'Romance' which reveals the underlying uncertainty and vulnerability of two 'average' lives.

'"We're happy, aren't we, darling?"' Irene Westcott's anxious question, with its special point and poignancy in the country dedicated to 'life, liberty and the pursuit of happiness', has a representative status in relation to the short story of the East Coast suburbs, and particularly to Cheever's. His people usually have enough money, pleasant homes, good jobs, flourishing families. And they share – together, one feels with the author – the sense that these things should be enough to make them happy. Usually, they are not. Cheever once wrote:

> I come from a Puritanical family and I had been taught as a child that a moral lies beneath all human conduct and that the moral is always detrimental to man. I count among my relations people who feel there is some inexpugnable nastiness at the heart of life and that love, friendship, Bourbon whisky, lights of all kinds – are merely the crudest deceptions. My aim as a writer has been to record a moderation of these attitudes – an escape from them if this seemed necessary . . .[7]

This Puritan legacy, and the ironic parables and 'Romance' stories suitable for the exploration of moral crisis or its avoidance, place Cheever in the line of Hawthorne. The attempt to 'escape' leads him frequently to comedy, and Alfred Kazin has commented penetratingly: 'My deepest feeling about Cheever is that his marvelous brightness is an effort to cheer himself up.'[8]

The stories where this 'cheering up' effect is strongest are those in which transgression is allowed to intrude only on the edges of a story, or where unhappiness is there but held at bay. 'The Day the Pig Fell into the Well' traces the way an unusual event is the node around which memory clusters, and how memory builds a sense of family identity and permanence out of different times and incidents, suppressing unhappiness and the sense of transience, and clinging to preferred versions of the past. But in some of Cheever's stories unhappiness is not escaped. 'The Hartleys' must be one of the saddest stories ever written. Mr and Mrs Hartley return with their seven-year-old daughter to an East Coast ski resort where eight years before (says Mr Hartley) 'we had such a wonderful time'. The couple are well liked in the hotel, but it becomes clear that something is wrong. The daughter Anne is too clingingly close to her father, wanting only to be with him, anxious when he is gone too long. A maid overhears the wife saying repeatedly, in a long monologue which rings with uncontrolled desperation: '"Why do we have to come back? . . . What good is it going to do? . . . Why can't we separate again?' And dreadfully to compound this unhappiness, the story ends with the shocking accidental death of Anne, caught in the tow-rope of the ancient ski-lift. This is one of the few short stories by Cheever which ends with unrelieved blackness, and the short story form focuses this tragedy with unusual force. It could be said that the couple's circumstances are too unexplained, and the daughter's death too much a merely accidental horror, for the complexity of tragedy: but this is partly what gives the story its bleak force. The sheer contingency of the death is part of its terrible sadness.

A more subtly memorable story – arguably Cheever's best, and a good example of both the parable and 'romance' (or surreal) element in his writing – is 'The Swimmer'. Neddy Merrill, a middle-aged suburbanite who still gives an impression of 'youth, sport and clement weather', decides one hot summer day at his neighbour's poolside to 'swim home', following the line of an imaginary river which he creates out of all his friends' and neighbours' swimming pools. The project is at once plausible and mythic, the epic journey home of a suburban Ulysses, who names the imaginary river Lucinda after his wife (a name faintly reminiscent of Lucina, Roman goddess of childbirth, one who 'brings to light'). The journey starts with a sense of exhilaration (and the story works partly because the suburban pool-sides and characters are so sharply delineated), but the mood gradually darkens. The visit to the pool of some old, left-wing friends ends with an uneasy feeling of friendship cooled and perhaps betrayed; the swim in the pool of an old flame, who is in the midst of hosting a party, leads to a sour rebuff; in a dry-land section of the journey he has to cross a main road and is caught ignominiously on the verge by the heavy traffic, amid the beer cans, rags and bits of blown-out tyres. Storm clouds begin to gather; and when he reaches home, instead of his wife and daughters awaiting him, he finds the doors locked and their handles rusty, the rain gutter hanging down and the house empty. In the course of the story its mode shifts gradually from a mythically tinged realism to a romance which never loses its realistic surface. The effect is an underlying emptiness powerfully and gradually 'brought to light', the allegory of a life hollowed out beneath its complacency and pool-surface glitter, a chilling miniature epic of empty homecoming.

The sense of life in the stories of John Updike (b. 1932) is more sanguine than in those of Cheever, and Updike's broad equanimity is perhaps one factor that has helped sustain a writing career of extraordinary longevity and productivity. He wrote his first short story, 'Ace in the Hole', in 1953 (publishing it soon after in *The New Yorker*) and has gone on to publish some thirteen independent volumes of stories, not to mention other story collections, as well as twenty novels, and several volumes of poems, memoirs and essays, and children's books. While he is doubtless best known for some of his novels – the *Rabbit* tetralogy (1960–90) and *Couples* (1968) in particular – his short stories have had an equally wide readership, and stories like 'Ace in the Hole', 'Pigeon Feathers', 'Friends from Philadelphia', 'Sunday Teasing' and 'The Music School' are among the classics of the short story in the second half of the twentieth century. 'I hate to be judgmental in this regard', Updike has written, 'in fact I don't know – but the short story may be what I do best. I certainly feel comfortable with it, whereas with the novel I occasionally feel uncertain.'[9] And on the difference between writing a novel and writing a short story he has commented: 'What you need in a novel is for several ideas to come somehow together in an interesting way. But with a short story you need only one spark to begin writing. So it is fairly spontaneous, and I think the better ones have been written with a fairly direct "delivery" from inspiration to production. Otherwise you tend to cool on the idea and forget what excited you.'[10]

Updike's short stories, as evidenced in his most recent collection, the 838-page *The Early Stories (1953–1975)*,[11] illustrate two important points about the genre: that the successful short story should be able to stand alone, but it can also benefit from its placing in a collection. In this particular collection Updike has arranged the stories roughly chronologically in terms of the events they record or reflect, so that the volume, with its groupings of stories into sections with titles like 'Olinger Stories', 'Out in the World', 'Married Life' and 'Family Life', charts not only the lives of its protagonists (usually male, and often kinds of surrogate for the author) but also middle-class American life in general across nearly a quarter of a century.

'Olinger' is a fictional town in rural Pennsylvania which is the counterpart of the real-life Shillington, where Updike grew up. And the 'Tarbox' of 'Tarbox Tales' is analogous to Ipswich, Massachusetts, to which Updike moved in 1957. In the matter of middle-class America which Updike explores, the terrain is similar in many ways to that of Cheever – business and professional protagonists and their wives, suburban domesticity, marriage and divorce – but moved a generation on and with distinctively new inflections. There is perhaps less unhappiness – or rather the anxieties and sexual uncertainties that so often rise disruptively to the surface in Cheever are still there, but are often allowed to be allayed. Divorce and extra-marital sex for example, felt as a constant possibility in Cheever but usually avoided or repressed, are frequently treated directly in Updike's stories. Divorce, for all its pain and embarrassment, is also portrayed as a positive step; yet sometimes that step proves unexpectedly difficult in the event. In 'Twin Beds in Rome' the Maples (a recurring couple in the stories) 'talked and thought about separation so long it seemed it would never come. . . 'Burning to leave one another, they left, out of marital habit, together': they take a holiday in Rome, where Richard sees Joan is happy, and at the end of the story, 'jealous of her happiness, he grew again reluctant to leave her'. In another story, 'The Music School', a man taking his daughter to a piano lesson and thinking about a recent conversation with a priest and about his own infidelity to his wife, has the curious reflection: 'We are all pilgrims, faltering towards divorce.' Sometimes the stirrings of infidelity are quite lightly and uncomplicatedly treated, as in 'The Persistence of Desire' (1958), in which an encounter with an old girlfriend in an eye clinic – particularly her blurred handwritten note to him (there is a *leitmotif* of 'seeing') – requickens the protagonist's desire for her. Moral questions are suspended here, as they are sometimes in Updike, and the brevity of a short story can particularly allow this. Updike's stories test various facets of modern relationships with an eye that is partly clinical (he is fond of hospitals, and doctors' and dentists' surgeries as locations for his stories) and partly sacerdotal.

One of the most interesting things about Updike's sensibility, indeed, is its religious element, indisputably American in the accommodations of its Protestant individualism. And the short story, with its roots in parable and exemplum, seems particularly suited to the examination of the tests and sustenances of faith. In one of his most famous stories, 'Pigeon Feathers', a fourteen-year-old boy discovers the atheism of H. G. Wells and his simple religious faith is deeply shaken. His mother's folksy superstitions about the soil, and his Sunday School teacher's earnest but textbook affirmations, fail to ward off his sudden anxieties about death. But he achieves a renewed belief in his own immortality, by chance, after he shoots some pigeons infesting the family's barn; burying them, he sees for the first time the finely intricate pattern of their feathers:

> As he fitted the last two, still pliant, on the top, and stood up, crusty coverings were lifted from him, and with a feminine, slipping sensation along his nerves that seemed to give the air hands, he was robed in this certainty: that the God who had lavished such craft upon these worthless birds would not destroy His whole Creation by refusing to let David live forever.

The story is finely written and the ending is a classic short story epiphany, though there is a curious paradox in the tale and an air of contrivance. The paradox is that the boy achieves his sense of eternal life not simply by *seeing* the beauty of God's creatures, but by killing them first. (Coleridge's Ancient Mariner did the same, but he had to go through a hell of guilt before being granted his insight, and his suffering is never entirely remitted.) And the contrivance is that so much is made to depend on this chance vision which hardly arises integrally out of the preceding incidents of the story: the well-established convention of the epiphanic ending is perhaps being made to do too much work here. Another interesting contrast would be with Hemingway's

'Indian Camp', where the young Nick goes through a violent experience of birth and death before reaching his sudden access of physical exhilaration on the lake: 'He knew he would never die.' One could interpret Updike's approach as ironic (this is after all a young boy's experience), but he must also have intended the story, with its earlier theological debates, as a general illustration of the 'argument from design': the idea that the existence of God is shown by the pattern of His creation.

Updike has been writing short stories for more than fifty years. There have been no dramatic shifts of style or changes of technique in this time (he might concur with Philip Larkin, who used to say his aim was to go on writing as he'd always done, but doing it better), but there have been experiments with subject and form. Two stories, for example, use respectively triptych and 'tetraptych' structures. 'The Blessed Man of Boston, My Grandfather's Thimble, and Fanning Island' puts together a portrait, a quasi-autobiographical narrative and a historical sketch of a vanished island race, all linked by the themes of blessedness, accident, transience and preservation. 'Packed Dirt, Churchgoing, a Dying Cat, a Traded Car' links two very brief sketches and two equally brief narratives in a fourfold evocation of habit and ceremony. As the narrator says at the end of the story, addressing the sailor who hitched a ride in his car and to whom he was unable to explain his job as a writer: 'We in America need ceremonies, is I suppose, sailor, the point of what I have written.' Ceremony is indeed a recurring theme throughout Updike's stories, and so is celebration, the aim 'to give the mundane its beautiful due'.[12] For the last fifty years, Updike has been the most fecund and characteristic bard of East Coast, middle-class, white Anglo-Saxon Protestant America and its quotidian life.[13]

Chapter 20

Two traditions and the changing idea of the mainstream

The Jewish American short story, 1950–1980

One of the most persistent functions of the American short story from the last decades of the nineteenth century has been to act as a kind of advance guard for new voices, particularly for new immigrant or older 'marginalized' sections of American society. Newness and marginality are no longer the appropriate words for any of the different American ethnic groups, but the short story still plays a significant role in giving them cognizance of each other, intimate glimpses into the very feeling and texture of life in different communities. One can hardly any longer talk of a 'mainstream', or if one can, it is no longer homogeneous: rather there is a sense of many different groups contributing to a kind of literary centre ground governed by the major writers from all groups, and the major short story magazines and publishing houses. No self-respecting writer would want to be mainly regarded in terms of ethnic or regional identity, but there is still a strong sense in many writers of allegiance to this. American Jewish writers of this period, like Isaac Bashevis Singer, Saul Bellow, Philip Roth, Bernard Malamud, Grace Paley, and Tillie Olsen (confining ourselves once again to writers who have made a significant contribution to the short story), have, to greater or lesser degrees, written about Jewish communities and issues. Isaac Bashevis Singer wrote in Yiddish and drew a great deal on traditional European Jewish culture and folk story traditions. Most Jewish American writers abandoned Yiddish, became a central part of American mainstream culture, and have helped to form that culture for over a century.

Saul Bellow (1915–2005) has been seen as the major American literary figure of the second half of the twentieth century. Philip Roth, in a generous tribute, has called him the 'backbone' of American literature during that period. And while his major contribution has undoubtedly been to the novel, the single volume of his collected short fiction, comprising thirteen stories and published in 2001, reveals a writer who added powerfully and distinctively to the tradition of the short form.[1] Several of the stories (like the richly peopled 'Cousins') are long, and best described as novellas: one feels that often Bellow's expansiveness and wide-ranging curiosity strains at the seams of the short story proper and needs the cut of longer forms. But a number of stories confine themselves to the short story compass and achieve the short story singleness of impression and unity of idea. 'Looking for Mr Green' (1956) is at once a realist story of the day in the life of a Chicago benefit distributor looking for an elusive cheque recipient in a black neighbourhood, and an essay on appearance and reality, phenomena and 'the thing-in-itself'. The cold, grimy streets and gnarled characters of wintry Chicago are done with unique evocativeness, but there is also a philosophical preoccupation (as in so much of Bellow): does Mr Green 'really' exist, or is he merely an 'effect' of bureaucratic records and neighbourhood rumours? In a final vivid scene the distributor, having found a house with 'Mr Green' on the mailbox and convinced he is there, confronts only a naked woman in the draughty hallway, and is left with a mixed sense of self-ridicule and elation: '"For after all," he says, "he *could* be found."' In 'Mosby's Memoirs' Mosby, an *alter ego* for Bellow, is in Mexico writing his memoirs. He tries to enliven them by introducing the story of Lustgarten, a fellow expatriate in Europe who in an attempt to save his financial situation imports a Cadillac which he then cannot sell. But why introduce Lustgarten? (thinks Mosby). He 'didn't *have* to happen'. He is there because Mosby is good at making fun of people. But the story also asks how seriously we should take Mosby himself, who is left confronting death, claustrophobic on a visit to an ancient Mexican tomb. Another story which raises deep questions of the relation of comedy to self-knowledge and morality is the wonderfully searching 'Him with His Foot in His Mouth' (1984), in which the ageing narrator tells of the pitfalls of his compulsive, eruptive wit, which has caused him lost deals and lost friends. (To one rich *grande dame* and potential sponsor, who has spent dinner talking about her millions and who announces she is going to write her autobiography, he responds: 'Will you use a typewriter or an adding machine?') Above all it has led him into one particularly cruel remark to an innocent recipient, which, looking back, he deeply regrets. The achievement of this story is to suggest the creativity, the vital energy of his wit (which at one point the narrator links to Nietzsche's 'will to power') and at the same time the sense of guilt into which it leads him.

Many of the stories in this collection involve an old or elderly narrator looking back on family relationships and formative experiences; a sense of the binding power of the Jewish family, and its function as a source of both human affections and moral laws, is at the heart of the best of them. 'The Old System' inclines, like several of Bellow's stories, towards an overload of character and subsidiary plot: but at its burning centre is the story of the estrangement, caused, typically, by money, between the narrator and his sister. And the climactic scene of hard-won reconciliation, in which the dying sister initially agrees to see her brother only if he pays her $20,000, is one of the most moving in the volume (and in modern American literature). But Bellow's short story masterpiece is undoubtedly the concise, strange, vividly narrated 'Something to Remember Me By', in which an elderly narrator leaves for his son the story of a day of shame and confusion, which despite its indignities seems to define his sense of himself. Seventeen years old, working as a flower-deliverer in Chicago, he is inveigled by a series of extraordinary circumstances into going back to the room of a woman who then steals his clothes, leaving him naked to get home through the freezing Chicago night as best he may. His mother is dying, and the shame of returning to face his fiercely patriarchal father and the family circle, in a woman's dress underneath slacks and trenchcoat borrowed from a drunk, burns in him. He works out a stratagem for climbing into his house unnoticed, but finally abandons it, meeting his father's angry blow to his head 'with gratitude': 'If my mother had already died, he would have embraced me instead.' The story is also about the boy's desperate longing for intellectual understanding, which drives him, absurdly, to scrounge for his lost book of philosophy beneath the window where the woman has thrown out his clothes to a waiting fellow thief. And what it achieves is an exemplary instance of how the short story can bring home to a reader the experience of a moral crisis which has had a profound effect on a life and its beliefs.

Philip Roth (b. 1933) is most celebrated as a novelist, for such works as *Portnoy's Complaint* (1969), *American Pastoral* (1997) and *The Plot Against America* (2004): like Bellow, he must certainly be seen as a major figure in any idea of a 'mainstream' in the second half of the twentieth century. And his first book, *Goodbye Columbus* (1959), consisting of the title novella and five short stories, is significant for the tradition of the short story in its strong preoccupation with moral parable, though in a realist rather than a Hawthornean 'Romance' mode. His most compelling subject in his stories is the tension, for American Jews, between the demands of modern secular life and traditional Jewish moral values. In 'Defender of the Faith' a non-observing Jewish American army sergeant has to cope with the seemingly devout demands of a difficult young Jewish recruit, who plays cleverly but unscrupulously on the sergeant's residual piety and nostalgia to gain special privileges and exemptions. The complexity of both characters is finely delineated – the sergeant's mixture of tough common sense and moral sympathy, and the recruit's canny self-righteousness. In 'Eli the Fanatic' realism is stretched to greater extreme, though never entirely abrogated, when a nervous young secular Jewish lawyer informally representing a predominantly gentile, middle-class neighbourhood has to negotiate with a traditional Jewish boarding school which may be contravening zoning laws. It also offends the community by its too obvious presence, particularly in the form of a devout Jew in long black habit and Talmudic hat who does not speak English and collects groceries for the school. The lawyer (who is already under strain from a difficult marriage to a possessive, pregnant wife) solves one problem by giving two of his suits to the pious Jew. The latter in turn presents his own clothes to the lawyer, who then feels neurotically compelled to don the clothes and parade around the town and into his wife's maternity clinic. Roth writes with a tough, witty energy and a keen eye for the paradoxes and problems of the moral and spiritual life; and the short story form allows him a concentration and moral meaning sometimes dissipated in the greater expansiveness of the novel.

The three volumes of stories by Bernard Malamud (1914–86) – *The Magic Barrel* (1958), *Idiots First* (1963) and *Rembrandt's Hat* (1973) – are remarkable for an imagination that can explore both realism and 'Romance' and for their strong, wry humour. In many ways the combination of parable and comedy is reminiscent of a moral ironist from a very different tradition, Nathaniel Hawthorne: what links them, perhaps, is the continuity of the Judaeo-Christian tradition, and the part that parable plays in both. In 'The Mourners' a landlord tries to evict an impoverished, ageing tenant, but is recalled to compassion by the opposition of the old man's neighbours, and the old man's own strange 'mourning' for the landlord himself. In 'The Magic Barrel' a young man fails to find a suitable bride from an impoverished and comically importunate marriage-broker – until he falls in love with a picture of the broker's daughter (who has become a streetwalker) and refuses to be put off by the broker's passionate denunciation of her. In the Romance fable 'The Jew Bird' a vividly described, decrepit crow – a grotesque parody of an old-fashioned, orthodox, down-on-his-luck immigrant – on the run from what it calls 'Anti-Semeets' takes up residence with a secular Jewish family, helps the son with his schoolwork but infuriates the father with its orthodoxy, and is turned out onto the streets where it is killed. This fable, with its Kafkaesque tragicomic strangeness, epitomizes with melancholy humour the plight of orthodoxy among modern assimilated Jews.

One notable strand of the American Jewish short story since 1950 has been the contribution of women writers and an involvement with feminist concerns. Grace Paley (b. 1922) is very much in the tradition of Malamud, although her stories are formally less plotted and parable-like, more given to interior monologue or stream of consciousness. In *The Little Disturbances of Man* (1959) and *Enormous Changes at the Last Minute* (1974) she explores the dilemmas of modern middle-class New York Jews, particularly women, in stories which confront experience with a remarkable compassion, quirky humour and political and philosophical reflectiveness. In 'Goodbye and Good Luck' Aunt Rose, 'a lady what they call fat and fifty', tells her story in a sharply characterized dramatic monologue to her young niece Lillie: of her youth ('I wasn't no thinner then, only more stationary in the flesh'), her hitherto unhappy love for Volodya, a Russian actor, and its late-flowering happy conclusion. After the death of his wife, Volodya has recently agreed to marry her. ('I'll have a husband, which as everybody knows, a woman should have at least one before the end of the story.') Rose's awareness of the conventions of 'story' is related to Paley's humane optimism and refusal to acquiesce in the bleakness of life she often sees around her. As the narrator says in 'A Conversation with My Father' (a humorous dialogue on Paley's essentially comic aesthetic), she generally despises 'plot, the absolute line between two points . . . Not for literary reasons, but because it takes all hope away. Everyone, real or invented, deserves the open destiny of life.' Her father, an old-school pessimist, wants her to write more straightforward stories ('Just recognizable people, and then write down what happened to them next'). Discussing her proposed story of a woman who becomes a drug addict to try and understand her son and is then abandoned by the son, he wants closure: 'Tragedy! Plain tragedy! Historical tragedy! No hope! The end!' But the narrator says, no, the woman recovered: she lost her son, but became the receptionist in a storefront community clinic, valued for her experience.

In contrast to Paley, Tillie Olsen (b. 1913), a West Coast Jewish writer from a socialist background, confronts tragedy directly in her collection of four stories, *Tell Me a Riddle* (1961). The first story, 'I Stand Here Ironing', is the monologue of a woman whose teenage daughter is in trouble at school. Looking back over her life, she is aware of the reasons for her difficult relations with her daughter but is also unable to see how they could have been different given her economic circumstances. The story is open-ended, but there seems no way out of her dilemma. In the title story, the last and longest of the four, there is the finality of death: a dying woman tries to find some respite from the loving but oppressive attentions of her cantankerous socialist husband and well-meaning family. The sad, comic, bitter struggle between competing claims – of love and society, of human independence and freedom – is powerfully portrayed, and the conclusion achieves a genuine tragic intensity.

Finally, any discussion of the Jewish American short story in these years should mention Cynthia Ozick (b. 1928) and Leonard Michaels (b. 1933). Ozick has published three volumes of stories. Her story 'The Shawl' (1980) is a powerful and horrifying glimpse of the experience of the death camps of the Second World War, while 'The Pagan Rabbi' is a fantastical and grotesque parable on the relation between Jewish belief and the natural world. Michaels, born in the same year as Roth and working on similar cultural material but in a more experimental and absurdist mode, has published three collections, *Going Places* (1965), *I Would Have Saved Them If I Could* (1975) and *A Girl with a Monkey: New and Selected Stories* (2000). 'City Boy' from the first volume is a tragicomedy in which a young man and his girlfriend are surprised by her father while having sex. He escapes naked into the street, walking on his hands past the doorman to distract him. Later he learns with genuine chagrin that the father has had a heart attack; but he returns with the girl to the house for even more zestful sex. The style has a staccato, anxiety-fuelled energy which exactly catches the character and the action. In 'Murderers', from the second volume, sex is again the spur but the outcome is tragic and grotesque: the narrator and a group of other boys go up on a roof to watch the rabbi making energetic love to his wife to the sound of Cuban music; but one of the boys falls off, leaving his ringed finger caught on a nail. Michaels's edgy vision compels the reader with its startling mix of the comic and the painful.

The African American short story, 1930–1980

African American writing, as we have already seen in the works of Chesnutt, Toomer, Wright and Baldwin, has from the first found the short story a powerful medium for exploring the often fragmented and uncentred experience of that group which Orlando Patterson has called 'the loneliest of all Americans'[2]. The short stories of Langston Hughes (1902–67), a leading black American writer from the 1920s onwards, are also an essential part of the tradition: in all Hughes published ten volumes of short stories from 1934 to 1965, including five of his popular 'Simple' stories, about a sharp, feckless, comic Harlem black called Jesse B. Semple whose plain-speaking and untutored philosophizing provides an acute commentary on his condition. Since 1960 the tradition has been extended and deepened by a wide range of voices. Ralph Ellison (1914–94) complemented the outstanding achievement of his novel *Invisible Man* (1952) with a number of short stories, posthumously reprinted in the collection *Flying Home* (1997). The title story is darkly comic, evoking the black protagonist's complicated sense of isolation, ambition and frustration, his fear of blind and twisted racism, and the exasperation he feels towards his less educated fellow blacks. An airman who crashes his army plane is tended by an old black man who tells him of his dreams of flying in heaven and infuriates him with his ignorance (or is it just teasing? 'Wasn't you scared they might shoot you for a crow?'). But his encounter with the racist owner of the land he has crashed on, together with the ultimate sympathy of the old black man, puts him in closer touch with his fellow blacks and 'back into the world of men'; and in a final brilliant image his sense of things is transformed: 'Then like a song within his head he heard the boy's soft humming and saw the dark bird glide into the sun and glow like a bird of flaming gold.' The poetic concentration of the short story form is used to convey a whole creative movement of experience.

Ernest J. Gaines (b. 1933) in *Bloodline* (1968) employs in several stories a child's-eye view of experience which has remarkable freshness, humour and insight. In 'The Sky Is Gray' a young boy is taken to a dentist's clinic on a freezing winter day.[3] He witnesses a sharp and revealing argument between an elderly black preacher and a young man who proclaims himself an atheist, saying 'A white man told you to believe in God', and bemuses the general company by his radical views on the arbitrariness of language. Later, when the boy and his mother are given food and shelter by an old white lady, the mother's proud, grudging acceptance and the old lady's delicacy and tact are finely caught in the tone of their dialogue: this is a story which holds a sharp critique of traditionalism and a sense of human possibility in a single vision. The stories of John Edgar Wideman (b. 1941) are more experimental in form and wide-ranging in subject: in 'Valaida', for instance, the experience of a black woman jazz artist in a German death camp is mediated through a number of voices and consciousnesses to suggest a commonalty of suffering which begins to break down barriers between races.

The experience of African American women has often found a natural form of expression in the short story, as can be seen in the work of Alice Dunbar-Nelson (of mixed Negro, Indian and white ancestry and writing in the 1890s), Zora Neale Hurston (see pp. 186–7 above), Nella Larsen (1891–1964),

Paule Marshall (b. 1929), Toni Cade Bambara (b. 1939) and Alice Walker (b. 1944). Paule Marshall was born in Brooklyn of Barbadian parents. Her collection of four long stories *Soul Clap Hands and Sing* (1961) tells of the lives of ageing men in four settings: Brooklyn, Barbados, British Guiana (now Guyana) and Brazil. 'Barbados' contains the finely drawn portrait of the austere Mr Watford, an elderly rich Barbadian plantation owner: his hard-working solitary life in his 'pure, proud' house, painted 'a pristine white', with the doves which he holds in his hands and whose sound – 'more the feel of that sound than the sound itself' – wakes him each morning; and his encounter with a spirited young woman who is sent to him as a servant. There is a strong sense here of the conflict between generations and the inevitable triumph of the younger, a conflict at once sensuous, emotional and political. The resurgence of Mr Watford's long dormant sexual feeling is disguised as Puritanical rage against the girl and her boyfriend, whose Barbados People's Party badge with its motto 'Vote for the Barbados People's Party: The Old Order Shall Pass' suddenly seems 'threatening' rather than 'ludicrous'. Who are 'the People?' The girl's angry contempt as he reaches for her gives a clear answer: '"you nasty, pissy old man . . . You ain't people, Mr Watford, you ain't people!"'

Toni Cade Bambara's first short story collection, *Gorilla, My Love* (1972), is an exploration of her striking sense of the possibilities of what she calls 'Black English', that 'verbal skill which is an obligatory aesthetic demand in Afro-American culture', in which language is used as much 'to mis-inform, to mis-direct, to smoke out, to screen out, to block out, to intimidate as it is to inform'.[4] The stories, often vibrantly comic, show characters using their skills in the conflicts between generations and political views, and in the general battle of black Brooklyn life. So in 'My Man Bovanne' Hazel Lee defends her corner to the reader against her three grown-up children, who object to her dancing so close to an old, blind 'Uncle Tom' at a local political festivity. 'An I press up close to dance with Bovanne who blind and I'm hummin and he hummin, chest to chest like talking. Not jamming my breasts into the man. Wasn't bout tits, Was bout vibrations . . . Comfy and cheery is what I'm trying to get across. Touch talking, like the heel of the hand on the tambourine or on a drum.' 'I was just talking on the drums' she says later, to confuse as much as to enlighten them. The image suggests a tactile mode of perception which is part of her human warmth and loving-kindness, a humanity which plays against the sharper political consciousness (and self-righteousness) of the younger generation.

Finally, among recent African American short story writers, Edward P. Jones (b. 1950) stands out as a sharply sensitive portraitist of mainly working-class black Americans in Washington DC. His feeling for character and subtle handling of narrative are exemplified in the moving story 'Marie' from his collection *Lost in the City* (1992). By means of a narrative which moves backward and forward in time, it portrays an ageing woman who has survived three husbands and whose life is now reduced to visiting the Social Security Office, being interviewed by a folklore student and (more perilously) defending herself against muggers with a knife she always carries with her. The form of the short story here, and in other stories by Jones, is used not so much for the focus on a single life-changing event as for the accumulation of selected narrative episodes which add up to the sense of a whole life.

Chapter 21

The postmodern short story in America

The history of the short story in mid-twentieth century America continues to be marked by a tension between the twin fictional poles of realism and romance, the story of accurate 'reportage' and the story of fantasy and imagination. The short story also encourages, and can accommodate in particular ways, a reflexive self-consciousness about literary form, a propensity to build into the story a commentary on itself. The closeness of the typical length of the short story to that of the essay, and the relationship of story to essay through the sketch, which shares features of both, also influences the short story's tendency towards self-reflection and a mingling of genres and registers.

In the twentieth century we can see the beginnings of an anti-realist playfulness in O. Henry. Sherwood Anderson's stories often accentuate the grotesque beyond the boundaries of realist report. Flannery O'Connor's tales, for all their compelling realism of detail and surface, relentlessly press their plots and characters towards the extreme revelations of transcendent parable. One of the most famous *New Yorker* stories by Shirley Jackson, 'The Lottery', is a tour de force of bland suburban realism suddenly shifting almost imperceptibly into an enigmatic fantasy in which social orthodoxy involves inhuman sacrificial violence. As we have seen, even a chronicler of contemporary suburban mores like Cheever often allows his imagination to lift his stories beyond the everyday into regions that border the surreal.

Some time beginning in the 1960s the questioning of the limits of realism became more self-conscious and programmatic. Writers like John Barth (b. 1930), Donald Barthelme (1931–89), Robert Coover (b. 1932) and William Gass (b. 1924) began to produce novels and stories which raised questions about the relation of language to reality in new and more conscious ways. One can call this kind of story 'postmodern' with reference either to a phase of literary and cultural history (if one sees postmodernism as a historical moment) or to a literary and artistic mode (if one sees it as a recurring feature in all art and literature). That is, it involves an antagonism to what Jean-François Lyotard called 'the grand narratives' (overarching modes of explanation like the great systems of Hegel or Marx or Freud, or like the epic novels and poems of the nineteenth century); a conscious sense of the way in which language does not just reflect but actually forms reality; a consequent self-consciousness about language; a tendency towards arbitrary, playful or parodic uses of language; and a mixing up of linguistic styles and registers in order to disconcert the reader's expectation and provoke new kinds of awareness. It differs from modernism in its more sceptical view both of the division between 'high' and popular culture and of the belief in reason as formulated by the Enlightenment. In the words of a character in Barthelme's novel *Snow White*, if modernists looked for Henry James's 'figure in the carpet' (see p. 84 above), postmodernists were aware only of 'carpet'.

John Barth

Although not among the earliest examples of the postmodern short story [1] John Barth's 'Lost in the Funhouse' (1968) is a good place to begin. The story involves a teenage boy going with his family to Atlantic City with his parents, his brother and their fourteen-year-old neighbour Magda, seeing a couple making love under the boardwalk and getting lost in a funhouse labyrinth; and the social history of America during the Second World War is implicit in the realist context. But Barth's reflections on the story and on writing explicitly problematize what the story is about, so that the funhouse becomes not just a symbol but a changing metaphor for sex, thought and imagination, fiction and life. Getting 'lost in the funhouse' is getting lost, variously, in an actual place, in the toils of sexual desire, in the winding ways of thought, in the multiple conventions of fiction and language and in the metaphysical quest for the meaning of life. In relation to sex and love, the story has a clear kinship with the traditional allegory of the Quest, like the medieval *Romance of the Rose*. Barth's use of language and typographic conventions (in particular italics) alerts us to the ways in which language is formed by convention, and how the simplest phrases can be quotations as much as 'original' utterances. The device of the broken-off sentence, for example, indicates that we know how it is going to end. It also draws our attention to the way in which any use of language conveys meaning beyond the original intention of its author, so that, particularly in fiction, the plainest and most prosaic denotative language can always carry metaphoric and symbolic significance, whether intended or unintended. Getting lost in the funhouse is partly getting lost in these possibilities of meaning. So the story is about a visit to the funhouse, about how this gets changed in memory and how it gets changed again in writing. It also makes fun of readers' and critics' expectations and habits. One view of postmodern fiction is that it grew up as a response to the ever-growing study of literature at universities, building into its procedures a mockery of pedagogic cliché (Ambrose listens to the laughter from under the boardwalk: 'If the joke had been beyond his understanding he could have said: "*The laughter was over his head.*" And let the reader see the serious wordplay on second reading'). Barth's text is witty from moment to moment, and the underlying narrative keeps us wanting to know 'what happens' in the traditional way – but with a new kind of awareness of what might be meant by 'what happens'. (Does Ambrose 'come out' of the funhouse? Have we?)

Donald Barthelme

If short stories often arise from the consideration of a single guiding idea or image, with the postmodern story the idea or image is often (as with 'Lost in the Funhouse') about the nature of story itself. Donald Barthelme's stories are rich and varied in their ideas and images,[2] but one strand of his artistic thinking is clearly preoccupied with exploring the nature of the fictive imagination itself, its inventions, and how they fare when they go out into the world. 'The Balloon' (1968) tells of the narrator's creation of a giant balloon which he has inflated in New York City and which covers 'forty-five blocks north-south and an irregular area east-west'. The story becomes a witty allegory of the public's reaction to a new and strange work of art:

> There were reactions. Some people found the balloon 'interesting'. As a response this seemed inadequate to the immensity of the balloon, the suddenness of its appearance over the city; on the other hand, in the absence of hysteria or other socially induced anxiety, it must be judged a calm 'mature' one.[3]

Meanwhile children run about on the high surface of the balloon, and others hang green and blue paper lanterns 'from the warm gray underside'. Barthelme has some satirical parody of critical reactions in a list of mock 'soundbite' or bill-poster quotations: '"monstrous pourings" . . . "large, square corners"... "conservative eclecticism that has so far governed modern balloon design"'. Satire is an element in much of his work, though perhaps never the predominant impulse behind it. Here the story's surrealism evokes the genuine strangeness of the new work of art, and also suggests a connection with its creator ('"The balloon [the narrator says to an unnamed partner] is a spontaneous autobiographical disclosure, having to do with the unease I felt at your absence . . ."'). So the balloon is a metaphor (here one might think of it as a pall of unease that hangs over the narrator), but it is also very concrete: at the end of the story it is carried away, deflated, to be stored in West Virginia. This mirrors the odd paradox by which a work of art is both a limited object and something that 'means' more than itself. Barthelme's switches between literal and metaphoric are both comic and conceptually suggestive.

Elsewhere in his work Barthelme explores a variety of topics – childhood, war, science, marriage, psychiatry, religion, jazz, television culture, a son's reaction to his father's death – but at the back of his preoccupations lies always the concern with the medium of language itself: its conventions, its clichés, the way it moulds thought and the way it never originates with its user. Behind every individual expression of language (or what linguistic philosophers have called 'la parole'), there is the is the world of the language system ('la langue'), and it is in this we live, as much as in the non-linguistic world.

Barthelme is fond of nonsense in a way close to T. S. Eliot's idea of it as a 'parody of sense', but his topics are also a subtle commentary on the actual contemporary world. In 'Me and Miss Mandible' the narrator is a former insurance claims adjuster who is masquerading as an eleven-year-old schoolboy. His teacher Miss Mandible vies for his affection with his fellow pupil Sue Ann Brownley. The children are eager devourers of tabloid stories about 'Debbie, Eddie, Liz' (presumably Reynolds, Fisher and Taylor respectively). The story is an ironic commentary on adult imaginings of childhood (how they are always coloured by adult preoccupations), the promises and delusions of education (the teacher's handbook enjoins a simplistic problem-solving mentality) and the fantasies of sexual love fostered by the newspapers. In 'A Shower of Gold' an artist signs up for an existentialist TV game show. The story is an absurdist satire on absurdism, in which the Existential world-view is harnessed for television and the satire cuts both ways. As the presenter explains to a perplexed protagonist, '"God is dead. Nothingness everywhere. Dread. Estrangement. Finitude. *Who Am I* approaches these problems in a root radical way." "On television?" "We're interested in basics, Mr Peterson, we don't play around."' In the end Peterson rebels against his role and, in an outburst of mythic and romantic archetypes, proclaims his mother '"was a royal virgin and my father a shower of gold. My childhood was pastoral and energetic"... [and although] he was, in a sense, lying, in a sense he was not'. The ending, despite its ironies, is affirmative, and belies the idea of Barthelme as simply a reflector of chaos and despair. Similarly, 'See the Moon' is a tale of science-induced paranoia (the narrator is absorbed in 'lunar hostility studies') and difficult family life (his son has started to ask critical questions about his upbringing, and the narrator keeps his wife in the background – 'just the odd bit of dialogue' – because he does not want her to intrude on the narrative with 'the freshness and originality of her observations'). But the general air of disillusion is lightened by his tender attitude to their unborn baby, Gog ('I'm just trying to give you a little briefing here. I don't want you unpleasantly surprised'). In other stories the aims are more directly satirical, as in the darkly hysterical farce of 'War', in which two soldiers in charge of a nuclear warhead get progressively more obsessive as they suspiciously watch the antics of the other; or 'The Report', in which a 'Software Man' talks to a group of secret weapons engineers 'to persuade them not to do what they were doing'. An engineer explains with relish all the horrors of the weaponry (earnestly conceding 'Yes. I realize that there is too much relish here'), but reassures him that 'the interesting thing is that we have a *moral sense*. It is on punched cards, perhaps the most advanced and sensitive moral sense the world has ever known.' Barthelme catches brilliantly not only the permeation of thought by technology, but the comic earnestness with which this is embraced.

Robert Coover

The writers of the postmodern story all share the attitude towards fiction epitomized in William Gass's statement: 'there are no descriptions in fiction, there are only constructions'.[4] Fiction does not describe but invents worlds which have no existence divorced from the words in which they are constructed. Robert Coover's short fictions, in his collection *Pricksongs and Descants* (1969),[5] characteristically make the reader aware of the author creating that world while telling the story. 'The Magic Poker' begins:

> I wander the island, inventing it. I make a sun for it, and trees – pine and birch and dogwood and firs – and cause the water to lap the pebbles of its abandoned shores.

It is a mark of Coover's powers as a writer that he can, in this story and others, create a strong sense of place and atmosphere while always keeping the reader aware of the imaginative process at work; this combination induces a more critical attitude towards meaning and towards the choices the writer makes. 'The Magic Poker' elaborates a story which is part mystery thriller, part fairy tale, with an abandoned island, house and harbour, a lurking, hirsute (possibly mad?) caretaker's son, two attractive young women who visit the island, and the magic poker itself, 'planted' deliberately by the narrator, which turns into a handsome young man when kissed.

What we experience is the narrator's imagination wandering the island, exploring narrative possibilities. The thriller and fairy-tale elements combine to achieve an ambiguous mixture of realism and romance which always keeps in play a sense of the narrator's choices. Coover often takes an established genre or a familiar story and explicitly explores its possibilities for comic or critical effect: in 'The Brother' (one of 'Seven Exemplary Fictions' dedicated to Cervantes) he tells the story of Noah's Ark from the point of view of Noah's incredulous relatives; in 'Morris in Chains' he tells a story of the demise of a pastoral idyll by having an old shepherd and his flock hunted down in a city park by a kind of federal bureau of technological progress; in 'The Romance of the Thin Man and the Fat Lady' he again puts 'romance' and myth into a realistic setting and tells of the fortunes of the real circus couple behind the folklore archetype.

Of all the postmodern writers considered here, Coover is the one most drawn to horror and violence and a kind of quasi-pornographic sexuality. In exploring the way fictions work he is also exploring the darker sides of the imagination. Sometimes this is mainly a matter of disrupting narrative order, returning at various points to paragraphs of development and suspense rather than resolving to threatened outcome, as in 'Quenby and Ola, Swede and Carl', in which Carl on a fishing trip gets sexually involved with the wife and daughter of his fishing guide and ends up alone with the guide on a small boat on the lake at night. Anxiety and tension are built up by the non-chronological narrative ordering, and the reader is left in an uncertain state of suspense – though with strong suspicions – about the facts of the matter and the final outcome. In 'The Baby Sitter' the fantasies and realities of sex and violence are confused, to create a critique of popular fiction and of the reader's own imaginings. It is sometimes difficult, however, to distinguish the titillation of those expectations from the critique of them: the story could be said to pander to what it parodies. In a comparable way 'The Hat Act' is the scenario of a short mime by a conjuror, which explores the imagining of sexuality and violence and the dangerous interplay of fantasy and reality, in such a way as to be both a criticism and an instance of that interplay.

William H. Gass

William Gass thought that Donald Barthelme's finest story was 'The Indian Uprising', an enigmatic tale of American Indians attacking New York City, 'a triumph of style, achieving with the most unlikely materials an almost lyrical grace and beauty'.[6] He was less impressed by those stories which were 'guilty of opportunism of subject' – which constituted comments on topical issues, 'war, street riots, launching pads, etc.'. Gass's judgement here points to the tendency in his own work towards an art which is self-contained and autonomous, which, in Larry McCaffery's words 'denies fiction any mimetic value at all'.[7] Or in Gass's words: 'the philosopher invites us to pass through his words to his subject: man, God, nature, moral law; while the novelist, if he is any good, will keep us kindly imprisoned in his language – there is literally nothing beyond'.[8]

While Gass has written two novels (*Omensetter's Luck*, 1966, and *The Tunnel*, 1994), his reputation as a writer of fiction rests equally on his short stories, and in particular his first collection *In the Heart of the Heart of the Country* (1968), which consists of the title short story and three others, and a novella. The preoccupation of all the short stories is with kinds of transcendence, the escape from quotidian life into a mental or spiritual other world. In 'Icicles' an ageing and unsuccessful real estate salesman becomes obsessed with the beauty of the icicles round his house and the houses he is trying to sell, while being progressively humiliated at work and filled with the sense that he himself is just the property of others and of houses themselves. It is the story of the mind's retreat into a world of non-human beauty. In 'Order of Insects' the female narrator, a wife and mother, similarly becomes absorbed in the strangeness and beauty of dead shells of cockroaches she finds on her rug every morning.

> But this bug I hold in my hand and know to be dead is beautiful, and there is a fierce joy in its composition that beggars every other, for its joy is the joy of stone, and it lives in its tomb like a lion.

But at the same time she knows she also lives in an ordinary world:

> Peace. How can I think of such ludicrous things – beauty and peace, the dark soul of the world – for I am the wife of the house, concerned for the house, tidy and punctual, surrounded by blocks.

The images and rhythms of Gass's sentences are the heart of the matter. Art for Gass transforms mundane life into another order of being. But he is also aware of a potential price (as in the breakdown of the protagonist in 'Icicles').

In 'Mrs Mean' the narrator's philosophical and aesthetic fascination with the neighbour to whom he gives that title leads him into an intense perception of human cruelty and banality, but one that leaves him cut off from life and longing to be inside it, inside the Means' house, inside their lives.

If Gass's project is the redemption of the mundane, then the title story in *The Heart of the Heart of the Country* is that project's biggest challenge. Here are thirty-six paragraphs, with (recurring) titles like 'Weather', 'My House', 'Vital Statistics' and 'Business', in which the narrator describes his town and his relationship to it. He is, he says, 'in retirement from love', and the sadness and regret for a lost love – addresses to an unnamed 'you' – are a recurring motif. But '[f]or all those not in love there's law: to rule, to regulate, to rectify'. And the description of the town, the narrator's house, his neighbours and the rest, with its gesture at a kind of 'guide-book' system (though in the end its logic is that of poetry), is a way of ordering and transforming loss and sadness. 'So I have sailed the sea and come . . . / to B . . .' read the first two lines (under the section title 'A Place'); and the quotation from the first stanza of Yeats's 'Sailing to Byzantium' is more than casual. It has been pointed out that the thirty-six paragraphs in the story correspond with the thirty-six lines of the poem.[9] And it becomes clear that the story is an attempt to create a different kind of 'artifice of eternity' – not romantic and exquisitely wrought like Yeats's nightingale and the poem that contains it, but made up of the banal as well as the beautiful: the electric wires that block the narrator's view, the crumbling asphalt, the list of the town's clubs and societies, the exact number of gas stations; but also the ample shade, the heavy red apple trees, the corn which has 'sifted from the chains of tractored wagons to speckle the streets with gold and with the russet fragments of the cob . . .'. The narrator seems to want to immerse himself, not socially but poetically, in the life of the town, as a replacement for his lost love. But does salvation come from living '*in*', as he puts it, or transcending the world? 'You, not I, live in: in house, in skin, in shrubbery' he says to his cat; and 'Your nature is not something you must rise to.' And there is the lure, or temptation, of 'out': 'Here a stair unfolds towards the street – dark, rickety and treacherous – and I always feel, as I pass it, that if I just went carefully up and turned the corner at the landing, I would find myself out of the world. But I've never had the courage.' Perhaps it is a question of living in the world but changing it through poetry. 'A bush in the excitement of its roses could not have bloomed so beautifully as you did then', he says, looking back. 'It was a look I'd like to give this page. For that is poetry: to bring within about, to change.' The metaphor of the bush is more than a metaphor qualifying the woman, for in 'the excitement of its roses' the bush itself is changed by its association with her, and 'within' is brought about.

It is clear that 'In the Heart of the Heart of the Country' is the short story as poem (postmodernist in its insistence on the 'dreck' of the town, in contrast to Yeats's modernist beauty).[10] It cannot be read for its 'story' (though there is the ghost of one), but it can and must be read and re-read for its subtle shifts of imagery and symbol, its play of tone, its rhythms and its occasional unobtrusive rhymes: all of these together build a complex artefact which is both the correlative of a state of mind and a critique of that state. Partly its aim is the one of poetry's traditional aims, to redeem the facts. Of his lonely, eccentric neighbour Billy the narrator says: 'I keep wondering whether, given time, I might not someday find a figure in our language which would serve him faithfully, and furnish his poverty and loneliness richly out.' But there is also the sense that intentions are vain things, and the finished work has its own voice which may run counter to positive intentions. The story ends in the week of Christmas (the section is ironically entitled 'Business') with a loudspeaker playing a Christmas carol: 'I believe it's one of the jolly ones, it's "Joy to the World". There's no-one to hear the music but myself, and though I'm listening, I'm no longer certain. Perhaps the record's playing something else.'

Chapter 22

Raymond Carver

In the 1970s and 1980s there was a notable revival of interest in the short story in America. And if there was one single figure who represented this revival and was the focus of this interest it was Raymond Carver. Born in Clatskanie, Oregon, in 1938, Carver worked with his father in a sawmill and took other menial jobs (gas station attendant, hospital orderly) before enrolling in Chico State College in California. Coming from this backgound, he represents another of those periodic shifts in American literature away from the predominance of the East Coast middle class. He also represents a return to realism as a literary mode after the postmodern experimentation of Barthelme, Gass and others; a realism which owes much to Hemingway but which also gives the mode a distinctively new inflection, exploring the strange turns of ordinary life, the odd corners within the familiar.

Carver professed an admiration for the early stories of Donald Barthelme, but felt that the movement he represented had run its course and that his widespread influence on other writers (particularly students in university creative writing classes) was not always a benign one.[1] Instead he turned to stories with 'lines of reference back to the real world': stories in a tradition which he saw as including Tolstoy, but above all Anton Chekhov ('the best short story writer who ever lived'), who often wrote about a 'submerged population' (Carver echoes Frank O'Connor here) and 'gave voice' to the inarticulate.[2] In terms of style the greatest influence was perhaps Hemingway: 'The cadences of his sentences I find very exciting. They get into the blood.'[3]

Carver's first collection of stories, *Will You Please Be Quiet, Please?* was published in 1976. Many of the stories are brief, between a thousand and three thousand words, and explore a world in which seemingly minor, slightly unusual experiences cause small seismic shifts in uneventful, 'ordinary' lives. In 'Fat', a waitress tells her friend about serving a very fat man with beautiful manners and a courtly way of referring to himself as 'we'. His size in combination with his gracefulness of manner and a certain philosophical melancholy have a profound effect on the waitress. Carver catches her voice with precision, and dialogue is unmarked, which puts her voice on a level with the narrator's and increases the sense of her talking directly to us. In 'Are You A Doctor?' a man receives a wrong-number call in the middle of the night, and is persuaded to visit the caller, a lonely woman with two children. The story, like a number of stories in the volume, reveals the precariousness of human identity, and how a small departure from the familiar can open up hidden uncertainties. The man gives his name on the phone, and immediately regrets it: the giving and withholding of names, as markers of identity, plays a central part in the story. When the man's wife telephones at the end of the story, he answers it with the nervous announcement 'This is Arnold Bright', and remains silent when his wife teases him about his formality. '"Are you there, Arnold?" she said. "You don't sound like yourself"' is the story's last line. Carver opens up a world in which identity is uncertain and the sense of it easily shaken.

Six of the twenty-two stories in this collection, like this one and the title story, have questions for titles; the stance taken towards ordinary life is interrogative. What keeps people going? What constitutes their sense of themselves? What makes them unhappy? In the title story the protagonist brings up the question of his wife's relationship with another man three years before, is violently shaken by her confession of infidelity, goes out and gets drunk and is beaten up, and is left at the end desperately trying to re-establish a dignified authority; the title question, shouted to his wife as he immures himself in the bathroom, perfectly catches his would-be firmness undermined by self-doubt. In 'What's In Alaska?' the question epitomizes the sense of emptiness that lies behind a couple's desire (typically American in the constant shifting of location) for a new start; and the story ends with a sense of anxiety and menace, the man in bed at night, seeing, or thinking he sees, 'something in the hall . . . a pair of small eyes'.

Carver's work has been labelled 'minimalism' by a number of critics, and the term catches something of these early stories in particular, though Carver himself later repudiated it, feeling that it 'smacks of smallness of vision and execution'.[4] But it is apt insofar as it suggests a concentration and economy of method, and also a focus on the small behavioural signs that register larger predicaments. Story titles, for instance, are often taken from a snatch of dialogue, seemingly banal or unimportant at the time. 'Nobody Said Anything' is an entirely incidental phrase from that story, which nevertheless points to the general lack of communication in the boy protagonist's family. The extreme brevity of the 'short short story' (as it has been dubbed)[5] is also the mode of one story here which chillingly evokes the loss or lack of identity preoccupying many of the stories in the collection. In 'The Father', barely five hundred words long, a family group coos over a baby, speculating on whom it looks like. '"He looks like *Daddy!*"' says one little sister. Another says '"But who does Daddy *look* like?"' And later adds '"Daddy doesn't look like *anybody*."' And they look at the father: 'He had turned around in his chair and his face was white and without expression.'

In Carver's second collection, *What We Talk About When We Talk About Love* (1981), the stories are generally shorter, aiming at concentrated effects that focus on single scenes or episodes. The brevity often arises too from the characters' inarticulacy and their lack of reflectiveness. Instead, what is going on inside them comes out in banal talk or in small actions, sometimes punctuated by sudden outbursts of violence. One thing Carver explores with particular subtlety is the need for, and the frequent breakdown or inefficacy of, talk. Attempts at 'serious talk' (the title of one of the stories) are usually baffled in a way that is both desperate and comic. Language is a way of trying to hold on to things, to maintain dignity, but it often fails. In 'One More Thing' a man has an inane but violent argument with his teenage daughter about whether illness originates 'in the mind' (as she claims); his wife comes in, the argument escalates, he throws a pickle jar through the window; she tells him to leave; he says he's going ('It suits me to a tee . . . Believe me, this is no picnic, this nuthouse'). His efforts at expression are ways of staying in control, but the story ends: 'He said: "I just want to say one more thing." But then he could not think what it could possibly be.' Much is written in short story criticism about 'epiphanies' – clinching moments of revelation or realization that come usually at the end: in Carver we are often left with 'anti-epiphanies', where the realization (at least for the characters) just does not come.

But what makes Carver's stories humane as well as artistically subtle is the feeling that his characters are striving, often desperately, for understanding; and that even where (as is usually the case) it is not achieved, its absence is felt and registered as a central element in the story. In 'So Much Water So Close To Home' a man is confronted by his wife after a fishing trip in which he and his buddies find a dead girl in the river but continue with their fishing and do not report the discovery for two days. Her confrontation is mainly silent – for the enormity of the men's callousness should surely be apparent. '"You know"', she says. And when he says '"She was dead"', she replies simply '"That's the point."' The rest of the story recounts the baffled progress of the wife's inarticulacy. She is telling the story, but the struggle to comprehend and respond adequately is internal as well as external. At the end of the story sexual love and habit erase her disgust with her husband. 'I can't hear a thing with so much water going', she thinks, completing the motif of water as the element of nature, wildness and danger – and giving a rare instance, for Carver, of pure metaphor. In the later, longer version of the story published in *Where I'm Calling From* (1988), there is much more space given to the woman's inner thoughts, and the ending is changed from the dulling of moral doubt by love and habit to a final assertion of the woman's moral unease: talking on the phone, she has just said '"It doesn't matter, Stuart."' But a few lines later the story ends with: 'Then I wake up and say: "For God's sake, Stuart, she was only a child."' Both endings 'work'; and it is a debatable point whether the longer, more deliberately humane version or the earlier, starker and more enigmatic one is more successful.[6]

With the next collection, *Cathedral* (1983), Carver's new humanity and generosity – exemplified in stories like 'Where I'm Calling From', 'A Small, Good Thing', 'The Bridle' and 'Cathedral' – lets his people find their voices and get some bearings on their still often dire emotional and spiritual predicaments. In 'Where I'm Calling From' it is notable that the characters find these bearings by telling stories. One of Carver's most distinctive characteristics is how he puts himself on a level with his characters – the absence of irony in the ordinary sense has often been commented on. So among other things he finds in them a recurring propensity to use narrative as a means of understanding their experience. The protagonist and narrator in 'Where I'm Calling From' is in an alcoholics' 'drying out' clinic (alcohol figures largely in Carver's stories, as it did in his life up to the moment in 1977 when, threatened with a complete breakdown of his health, he gave it up for good). And the thing that gets him going again, spurs him out of mindlessness, is listening to the stories of other inmates. One of them, J. P., tells vividly of a boyhood incident when he fell into a well ('Way up at the top he could see a circle of blue sky. Every once in a while a white cloud passed over'). J. P.'s story is told by the protagonist rather than in direct speech, which makes us feel his assimilation of it, his entering into the possibilities of other lives. At the end of the story the narrator feels enough strength and optimism to decide to telephone his girlfriend (before his wife: his problems are clearly by no means over), and the last line is: '"Hello, sugar," I'll say when she answers. "It's me."' The casual phrase is a small but significant achievement of identity.

One of the most important qualities of Carver's writing, and a key to his particular kind of realism, is what could be called his metonymic imagination. In the figure of metonymy the part stands for the whole. Carver's stories show a marked absence of metaphor or simile, but his method is instead metonymic. Everyday objects take their place in the story in a descriptive, realist manner, relating to each other in a mode of contiguity both in the 'world' of the story and in the syntax of its sentences.[7] But they often come to take on a quasi-symbolic significance in the characters' lives.

In 'The Bridle', for example, the narrator is a hairdresser who runs an apartment block with her husband. Her husband is lazy and she does all the work. A Swede called Holits, an unemployed farmer who has moved from Minnesota with his family, takes one of the apartments. Holits's wife is a waitress, anxious about their lack of money, and the narrator is kind and sympathetic towards her. She also disapproves of the other apartment tenants who sit around the pool doing nothing. Through very simple means, the portrait is built up of a simple-minded but kind and conscientious woman, living in an arid and aimless world. The literal lack of water in the region is a motif that arises quite contingently in her narrative, but it becomes a metonymic detail that stands for the whole. Towards the end, Holits, drinking with the other tenants, jumps into the empty swimming pool, but refuses to go to hospital and leaves with his family soon after. (In a tellingly bleak detail, Holits looks at the other tenants 'like he doesn't know them' when they wave goodbye, raises his right hand, and then goes on waving after the others have stopped.) The narrator later finds a bridle in the Holitses' rooms and gets to thinking about it. She describes it in detail and concludes: 'When you felt it pull, you'd know it was time. You'd know you were going somewhere.' Carver said 'When I'm writing I don't think in terms of developing symbols';[8] but this could nevertheless be called a metonymic symbol – a detail that arises naturally out of the contingent world of the story and comes as the culmination of our sense of the narrator's sense of order, the state of mind that prosaically but effectively resists the aimlessness and vacuity of her surroundings.

It has often been suggested that the short story as a form has as much in common with poetry as with the novel. And Carver, who was also successful as a poet, was himself fond of noting the parallels between the two. The strong sense of form and structure, close attention to verbal detail, rhythm of sentences and tone of voice: all these elements are of crucial importance in both genres. Carver added others:

> economy and unity. There's nothing extraneous or baggy or shapeless about the story or poem as there sometimes is with a novel. And I write my stories and poems in the same way, building from one word to the next, one line or sentence to the next. There's also the spirit. You're trying to capture and hold a moment. A novel is an accretion of detail that may cover weeks or months or years – generations, God forbid. The story takes place in a much smaller compass of time, just like the poem. The impulse is to say it now, get it into the corral rather than let it roam around the range.

There is also 'preciseness, meaningful detail, along with a sense of mystery, of something happening just under the surface of things'.[9]

This 'sense of mystery', often allied with the element of 'threat or sense of menace' which Carver also said he liked in stories, is marked throughout his earlier work ('The Bath', 'What's In Alaska?', 'Viewfinder', 'The Student's Wife') and developed with particular resonance and subtlety in his two final volumes, *Cathedral* (1983) and *Elephant* (1988). The threat and menace usually remain latent, their immediate cause standing for something larger than itself. And in the later volumes there is also a new sense of menace transcended or dissolved, leading not necessarily to a 'happy ending' but to a new awareness, a deepening of the sense of life. In 'Feathers', from *Cathedral*, the narrator Jack and his wife Fran go to supper with friends, Bud and Olla. The latter couple have a small baby and a pet peacock; and they keep a plaster cast of Olla's teeth on the television set. Jack and Fran first encounter the peacock in the front yard: they have never seen one before and are transfixed by its beauty and its strange cry. The baby, Jack recalls, 'was the ugliest baby I'd ever seen' (he has already told us of his own marriage: 'the one thing we didn't wish for was kids'). Olla cooks them a huge and satisfying meal; Fran plays 'patty-cake' with the baby. The peacock is in the living room 'turning its head this way and that, like you'd turn a hand-mirror'; then it comes in and up to the table.

> The peacock walked quickly around the table and went for the baby. It ran its long neck across the baby's legs. It pushed its beak in under the baby's pajama top and shook its stiff head back and forth. The baby laughed and kicked its feet. Scooting onto its back, the baby worked its way over Fran's knees and down onto the floor. The peacock kept pushing against the baby, as if it was a game they were playing.

In this extraordinary moment, a sudden sense of possible violence ('went for the baby') is resolved in the next two sentences into our awareness of harmless playfulness. Threat is dissolved. The evening with Bud and Olla, the sense of contented family life, also dissolves the visitors' original ill-tempered, comically trivial, suspicions of the couple and arouses afresh their feelings for each other and back at home they make love. At the end of the story Jack looks back with a kind of perplexed, not fully articulated wonder at that time. What followed it was a change for him and Fran, and not a change for the better: a son (conceived, we infer, on that evening) has grown up with a 'conniving streak'; Fran 'has gotten fat on me, too'. Fran blames that evening: '"Goddamn those people and their ugly baby . . . And that smelly bird."' But we pick up – not from what Jack says explicitly but from the way he remembers the details of the evening – that it has stayed with him as a kind of barely perceived, half-understood emblem of the possibilities of life, its beauty and strangeness and potential happiness. The story is a masterly demonstration of Carver's ability to evoke a deeper sense of these things through a poetically precise notation of surface banality and oddity, and through his characters' own real but limited insight.

One of the most interesting aspects of Carver's short stories is their relation to irony. It could be said that they are marked by the absence of irony, at least of that kind of irony which suggests an authorial or narratorial insight superior to that of the characters (or, where there is a first-person narrator, the other characters). Asked about irony in an interview, Carver expressed a certain discomfort with it:

> I see irony as a sort of pact or compact between the writer and the reader in that they know more than the characters do. The characters are set up and then they're set down again in some sort of subtle pratfall or awakening. . . . I'm uncomfortable with irony if it's at the expense of someone else, if it hurts the characters.[10]

And in another interview: 'These are my people. I can't offend them, and I wouldn't.' The humanity of this concern for his characters is striking. But it does not preclude a sense of authorial perspective – the perspective one feels a work of fiction must have to enable it to reveal anything. In 'Feathers', for example, we presumably feel that the author's attitude to the teeth on the television set is not the same as Olla's, and that his sense of the peacock is not quite the same as either Fran's or Jack's. But at the same time he feels with them, he enters into their point of view (which itself often consists of different elements and is subject to change). This means that the frequent elements of comedy in the stories are benign: they allow readers a wider perspective but they also deepen the latter's sympathy for and empathy with all the characters, particularly with any first-person narrator. The form of the short story may be especially suited to this. The exploration of the consciousness of an unsophisticated first-person narrator, which remains throughout limited to his or her words, might pall over the long duration of a novel (Henry James famously found this to be the case with Flaubert's *L' Education Sentimentale*), but can be sustained throughout a short story.

Carver, as has been noted above, is usually seen as a 'realist' writer, as he certainly is in contradistinction to say Barthelme or Gass, but his stories raise interesting questions about the problematic nature of the term, particularly in relation to the short story. One is tempted to say that realism in fiction cannot exist: at least if the term connotes a simple reflection of the real. Historiography or reportage might be seen to aim at such a direct reflection (though also not unproblematically), but fiction involves invention: the writer of fiction *qua* fiction is not writing about anything that has actually happened. (Carver said that he drew on his own experience, using 'a little autobiography but a lot of imagination'.) Realist fiction can at most delineate things that *could* happen. And with invention comes unlimited scope for shaping, for imaginative choice, for form. Even Carver's most 'realist' stories, describing simple and commonplace events, are shaped towards meaning – towards the symbolic, the representative, the revelatory – by form. In 'Nobody Said Anything' (from his first volume) the title raises a casual phrase to a representative status; and the form of the ending, the syntax and punctuation (Carver once quoted Isaac Babel: 'No iron can pierce the heart with such force as a period put just at the right place')[11] transforms the messy trophy of half a fish into a kind of triumph for the boy protagonist:

> I went back outside. I looked into the creel. What was there looked silver under the porch light. What was there filled the creel.
> I lifted him out. I held him. I held that half of him.

Carver employs these powers in all his stories: but one great interest of the last volume he published before his death, *Elephant*, is its new reflexive awareness of and experiments with form. Three stories in particular, 'Intimacy', 'Blackbird Pie' and 'Errand', show a new sense of the possibilities of the short story medium, and constitute reflections on the art of the short story itself. In 'Intimacy' the narrator, a writer, goes to visit his ex-wife. In the course of the visit, the wife 'comes out with what's on her mind' – about their life together and his writing about it – and the narrator listens. The unusual achievement of the story is to create a distinctive voice for the woman, but to mediate this through the narrator's voice. So we hear him, and hear her through him. The dialogue (mainly the woman's monologue) is without quotation marks, but each of her paragraphs of speech begins with 'She says', and his replies are similarly marked. This technique, which mixes direct with free indirect speech, not only allows the woman's point of view to emerge strongly and vigorously, but also makes us feel the way the man is impressed by it and enters into its spirit (his use of the present tense is clearly of the essence here), catching its mixture of cliché, bitter wit and unconscious humour. Sometimes these latter elements are difficult to distinguish, which is itself a mark of her passionate sincerity:

> She wishes I'd get off that other subject [the bad times]. She's bored with it. Sick of hearing about it. Your private hobbyhorse, she says. What's done is done and water under the bridge, she says. A tragedy, yes. God knows it was a tragedy and then some. But why keep it going?

Her tirade leaves him virtually speechless, but towards the end he finds himself going down on his knees ('What am I doing on the floor? I wish

I could say') and taking the hem of her dress. At which point her speech registers that she is embarrassed, moved and exasperated at once, in a mixture of irony and compassion:

> She says, I forgive you.
>
> She says, Are you satisfied now? Is that better? Are you happy? He's happy now, she says.

The effect is on a knife-edge between sentiment and sentimentality, but her tone of voice saves it; and saves the narrator. We feel that something has been genuinely brought to light: the difficult relation between art and life – the necessary freedom of the artist and his responsibility to deal justly with his material – has been clarified.

'Where Is The Voice Coming From?' The title of one of Eudora Welty's later stories might serve as an epigraph to the three stories I am considering. In 'Blackbird Pie' it should perhaps be recast as 'Whose writing is this?' This is a kind of mystery story (with shades of Poe: an obsessive narrator, a foggy night and a woman in a darkened house) which again explores the relation between experience and writing, but in a non-realist way which Carver has not attempted before. One evening the narrator finds a letter from his wife, pushed under the door. The letter (of which we are given snatches) gives her reasons for leaving him. But what perplexes him is that it is not in her handwriting. 'Secondly, my wife *never* underlines her words for emphasis' (he says, or writes, with these emphases or underlinings), adding however that 'anyone . . . *given the pressure of the moment* [could] do something totally out of character'. We begin to wonder if he has written the letter himself. Is he mad? Or is he just a writer of fiction? He has an interest in history, and his reflections on the origin of the letter and the facts of their life together are mixed up with historical allusions. History aims both at factual accuracy and at evaluation of significance, giving the truth of, and an appropriate dignity to, events; and the narrator is garrulously and comically preoccupied with both, striking heroic analogies and falling into bathos:

> Suddenly it was too late for any decisive action. The moment had come and gone, and could not be called back. Just so did Darius hesitate and then fail to act at the battle of Granicus, and the day was lost, Alexander the Great rolling him up on every side and giving him a real walloping.

The story also has a sense of mystery, and the final scene, in which he finds two stray horses on the lawn at the moment his wife is about to leave, is both comic and surreal, recalling Carver's poem 'Late Night with Fog and Horses' and the line 'Whatever was / happening now was happening in another time'. The mystery of the handwriting is never solved and is in a sense unimportant (just as the biographical connections of the story – where is the writing coming from? – are in the end irrelevant). And the narrator is left with the realization that 'autobiography is the poor man's history', and that with the end of his marriage and its passionate communal life, 'I am saying goodbye to history. Goodbye, my darling.' The short story has focused on and realized another turning point, a scene of revelation, the coming to consciousness of an idea.

Biography, and the connection between the writer's life and that of his protagonists, may give explanations that have their proper interest, but they are finally irrelevant to artistic effect. Yet the author's placing of stories in a collection is a part of that effect, and it is surely no accident that 'Blackbird Pie', which ends with the lines just quoted, should be followed by 'Errand', which begins: 'Chekhov. On the evening of 22 March 1897 . . .' The narrator of 'Blackbird Pie' said goodbye to history – to the poor man's history, autobiography – but the author of 'Errand' confronts a wider history. As the last story published in Carver's lifetime it shows an entirely new creative direction, a looking outward for subject matter, towards other kinds of lives and towards a more conscious consideration of the short story tradition and of story's relation to truth. At the same time it is a homage (as Carver himself said) to the short story writer Carver most admired, Anton Chekhov. The story tells of Chekhov's death in a German spa hotel in 1904. It keeps close to the biographical facts – drawn from Henri Troyat's biography, which itself draws on the eye-witness account of Olga Knipper, Chekhov's wife – including the moving detail of the doctor's ordering champagne. But with the role of the bellboy who brings the champagne Carver enters the realm of imaginative creation, not so much redeeming the character for history as creating him for story, so that he lives in the story with as much reality as the historically recorded events. The extraordinary passage in which Olga tells the young man exactly how he should go and summon the coroner enacts an imagining within an imagining, in which Olga's contribution to the dignity and propriety of the event is given its due. It leads to the delicate crowning moment when the boy bends down and picks up the fallen champagne cork. This completes the fictional picture by allowing the young man his creative contribution to the action. Like Chekhov's own stories, it reveals the moral significance and dignity in the ordinary. As such, it is an unusually fitting conclusion to Carver's work, and an exemplary instance of the modern short story.

Chapter 23

Epilogue: the contemporary American short story

I have chosen to conclude my account of the American short story with Carver, both because of his special distinction and because of the undoubted influence his example has had on the prestige and status of the form in our own time. But other major contemporary writers like John Updike (discussed in Chapter 19) and Joyce Carole Oates have produced several volumes of short stories since the 1950s and 1960s respectively; and since the 1980s, too, the short story has inspired a remarkable fecundity and brilliance among newer writers. Labels are always indadequate, but from among those who have been called 'the new realists' one would want to single out the names of Tobias Wolff, Richard Ford, Bobbie Ann Mason, Mary Robison, Andre Dubus and Richard Bausch. From those writers who have experimented with very short forms two of the most striking are Amy Hempel and Jayne Ann Phillips, and the latter's work often includes a lyrical, visionary element which is notable also in the stories of Denis Johnson. Anne Beattie and Lorrie Moore are two writers who have penetratingly explored the world of a new generation of middle-class professional characters, with a comic and witty emphasis. Annie Proulx has explored the territory of the contemporary rural East and 'cowboy' West in stories which have a sharp, grainy sense of landscape, weather and human oddity. African American writing has seen strong recent collections from Jamaica Kincaid and Edward P. Jones. The Native American short story is becoming increasingly important through the work of Gerald Vizenor, Leslie Marmon Silko, Louise Erdrich and Sherman Alexie. Hispanic American writing has been especially distinguished by collections from Sandra Cisneros and Dagoberto Gilb. Recent volumes by Amy Tan and David Wong Louie have continued a tradition of Asian American writing began at the end of the nineteenth century with the work of Sui Sin Far. From the East Coast, any account of the most significant recent American publications in the last five years would have to include the brilliant short story collections of David Means and David Foster Wallace – both writers who achieve a fresh and sometimes startling handling of the form.

The short story has also come to be seen as playing a distinctive part in defining and exploring the life of particular social groups: the American working-class short story, the ecological short story and lesbian and gay short stories (as in the work of David Leavitt) all get separate essays in *The Columbia Companion to the Twentieth Century American Short Story.* Of writing in any genre on the Vietnam War the short story collections of Tobias Wolff (*In Pharaoh's Army,* which mingles short story and memoir) and Tim O'Brien (*The Things They Carried*) are among the most significant. Mention should also be made of the new recognition of the short story cycle. As a distinct genre, it goes back to Crane and Jewett, but it has proved especially important during the last thirty years, particularly in relation to the changing sense of American ethnicity, in the work of Erdrich, Kincaid, Cisneros, Susan Minot, Julia Alvarez and Robert Olen Butler.[1]

Lists like these point to the vitality of the tradition, but they should also be read as rolls of literary honour. The short story in the United States has undoubtedly established itself in two centuries as a major literary form and can no longer be seen merely as a kind of baby brother to the novel. Of a number of pre-eminent writers in the American tradition, among them Irving, Hawthorne, Poe, Bierce, Anderson, Hemingway, Welty, Flannery O'Connor and Carver, it can be convincingly argued that their most important work lies in their short stories. More recently, Cheever, Tobias Wolff, Dubus, Moore, Mason and Phillips have all made what is arguably their most important contribution (or contribution so far) in the short story form.

The short story is still, as it has been from the first, an ideal form for experimentation, for breaking new literary ground and for introducing new regional and ethnic voices into the mainstream of literature. The form is flourishingly represented in a large number of magazines, both best-selling and 'little': out of the many one might particularly mention *The New Yorker, The Atlantic Monthly, Vanity Fair, Esquire, Granta, The Kenyon Review, Harper's* and *McSweeney's.* Notable annual anthologies – in particular *The O. Henry Memorial Prize Stories* (published since 1919, with only one two-year break in 1952–3), *The Best American Short Stories* (published continuously since 1915) and the *Pushcart Prize Stories* (published from 1977) – focus on the best stories from 'little' magazines. There are also a number of recent anthologies from major publishers, such as the lively and surprising collection *The Anchor Book of New American Short Stories* (2004). Critical writing on the form – with a few notable exceptions – has not perhaps entirely kept pace with the fecundity of the form itself. But, as I hope the works cited in the Notes and the Guide to Further Reading make clear, there has in the last thirty or forty years been a welcome expansion of academic attention to the form, with a number of useful collections of essays exploring the aesthetic of the short story, and more than one periodical dedicated to its critical study. One might mention particularly *Studies In Short Fiction*, published by Newberry College, South Carolina, and *The Journal of The Short Story in English*, published jointly by the University of Angers in France and Belmont University in Nashville, Tennessee.

A surprising number of American writers have spoken of the short story as a form to which they feel particularly attracted artistically, or which they feel makes bracing demands on – or calls out the best in – a writer. Edith Wharton, it will be remembered, spoke of 'the sense of authority with which I take hold of the short story'. Henry James felt that 'to write a series of good little tales I deem ample work for a lifetime'. Richard Ford has said: 'Unlike novels, short stories seem perfectible, but getting them perfected is very frustrating . . . There is such economy of gesture in short stories, that everything takes on added weight.'[2] Joyce Carol Oates, despite her prolific production of novels, has described the role of her short stories as 'virtually indistinguishable from my life! . . . The short story lends itself most gracefully to experimentation . . . I like the freedom and promise of the form.'[3]

The short story is perhaps the exemplary form for the perception of crisis, crux, turning point; and as such it has proved ideal for recording decisive moments, intimately private but often with broad social resonances, in the swift development of the psyche of post-independence America. Its ratio of insight to length is greater than that of the novel. Like the lyric poem, but always with the emphasis on narrative and event, it focuses on the most intense and life-changing experiences. 'And suddenly, everything became clear to him.' That line from Chekhov, which Raymond Carver kept on a three-by-five card on his desk, might serve as an expression of the essential short story effect. And across two centuries in America the short story has been like a torch whose stabs of light, brilliant, intermittent, startling, have illuminated the most crucial areas of American experience.

Notes

1 Introduction

1. Frank O'Connor, *The Lonely Voice: A Study of the Short Story* (first published 1963; Hoboken, NJ: Melville House Publishing, 2004), p. 39. O'Connor was referring to the short story in the United States: I, too, will restrict myself to that country for reasons of length – though with some regret at having to omit all mention, for instance, of such fine contemporary Canadian short story writers as Alice Munro and Alistair MacLeod, to name only two.
2. See 'The Bungling Host (Hitchiti)', in Paul Lauter (ed.), *The Heath Anthology of American Literature*, 2nd edn (Lexington and Toronto: D. C. Heath & Co., 1994), vol. I, p. 69–70; and 'The Bungling Host (Koasati)', in Nina Baym (ed.), *The Norton Anthology of American Literature*, 4th edn (New York and London: W. W. Norton & Co., 1974), vol. I, pp. 131–6.
3. *The Norton Anthology of American Literature*, vol. I, p. 131.
4. See for example Gerald Vizenor, *Landfill Meditation: Crossblood Stories* (Middletown, Conn.: Wesleyan University Press, 1992).
5. See for example John Bayley, *The Short Story: Henry James to Elizabeth Bowen* (New York: St Martin's Press), 1988; and Douglas Tallack, *The Nineteenth Century American Short Story: Language, Form and Ideology* (London and New York: Routledge, 1993).
6. See for example Eileen Baldeshwhiler, 'The Lyric Short Story: the Sketch of a History', and Nadine Gordimer, 'The Flash of Fireflies', in Charles E. May (ed.), *The New Short Story Theories* (Athens: Ohio University Press, 1994), pp. 231–43 and 263–7.
7. See e.g. Charles E. May, 'The Nature of Knowledge in Short Fiction', in May (ed.), *The New Short Story Theories*, pp. 131–43.
8. See e.g. Mary Louise Pratt, 'The Short Story: the Long and the Short of It', in May (ed.), *The New Short Story Theories*, p. 92.
9. Henry James, *The Novels and Tales of Henry James* (New York: Charles Scribner's Sons, 1908–9), vol. XV, p. vii; passage repr. in Richard A. Hocks, *Henry James: A Study of the Short Fiction* (Boston: Twayne, 1990), p. 126.
10. Richard Ford (ed.), *The Granta Book of the American Long Story* (London: Granta Books, 1998).

11. Poe in his 'Review of *Twice-Told Tales*' (1842); repr. in *The American Tradition in Literature*, 4th edn (New York: Grosset and Dunlap/W. W. Norton, 1974), p. 875.
12. Henry James, Notebook entry for 22 February 1891, *The Notebooks of Henry James*, ed. F. O. Mattheson and Kenneth B. Murdock (Oxford: Oxford University Press, 1947); repr. in Eugene Current Garcia (ed.), *What is The Short Story?* (Glenview, Ill. and Brighton: Scott, Foresman & Co., 1974), pp. 25–7.
13. Ralph Waldo Emerson, 'The American Scholar', in Baym (ed.), *The Norton Anthology of American Literature*, pp. 1113, 1104.
14. Washington Irving, *The Sketch-Book of Geoffrey Crayon, Gent.*, ed. Susan Manning (Oxford: Oxford World's Classics, 1996); quoted in the editor's Introduction, p. xxviii.
15. See Andrew Levy, *The Culture and Commerce of the American Short Story* (Cambridge: Cambridge University Press, 1993), pp. 32–3.
16. Quoted in ibid., p. 11.
17. Letter to Charles Anthon, *Letters of Edgar Allan Poe*, ed. John Ward Ostrom (New York: Gordian Press, 1966), vol. I, p. 168; quoted in Levy, *Culture and Commerce*, p. 17.
18. Levy, *Culture and Commerce*, p. 18.
19. Alexis De Tocqueville, *Democracy in America* (London: Collins, 1968), vol. II, pp. 608–9.
20. See O'Connor, *Lonely Voice*, pp. 15, 17.
21. Emerson, 'The American Scholar', p. 1113.
22. Henry James, letter to W. D. Howells, 31 January 1880; quoted in Edward O'Brien, *The Advance of the American Short Story* (New York: Dodd, Mead & Co., 1931), p. 120.
23. Henry James, *Letters*, ed. Leon Edel, 4 vols. (Cambridge, Mass.: Harvard University Press, 1980), vol. III, p. 240; quoted in Valerie Shaw, *The Short Story: A Critical Introduction* (London and New York: Longman, 1994), p. 12.
24. Raymond Carver, *Fires: Essays, Poems, Stories* (London: Pan Books Ltd., 1986), p. 22.

2 The short story as ironic myth: Washington Irving and William Austin

1. Nathaniel Hawthorne, *The Scarlet Letter* (New York: New American Library, 1959), p. 45.
2. For the category of the fantastic, a literary domain which hovers ambiguously between the supernatural and the realistic, see Tzvetan Todorov, *The Fantastic: A Structural Approach to a Literary Genre* (Ithaca, NY: Cornell University Press, 1975).
3. See e.g. Louis Le Fevre, 'Paul Bunyan and Rip Van Winkle', *Yale Review*, 36 (1946), pp. 66–76; abstracted in J. K. Bowen and R. Van Der Beets (eds.), *American Short Fiction: Readings and Criticism* (Indianapolis: Bobbs Merrill, 1990), pp. 22–3.

4. Letter of 11 December 1824; quoted in Washington Irving, *The Sketch-Book of Geoffrey Crayon, Gent.*, ed. Susan Manning (Oxford: Oxford World's Classics, 1996), p. xxviii.
5. William Austin, *The Man With the Cloaks and Other Stories*, ed. Alain Geoffroy, *Alizés*, 15 (Faculté des Lettres et Sciences Humaines, Université de la Réunion, 1998). See also the critical edition of 'Peter Rugg, the Missing Man' in *Alizés*, 11 (1996).
6. Todorov, *The Fantastic.*
7. Cited in F. L. Pattee, *The Development of the American Short Story* (New York: Biblo & Tannen, 1975), pp. 37–8.
8. Ibid.
9. Alain Geoffroy, 'The Schoolmaster of Stingy Hollow', *Alizés*, 15 (1998), pp. 135–45.

3 Nathaniel Hawthorne

1. For 'the idea as hero', see above, pp. 5–6.
2. For documentation of the magazines in which Hawthorne's story appeared, see F. L. Pattee, *The Development of the American Short Story* (New York: Biblo & Tannen, 1975), pp. 111–14.
3. *The Scarlet Letter* (New York: New American Library, 1959), p. 21.
4. Henry James, *Hawthorne* (London: Macmillan; New York: St Martin's Press, 1967), p. 69.
5. See Hawthorne, *Young Goodman Brown and Other Tales*, ed. Brian Harding (Oxford: Oxford World's Classics, 1998), p. 361.
6. The story is based on the actual community founded by Captain Wollaston and later led by William Morton, who came into conflict with the sterner Endicott. See Bradford's *Of Plymouth Plantation*, Book II, Chapter XIX, *The Norton Anthology of American Literature*, 5th edn (New York and London: W. W. Norton & Co., 1998), vol. I, pp. 187–90.
7. *The Norton Anthology of American Literature*, 5th edn, vol. I, p. 2264.
8. See Daniel G. Hoffman, *Form and Fable in American Fiction* (New York: W. W. Norton & Co., 1961), cited in Harding's notes to 'Young Goodman Brown' p. 350.
9. See the arguments of E. Earle Stibitz, 'Ironic Unity in Hawthorne's "The Minister's Black Veil"', *American Literature*, 34 (1962), pp. 182–90 and Nicholas J. Canaday Jnr., 'Hawthorne's Minister and the Veiling Deceptions of Self', *Studies in Short Fiction*, 4 (1967), pp. 135–42; cited in Harding's notes to 'Young Goodman Brown', p. 350.
10. J. Hillis Miller, *Hawthorne and History: Defacing It* (Cambridge, Mass. and Oxford: Blackwell, 1991), p. 51.
11. Ralph Waldo Emerson, 'Nature', *The Norton Anthology of American Literature*, p. 1081.
12. James, *Hawthorne*, pp. 70–1.

4 Edgar Allan Poe

1. Poe, *Essays and Reviews* (New York: The Library of America, 1984), p. 571.
2. Ibid., p. 572.
3. Brander Matthews, *The Philosophy of the Short-Story* (New York: Folcroft Library Editions, 1971).
4. Poe, 'The Philosophy of Composition', in *Essays and Reviews*, pp. 13–25.
5. Ibid., p. 19.
6. For a persuasive Freudian reading of these stories, which relates them to the trauma of Poe's early loss of his mother and the subsequent early deaths of a number of other mother-figures, see Marie Bonaparte, *Edgar Allan Poe*, trans. John Rodker (London: Imago, 1949).
7. D. H. Lawrence, *Studies in Classic American Literature* (1923; New York: The Viking Press, 1973), p. 68.
8. See Roy P. Basler, 'The Interpretation of "Ligeia"', in R. Regan (ed.), *Edgar Allan Poe: a Collection of Critical Essays* (Englewood Cliffs, NJ: Prentice Hall, 1967).
9. See Poe's 'Review of Hawthorne's "Twice-Told Tales"' in *Essays and Reviews*, pp. 574–5.
10. Tzvetan Todorov, *The Fantastic: A Structural Approach to a Literary Genre*, trans. Richard Howard (Ithaca, NY: Cornell University Press, 1975).
11. Fyodor Dostoyevsky, *Notes from Underground* (1864), trans. J. Courson (Harmondsworth: Penguin Books, 1977).
12. For a view that argues that the narrator is also affected by Usher's madness, and that the return of Madeline is an hallucination shared by both, see John S. Hill, 'The Dual Hallucination in "The Fall of the House of Usher"', in William L. Howarth (ed.), *Twentieth Century Interpretations of Poe's Tales* (Englewood Cliffs, NJ: Prentice Hall, 1971), pp. 55–62.
13. See Mario Praz, *The Romantic Agony*, trans. A. Davidson, 2nd edn (Oxford: Oxford University Press, 1970).
14. See Christopher Benfey, 'Poe and the Unreadable: "The Black Cat" and "The Tell-Tale Heart"', in Kenneth Silverman (ed.), *New Essays on Poe's Major Tales* (Cambridge: Cambridge University Press, 1993), pp. 36, 38.
15. See John Dickson Carr, *The Life of Sir Arthur Conan Doyle* (London: Murray, 1949), pp. 29, 237.
16. See Poe, *Letters*, ed. J. W. Ostrom, 2 vols. (New York: Gordian Press, 1966), vol. II, p. 38; quoted in Kenneth Silverman, *Edgar Allan Poe: Mournful and Never-Ending Remembrance* (New York: Weidenfeld & Nicolson, 1991), p. 172.
17. G. K. Chesterton, 'A Defence of Detective Stories', in *The Defendant* (London: Dent, 1914), pp. 161–2.
18. Louise J. Kaplan, 'The Perverse Strategy in "The Fall of the House of Usher"', in Silverman (ed.), *New Essays on Poe's Major Tales*, pp. 46–7.
19. Lacan, *The Seminar*, Book III: *The Psychoses*, trans. Russell Griggs (London: Routledge, 1993), p. 167.

20. See Barbara Johnson, 'The Frame of Reference: Poe, Lacan, Derrida', in J. P. Muller and W. J. Richardson (eds.), *The Purloined Poe: Lacan, Derrida and Psychoanalytic Reading* (Baltimore and London: Johns Hopkins University Press, 1988), pp. 213–51.
21. See R. Morrison and C. Baldick (eds.), *Tales of Terror from Blackwood's Magazine* (Oxford: Oxford World's Classics, 1995).
22. A version of this point was first suggested to me in a seminar by Professor Stephen Bann.

5 Herman Melville

1. See 'Introduction' to Herman Melville, *Billy Budd, Sailor and Selected Tales*, ed. Robert Milder (Oxford: Oxford World's Classics, 1997), p. viii.
2. See Leo Marx, 'Melville's Parable of the Walls', *Sewanee Review*, 61 (1963), pp. 602–67.
3. Henry Thoreau, *Walden* (London: Penguin Books, 1986), p. 135.
4. See Merton M. Sealts Jnr., 'Herman Melville's "I and My Chimney"', in *Pursuing Melville 1940–1980* (Madison: University of Wisconsin Press, 1982), pp. 11–22.

6 New territories: Bret Harte and Mark Twain

1. See Paul Johnson, *A History of the American People* (London: Phoenix Press, 1997), p. 393.
2. Bret Harte, *Selected Stories and Sketches*, ed. David Wyatt (Oxford: Oxford World's Classics, 1995), p. xvi. All subsequent quotations from Harte's stories are taken from this edition.
3. Mark Twain, *Selected Stories*, ed. Justin Kaplan (London and New York: Penguin Books, 1985), p. 61.
4. *Cornhill Magazine*, July, 1899; repr. in Eugene Current-García and Walton R. Patrick, *What Is the Short Story?*, revised edn (Glenview, Ill.: Scott, Foresman & Co., 1974), p. 32.
5. Ibid., p. 29.
6. Ibid., p. x.
7. Repr. in Paul Lauter (ed.), *The Heath Anthology of American Literature*, vol. I, 2nd edn (Lexington, Mass. and Toronto: D. C. Heath Co., 1994), pp. 1470–4.
8. Quoted by R. J. Krause in *Mark Twain: Critical Assessments*, vol. III, ed. Stuart Hutchinson (Mountfield: Helm Information, 1993), p. 16.
9. See Ronald J. Gervais, 'What Remains When Everything Is Left Out: the Joke of "Jim Baker's Blue Jay Yarn"', *Mark Twain Journal*, 21/4 (Fall, 1983), pp. 12–14. Quoted in J. D. Wilson, *A Reader's Guide to the Short Stories of Mark Twain* (Boston: G. K. Hall, 1987), p. 158.

10. The controversial question of the ideological implications of Harris's Uncle Remus is discussed more fully in Chapter 18 below.
11. In a remarkably suggestive book, Shelley Fisher Fishkin has demonstrated the similarity of Huck's voice to that of the African American boy in 'Sociable Jimmy'. This is significant in a number of ways, but from the point of view of the present study it shows the fruitfulness of the sketch and short story form for literary experiment and for preliminary sortees into entirely new literary territory, particularly in relation to 'voice'. See Fishkin, *Was Huck Black?: Mark Twain and African American Voices* (Oxford: Oxford University Press, 1993).

7 Realism, the grotesque and impressionism: Hamlin Garland, Ambrose Bierce and Stephen Crane

1. William Dean Howells, *The Editor's Study* (1887), *The Heath Anthology of American Literature*, 2nd edn, ed. Paul Lauter (Lexington: D. C. Heath and Co., 1994) vol. II, p. 539.
2. Ibid., p. 542.
3. Hamlin Garland, *Main Travelled Roads* (New York: Harper & Row, 1956), p. ix.
4. Ambrose Bierce, *Collected Works*, vol. X, p. 277; quoted in Cathy N. Davidson, *The Experimental Fictions of Ambrose Bierce: Structuring the Ineffable* (Lincoln and London: University of Nebraska Press, 1984), p. 116.
5. See Davidson, *Experimental Fictions of Ambrose Bierce*, p. 116.
6. Ibid., pp. 48–9.
7. See M. E. Grenander, *Ambrose Bierce* (New York: Twayne, 1971), p. 161.
8. Quoted in John Berryman, *Stephen Crane* (Cleveland: Meridian, 1962), p. 54.
9. See James Nagel, *Stephen Crane and Literary Impressionism* (University Park, Pa.: Pennsylvania State University Press, 1980), p. 1.
10. Ibid., p. 20.
11. See Daniel Weiss, '"The Blue Hotel": A Psychoanalytic Study', in M. Bassan (ed.), *Stephen Crane: A Collection of Critical Essays* (Englewood Cliffs, NJ: Prentice Hall, 1967), pp. 154–64.
12. Berryman, *Stephen Crane*, p. 291.

8 Henry James

1. Henry James, letter to Charles Eliot Norton, 16 January 1871; excerpted in Richard A. Hocks, *Henry James: A Study of the Short Fiction* (Boston: Twayne, 1990), p. 123.
2. Ibid., p. 116.
3. Ibid., p. 117.

4. Henry James, 'Guy de Maupassant', in *Literary Criticism* (vol. II), ed. Leon Edel and Mark Wilson (New York: The Library of America, 1984).
5. Letter to Vernon Lee, 27 April 1899; cited in T. J. Lustig, *Henry James and the Ghostly* (Cambridge: Cambridge University Press, 1994), p. 86.
6. See above, pp. 10 and 19.
7. For the ten 'ghost' stories see *The Ghost Stories of Henry James*, ed. Martin Scofield (Ware: Wordsworth Classics, 2001); for all eighteen of the 'ghostly' tales see *The Ghostly Tales of Henry James*, ed. Leon Edel (Piscataway, NJ: Rutgers University Press, 1949).

9 Rebecca Harding Davis, Sarah Orne Jewett and Mary Wilkins Freeman

1. See F. L. Pattee, *The Development of the American Short Story* (New York: Biblo & Tannen, 1975), p. 70.
2. Quoted in ibid.
3. Hawthorne, *Letters*, quoted in Cynthia Griffin Wolff (ed.), *Four Stories by American Women* (Harmondsworth: Penguin Books, 1990), p. vii.
4. See e.g. Karen Kilcup (ed.), *Nineteenth-Century Women Writers: An Anthology* (Oxford: Blackwell, 1997); *Scribbling Women: Short Stories by 19th Century American Women*, selected and introduced by Elaine Showalter (London: Dent, 1997); and Karen Kilcup (ed.), *Nineteenth-Century Women Writers: A Critical Reader* (Oxford: Blackwell, 1998).
5. For these and then other striking stories by lesser-known figures the reader should consult the anthologies by Kilcup and Showalter (see n. 4).
6. The story is reprinted in *Scribbling Women*, pp. 87–94.
7. See e.g. Elizabeth Ammons, in ibid., p. 488.
8. See Perry D. Westbrook, *Mary Wilkins Freeman* (Boston: Twayne, 1967), pp. 72ff.
9. See e.g. Peter Coveney, *The Image of Childhood* (Harmondsworth: Penguin Books, 1967).

10 Charlotte Perkins Gilman, Kate Chopin, Edith Wharton and Willa Cather

1. Charlotte Perkins Gilman, *The Yellow Wall-Paper and Other Stories*, ed. Robert Shulman (Oxford: Oxford World's Classics, 1995), p. 5. All quotations from Gilman, unless otherwise indicated, are from this edition.
2. Elizabeth Ammons, *Conflicting Stories: American Women Writers at the Turn into the Twentieth Century* (New York and Oxford: Oxford University Press, 1992), p. 37.

3. Quoted in Janet Beer, *Edith Wharton* (Tavistock: Northcote House in association with the British Council, 2002), p. 24.
4. *The Collected Short Stories of Edith Wharton*, ed. R. W. B. Lewis (New York: Scribner, Macmillan, 1987), p. xxxvi.
5. Ibid., pp. xxxvi–xxxvii.
6. Ibid., p. xxxvii.
7. *The Letters of Robert Louis Stevenson*, ed. Sidney Colvin, vol. I, p. 134; quoted in Valerie Shaw, *The Short Story: A Critical Introduction* (London and New York: Longman, 1994), p. 30.
8. *'The Reckoning' and Other Stories*, ed. Janet Beer (London: Phoenix Publications, 1999), p. 69.
9. E.g. Beer, *Edith Wharton*, p. 44; Margaret B. McDowell, *Edith Wharton* (Boston: Twayne, 1976), pp. 88–9; Gloria Erlich, 'The Female Conscience in Wharton's Shorter Fiction: Domestic Angel of Inner Demon', in Millicent Bell (ed.), *The Cambridge Companion to Edith Wharton* (Cambridge: Cambridge University Press, 1995) pp. 106–7.
10. Cynthia Griffin Wolff (ed.), in Willa Cather, *Coming, Aphrodite! and Other Stories* (Harmondsworth: Penguin Books, 1999), p. xix.

11 Growth, fragmentation, new aesthetics and new voices in the early twentieth century

1. See Andrew Levy, *The Culture and Commerce of the Short Story* (Cambridge: Cambridge University Press, 1993), p. 31.
2. Ibid., p. 83. This standardization and mechanization in the short story was also often attacked in the first half of the century. See e.g. Henry S. Canby, 'Free Fiction', *Atlantic Monthly*, 116 (1915), pp. 60–8; and Edward J. O'Brien, *The Dance of the Machines: The American Short Story and the Industrial Age* (New York: The Macaulay Co., 1929).
3. James T. Farrell, author of *Studs Lonigan* and a number of short story collections, has a wittily scathing essay on such handbooks: see 'Nonsense and the Short Story', in *The League of Frightened Philistines and Other Papers* (London: Routledge, 1947).
4. For Anderson see below, p. 128; Willa Cather, 'The Novel *Démeublé*' (1922), in R. K. Miller (ed.), *Great Short Works of Willa Cather* (New York: Harper & Row, 1989), pp. 325–30.
5. Friedrich Nietzsche, *The Gay Science* (1882); for Sigmund Freud, see particularly *The Interpretation of Dreams* (1900) and *Introductory Lectures on Psychoanalysis* (1915–17).
6. Cf. Raymond Carver: 'The short story writer's task is to invest the glimpse with all that is in his power.' 'On Writing', *Fires: Essays, Poems, Stories* (London: Picador, 1986), p. 27.

7. Quoted in Brander Matthews, *The Philosophy of the Short Story* (Folcroft, Philadelphia: Folcroft Library Editions, 1971), p. 55.
8. *A Story Teller's Story* (New York: Huebsch, 1924), p. 402; quoted in Valerie Shaw, *The Short Story: A Critical Introduction* (London: Longman, 1983), p. 15.
9. 'Some Aspects of the Short Story', in Charles E. May (ed.), *The New Short Story Theories* (Athens: Ohio University Press, 1994), pp. 246–7.
10. William Carlos Williams, *Selected Essays* (New York: New Directions Books, 1969), p. 300.
11. 'Alibi Ike'. This and the other stories discussed here, except for 'Who Dealt?', are collected in a recent edition, *The Best of Ring Lardner*, ed. David Lodge (London: Everyman, J. M. Dent, 1999). In his lifetime, Lardner's stories were published in some twelve volumes from 1915 to 1933, the best collection being *How to Write Short Stories* (New York: Scribner, 1924). *The Collected Stories of Ring Lardner* was published by The Modern Library, 1941.
12. Edmund Wilson, 'Mr Lardner's American Characters', *The Dial*, 77/1 (July, 1924), pp. 69–72. Also online at http://galenet.galegroup.com.
13. H. L. Mencken, 'Ring W. Lardner', *The American Mercury*, 2/7 (July, 1925), pp. 376–7. Also online at http://galenet.galegroup.com.

12 O. Henry and Jack London

1. The biographical details in this and later paragraphs are taken from Eugene Current-Garcia, *O. Henry* (New York: Twayne, 1965).
2. H. L. Mencken, *Prejudices* (Second Series), 1920, quoted in Current-Garcia, *O. Henry*, p. 163; F. L. Pattee, *The Development of the American Short Story* (1923; New York: Biblo & Tannen, 1975), p. 364. In later works on American literature O. Henry has fared even less well: he gets one mention in passing in *The New Pelican Guide to English Literature*, vol. IX: *American Literature*, ed. Boris Ford (London: Penguin Books Ltd., 1988); and he is not mentioned at all in *American Literature Since 1900*, ed. Marcus Cunliffe (London: Penguin Books Ltd., 1993).
3. E.g. by Current-Garcia, *O. Henry*; and see also the Intoduction to Ian F. A. Bell (ed.), *The Best of O. Henry* (London: J. M. Dent; Rutland, Vt.: Charles E. Tuttle Co. Inc., 1993).
4. Trans. in L. Matejka and K. Pomorska (eds.), *Readings in Russian Poetics* (Cambridge, Mass.: Massachusetts Institute of Technology Press, 1971).
5. Ibid., pp. 231, 247.
6. See e.g. John Gerlach, *Towards the End: Closure and Structure in the American Short Story* (Tuscaloosa: University of Alabama Press, 1985).
7. The whole question of the reproduction of African American dialect, particularly by white writers, is of course controversial. But cultural critics have recently come to take a more complex view of the process, seeing it as analogous to the

phenomenon of blackface minstrelsy. Rather than simply as an expression of mockery and racial superiority, white mimicry is seen as an ambiguous mixture of hostility, fascination and 'the vagaries of racial desire' (Eric Lott, *Love and Theft: Blackface Minstrelsy and the American Working Class* (Oxford: Oxford University Press, 1993), p. 6). See also *Raising Cain: Blackface Performance from Jim Crow to Hip Hop* (Cambridge, Mass.: Harvard University Press, 1998).

8. Letter of 14 October 1904; quoted in James McClintock, *Jack London's Strong Truths: A Study of the Short Stories* (East Lansing: Michigan State University Press, 1997), p. 14.
9. Ibid., pp. 30–1.
10. Earle Labor (ed.), *The Portable Jack London* (New York and London: Penguin Books, 1994), p. xxix.
11. See, respectively, Clell Peterson, 'The Theme of Jack London's "To Build a Fire"' and James M. Mellard, 'Dramatic Mode and Tragic Structure in "To Build a Fire"', in Susan M. Nuernberg (ed.), *The Critical Response to Jack London* (Westport, Conn. and London: Greenwood Press), 1995.
12. Jack London, 'Letter to "Mr Revision Editor" at *Youth's Companion*', in Nuernberg (ed.), *Critical Response*, p. 1.
13. Andrew Sinclair, *Jack: A Biography of Jack London* (London: Weidenfeld & Nicolson, 1978), p. 221.

13 Sherwood Anderson

1. See for example Rex Burbank, *Sherwood Anderson* (New York: Twayne, 1964); Keith Carabine, '"A Pretty Good Unity": A Study of Sherwood Anderson's *Winesburg, Ohio* and Ernest Hemingway's *In Our Time*', unpublished Ph.D. dissertation (Yale University, 1978).
2. Sherwood Anderson, *A Story Teller's Story*, ed. Ray Lewis White (Cleveland: Case Western Reserve University Press, 1968), p. 255.
3. Quoted in William C. Phillips, 'How Sherwood Anderson Wrote *Winesburg, Ohio*', in R. L. White (ed.), *The Achievement of Sherwood Anderson* (Chapel Hill, University of North Carolina Press, 1966), p. 74.
4. All quotations from *Winesburg, Ohio* are from the Norton Critical Edition, ed. Charles E. Modlin and Ray Lewis White (New York and London: W. W. Norton & Co., 1996).
5. John Updike, 'Twisted Apples', repr. in Sherwood Anderson, *Winesburg, Ohio* (New York and London: W. W. Norton & Co., 1996), pp. 189–94.
6. Biographical details in this paragraph are taken from Burbank, *Sherwood Anderson.*
7. Letter of 26 November 1932, *Selected Letters*, ed. Charles E. Modlin (Knoxville: University of Tennessee Press, 1984), pp. 152–6; repr. in Anderson, *Winesburg, Ohio*, p. 145.

8. Irving Howe, *Sherwood Anderson: A Biographical and Critical Study* (Stanford: Stanford University Press, 1966), p. 107.
9. Ibid., pp. 107–8.
10. See Chapter 4, n. 3, p. 242 below.
11. See e.g. Shlomith Rimmon-Kenan, *Narrative Fiction: Contemporary Poetics* (London and New York: Routledge, 1994), pp. 52–3.
12. Quoted in Burbank, *Sherwood Anderson*, p. 64.
13. Ibid.
14. Sherwood Anderson, *The Egg and Other Stories*, ed. Charles E. Modlin (London: Penguin Books, 1998), p. 12. All subsequent quotations of Anderson's stories are from this edition.

14 Ernest Hemingway

1. Cited by Charles Fenton, *The Apprenticeship of Ernest Hemingway: The Early Years* (1954; New York: Octagon Books, 1975), pp. 33–4.
2. Ibid.
3. Ernest Hemingway, *Death in the Afternoon* (1932; London: Jonathan Cape, 1963), p. 183.
4. See *Journal of the Short Story in English*, 40 (Spring, 2003), special edition on 'The Implicit in the Short Story in English'.
5. *A Farewell To Arms* (1929; London: Collins, 1986), p. 133.
6. *The First Forty-Nine Stories* (1938; London: Arrow Books, 1993), p. 89. All subsequent page references are to this edition.
7. Despite Hemingway's famous 'iceberg' theory, Tom Stoppard points to the vitalizing randomness, as here, of what Hemingway sometimes *leaves in*. See James Nagel (ed.), *Ernest Hemingway: The Writer in Context* (Madison: University of Wisconsin Press, 1984), p. 22.
8. Edmund Wilson, 'Hemingway: Gauge of Morale', in *The Wound and the Bow* (1941; London: Methuen, 1961), p. 212.
9. Ibid., p. 199.
10. See Wendolyn E. Tetlow, *Hemingway's* In Our Time: *Lyrical Dimensions* (Lewisburg, Pa: Bucknell University Press; London and Toronto: Associated University Presses, 1992), pp. 47 and 125 n. 2.
11. See Susan Swartzlander, 'Uncle Charles in Michigan', in Susan F. Beegel (eds.), *Hemingway's Neglected Short Fiction* (Tuscaloosa, Ala. and London: University of Alabama Press, 1992), pp. 31–41. On free indirect discourse, see Shlomith Rimmon-Kenan, *Narrative Fiction: Contemporary Poetics* (London and New York: Routledge, 1994), pp. 110–16.
12. The view that it also alludes to the term 'white elephant' for something expensive but unwanted (and hence relates to the unborn child) seems to me less convincing:

Hemingway's imagery evokes more than itself, but it works subtly through poetic suggestion rather than conventional metaphoric displacement.

13. See Paul Smith, 'From the Waste Land to the Garden with the Elliots', in Beegel (ed.), *Hemingway's Neglected Short Fiction*, pp. 123–9. Hemingway changed the protagonists' name from Smith (after Chard Powers Smith) to 'Eliot' and then 'Elliot' after the first publication of the story.
14. See Warren Bennett, '"That's Not Very Polite": Sexual Identity in Hemingway's "The Sea Change"', in Beegel (ed.), *Hemingway's Neglected Short Fiction*, pp. 225–45. Bennett, however, has some well-observed suggestions about the nature of the couple's sexual relationship, and its connection with Hemingway's later novel *The Garden of Eden*.

15 F. Scott Fitzgerald

1. *The Letters of F. Scott Fitzgerald*, ed. Andrew Turnbull (New York: Scribner, 1963), p. 206; *Dear Scott/Dear Max: The Fitzgerald–Perkins Correspondence*, ed. John Kuehl and Jackson R. Bryer (New York: Scribner, 1971), p. 70; quoted in John Kuehl, *F. Scott Fitzgerald: A Study of the Short Fiction* (Boston: Twayne, 1991), p. 4.
2. Kuehl, *F. Scott Fitzgerald*, p. 5. The figures are around $260,000 for the stories and around $107,300 for the novels.
3. *Letters*, pp. 571–2; quoted in Kuehl, *F. Scott Fitzgerald*, p. 142.
4. Kuehl, *F. Scott Fitzgerald*, p. 144.
5. See Susan F. Beegel, '"Bernice Bobs Her Hair": Fitzgerald's Jazz Elegy for *Little Women*', in Jackson R. Bryer (ed.), *New Essays on F. Scott Fitzgerald's Neglected Short Stories* (Columbia and London: University of Missouri Press, 1996), pp. 58–73.
6. *The Collected Short Stories of F. Scott Fitzgerald* (Harmondsworth: Penguin Books, 1986), p. 350.
7. For a discussion of this story, which was originally included in *Taps for Reveille* (1935), see Scott Donaldson, '"Two Wrongs" or One Wrong too many', in Bryer (ed.), *New Essays*, pp. 165–74.
8. *The Collected Stories of F. Scott Fitzgerald.*
9. Bryer (ed.), *New Essays.*

16 William Faulkner

1. *Collected Stories* (New York: Random House, 1950); *Collected Short Stories of William Faulkner* (London: Duckworth, 1958); *Uncollected Stories,* ed. Joseph Blotner (New York: Random House, 1979).

2. Malcolm Cowley (ed.), *The Portable Faulkner* (Harmondsworth: Penguin Books, 1977), p. xxv.
3. Irving Howe, *Faulkner: A Critical Study* (1951; Chicago: Ivan R. Dee, 1995), pp. 260–1.
4. Michael Millgate, *Faulkner* (Edinburgh and London: Oliver and Boyd, 1961), p. 65.
5. There is an interesting essay by Judith Fetterley which reads the story from a feminist perspective on the corrupting effect of the male chivalric ideal. See 'A Rose for "A Rose for Emily"', in *The Resisting Reader: A Feminist Approach to American Fiction* (Bloomington: Indiana University Press, 1978), pp. 34–45; also reprinted in Henry Claridge (ed.), *William Faulkner: Critical Assessments*, vol. IV (Mountfield: Helm Information, 1999), pp. 50–8.
6. The story is also included in Malcolm Cowley's *The Portable Faulkner* (New York: Penguin Books, 1977).
7. See Caroline Gordon and Allen Tate, 'Commentary on "Spotted Horses"', in Gordon and Tate (eds.), *The House of Fiction* (New York: Scribner, 1966), pp. 332–4; repr. in Claridge (ed.), *William Faulkner: Critical Assessments*, vol. IV, pp. 59–62.

17 Katherine Anne Porter, Eudora Welty and Flannery O'Connor

1. See e.g. Cleanth Brooks, 'On "The Grave"', in Robert Penn Warren (ed.), *Katherine Anne Porter: A Collection of Critical Essays* (Englewood Cliffs, NJ: Prentice-Hall Inc., 1979), pp. 112–16.
2. See for example her essay 'The Eye of the Story' in ibid., pp. 72–80.
3. See Eudora Welty, *Photographs* (Jackson: University Press of Mississippi, 1989).
4. Eudora Welty, *One Writer's Beginnings* (Cambridge, Mass. and London: Harvard University Press, 1984; repr. 2000), p. 9.
5. Ibid., p. 10.
6. Katherine Anne Porter, '*A Curtain of Green*', in Harold Bloom (ed.), *Eudora Welty*, Modern Critical Views (New York: Chelsea House Publishers, 1986), p. 15.
7. For an account of various interpretations, see e.g. Diana R. Pingatore, *A Reader's Guide to the Stories of Eudora Welty* (Boston: G. K. Hall & Co., 1996), pp. 69–79.
8. Flannery O'Connor, *Mystery and Manners* (1961; London: Faber and Faber, 1972), p. 91.
9. Ibid., p. 112.
10. Letter of 25 August 1955, *The Habit of Being: Letters of Flannery O'Connor*, ed. Sally Fitzgerald (New York: Farrar, Straus and Giroux, 1998), p. 98.
11. Ibid., p. 118.
12. Ibid., p. 437.
13. Letter of January 1961, *The Habit of Being*, p. 438. Teilhard de Chardin, *The Phenomenon of Man* (London: Fontana Religious Books, 1965).

18 Charles Chesnutt, Richard Wright, James Baldwin and the African American short story to 1965

1. For a representative selection of these, see Paul Lauter et al. (eds.), *The Heath Anthology of American Literature*, 2nd edn, 2 vols. (Lexington, Mass.: D. C. Heath and Co., 1994), vol. II, pp. 191–212.
2. See introductory note by George Friedman, ibid., p. 446. The status of Harris's Brer Rabbit stories is of course a highly controversial one. But recent commentators have begin to stress either the distinction between the 'paternalistic' view of Uncle Remus and the subversive freedom of the Brer Rabbit figure; or in a more complex reading, the double nature of Harris himself and the internal 'other fellow' (the often slily subversive black story-teller) who 'takes charge', as Harris put it, of the writing. See the Introduction to Robert Hemenway (ed.), *Uncle Remus, His Songs and Sayings* (Harmondsworth: Penguin Books, 1982); and Robert Cochran, 'Black Father: the Subversive Achievement of Joel Chandler Harris', *African American Review*, 38 (Spring, 2004), pp. 21–35.
3. See the Introduction to Charles W. Chesnutt, *The Conjure Woman and Other Conjure Tales*, ed. Richard Brodhead (Durham, NC: Duke University Press, 1993), pp. 11–12.
4. Earl Schenck Miers in his Introduction to Charles W. Chesnutt, *The Wife of his Youth and Other Stories* (Ann Arbor: University of Michigan Press, 1977), p. xiv.
5. For examples of short stories by these and later African American writers, see Langston Hughes (ed.), *The Best Short Stories by Negro Writers* (Boston and Toronto: Little, Brown and Co., 1967).
6. James D. Hart, *The Oxford Companion to American Literature* (Oxford: Oxford University Press, 1986), p. 451.
7. See James Baldwin, 'Alas, Poor Richard', in *Nobody Knows My Name* (New York: Dell Publishing Co., 1961), pp. 149–50.
8. Ibid., p. 18.
9. Isaiah 51: 17–22.
10. Frank O'Connor, *The Lonely Voice: A Study of the Short Story* (Cleveland: The World Publishing Co., 1963), p. 115.
11. The title is from a well-known jazz song by Milton Browne.

19 Aspects of the American short story 1930–1980

1. Kurt Vonnegut, *Bagombo Snuff Box: Uncollected Short Fiction* (London: Vintage, 2000), p. 4.
2. Among other notable magazines which published important writers in this period one might mention also *Collier's*, *Reader's Digest*, *Playboy* and *Story*.
3. A richly informative study of the world of *The New Yorker* and its influence on the short story can be found in Ben Yagoda's *About Town: 'The New Yorker' and the World It Made* (New York: Da Capo Press, 2001).

4. Quoted by Jay Parini in Blanche H. Gelfant (ed.), *The Columbia Companion to the American Short Story* (New York: Columbia University Press, 2000), p. 523.
5. Surprisingly, Powers is not mentioned in Abby H. P. Werlock (ed.), *Facts on File Companion to the American Short Story* (New York: Checkmark Books, Facts on File Inc., 2000), and only gets one brief mention in passing in *The Columbia Companion.* But his reputation deserves to be sustained and re-examined.
6. Letter of 1934, repr. in James O'Hara, *John Cheever: A Study of the Short Fiction* (New York: Twayne Publishers, 1989), pp. 97–8.
7. From *Understanding Fiction*, ed. Cleanth Brooks and Robert Penn Warren, 2nd edn (New York: Appleton-Century-Crofts, 1959), p. 570; repr. in O'Hara, *Cheever*, p. 106.
8. Alfred Kazin, 'O'Hara, Cheever and Updike', in O'Hara, *Cheever*, p. 126.
9. John Updike in an interview with Charles Reilly, repr. in Robert M. Luscher (ed.), *John Updike: A Study of the Short Fiction* (New York: Twayne Publishers, 1993), p. 171.
10. Ibid., p. 174.
11. *The Early Stories* (New York: Alfred A. Knopf, 2003; London: Hamish Hamilton, 2004).
12. Updike in the Foreword to ibid., p. xv.
13. With reference to 'white Anglo-Saxon Protestant' it should be noted that Updike has also published three volumes of stories which have as their narrator a Jewish writer: *Bech: A Book* (1970), *Bech Is Back* (1982) and *Bech: A Quasi-Novel* (1998); a playful gesture (or an act of mischievous cultural imperialism perhaps), intended to extend his scope into that other great intellectual and cultural tradition of modern America, and challenge the hegemony of his great contemporaries Saul Bellow and Philip Roth.

20 Two traditions and the changing idea of the mainstream

1. Saul Bellow, *Collected Stories*, ed. Janis Bellow, with an introduction by James Wood (New York: Viking; London: Penguin Books, 2001).
2. Orlando Patterson, *Rituals of Blood: Consequences of Slavery in Two American Centuries* (Washington: Civitas/Counterpoint, 1998), p. xii; quoted in J. Gerald Kennedy and Robert Beuka, 'Imperilled Communities in Edward P. Jones's *Lost in the City* and Dagoberto Gilb's *The Magic of Blood*', *Yearbook of English Studies*, 31 (2001), p. 14.
3. This story is also reprinted in Paul Lauter et al. (eds.), *The Heath Anthology of American Literature*, 2nd edn, 2 vols. (Lexington, Mass.: D. C. Heath and Co., 1994), vol. II, pp. 2594–2614.
4. Toni Cade Bambara, 'Black English', quoted in ibid., p. 2693.

21 The postmodern short story in America

1. Barthelme's first story, 'L'Lapse', was published in *The New Yorker* in 1963.
2. Barthelme published seven original volumes of stories and four novels.
3. Donald Barthelme, *Sixty Stories* (London: Minerva, 1991). Subsequent quotations are from this edition.
4. William Gass, 'Philosophy and the Form of Fiction', in *Fiction and the Figures of Life* (New York: Vintage Books, 1971), p. 17; quoted in Larry McCaffery, *The Metafictional Muse: The Works of Robert Coover, Donald Barthelme and William H. Gass* (Pittsburgh: University of Pittsburgh Press, 1982), p. 23.
5. The title puns on the sexual meaning of 'pricksongs' and the musical meaning of an embellishment or counterpoint to a main theme (cf. also 'descants'). Coover's stories are often variations on traditional stories.
6. William Gass, 'The Leading Edge of the Trash Phenomenon', in *Fiction and the Figures of Life*, p. 102.
7. McCaffery, *Metafictional Muse*, p. 152.
8. Gass, *Fiction and the Figures of Life*, p. 8.
9. McCaffery, *Metafictional Muse*, p. 216.
10. 'Dreck', trash, is a term of Barthelme's which Gass uses to characterize a central preoccupation of the former's stories. See 'The Leading Edge of the Trash Phenomenon', pp. 97–103.

22 Raymond Carver

1. Review of Barthelme's *Great Days* (1979), repr. in Raymond Carver *No Heroics, Please* (London: Harvill, 1991), pp. 167–8.
2. See Marshall Bruce Gentry and William H. Stull (eds.), *Conversations with Raymond Carver* (Jackson and London: University Press of Mississippi, 1990), pp. 210, 139 and 112.
3. Ibid., p. 213.
4. Ibid., p. 44.
5. See e.g. Robert Shapard and James Thomas (eds.), *Sudden Fiction: American Short-Short Stories* (Salt Lake City: Gibbs M. Smith Inc., 1986).
6. The question of Carver's revisions in this and other stories has been extensively discussed by Hiromi Hashimoto, 'Trying to Understand Raymond Carver's Revisions', *Tokai English Review*, 5 (December, 1995), pp. 113–57. Also online at http://www/whitman.edu/english/carver/precision.html
7. On the distinction between the metaphoric and the metonymic, see Roman Jakobson, 'Two Aspects of Language', in *On Language* (Cambridge, Mass.: Harvard University Press, 1990); repr. in J. Rivkin and M. Ryan (eds.), *Literary Theory: An Anthology* (Oxford: Blackwell, 1998), pp. 91–5.

8. Gentry and Stull (eds.), *Conversations with Raymond Carver*, p. 106.
9. Ibid., pp. 187 and 198.
10. Ibid., p. 185.
11. Author's Foreword to *Where I'm Calling From* (London: The Harvill Press, 1995) p. xi.

23 Epilogue: the contemporary American short story

1. For a recent study see James Nagel, *The Contemporary American Short Story Cycle: The Ethnic Resonance of Genre* (Baton Rouge: Louisiana State University Press, 2001).
2. Interview with Richard Marshall, *Seattle Post-Intelligencer*, 29 March 2002, p. 21. Cited in 'Richard Ford', *Contemporary Authors Online*, Thomson Gale, 2004, http://80-galenet.galegroup.com
3. Quoted in Patrick Meanor and Joseph McNicholas (eds.), *American Short Story Writers Since World War II*, 4th series (Detroit: Gale Group, 2001), p. 245.

Guide to further reading

American short story anthologies, and other anthologies of American literature containing short stories

Baym, Nina (ed.), *The Norton Anthology of American Literature*, 5th edn, 2 vols., New York: W. W. Norton & Co., 2003

Best American Short Stories, New York: Houghton Mifflin, annually 1915 to present

Carver, Raymond, and Tom Jenks, *American Short Story Masterpieces*, New York: Dell Publishing, 1987

Chan, Jeffrey Paul et al. (eds.), *Aiiieeeee! An Anthology of Asian American Writers*, Washington DC: Howard University Press, 1974

Charters, Ann (ed.), *The Short Story and its Writer*, New York: St Martin's Press, Inc., 1983

Cochrane, James, *The Penguin Book of American Short Stories*, Harmondsworth: Penguin Books, 1969

Current-Garcia, Eugene (ed.), *What Is the Short Story?* Glenview, Ill.; Brighton: Scott, Foresman & Co., 1974

Ford, Richard (ed.), *The Granta Book of the American Short Story*, London: Granta Books, 1992

Gates, Henry Louis (ed.), *The Norton Anthology of African American Literature*, New York: W. W. Norton & Co., 2004

Gioia, Dana and Gwynn, R. S. (eds.), *The Longman Masters of Short Fiction*, New York; London: Longman, 2002

Hughes, Langston (ed.), *The Best Short Stories by Negro Writers: An Anthology from 1899 to the Present*, Boston: Little, Brown and Co., 1967

Lauter, Paul et al. (eds.), *The Heath Anthology of American Literature*, 4th edn, New York: Houghton Mifflin, 2002

Litz, A. Walton (ed.), *Major American Short Stories*, 3rd edn, New York and Oxford: Oxford University Press, 1993

Major, Clarence (ed.), *Calling the Wind: Twentieth Century African-American Short Story Writers*, New York: HarperPerennial, 1993

Marcus, Ben (ed.), *The Anchor Book of New American Short Stories*, New York and Toronto: Anchor Books, 2004

McMillan, Terry, *Breaking Ice: An Anthology of Contemporary African American Fiction*, New York: Penguin Books, 1990

Oates, Joyce Carol, *The Oxford Book of the American Short Story*, Oxford: Oxford University Press, 1992

O. Henry Memorial Prize Stories, New York: Doubleday, annually 1919 to present (except 1951–2)

The Pushcart Prize Stories, Yonkers, NY: Pushcart Press, annually 1977 to present

Trafzer, Clifford (ed.), *Earth Song, Sky Spirit: Short Stories of the Contemporary Native American Experience*, New York: Anchor Doubleday, 1993

Wolff, Tobias (ed.), *The Picador Book of Contemporary American Stories*, London: Picador, 1993

Volumes of short stories by individual author, and related critical works

This section gives recent editions of collected stories by author and the standard scholarly edition of the complete stories (or complete works) where one exists. Where applicable, author entries also include (1) critical writing on the short story by the same author and (2) selected critical studies of that author. Where stories have been republished in collected or complete editions, the titles of earlier volumes are not listed.

Alexie, Sherman

The Business of Fancydancing: Stories and Poems, Brooklyn, NY: Hanging Loose Press, 1992

The Lone Ranger and Tonto Fistfight in Heaven, New York: Atlantic Monthly Press, 1993

Reservation Blues, New York: Warner Books, 1996

Ten Little Indians, New York: Grove Press, 2003; London: Secker and Warburg, 2004

Alvarez, Julia

How the Garcia Girls Lost Their Accents (short story cycle), Chapel Hill, NC: Algonquin Books, 1991

Sirias, Silvia, *Julia Alvarez: A Critical Companion*, Westport, Conn.: Greenwood Press, 2001

Austin, William

Peter Rugg, the Missing Man, ed. Alain Geoffroy (*Alizés*, 11), Saint-Denis, Réunion: Université de la Réunion, 1996
The Man with the Cloaks and Other Stories, ed. Alain Geoffroy (*Alizés*, 15), Saint-Denis, Réunion: Université de la Réunion, 1998
'Peter Rugg, the Missing Man', in Joyce Carol Oates (ed.), *The Oxford Book of the American Short Story*, Oxford: Oxford University Press, 1992

Baldwin, James

Going to Meet the Man, New York: Vintage Books, 1993
Porter, Horace, *Stealing the Fire: The Art and Protest of James Baldwin*, Middletown, Conn.: Wesleyan University Press, 1989
Standley, Fred L. (ed.), *Critical Essays on James Baldwin*, Boston: G. K. Hall, 1988

Bambara, Toni Cade

Gorilla, My Love, New York: Random House, 1972
The Sea Birds Are Still Alive, New York: Random House, 1977
Evans, Mari (ed.), *Black Woman Writers of the Contemporary South*, Garden City, NY: Anchor Books, 1984
Prenshaw, Peggy (ed.), *Women Writers of the Contemporary South*, Jackson: University Press of Mississippi, 1984

Barth, John

Lost in the Funhouse: Fiction for Print, Tape, Live Voice, Garden City, NY: Doubleday, 1968
Morrell, David, *John Barth: An Introduction*, University Park, Pa.: Pennsylvania State University Press, 1976
Waldmeir, Joseph (ed.), *Critical Essays on John Barth*, Boston: G. K. Hall, 1980

Barthelme, Donald

Sixty Stories, New York: Putnam, 1981
Forty Stories, New York: Putnam, 1987
McCaffery, Leonard, *The Metafictional Muse: the Works of Robert Coover, Donald Barthelme and William Gass*, Pittsburgh: University of Pittsburgh Press, 1982
Trachtenberg, Stanley, *Understanding Donald Barthelme*, Columbia, SC: University of South Carolina Press, 1990

Bausch, Richard

The Stories of Richard Bausch, New York: HarperCollins, 2003

Beattie, Ann

Distortions, New York: Doubleday, 1976
Secrets and Surprises, New York: Random House, 1976
The Burning House, New York: Random House, 1982
What Was Mine, New York: Random House, 1991
Park City: New and Selected Stories, New York: Knopf, 1998
Perfect Recall, New York: Scribner, 2001

Bierce, Ambrose

The Complete Short Stories of Ambrose Bierce, compiled by Ernest Jerome Hopkins, Lincoln and London: University of Nebraska Press, 1984
Davidson, Cathy N., *The Experimental Fictions of Ambrose Bierce: Structuring the Ineffable*, Lincoln and London: University of Nebraska Press, 1982
Critical Essays on Ambrose Bierce, Boston: G. K. Hall, 1982
Woodruff, Stuart C., *The Short Stories of Ambrose Bierce*, Minneapolis: University of Minnesota Press, 1964

Bowles, Jane

The Collected Works of Jane Bowles, New York: Farrar, Straus & Giroux, 1966

Bowles, Paul

Collected Stories, 1939–1976, Santa Barbara, Calif.: Black Sparrow Press, 1979
Stories, Harmondsworth: Penguin Books, 2000
Caponi, Gena Dagel, *Paul Bowles*, New York: Twayne, Prentis Hall, 1998
Dillon, Millicent, *You Are Not I: a Portrait of Paul Bowles*, Berkeley: University of California Press, 1998

Butler, Robert Olen

A Good Scent from a Strange Mountain: Stories, New York: Viking Penguin, 1992
Tabloid Dreams, New York: Holt, 1996
Had a Good Time, Grove Press: New York, 2004

Carver, Raymond

The Stories of Raymond Carver, London: Picador/Pan, 1985
Where I'm Calling From, New York: Atlantic Monthly Press, 1988
Call Me If You Need Me: The Uncollected Fiction and Prose, London: Harvill Press, 2000; New York: Vintage, 2001
Meyer, Adam, *Raymond Carver*, New York: Twayne, 1995
Nesset, Kirk, *The Stories of Raymond Carver: A Critical Study*, Athens: Ohio University Press, 1995
Runyon, Randolph, *Reading Raymond Carver*, Syracuse, NY: Syracuse University Press, 1992

Cather, Willa

Great Short Works of Willa Cather, ed. Robert K. Miller, New York: Harper & Row, 1989
The Novels and Stories of Willa Cather, 2 vols., Library of America, New York: Literary Classics of the United States, 1987, 1990
Coming, Aphrodite! and Other Stories, ed. Margaret Anne O'Connor, Harmondsworth: Penguin Books, 1999
Arnold, Marilyn, *Willa Cather's Short Fiction*, Athens: Ohio University Press, 1993
Slote, Bernice (ed.), *The Kingdom of Art: Willa Cather's First Principles and Critical Statements*, Lincoln: University of Nebraska Press, 1967

Cheever, John

The Stories of John Cheever, New York: Alfred A. Knopf, 1979
Bosha, Francis J., *The Critical Response to John Cheever*, Washport, Conn.: Greenwood Press, 1994
Coale, Samuel Chase, *John Cheever*, New York: F. Ungar, 1977
O'Hara, James Eugene, *John Cheever: A Study of the Short Fiction*, Boston: Twayne, 1989

Chesnutt, Charles W.

The Short Fiction of Charles W. Chesnutt, ed. Sylvia L. Render, Washington DC: Howard University Press, 1974
The Collected Stories of Charles W. Chesnutt, ed. William L. Andrews, New York: Signet Books, 1992
The Conjure Woman and Other Tales, ed. Richard H. Brodhead, Durham, NC: Duke University Press, 1993

Andrews, William L., *The Literary Career of Charles W. Chesnutt*, Baton Rouge: Louisiana State University Press, 1980
Render, Sylvia L. *Charles W. Chesnutt*, Baton Rouge: Louisiana State University Press, 1980
Steptoe, Robert B., 'Charles Chesnutt: The Uncle Julius Stories', in Günter H. Lenz (ed.), *History and Tradition in Afro-American Culture*, Frankfurt and New York: Campus, 1984

Chopin, Kate

The Complete Works of Kate Chopin, ed. Per Seyersted, Baton Rouge: Louisiana State University Press, 1969
The Awakening and Selected Stories, ed. Sandra M. Gilbert, Harmondsworth: Penguin Books, 1986
Seyersted, Per, *A Critical Biography*, Baton Rouge: Louisiana State University Press, 1969
Toth, Emily, *Kate Chopin*, Austin: University of Texas Press, 1993

Cisneros, Sandra

The House on Mango Street, Houston: Arte Publico, 1984
Woman Hollering Creek and Other Stories, New York: Vintage, 1992; London: Bloomsbury, 2004
Quintana, Alvina E., *Home Girls: Chicana Literary Voices*, Philadelphia: Temple University Press, 1996
Simmen, Edward (ed.), *North of the Rio Grande: The Mexican American Experience in Short Fiction*, New York: Mentor, 1992

Coover, Robert

Pricksongs and Descants, New York: Dutton, 1969
Cope, Jackson I., *Coover's Fictions*, Baltimore: Johns Hopkins University Press, 1986

Crane, Stephen

The Open Boat and Other Stories, New York: Dover Publications Inc., 1983
Prose and Poetry, The Library of America, New York: Literary Classics of the United States, 1984
The Red Badge of Courage and Other Stories, Harmondsworth: Penguin Books, 1985

La France, Marston, *A Reading of Stephen Crane*, Oxford: Oxford University Press, 1971
Nagel, James, *Stephen Crane and Literary Impressionism*, University Park, Pa.: Pennsylvania State University Press, 1980

Davis, Rebecca Harding

'Life in the Iron Mills', in *Four Stories by American Women*, ed. Cynthia Griffin Wolff, Harmondsworth: Penguin Books, 1990
'Marcia', in *Scribbling Women: Short Stories by 19th Century American Women*, London: Dent, 1997

Dubus, André

Selected Stories, London: Picador, 1991; New York: Random House, 1996
Dancing after Hours, New York: Random House, 1996
Kennedy, Thomas E., *André Dubus: A Study of the Short Fiction*, Boston: Twayne, 1988

Ellison, Ralph

Flying Home and Other Stories, New York: Random House, 1996
Bloom, Harold (ed.) *Ralph Ellison*, New York: Chelsea House, 1986
Hersey, John (ed.), *Ralph Ellison: A Collection of Critical Essays*, Englewood Cliffs, NJ: Prentice Hall, 1973

Erdrich, Louise

Tracks, New York: Harper, 1988
Love Medicine, New York: H. Holt and Co., 1993
The Bingo Palace, New York: HarperCollins, 1993
Tales of Burning Love, Rockland, Mass.: Wheeler, 1996
Chavkin, Allan and Nancy Feyl Chavkin, *Conversations with Louise Erdrich and Michael Dorris*, Jackson: University of Mississippi Press, 1994

Faulkner, William

Collected Stories of William Faulkner, New York: Vintage Books, 1950
Uncollected Stories of William Faulkner, ed. Joseph Blotner, New York: Vintage Books, 1979

Ferguson, James, *Faulkner's Short Fiction*, Knoxville: University of Tennessee Press, 1991
Shei, Hans H., *William Faulkner: The Novelist as Short Story Writer*, Oslo: Universitetsforlaget, 1985

Fitzgerald, F. Scott

The Collected Short Stories of F Scott Fitzgerald, Harmondsworth: Penguin Books, 1986
Bryer, Jackson R. (ed.), *The Short Stories of F. Scott Fitzgerald: New Approaches in Criticism*, Madison: University of Wisconsin Press, 1982
New Essays on F. Scott Fitzgerald's Neglected Short Stories, Columbia and London: University of Missouri Press, 1996
Kuehl, John, *F. Scott Fitzgerald: A Study of the Short Fiction*, Boston: Twayne, 1991
Way, Brian, *F. Scott Fitzgerald and the Art of Social Fiction*, London: Edward Arnold, 1980

Ford, Richard

Rock Springs, New York: Atlantic Monthly Press, 1987; London: Collins Harvill, 1988
A Multitude of Sins, London: Harvill, 2001; New York: Knopf, 2002
Guagliado, Huey (ed.), *Perspectives on Richard Ford*, Jackson: University Press of Mississippi, 2000
Conversations with Richard Ford, Jackson: University Press of Mississippi, 2001

Freeman, Mary Wilkins

Mary Wilkins Freeman Reader, ed. Mary R. Reichardt, Lincoln and London: University of Nebraska Press, 1997
The Uncollected Stories of Mary E. Wilkins Freeman, ed. Mary R. Reichardt, Jackson: University Press of Mississippi, 1992
Glasser, Leah Blatt, *In a Closet Hidden: The Life and Work of Mary E.Wilkins Freeman*, Amherst: University of Massachusetts Press, 1996
Reichardt, Mary R. *Mary Wilkins Freeman: A Study of the Short Fiction*, Boston: Twayne, 1997
Women in the Short Stories of Mary Wilkins Freeman, Jackson: University Press of Mississippi, 1982

Gaines, Ernest J.,

Bloodline, New York: Dial, 1968
Babb, Valerie Melissa, *Ernest Gaines*, Boston: Twayne, 1991
Estes, David C., *Critical Reflections on the Fiction of Ernest Gaines*, Athens: University of Georgia Press, 1994
Lowe, John, *Conversations With Ernest Gaines*, Jackson: University Press of Mississippi, 1995

Garland, Hamlin

Main Travelled Roads (with Introduction by William Dean Howells), Lincoln: University of Nebraska Press, 1995
Collected Works, New York: New York University Press, 1998
McCullough, Joseph B., *Hamlin Garland*, Boston: Twayne, 1978
Nagel, James, ed., *Critical Essays on Hamlin Garland*, Boston: G. K. Hall, 1982
Pizer, Donald, *Hamlin Garland's Early Work and Career*, Berkeley: University of California Press, 1960
Schorer, Mark, 'Hamlin Garland', in *The World We Imagine: Selected Essays*, New York: Farrar, Straus and Giroux, 1968

Gass, William H.

In the Heart of the Heart of the Country and Other Stories, New York: Harper, 1981
Gass, William H., *Facts and Figures of Life*, New York: Harper & Row, 1970

Gilb, Dagoberto

The Magic of Blood, Albuquerque: University of New Mexico Press, 1993
Woodcuts of Women, New York: Grove, 2001

Gilman, Charlotte Perkins

The Charlotte Perkins Gilman Reader, ed. Ann J. Lane, Charlottesville: University of Virginia Press, 1980
The Yellow Wall-Paper and other Stories, ed. Robert Shulman, Oxford: Oxford World's Classics, 1995
Bauer, Dale M., *The Yellow Wallpaper: Charlotte Perkins Gilman*, Bedford Cultural Editions, New York: Bedford Books, 1998

Dock, Julie Bates (ed.), *Charlotte Perkins Gilman's 'The Yellow Wall-Paper' and the History of its Publication and Reception: A Critical Edition and Documentary Casebook*, University Park, Pa.: Pennsylvania State University Press, 1998

Golden, Catherine (ed.), *The Captive Imagination: A Casebook on 'The Yellow Wallpaper'*, New York: The Feminist Press at the City University of New York, 1991

Knight, Denise D., *Charlotte Perkins Gilman: A Study of the Short Fiction*, Boston: Twayne, 1997

Meyering, Sheryl L., *Charlotte Perkins Gilman: The Woman and Her Work*, Ann Arbor: UMI Research Press, 1989

Harris, Joel Chandler

The Complete Tales of Uncle Remus, ed. Richard Chase, New York: Houghton Mifflin, 1955

Uncle Remus: His Songs and Sayings, Harmondsworth: Penguin Books, 1982

Bickley, Bruce R,. *Joel Chandler Harris*, Athens: University of Georgia Press, 1987

Critical Essays on Joel Chandler Harris, Boston: G. K. Hall, 1981

Harte, Bret

The Writings of Bret Harte, Standard Library Edition, Boston and New York: Houghton Mifflin, 1896–1904

The Luck of Roaring Camp and Other Writings, ed. Gary Scharnhorst, New York: Pengiun Books, 2001

Selected Stories and Sketches, ed. David Wyatt, Oxford: Oxford University Press, 1995

Barnett, Linda Diz, *Bret Harte: A Reference Guide*, Boston: G. K. Hall, 1980

Kolb, Harold H., Jr., 'The Outcasts of Literary Flat: Bret Hart as Humorist', *American Literary Realism*, 23 (Winter, 1991), pp. 52–63

Scharnhorst, Gary, *Bret Harte*, Boston: Twayne, 1992

Hawthorne, Nathaniel

Hawthorne's Short Stories, ed. Newton Arving, New York: Knopf, 1946; repr. Columbus: Ohio State University Press, 1963

Works, Centenary Edition ed. William Charvat et al., Columbus: Ohio State University Press, 1974 (vol. IX, *Twice-Told Tales*; vol. X, *Mosses from an Old Manse*; vol. XI, *Miscellany*)

Selected Tales and Sketches, ed. Michael J. Colacurcio, Harmondsworth: Penguin Books, 1987
Young Goodman Brown and Other Tales, ed. Brian Harding, Oxford: Oxford University Press, 1987; repr. 1998
Bell, Millicent (ed.), *New Essays on Hawthorne's Tales*, Cambridge: Cambridge University Press, 1993
Colacurcio, Michael J., *The Province of Piety: Moral History in Hawthorne's Early Tales*, Cambridge, Mass. and London: Harvard University Press, 1984
Crews, Frederick, *The Sins of the Father: Hawthorne's Psychological Themes*, New York: Oxford University Press 1966
Fogle, Richard Harter, *Hawthorne's Fiction: the Light and the Dark*, Norman: University of Oklahoma Press, 1952; rev. edn 1964
James, Henry, *Hawthorne*, London: Macmillan; New York: St Martin's Press, 1967
Kaul, A. N. (ed.), *Hawthorne: A Collection of Critical Essays*, Englewood Cliffs, NJ: Prentice Hall, 1966

Hemingway, Ernest

The First Forty-Nine Stories, London: Arrow Books, 1993
Baker, Carlos, *Ernest Hemingway: A Life Story*, New York: Scribner, 1976
Benson, Jackson J. (ed.), *New Critical Approaches to the Short Stories of Ernest Hemingway*, Durham, NC: Duke University Press, 1995
Smith, Paul, *A Reader's Guide to the Short Stories of Ernest Hemingway*, Boston: G. K. Hall, 1989

Hempel, Amy

Reasons To Live, New York: Knopf, 1985
At The Gates of the Animal Kingdom, New York: Knopf, 1990
Tumble Home: A Novella and Short Stories, New York: Scribner, 1997

Henry, O. (William Sydney Porter)

The Best of O. Henry, ed. Ian F. A. Bell, London: Dent, 1989
Selected Stories, ed. Guy Davenport, Harmondsworth: Penguin Books, 1993
100 Selected Stories, Ware: Wordsworth Classics, 1995
Current-Garcia, Eugene, *O. Henry*, Boston: Twayne, 1965
Ejxenbaum, Boris M., 'O. Henry and the Theory of the Short Story', in Ladislav Matejka and Krystyna Pomorska (eds.), *Readings in Russian Poetics: Formalist and Structuralist Views*, Cambridge, Mass.: MIT Press, 1971

Hughes, Langston

Short Stories, ed. A. S. Harper, New York: Hill & Wang, 1996
Ostrom, Hans, *Langston Hughes: A Study of the Short Fiction*, New York: Twayne, 1993

Hurston, Zora Neale

Zora Neale Hurston: The Complete Stories, ed. Henry Louis Gates Jnr. and Sieglinde Lemke, New York: Harper Perennial, 1996

Irving, Washington

The Complete Works of Washington Irving, 30 vols., Madison: University of Wisconsin Press, 1969–70; Boston: Twayne, 1976–89 (*The Sketch-Book of Geoffrey Crayon, Gent.*, ed. William Haskell, is vol. VIII)
The Sketch-Book of Geoffrey Crayon, Gent., ed. Susan Manning, Oxford: Oxford University Press, 1996
Aderman, Ralph M., *Critical Essays on Washington Irving*, Boston: G. K. Hall, 1990
Myers, Andrew B., *A Century of Commentary on the Works of Washington Irving*, Tarrytown, NY: Sleepy Hollow Restoration, 1976

Jackson, Shirley

The Lottery; or, the Adventures of James Harris, New York: Farrar, Straus, 1949

James, Henry

Fifteen Short Stories, ed. M. D. Zabel, New York: Bantam Books, 1961
Selected Tales, London: Dent, 1982
The Complete Tales of Henry James, ed. Leon Edel, 12 vols., London: Rupert Hart–Davis, 1984
The Figure in the Carpet and Other Stories, Harmondsworth: Penguin, 1986
Collected Stories, 2 vols., London: Dent, 1999
Clarke, Graham (ed.), *Henry James: Critical Assessments*, 4 vols., Mountfield: Helm Information, 1991
Hocks, Richard A., *Henry James: A Study of the Short Fiction*, Boston: Twayne, 1990

Kraft, James, *The Early Tales of Henry James*, Carbondale: University of Southern Illinois Press, 1969
Wagenknecht, Edward, *The Tales of Henry James*, New York: F. Ungar, 1984

Jewett, Sarah Orne

The Best Stories of Sarah Orne Jewett, ed. Willa Cather, 2 vols., Boston and New York: Houghton Mifflin, 1925
Deephaven and Other Stories, ed. Richard Cary, New Haven: College and University Press, 1966
The Country of The Pointed Firs, ed. Alison Easton, Harmondsworth: Penguin Books, 1995
Cary, Richard, *Sarah Orne Jewett*, New York: Twayne 1962
Nagel, Gwen L., *Critical Essays on Sarah Orne Jewett*, Boston: G. K. Hall, 1984

Johnson, Denis

Jesus' Son, New York: Farrar, Straus, 1992

Jones, Edward P.

Lost in the City, New York: Morrow, 1992

Keillor, Garrison

Leaving Home: A Collection of Lake Wobegon Stories, New York: Viking, 1987
We Are Still Married: Stories and Letters, New York: Viking, 1989
The Book of Guys, New York: Viking, 1993

Kincaid, Jamaica

At the Bottom of the River, New York: Farrar, Straus, 1983
Annie John (short story cycle), New York: Farrar, Straus, 1985
Simmons, Diane, *Jamaica Kincaid*, New York: Macmillan, 1994

Lardner, Ring

The Portable Ring Lardner, New York: Viking Press, 1949
The Ring Lardner Reader, New York: Scribner's, 1963

The Best of Ring Lardner, ed. David Lodge, London: Dent, 1984
Evans, Elizabeth, *Lardner*, New York: Ungar, 1979
Patrick, Walton R., *Lardner*, New York: Twayne, 1963
Yardley, Jonathan, *Ring Lardner: A Biography*, New York: Random House, 1977

Leavitt, David

Collected Stories: New York: Bloomsbury, 2003

London, Jack

Tales of the Pacific, London: Penguin Books, 1989
The Sea Wolf and Other Stories, London: Penguin Books, 1989
Short Stories of Jack London, ed. Earle Labor et al., Stanford: Stanford University Press, 1993
Northland Stories, London: Penguin Books, 1997
Cassuto, Leonard and Jeanne Campbell Reesman (eds.), *Rereading Jack London*, Stanford: Stanford University Press, 1993
McClintock, James I., *White Logic: Jack London's Short Stories*, Grand Rapids: Wolfhouse Books 1975
Reesman, Jeanne Campbell, *Jack London: A Study of the Short Fiction*, Boston: Twayne, 1989
Tavernier-Courbin, Jacqueline (ed.), *Critical Essays on Jack London*, Boston: G. K. Hall 1983

Louie, David Wong

The Pangs of Love: Stories, New York: Knopf, 1991
The Barbarians Are Coming, New York: Putnam, 2000

McCullers, Carson

'*The Ballad of the Sad Café' and Collected Short Stories*, Boston: Houghton Mifflin, 1955

Malamud, Bernard

The Magic Barrel, New York: Farrar, Straus & Cudahy, 1958
Idiots First, New York: Farrar, Straus, 1963
Rembrandt's Hat, New York: Farrar, Straus, Giroux, 1973

Astro, Richard and Benson Jackson (eds.), *The Fiction of Bernard Malamud*, Corvallis: Oregon State University Press, 1977
Field, Leslie and Joyce Field (eds.), *Bernard Malamud: A Collection of Critical Essays*, Englewood Cliffs, NJ: Prentice Hall, 1975
Helterman, Jeffrey, *Understanding Bernard Malamud*, Columbia, SC: University of South Carolina Press, 1985
Richman, Sidney, *Bernard Malamud*, New York; Twayne, 1967

Marshall, Paule

Soul Clap Hands and Sing, Washington, DC: Howard University Press, 1988
Merle: A Novella and Other Stories, London: Virago Press, 1985
Reena and Other Stories, Old Westburg, NY: Feminist Press, 1983

Mason, Bobbie Ann

Shiloh and Other Stories, New York: Harper, 1982
Love Life: Stories, New York: Harper, 1989
Zigzagging Down a Wild Trail, New York: Random House, 2001

Means, David

A Quick Kiss of Redemption: And Other Stories, New York: Morrow, 1991
Assorted Fire Events: Stories, New York: Context Books, 2000
The Secret Goldfish, New York: 4th Estate/HarperCollins, 2004

Melville, Herman

Great Short Works of Herman Melville, ed. Warner Berthoff, New York: Harper & Row, 1969
Billy Budd, Sailor and Other Stories, ed. Harold Beaver, Harmondsworth: Penguin Books, 1967; repr. 1986
The Piazza Tales and Other Prose Pieces, 1839–1860, ed. Harrison Hayford et al., Evanston and Chicago: Northwestern University Press and the Newberry Library, 1987
Billy Budd and Other Stories, ed. A. Robert Lee, London: Dent, 1993
Billy Budd, Sailor and Selected Tales, ed. Robert Milder, Oxford: Oxford University Press, 1997

Fogle, Richard Harter, *Melville's Shorter Tales*, Norman: University of Oklahoma Press, 1960
Lee, A. Robert (ed.), *Herman Melville: Critical Assessments*, 4 vols., Mountfield: Helm Information, 2001
Pullin, Faith (ed.), *New Perspectives on Melville*, Edinburgh: Edinburgh University Press and Kent, Ohio: Kent State University Press, 1978

Michaels, Leonard

A Girl with a Monkey, New and Selected Stories, San Francisco: Mercury House, 2000

Minot, Susan

Monkeys (short story cycle), New York: Dutton, 1986
Lust and Other Stories, Boston: Houghton/Seymour Lawrence, 1989

Moore, Lorrie

Like Life, New York: Plume, 1991
Self-Help, New York: Warner Books, 1995
Birds of America, New York: Knopf, 1998

Oates, Joyce Carol

Where Are You Going, Where Have You Been?: Selected Early Stories, New York: Ontario Review Press, 1993.
Haunted: Tales of the Grotesque, New York: Dutton, 1994
Will You Always Love Me? and Other Stories, New York: Dutton, 1995.
The Collected of Hearts: New Tales of the Grotesque, New York: Dutton, 1999
Faithless: Tales of Transgression, New York: Ecco Press, 2001
I Am No One You Know, New York: Ecco Press, 2004
Johnson, Grey, *Joyce Carol Oates: A Study of the Short Fiction*, Boston: Twayne, 1994

O'Brien, Tim

The Things They Carried: A Work of Fiction, New York: Houghton, 1990; London: Flamingo, 1991
Herzog, T. C., *Tim O'Brien*, London: Prentice Hall, 1997

Kaplan, Steven, *Understanding Tim O'Brien*, Columbia: University of South Carolina Press, 1995

O'Connor, Flannery

The Complete Stories of Flannery O'Connor, New York: Farrar, Straus & Giroux, 1971; London: Faber & Faber, 1990
Collected Works, New York: The Library of America, 1988
O'Connor, Flannery, *Mystery and Manners*, ed. Sally and Robert Fitzgerald, New York: Farrar, Straus & Giroux, 1969; London: Faber & Faber, 1972
The Habit of Being: The Letters of Flannery O'Connor, ed. Sally Fitzgerald, New York: The Noonday Press, 1979
Brinkmeyer, Robert H., *The Art and Vision of Flannery O'Connor*, Baton Rouge: Louisiana State University Press, 1989
Kessler, Edward, *Flannery O'Connor and the Language of Apocalypse*, Princeton: Princeton University Press, 1986
Paulson, Suzanne Morrow, *Flannery O'Connor: A Study of the Short Fiction*, Boston: Twayne, 1988
Walters, Dorothy, *Flannery O'Connor*, Boston: Twayne, 1973

Olsen, Tillie

Tell Me a Riddle, Philadelphia: Lippincott, 1960
Frye, Joanne S., *Tillie Olsen: A Study of the Short Fiction*, New York: Twayne, 1995
Nelson, Kay Hoyle and Nancy Huse (eds.), *The Critical Response to Tillie Olsen*, Westport, Conn.: Greenwood Press, 1994
Pearlman, Micky and Abby H. P. Werlock (eds.), *Tillie Olsen*, Boston: Twayne, 1991

Ozick, Cynthia

The Pagan Rabbi and Other Stories, New York: Knopf, 1971
Bloodshed and Three Novellas, New York: Knopf, 1976
Levitations: Five Fictions, New York: Knopf, 1982

Paley, Grace

Collected Stories, New York: Farrar, Straus & Giroux, 1994
Wilde, Alan, 'Grace Paley's Word Investing Words', in Alan Wilde (ed.), *Middle Ground*, Philadelphia: University of Pennsylvania Press, 1987

Parker, Dorothy

Collected Stories of Dorothy Parker, New York: Modern Library, 1942
The Penguin Dorothy Parker, Harmondsworth: Penguin, 1977

Phillips, Jayne Anne

Black Tickets, New York: Delacourte, 1979
Fast Lanes, New York: E. P. Dutton/Seymour Lawrence; London: Faber & Faber, 1987

Poe, Edgar Allan

Complete Works of Edgar Allan Poe, New York: AMS Press, 1965
The Science Fiction of Edgar Allan Poe, ed. Harold Beaver, Harmondsworth: Penguin Books, 1976
The Fall of the House of Usher and Other Writings, ed. David Galloway, Harmondsworth: Penguin Books, 1986
Tales of Mystery and Imagination, ed. Graham Clarke, London: J. M. Dent, 1993
Selected Tales, ed. David Van Leer, Oxford: Oxford University Press, 1998
Bonaparte, Marie, *The Life and Works of Edgar Allan Poe: A Psychoanalytic Interpretation*, trans. John Rodker, foreword by Sigmund Freud, London: Imago, 1949
Carlson, Eric W. (ed.), *The Recognition of Edgar Allan Poe: Selected Criticism from 1829*, Ann Arbor: University of Michigan Press, 1970
Clarke, Graham (ed.), *Edgar Allan Poe: Critical Assessments*, Mountfield: Helm Information, 1991
Davidson, Edward H., *Poe: A Critical Study*, Cambridge, Mass.: Harvard University Press, 1957
May, Charles E., *Edgar Allan Poe: A Study of the Short Fiction*, Boston: Twayne, 1991
Silverman, Kenneth (ed.), *New Essays on Poe's Major Tales*, Cambridge: Cambridge University Press, 1993

Porter, Katherine Anne

The Collected Stories of Katherine Anne Porter, London: Jonathan Cape, 1964
Brinkmeyer, Robert H., *Katherine Anne Porter's Artistic Development*, Baton Rouge: Louisiana State University Press, 1993
DeMouy, Jane Krause, *Katherine Anne Porter's Women: The Eye of Her Fiction*, Austin: University of Texas Press, 1983

Unrue, Darlene Harbour (ed.), *Critical Essays on Katherine Anne Porter's Fiction*, New York: G. K. Hall, 1997

Powers, J. F.

The Collected Stories of J. F. Powers, New York: The New York Review of Books, 2000
Hagopian, John V., *J. F. Powers*, New York: Twayne, 1968
Evans, Fallon (ed.), *J. F. Powers*, St. Louis: Herder, 1968

Proulx, Annie

Heart Songs and Other Stories, New York: Scribner, 1988; London: Fourth Estate, 1995
Close Range: Wyoming Stories, New York: Scribner; London: Fourth Estate, 1999
Bad Dirt, New York: Scribner; London: Fourth Estate, 2004

Robison, Mary

Days, New York: Knopf, 1979
An Amateur's Guide to the Night, New York: Knopf, 1983
Believe Them, New York: Knopf, 1988
Tell Me: 30 Stories, New York: Counterpoint, 2002

Roth, Philip

Goodbye Columbus and Five Short Stories, Boston: Houghton Mifflin, 1993
Baumgarten, Murray and Barbara Gottfried, *Understanding Philip Roth*, Columbia: University of South Carolina Press, 1990
Halio, Jay L., *Philip Roth Revisited*, New York: Twayne, 1992
Roth, Philip, *Reading Myself and Others*, New York: Farrar, Straus & Giroux, 1961

Sin Far, Sui

Mrs Spring Fragrance and Other Writings, Urbana: University of Illinois Press, 1995

Stein, Gertrude

Three Lives, New York and London: Penguin Books USA, 1990
Tender Buttons, Toronto and London: Dover Publications, 1997

Three Lives and Tender Buttons, New York: Signet Books, 2003
Hoffman, Frederick J., *Critical Essays on Gertrude Stein*, Boston: G. K. Hall, 1986

Steinbeck, John

The Pastures of Heaven, New York: Brewer, Warren and Putnam, 1932
The Long Valley, New York: Viking, 1938
McCarthy, Paul, *John Steinbeck*, New York: Unger, 1980
Parini, Jay, *John Steinbeck*, New York: Holt, 1995

Tan, Amy

The Joy Luck Club, New York: Putnam, 1989
Brown, Anne E. et al. (eds.), *International Women's Writing: New Landscapes of Identity*, Westport, Conn.: Greenwood Press, 1995
Palumbo-Lin, David (ed.), *The Ethnic Canon*, Minneapolis: University of Minnesota Press, 1995

Taylor, Peter

The Collected Stories of Peter Taylor, New York: Farrar, Straus & Giroux, 1969
The Old Forest and Other Stories, New York: Picador, 1985
McAlexander, Hubert H., *Critical Essays on Peter Taylor*, Boston: G. K. Hall, 1993
Robinson, David M., *World of Relations: The Achievement of Peter Taylor*, Lexington: University Press of Kentucky, 1998
Robinson, James Curry, *Peter Taylor: A Study of the Short Fiction*, Boston: Twayne, 1988

Thurber, James

My Life and Hard Times, New York: Harper & Bros., 1933
The Thurber Carnival, New York: Harper & Bros., 1945

Toomer, Jean

Cane, New York: Boni & Liveright, 1923
Benson, Brian Joseph and Mabel Mayle Dillard, *Jean Toomer*, Boston: Twayne, 1980

Twain, Mark (Samuel Clemens)

The Writings of Mark Twain (37 vols.), ed. Albert Bigelow Paine, New York: Gabriel Wells, 1922–25
Great Short Works of Mark Twain, ed. Justin Kaplan, New York: Harper & Row, 1969
Short Stories, ed. Justin Kaplan, Harmondsworth: Penguin Books, 1993
Short Stories and Tall Tales, Philadelphia and London: Running Press, 1993
Camp, J. and X. J. Kennedy, *Mark Twain's Frontier*, Holt, Reinhart and Wilson, 1963
Hutchinson, S., *Humour On the Run*, Amsterdam: Rodopi, 1994
Walker, I. M., *Mark Twain*, London: Routledge & Kegan Paul, 1970
Wilson, J. D., *A Reader's Guide to the Short Stories of Mark Twain*, Boston: G. K. Hall, 1987
Wonham, Henry B., *Mark Twain and the Art of the Tall Tale*, Oxford: Oxford University Press, 1983

Updike, John

Trust Me: Short Stories, New York: Knopf, 1987
Afterlife and Other Stories, New York: Knopf, 1994
The Complete Henry Bech: 20 Stories, New York: Knopf, 2001
The Early Stories, 1953–1975, New York: Alfred A. Knopf, 2003; London: Hamish Hamilton, 2004
Luscher, Robert M., *John Updike: A Study of the Short Fiction*, Boston: Twayne, 1993
Newman, Judie, *John Updike*, New York: St Martin's Press, 1988

Vizenor, Gerald

Wordarrows: Indians and Whites in the New Fur Trade, Minneapolis: University of Minnesota Press, 1978
Earthdivers: Tribal Narratives on Mixed Descent, Minneapolis: University of Minnesota Press, 1981
Landfill Meditation: Crossblood Stories, Hanover and London: Wesleyan University Press, 1991

Walker, Alice

The Complete Stories, London: The Women's Press, 1994
Petry, Alice Hall, 'Walker: The Achievement of the Short Fiction', *Modern Language Studies*, 19 (Winter 1989), pp. 12–27

Wallace, David Foster

Oblivion: Stories, New York: HarperCollins, 2004

Welty, Eudora

The Collected Stories of Eudora Welty, New York: Harcourt Brace, 1982; Harmondsworth: Penguin Books, 1983
Mortimer, Gail, *Daughter of the Swan: Love and Knowledge in Eudora Welty's Fiction*, Athens: University of Georgia Press, 1994
Prenshaw, Peggy (ed.), *Eudora Welty: Critical Essays*, Jackson: University Press of Mississippi, 1984
Vande Kieft, Ruth M., *Eudora Welty*, Boston: Twayne, 1962

Wharton, Edith

The Reckoning and Other Stories, London: Phoenix, 1999
The Collected Short Stories of Edith Wharton, ed. R. W. B. Lewis, 2 vols., New York: Scribner's, 1968
Bendixen, Alfred and Annette Zilversmit, *Edith Wharton: New Critical Essays*, New York: Garland, 1992
McDowell, Margaret B., *Edith Wharton*, Boston: Twayne, 1976
Vita-Finzi, Penelope, *Edith Wharton and the Art of Fiction*, New York: St Martin's Press, 1990

Wideman, John Edgar

The Stories of John Edgar Wideman, New York: Pantheon Books, 1982; published in UK as *All Stories Are True: The Collected Stories of John Edgar Wideman*, London: Pan Books, 1983
Coleman, James William, *Blackness and Modernism: The Literary Development of John Edgar Wideman*, Jackson: University Press of Mississippi, 1989

Williams, William Carlos

The Farmers' Daughters: The Collected Stories of William Carlos Williams, Norfolk, Conn.: New Directions, 1961
Wagner, Linda, *The Prose of William Carlos Williams*, Middletown, Conn.: Wesleyan University Press, 1970

Wolff, Tobias

The Stories of Tobias Wolff, London: Picador/Pan, 1988
The Night in Question: Stories, New York: Alfred A. Knopf; London: Bloomsbury, 1996
Hannah, Barry, *Tobias Wolff: A Study of the Short Fiction*, New York: Twayne, 1996

Wright, Richard

Uncle Tom's Children: Four Novellas, New York: Harper, 1938
Eight Men, New York: World, 1961
Butler, Robert J. (ed.), *The Critical Response to Richard Wright*, Westport, Conn.: Greenwood Press, 1995
Gates Henry Louis Jnr. and K. A. Appiah (eds.), *Richard Wright: Critical Perspectives Past and Present*, New York: Amistad, 1993

Yamamoto, Hisaye

Seventeen Syllables and Other Stories, New Brunswick, NJ: Rutgers University Press, 2001

Critical works on the American short story

Ammons, Elizabeth, *Conflicting Stories: American Women Writers at the Turn into the Twentieth Century*, Oxford: Oxford University Press, 1992
Bone, Robert, *Down Home: Origins of the Afro-American Short Story*, New York: Columbia University Press, 1988
Brown, Julie (ed.), *American Women Short Story Writers: A Collection of Critical Essays*, New York and London: Garland, 1995
Ethnicity and the American Short Story, New York and London: Garland, 1997
Bowen, James K. and Richard Van Der Beets (eds.), *American Short Fiction: Readings and Criticism*, Indianapolis: Bobbs Merrill, 1970
Current-Garcia, Eugene, *The American Short Story Before 1850: A Critical History*, Boston: Twayne, 1985
Gelfant, Blanche H. (ed.), *The Columbia Companion to the Twentieth-Century American Short Story*, New York: Columbia University Press, 2000
Gerlach, John, *Towards the End: Closure and Structure in the American Short Story*, Tuscaloosa: University of Alabama Press, 1985

Lee, A. Robert (ed.), *The Nineteenth Century American Short Story*, London: Vision, 1985
Levy, Andrew, *The Culture and Commerce of the American Short Story*, Cambridge: Cambridge University Press, 1993
Logsdon, Lauren and Charles Mayer, W., (eds.), *Since Flannery O'Connor: Essays on the Contemporary American Short Story*, Macomb: Western Illinois University Press, 1987
Mann, Susan Garland, *The Short Story Cycle: a Genre Companion and Reference Guide*, Westport, Conn.: Greenwood Press, 1989
McClave, Heather (ed.), *Women Writers of the Short Story*, Englewood Cliffs, NJ: Prentice Hall, 1980
Meanor, Patrick and Joseph McNicholas (eds.), *American Short Story Writers Since World War II*, 4th Series, Detroit: Gale Group, 2001
Nagel, James, *The Contemporary American Short Story Cycle: The Ethnic Resonance of Genre*, Baton Rouge: Louisiana State University Press, 2001
O'Brien, Edward, *The Advance of the American Short Story (1931)*, Norwood, Pa.: Norwood Editions, 1977
Pattee, F. L., *The Development of the American Short Story (1923)*, New York: Biblo & Tannen, 1975
Peden, William, *The American Short Story: Front Line in the National Defence of Literature*, Boston: Houghton Mifflin, 1964
The American Short Story: Continuity and Change, 1940–1975, Boston: Houghton Mifflin, 1975
Ross, Danforth, *The American Short Story*, Minneapolis: University of Minnesota Press, 1961
Stevick, Philip (ed.), *The American Short Story, 1900–1945*, Boston: Twayne, 1984
Tallack, Douglas, *The Nineteenth Century American Short Story: Language, Form and Ideology*, London and New York: Routledge, 1993
Voss, A., *The American Short Story: A Critical Survey*, Norman: University of Oklahoma Press, 1973
Weaver, Gordon (ed.), *The American Short Story, 1945–1980*, Boston: Twayne, 1983
Werlock, Abby H. P. (ed.), *Facts on File Companion to the American Short Story*, New York: Checkmark Books, Facts on File Inc., 2000
West, Ray B., Jnr., *The Short Story in America: 1900–1950*, Freeport, NY: Books for Libraries Press, 1952
Yagoda, Ben, *About Town: 'The New Yorker' and the World It Made*, New York: Da Capo Press, 2001

General works on American literature containing discussions of short story writers

Cunliffe, Marcus (ed.), *The Literature of the United States*, Harmondsworth: Penguin Books, 1987

American Literature to 1900, Harmondsworth: Penguin Books, 1993
American Literature Since 1900, Harmondsworth: Penguin Books, 1993
Lawrence, D. H., *Studies in Classic American Literature*, New York: Viking, 1973

General critical and theoretical works on the short story

Burke, Daniel, *Beyond Interpretation: Studies in the Modern Short Story*, New York: Whitston, 1991
Head, Dominic, *The Modernist Short Story*, Cambridge: Cambridge University Press, 1992
Lohafer, Susan, *Coming to Terms with the Short Story*, Baton Rouge and London: Louisiana State University Press, 1983
Lohafer, Susan, and Jo Ellen Clary, (eds.), *Short Story Theory at the Crossroads*, Baton Rouge: Louisiana University Press, 1989
Matthews, Brander, *The Philosophy of the Short Story (1901)*, Philadelphia: R. West, 1977
May, Charles B. (ed.), *Short Story Theories*, Athens: Ohio University Press, 1976
The New Short Story Theories, Athens: Ohio University Press, 1994
The Short Story: The Reality of Artifice, New York: Twayne; London: Prentice International, 1995
O'Connor, Frank, *The Lonely Voice: A Study of the Short Story (1960)*, Hoboken, NJ: Melville House, 2004
O'Faolain, Sean, *The Short Story*, London and Mercier Press, 1972
Reid, Ian, *The Short Story*, London and New York: Routledge, 1977
Shaw, Valerie, *The Short Story: A Critical Introduction*, London and New York: Longman, 1983

Bibliographies of criticism of the short story

Thurston, Jarvis, *Short Fiction Criticism: A Checklist of Interpretation since 1925 of Stories and Novelettes (American, British, Continental) 1800–1958*, Denver: A. Swallow, 1960
Weixlmann, J., *American Short Fiction: Criticism and Scholarship, 1959–1977: A Checklist*, Chicago: Swallow Press, 1982

Index

Lightning Source UK Ltd.
Milton Keynes UK
UKOW042349201212

203963UK00001B/62/P

9 780521 533812